ALL
AROUND
ME
PEACEFUL

ALL AROUND ME PEACEFUL

KENT NELSON

A Delta Book
Published by
Dell Publishing
a division of
Bantam Doubleday Dell Publishing Group, Inc.
666 Fifth Avenue
New York, New York 10103

Book design by Richard Oriolo

The trademark Delta ® is registered in the U.S. Patent and
Trademark Office.

Library of Congress Cataloging in Publication Data

Nelson, Kent, 1943–
    All around me peaceful / Kent Nelson.
        p.   cm.
    ISBN 0-385-29715-7
    I. Title.
PS3564.E467A78   1989
813'.54—dc19   88-38683
                                                              CIP

Printed in the United States of America
Published simultaneously in Canada

May 1989

10 9 8 7 6 5 4 3 2 1

BG

For Blue
—part of the journey.

The author thanks the Brown Foundation of the
University of the South, the Ingram-Merrill Foundation,
and the New Hampshire State Council on the Arts
for financial assistance in the writing of this book.

PART I

PART I

1

The word around town was that John "Pork" Meeker, the sheriff's new deputy, had blown up the hot springs pools at the river. No one knew for certain what had happened except that at eight o'clock in the morning on the Friday before elk season opened, there were five explosions —three one after another, and then two more a few minutes later. The blasts had come from the river at the bottom of Prosperity Street, and the sound had ricocheted from the sandstone cliffs above the town. Neil Shanks said he'd seen Meeker's patrol car right afterward raising dust down the River Road.

The rumors and arguments went on all morning in the cafés and at the post office where the people collected their mail and talked in the high-altitude sun. Some people were mad that Ed Wainwright hadn't cleaned up the hot springs long before. "He's the sheriff," Walt Cogswell said. "There's no reason to let that riffraff take over."

"The pools will get built back," said Mary Dwyer, who owned the New Wiesbaden Spa and Motel. "That's what I worry about. How's he going to keep them closed?"

"His own boy goes down there," Walt Cogswell said. "You'd think he'd worry."

Father Shonnard, the Catholic priest, paused on the sunny sidewalk. "But don't you think it's a shame that in a civilized society we resort to violence? I don't think Ed meant for the deputy to blow them up."

"He probably didn't know," Mary Dwyer said. "Anyway, who says this is a civilized society? We have hoodlums naked in public."

"We don't know who did it, really," Walt Cogswell went on. "All we know is what Neil Shanks said."

"The Indians went naked," Weedy Garcia said, smiling as he always did. "The hot springs have a religious significance. Pork had no right—"

"Pork?"

"Why shouldn't we believe Neil?" someone else said. "What's there to lie about?"

"Whoever did it picked a hell of a time," Father Shonnard said. "Hunting's about to start. We won't have time to think about anything with all the people coming in."

"Where's Ed?" Walt Cogswell asked. "Maybe he hasn't even heard about it yet."

By early that afternoon the back-and-forth had died down to a whisper. Jeeps and pickup trucks and four-wheel-drives clogged Main Street from the liquor store to the Panorama Motel, and the rush was under way. Blaze-orange jackets and hats sprang up like poppies along the sidewalks and the streets—brilliant and obvious and eerie. The talk was of elk and booze and guns.

School had let out early, too, so the children were free. Many of them were getting their own hunting gear in order or meeting relatives where they'd spend the weekend while their parents were up in the mountains. The motels were jammed. So were Rita's Diner and the Nugget Café and the bars along Main—the Outlaw and the Longbranch and the Golddigger.

Furze's Sporting Goods was doing a land-office business. A long line of hunters shouted impatiently at the front cashier, trying to buy thermal underwear and ski gloves, camping gear and Coleman fuel, wool socks and sunglasses. At the back of the store was an even longer line for ammunition, gun oil, and Colorado hunting licenses.

Lazy Miner Liquor had a special on Scotch and vodka by the case, but the price of bourbon, beer, and ice had been jacked up sixty percent. Hunters loaded their coolers right on the sidewalk in front of the store.

People crowded into the food markets too. Hamburger, bologna, and Wonder bread were sold out. So were apples and oranges, matches, peanut butter, canned stew, and Bisquik.

Gold Hill had been a mining boomtown. A century before, men had poured into the mountains surrounding the town from every state east of the Mississippi. They'd tunneled and blasted and dug into the hills, into the gullies, into the cliffs. They'd sieved the creeks and rivers, carved up the high meadows, sluiced tons of earth and rock through makeshift boxes. A city was christened in 1876, the same year Colorado had become a state, and for three decades it had flashed brightly on the horizon.

But when the gold and silver were gone, the rampage ended. The railroad tore up its track. The opera house closed down. One of the grand hotels, the Crystal Palace, caught fire under suspicious circumstances and collapsed into ashes. Businesses shut down, moved, went bankrupt. And the invisible men whose dreams were still in the ground drifted away to the iron mills of Pueblo or to the stockyards just starting in Denver or to the hazy places they had come from.

A few of the mines struggled on through the First World War, hollowing out the lesser grades of gold and silver or converting to the production of lead, tin, zinc, and copper. As ore prices fluctuated and fell, the mines lapsed piecemeal into the hands of conglomerates in distant cities. The Molly McGee closed in 1957, the Camp Langdon and the Southern Belle in 1968. Taylor's Mill, which in its heyday had employed two hundred people and produced gold ore worth millions a year, was boarded up in 1980.

But still the people stayed because the country was so beautiful. The town lay on a hillside on the eastern slope of the Uncompahgre River, stair-stepping up toward Main Street, which was Colorado Highway 550, and beyond five blocks to the scrub oak hills that rose into the Amphitheater far above. Red sandstone cliffs rimmed the town to the west and south. All around were mountains.

Highway 550 began in Chipeta Springs thirty miles north and ran upward through the ranch country along the river bottom and into the narrow valley which fed into Gold Hill. From the town Ptarmigan Pass wound up higher still, along the river gorge to the saddle at 11,704 feet between Mt. Abrams and Mt. McConnell.

The river ran south to north out of the mountains. It began as springs and snowmelt in the high meadows and tundra flats, collected into rivulets and streams, fell through the spruce forests, always aimed toward the center of the earth. Water cascaded down Dexter Creek, Oak Creek, Owl Creek, Cutler Creek, Bear Creek, down to the Uncompahgre, down to the Gunnison, down slowly into the great Colorado.

It was a land of mountains. A hawk whose terrain it was, soaring on a thermal, would have gained the panorama of peaks stretching away in every direction across the horizon. Summits and ridges and valleys—red from iron ore, white from unmelted snow, blue from the distant glaze of air— were both delicate and terrible. It was a land of plenty and a land of need.

From town the perspective was closed in. The granite cirque of the Amphitheater cut off the sky to the east. Cliffs and aspen benches and spruce forests rose like the broad shoulders and jutting elbows of giants. And still there were mountains—Whitehouse Peak, Mt. Hayden, Potosi Peak, Mt. Walcott, Mt. Abrams, Brown Mountain. These were the peaks one could see from town.

The town had diminished over the years, but the people had not let it die. They converted houses to bed-and-breakfast inns, built motels, opened shops catering to hunters and fishermen and mountain climbers and campers. They advertised the curative powers of the natural hot springs which bubbled from the river and seeped from the cliffs. The air was clean and invigorating. A new town was born and summer was its season. There were horseback rides, hayrides, gold panning, miniature golf, old-fashioned ice cream parlors, a movie house, restaurants and bars. Jeep tours careened into the mountains to the ghost towns of El Dorado, Taylor Springs, and Paradox, and to the grave of Molly McGee, who, it was said, committed suicide by ingesting a million dollars' worth of gold dust.

But summer ended. Families from Illinois and Texas and Massachusetts went home. School started in California and Florida. The days winnowed down and night tightened around the town. The aspens melted to yellow. But still to come was the season for deer and elk, the last revelry, a final fling before the winter's long wait for spring.

2

Neil Shanks liked the frenzy of the start of elk season. He had come from Michigan two years before, and though he wasn't a hunter anymore, he still felt the crispness of the air and the anticipation of the people who swarmed into town. Perhaps it was the mountains. In Michigan he'd thought the hunters were muted, stealthier, more stolid in pursuit, but out West they yelled in the streets and rolled through town blaring their horns.

He could not claim he had ever been a hunter. For most of his boyhood he had stalked white-tailed deer and grouse on his family's timberland around Grayling, but he'd only shot one deer and a few ruffed grouse. And the fall he was fourteen he'd shot a turkey. He'd seen the bird through the green willows in a bog—could still see it, with the crimson wattles and the black breast tuft. He'd squeezed off a soft shot the way his father had taught him, and the turkey had jumped with the hit. It skittered into the brush, though, and he'd chased it, crashing and snapping branches. His father had called to him from somewhere in the trees not to run, and he'd called back, "I hit one."

He'd felt proud and scared both. He'd slowed through the brush and then he'd seen the turkey lying in a puddle of water and dead leaves, oozing blood from its feathers. It was a hen. Her eyes were closed and she was crouching down in the muck, and he thought she was dead. He'd reached for her, and when he closed his hands, she burst from his grasp and flew up through the leaves, leaving him startled and crying, with blood still on his hands.

After that he had never hunted again. But he imagined it was different in the West, where you could look across the valleys so far away. You could see in the clean air and the spruce forests and the aspens. There was distance.

But what fascinated him still was that anything, even bloodlust, could stir so many people to such feverish action. The hunters—men and women both—behaved like people possessed. They shouted across Main Street to one another as if they were at a football game. All they cared about was how much they could pack into their Jeeps, how fast they could get into the mountains. It was as if they felt every moment wasted would be subtracted from their last week on earth.

That afternoon Shanks was on his way to his shop farther up Main when he spotted Becky and Finn Carlsson cruising slowly up the street. Finn's maroon truck with the wide tires and the jumping-buck decal on the driver's door was a common sight in town, particularly in front of the Gold-digger after five o'clock. And no one could miss the broom he had stuck handle down into a pole behind the cab.

They were pulling a double-horse trailer, and Finn had his arm akimbo out the open window, a slice of the blaze orange of his sleeve shining in the sun. He double-parked and let Becky out in the middle of the block.

Becky was furious about something, and Shanks could hear her swearing at Finn all the way down the block. Becky wasn't a big woman either. She was tough, and listening to her now made Shanks smile.

Finn gave her the finger, and when someone behind him honked, Finn gave that driver the finger too. Then he pulled ahead and turned the corner. Becky was still yelling at him and shaking her fist.

When Finn was gone, Becky jaywalked through a welter
of cars and went into Matheson's Market.

Shanks had first met Becky not long after he'd arrived in
Gold Hill. It had been a warm day in July, and he'd been on
a scouting mission out the Pinnacle Ridge Road, looking for
a family named Wilkerson, which, he thought, might have
some connection to Thomas Shanks, his great-grandfather.
The road was in the mesa-and-moraine country east of the
highway, five miles down the valley from town. Cattle
ranches and irrigated pastureland had been carved from the
dry hills, and the holdings of the families were both large
and poor. A man who could irrigate might get two cuttings
of timothy and alfalfa in a summer, but above the ditches
the arid land supported only gray sage and yucca and a few
scattered pinyons and cedars. Wilkerson owned two hundred acres on which he had a small ranch house and a lot to
feed cattle.

Shanks hadn't been encouraged about the connection to
Thomas Shanks. All he knew from the county archives was
that Wilkerson had owned land abutting a mining claim
Thomas Shanks had staked out in Dexter Creek. But he
thought the old man might remember something about
Thomas, so he'd brought along a plat map and a tape re-
corder and a tintype photograph of Thomas Shanks, along
with some of the letters Thomas had written home to his
family.

The road was gravelly and dusty, and as he had driven
along the hills he'd been distracted by a bird fluttering in an
alfalfa field—a hawk, he could tell. At first he'd thought the
hawk had captured a snake because it was twisting in circles, struggling and flapping. Then he decided it was injured, so he stopped. He sneaked under the barbed wire
fence and ran across the field, stripping off his jacket as he
ran. The hawk had a broken wing, and Shanks trapped it in
the jacket to keep its wings down. Then he'd taken it to
Wilkerson's.

Wilkerson had been in town, but his wife came out into

was. I heard he took out Witches' Brew and the Ladle and Star Trek."

"But not the Xanadu?"

"I don't know about the Xanadu. I thought I'd check tomorrow when the crowd thins out."

Becky selected three dinners from the bin and read the labels on the back. "And goddamn Finn," she said. "I've been trying to get him moving. He had the whole week. But no, he goes out to the Golddigger and shoots pool. He doesn't even sight in his rifle until this afternoon." She paused and let her voice ease. "Which of these would you want?" she asked. "Beef and noodles, Oriental stew, or ham and eggs?"

"Freeze dried?"

"Yes. If you were up the mountain on a cold night?"

"You." Shanks grinned and felt the smooth heat go into his face. "I mean, if I were Finn."

"You aren't Finn."

"Oriental stew," he said.

"I like beef and noodles." She threw two beef and noodles into her cart and pushed it up the busy aisle.

"I thought you had everything at camp on Wednesday," Shanks said. "You made that trip up."

"Not trail food. We have the cache at camp, but Finn was supposed to get trail food." She turned the corner and picked out two sacks of candy—Milky Way bars and M&M's—and a large bag of mixed nuts.

"You're mad about that?"

"I'm mad that Finn invited Hank Tobuk. Weedy is okay. I can take Weedy because I grew up with him. But not Hank Tobuk."

"They aren't going up now?"

"Monday. Weedy has the weekend shift, and Hank has business. Hank's bad news, and he makes Finn crazy. Besides, I don't want to be in the mountains with three drunk men."

Shanks had never seen the camp, but Becky had described the place to him many times, and the trail too. The

trail was dangerous. It hairpinned from the parking turnout
on the pass and wound up through spruce on the lower
slope. Then it crossed an open pitch of slippery shale to an
outcropping of rock. To the south you could see the summit
of Ptarmigan Pass and the river below, and to the east, the
Bear Creek Gorge, which fell straight off a thousand feet to
the creek. The trail traversed the face of the cliff for another
mile until it ran out into the dark timber again.

Shanks had read about the trail in the mining-history
books. To be able to transport their equipment on mules,
the miners had dynamited a three-foot-wide roadway along
the cliff. The Flora Dora, the God's Gift, and the Bear's
Tooth had operated in the area just beyond the cliff, and
farther on were a jumble of one-man mines. The Yellow
Jacket was the biggest mine, with a crude smelter and an
ore house. That lay two miles farther along the trail where
Bear Creek split into separate valleys.

Becky didn't know about the mines. She knew a different
country. She liked the aspen glades and the ravines and the
patches of dark timber where the elk hid out. Meadows
flowed right up to the sky, she said, and all around were
ridges and mountains without names.

"Finn's waiting," she said. "I have to go." She pointed
out through the plate-glass window to where Finn had
pulled his truck and horse trailer into a space in front of the
post office. He was standing beside the cab with one foot
propped up on the floorboard, slapping his hand on the roof
to an inaudible rhythm.

"Okay," Shanks said.

"You ought to go hunting sometime, Neil. You could
close your shop for a few days."

"Oh, not me. I got fear of heights."

"Bullshit."

"True," Shanks said.

Becky moved along. At the end of the aisle she tried on a
blaze-orange hat and made a face at him. "How do I look?"

"Young."

"No, really?"

The cap made her blond hair puff out like a wind was blowing in her face. "Beautiful," he said.

"So what are you doing this weekend?" she asked. "Are you finally finishing off Thomas Shanks?"

"Maybe."

"Are you seeing Earlene?"

"Not that I know of."

"Is she on at the Golddigger?"

"Friday and Saturday. She usually is." He followed Becky along.

"I thought you liked her."

"I like her all right." He glanced at Finn again. He was talking now to Weedy Garcia, and even in conversation he looked edgy. Finn had a thin, wiry frame, pale arms, long hair, blond, past his shoulders. The sun glinted from his hair as if from metal.

"What do you think they're talking about?" Becky asked.

"Music." Shanks could almost hear Finn's thin, whiny voice.

"I'll bet they're talking about women or elk. Or maybe horses. Finn thinks Bo Jack is a saint."

"Local politics," Shanks said.

Becky smiled. "I know you'll go drink in the bars, won't you? That's what you always do." She pushed her cart into the checkout line.

"I might."

"I just talked to Lorraine, and she isn't doing anything. Maybe you should call her."

"I barely know Lorraine. Anyway, I'm going to keep the shop open late. There'll be hunters in town. Maybe someone will come in and buy a book."

"Speaking of books," Becky said, "I still have those two of yours. *Ceremonies* was one of them, and I forget the other."

"*Tell Me a Riddle*." Shanks said. "Keep them awhile. I can get along with all the other books in the world."

3

Weedy and Finn were discussing the relative merits of blunt-nosed bullets versus the pointed kind when Becky and Neil Shanks came across the street.

"Blunts make the big exit," Finn said. "You hit a man with one of these, and he's dead." He tossed the shell into the air and caught it again. "Well, looky here. If it ain't Tammy Wynette in an orange hat and Nelly Shanks. It's about time."

Shanks nodded and smiled.

Becky said, "Fuck you."

"But they're not so accurate from two hundred yards," Weedy said. "And we aren't shooting people."

"We might."

"Finn thinks we ought to use blunt-nosed," Weedy said. "I got ten boxes of each. It'd be a shame to waste them."

"Blunt-nosed will ruin the insides," Becky said. "And what if you hit one in the back? You'll lose all that meat."

"Hank'll bring regulars," Finn said. "You can bet the family jewels on it. He'll have another dozen boxes."

Weedy grinned and shook his head. He had a kindly face with wobbly black eyes that appeared filmy as a springer spaniel's. He was dark skinned, thick through the chest and

"That's Bert Parks," Wendell said. "He'll tear you apart if you don't know his name."

Wendell was dressed up in a black suit and a tie and black, polished shoes that looked too small for him. He was a shortish man, younger than he looked probably, Shanks thought. He had gray hair that fell to his shoulders, and at ten in the morning, whiskey on his breath.

"What's that you got?" he asked, standing up and peering from the porch. "That a red-tail?"

"Yes. I know you have a wedding in the family today, but Mrs. Wilkerson thought you might look at it."

"I hate weddings," Wendell said. "Bring the bird out here."

Shanks brought the hawk out through the car window still wrapped up in his jacket.

"Wilkerson shoot the hawk?" Wendell asked.

"He didn't say."

Wendell came down the steps and took the bird gently into his own shaking hands. He stretched the injured wing as if he were caressing a child's hair. "Thirty-thirty," he said. "That's what Wilkerson used. If it had been a twenty-two, he might have been all right. I can mount him for you. That's all. He'll die anyway."

"You mean kill him?"

Wendell handed the bird back to Shanks. It flapped and Bert Parks barked once, and then Shanks noticed the two women who'd come out onto the porch. One was dark haired, tall and thin, though her slenderness was disguised by the light blue dress she wore. He guessed she was the older sister, in her twenties somewhere. The other one was sturdier, blond, boyish looking. She was the one in the white dress with lace at the sleeves.

"What happened to it?" asked the one in the white dress.

"Shot," Wendell called back. "It's a red-tail."

Shanks held the bird up.

"Can we keep him?" the girl asked.

She jumped down from the porch, and her white dress floated up over her legs. She hit the ground running.

the yard. She was a tall woman, rough looking, fiftyish. "What're you doing on our property?" was the first thing she said.

"I was hoping to ask some questions."

"We don't like questions," Mrs. Wilkerson said.

Shanks showed her the old tintype of bearded miners posing in front of the livery barn. "Would Mr. Wilkerson's father recognize any of these people?" Shanks asked.

"Not likely," the woman said. "The old man's been dead three years. We tossed his junk too. He had some pictures like that." She looked past Shanks at his car. "What you got that buzzard in there for?"

"It's a hawk," Shanks said. "I was going to find a vet."

The woman squinted. "Hawk, huh? Darryl said it was a buzzard. You could take it up the road to Wendell Blythe. He does birds and things. But his daughter's getting married today."

"How far up the road?"

"Two miles. You'll see a mailbox."

Shanks hadn't been able to get any more information from her, and she didn't promise much cooperation from her husband either. So he'd driven on two miles until he came to the silver mailbox that said BLYTHE on it.

He turned in and bounced down a long driveway to the yard.

Wendell was sitting on the back porch playing the guitar, and an old mongrel had got up from in front of the door and started barking in a hoarse voice. When Shanks shut off the engine, the dog stopped barking and limped away. But Wendell was still singing.

The ditch rider named Crider was up in the trees
Singing songs about women and shooting the breeze.

He stopped singing but kept picking the melody a little off-key. Then he stopped that too.

Shanks got out of the car. "Is the dog dangerous?" he asked.

"That's Becky," Wendell said. "I guess you can tell she's the one getting married."

Shanks held the hawk against his stomach and shook her hand. "Neil Shanks."

"What're you going to do with it?" Becky asked.

"I live in Gold Hill," he said. "I don't have a place to keep it. Your father says he can mount it."

"We had a golden eagle out here once. Lorraine found it up on the ridge. That's Lorraine on the porch. The eagle wouldn't eat anything unless we tied a live rabbit or a mouse to a string and let it go in the yard. Some birds, if they can't hunt, won't eat."

"He's still in pain," Wendell said. "That's the trouble."

Shanks looked up at Lorraine on the porch. She was listening to them and watching. He was aware of her attention the way he sometimes was aware of the effect of weather in his bones.

The door opened and a little boy peered outside. "I want to see."

"Go back inside, Christopher," Lorraine said. "This isn't for you."

"I want to see, though," he said. He came out onto the porch.

Lorraine picked him up and carried him into the house.

"My dad's probably right," Becky said. "It's better to kill him if he can't ever fly."

He'd believed her. It was the way her voice soothed the bird and the way she ran her hand over the feathers of its head. Her eyes were angry and sad at the same time.

Wendell had fetched a plastic sack from his workroom out in the barn, and they had put the hawk in a piece of PVC pipe so it couldn't flap its wings or tear the sack. Wendell put the piece of pipe in the sack and attached the open end to the exhaust of the tractor parked at the edge of the yard.

"You want to start it up?" he asked Shanks.

"No, sir."

Becky got up onto the tractor seat in her wedding dress

and turned the engine over. Once the engine was going, Shanks hadn't watched anymore.

A week later Wendell had delivered the bird to Shanks's post office box in Gold Hill. "No charge," he said in the note. "Maybe we can save the next one."

It was crowded that afternoon in Matheson's Market, and Shanks carried only a basket. He was a browser, not a list shopper, and he knew by now where everything was on the shelves. He wended his way along the depleted aisles, looking for nothing in particular. As a pretense for being there, he picked up a six-pack of Pepsi and a sack of potato chips. Even in the crowd of hunters he knew he couldn't avoid running into Becky.

She was one aisle over, sorting through a new shipment of freeze-dried dinners.

"You," she said. "What are you doing here?"

"Stocking up," he said. "It's a free country."

"I thought you ran a store."

"I do, but not very well. That's why it's for sale. You have a fight with Finn?"

"No."

"I thought you were ready."

"I was ready. Finn was supposed to do this shopping days ago."

Shanks stepped out of the way of two bearded men pushing a cart down the aisle, then looked back at Becky. She was short like her father, freckle faced, a natural streaked blond. She was twenty-three, but looked more like seventeen, and her eyes seemed as though they were constantly asking *What next?* or *Tell me something more.* But right then she looked mad, even at him.

"You hear what Pork did?" Shanks asked.

"Of course I heard. He got some TNT. Can you believe it?"

"I believe it. I saw him drive away."

"I mean, is it legal?"

"It happened. Watergate wasn't legal, either, but there it

arms, a blocking back's body. "You really have twenty boxes, man?" he asked.

"We got ten days," Finn said in his reedy voice. "If we ever get started." He measured Becky. "Where the hell have you been?"

"Doing what you should've already done," she said. "And you stand here worrying about your complexion."

"I been busy," Finn said. "I'm listening for the weather."

"So what is it?"

He tilted his head into the sun. "Sunny."

"Where do you want the bag?" Shanks asked.

"In back," Becky said. "Just set it in anywhere."

The bed of the truck was nearly empty except for two saddlebags and a red day pack and two rifles still in their leather cases and nestled into a down jacket. Shanks lifted the sack in over the side.

"So what'd you buy?" Finn said.

"We owe Neil ten dollars," Becky said. "I didn't have enough money."

"Ten," Finn said. "Is that what the hat cost?"

"I like the hat."

"Keep it on," Weedy said. "There are nuts running around these mountains with blunt-nosed bullets."

The music on the radio stopped, and Finn climbed into the truck cab. "High clouds," he called out. "Fifties high, forties low. Chance of rain late . . . snow in the higher elevations. . . . Sunday, clearing and colder. Hot damn. Maybe we'll get a couple of inches Saturday night."

"Like a man," Becky said. "You never know how many inches you'll get or how long it'll last."

"A white Christmas for elk," Finn said.

Weedy smiled. "Shit, by tomorrow you'll have them poor buggers spooked all over the mountain. I have my money on Becky."

"How much of it?" Finn said.

"Twenty says Becky gets an elk down before you do."

"That'll pay for my license," Finn said. "It's a deal."

Weedy took a toothpick from his shirt pocket and stuck it

into his mouth. "You already owe me fifty on the Rams. And you owe Neil ten."

"Let's make it sixty, then," Finn said.

"No cheating. Becky, you can't let him cheat."

"How would I cheat?"

"I don't know," Becky said. "How do you usually cheat?"

Weedy looked down the street. "Uh-oh, don't look at who's coming to dinner."

Shanks had the best angle down Main. There was a maze of Jeeps and trucks, but by degrees a beige car took shape. Heat waves shimmered above the road. Cars turned off in front of it, but the beige car kept coming. The light-panel on the top crystallized first, then the headlights and the grille, and finally the bulky form of John Meeker over the steering wheel.

"It's the A-Team," Weedy said. "Captain Pork."

Meeker turned on the blue flasher a half block away, before Finn had a chance to do anything.

Meeker had been hired from Big Spring, Texas, to give Ed Wainwright a hand with the local rabble. He'd come to town with the mentality of a frontier marshal, and in the space of a few weeks he'd made a lifetime's worth of enemies. He stopped alongside the pickup truck and got out his ticket book.

Weedy sat down on the curb and emptied out his boots of rocks and grass.

"Gentlemen," John Meeker said, nodding around. "Becky." He circled the cruiser and stood in front of the truck. "This your truck, Finn?"

"Which one?"

"This maroon one here with the deer on the side and the broom sticking up its ass. This one," he said, slapping the fender with his ticket book, "the one parked here in this no-parking zone."

"Never saw it before."

Meeker started writing.

"Come on, man. I was just waiting for Becky to get done at the store."

"Why don't you ask him real polite to move it?" Weedy said. "I bet he'd get going fast up to the mountain."

"I don't care if you've been waiting for Nancy Reagan to jump naked out of a cake," Meeker said. "Can I see the registration?"

Finn went around to the suicide, elbowed past Becky, and started pulling out maps and papers from the glove compartment. "If you'd moved your butt, we'd have been out of here."

"If you'd done it yesterday, we'd be up the trail," Becky said.

Weedy snapped off the toothpick in his teeth and threw the pieces in the gutter. "Hey, Pork, did you really blow up the hot springs?"

"What hot springs?" Meeker smiled, jowls bunching over his shirt collar.

"The sheriff wouldn't have done it. He didn't even know, did he, Pork?"

"I do my job," Meeker said. "And I don't like being called Pork." He took the registration from Finn and scanned it quickly. "This is expired."

"You know that," Finn said. "You stopped me last week."

"He's been here all of five minutes, Pork," Weedy said. "He was checking his tires out of concern for the public safety. Not one single cripple has wanted to park here."

"You keep your mouth shut," Meeker said.

Weedy grinned and stuck his hands into the air and held them high.

Meeker wrote on his pad.

"This is why Pork is so popular," Weedy said to Shanks. "He doesn't play favorites. He's a shit to everyone across the board."

Meeker looked up. "You got deaf ears, spick-o?"

Weedy kept his hands up. "I wasn't talking to you. I was

talking to Neil. Hey, Finn, you ever read the *Texas Sex Manual*?"

"No."

"It goes, one, push in. Two, pull out. Three, repeat if necessary. Four, let the steer go."

Finn laughed, and even Becky smiled.

Meeker tore off the ticket and handed it to Finn. "I could order this vehicle off the road," he said, "but being that it's hunting season, I'll give you to the end of the week. When you come down, register it first thing, you hear?" He tipped his hat to Becky. "You folks have a nice day."

Finn was still shaking when Meeker turned off the blue lights and moved on up Main.

"Forget it," Weedy said. "Get going. Have a good time. I'll see you Monday. Don't forget the bet, Becky. Shoot first, ask questions later."

Becky nodded. "Bye, Neil," she said. "I'll bring you a steak."

Finn got into the cab and revved the engine. "I just hope we get snow," he said.

He popped the clutch and jerked away from the curb, nearly taking Weedy down. Becky waved. And then the truck was burning oil up the state highway toward the pass.

4

Ed Wainwright spent most of Friday in Chipeta Springs organizing a tri-county message service for hunters. Chipeta was the hub city for the ranches and small towns in a hundred-mile radius of southwestern Colorado, the place people went for plumbing fixtures, new cars, birthday cakes, and McDonald's hamburgers. It was forty miles north and two thousand feet lower than Gold Hill, warmer and dryer, especially in fall and winter. It was the logical place for the message headquarters.

Together with Sidney Towe, the Chipeta Springs sheriff, and Jake Brannon from Lakeland, Ed had worked out a plan for the television and radio stations to broadcast emergency messages twice a day. If a hunter heard his name called, he was to get in touch with the station or with the nearest sheriff's department.

Ed knew that Friday, hectic as it was, would be his last day of peace for a while. The tourist season was bad enough, but families were generally well behaved. Airstream trailers with kids, retirees, backpackers anxious for a tramp across timberline, people sitting in the mountain air—those people were easy. But hunters were fanatics. They came out of the woodwork in October and November—bloodthirsty locals (even women he never thought were killers), out-of-staters who thought hunting was an excuse for war maneuvers, out-of-towners who wanted a couple weeks away from their wives and families. It was a nightmare come to life.

And almost all hunters were drinkers. Beer, wine, whiskey, gin—it didn't matter what. They could raise more flies than a buffalo herd, and all of them were carrying guns.

There were bound to be accidents. Last year there were two or three that still lodged in his mind. Robert Ballard had tugged his 30.06 loose from a pile of dirty clothes in his closet and woke up in the clinic with a bullet hole in his shoulder. And Flossie Jiminez had shot her poodle in the kitchen of her house on Mineral Street. In the west end of the county three hunters from Arizona had leveled one of Winifred Scott's prize Hereford steers from a roadside rest area and proceeded to butcher the animal right next to the highway.

The incidents of mayhem and misfortune were too numerous to remember. There were bar fights, poachers on private land, windshields shot out of cars. Hunters rolled their Jeeps and ran their trucks into trees. With so much raw energy on the loose something bad had to happen and it usually did. Meeker's blowing up the hot springs that morning was just a prelude.

He was thinking these things out loud to Jake Brannon over a beer in the Cubs' Lounge that afternoon in Chipeta Springs. "My own deputy," Ed said. "Can you imagine that?"

"You can't get good help nowadays," Brannon said. "People don't have no sense anymore. Over in Lakeland we had this man feeding his kids dog food." He paused and looked over toward the bar. "You want another one, Ed?"

"No, thanks, I've got to drive."

"And you remember a couple years back that fellow over in Dove Creek shot his wife between the eyes and testified in court he thought she was a jackrabbit."

"I remember it," Ed said.

"You sure you don't want another one? On me. It's going to be a tough couple of weeks."

"You know Sharon," Ed said, though he knew Brannon didn't. "She'll get on me if I drink."

He had never been much of a drinker anyway. Two or three beers was all he could handle, though he was a big man, paunchy and two hundred pounds. He looked at his watch.

Brannon ordered another Coors.

"In fact," Ed said, "I've got to get home. My kids are out of school, and I want to have a talk with my deputy before he starts blowing up streets and cars." Ed got up and shrugged generously and tucked in his khaki shirt. "Let me get these." He dropped down a five.

He had never been much of a liar either. There had never been much in his life to lie about, at least not to Jake Brannon. Not to Sharon, either, until now. He was too old to lie, though forty-six wasn't that old. He felt old. Lying made him feel old.

But he lied about Paula Esquebel. She had given him a sense of unease he hadn't felt in years—more like the intimation of something other than the real thing, and whatever it was made him feel good. It was like having a fever from which he knew he'd recover. It was devastating and temporary, and while it lasted he could not think about much else. He intended to recover from it soon. But while it lasted, it was oddly brilliant, like visions.

He had never meant for it to happen. That went without saying. When Paula Esquebel got tired of him, which would be soon, that would be the end of it. He wasn't deceiving himself on that score. It would be over quickly and he'd forget about it and go back to his normal life.

He left the Cubs' Lounge at dusk and headed south on the state highway. The road climbed steadily, mostly following the river course, though he couldn't feel the rise of the land in the Blazer. The arc lights of the farms and ranches were just coming on, separating from the dusk, and the mountains in the distance were silhouetted against the light blue sky. The Blazer droned smoothly, cutting through cornfields broken and yellow, through alfalfa pastures with bales of hay lying on the ground.

He had met Paula Esquebel at the Chipeta Springs hospital the summer before when he'd brought in a little girl from Iowa. A fishhook had pulled the girl's eye halfway from its socket. She was a beautiful kid too. The father had been flyfishing the river, and the mother had been fixing a picnic lunch. The little girl, who was six, had climbed down the embankment behind her father just as he was making a cast.

Ed had cried. He'd sat out in the emergency room, and Paula, who was the nurse on duty, had had to take him across the street to a diner. "What'll those people think?" she asked him. "You're an officer and I'm a nurse. We can't be going around in hysterics."

He hadn't been able to answer her. He had no voice, no way to stop. How could such things happen?

Paula had put her hand on his arm. "What if a kidnapper or a robber pointed a gun at someone?" she asked. "You wouldn't panic, would you? You'd be a brave man."

He understood what she meant. A sheriff was supposed to act in a certain manner. He'd had his job eighteen years, and he'd never cried before. Five years ago he wouldn't have. He'd have sat with the father and comforted him. He'd have filed reports.

But there he'd been. No excuses. In eighteen years he had come to see himself as a man of good behavior, a husband and a father and a public servant. But some loss had come to him. That was how he thought of it. He was getting soft. He thought of things in ways that he'd never considered before. Sometimes he sat around in his office as if he were stunned, wondering what he had done to himself.

Ten miles out of Chipeta Springs, almost to the county line, he turned west past the Indian Museum on White Mesa Road. The gravel paralleled a dry streambed and skirted a plateau which long ago had been the last encampment of the Uncompahgres before they had embarked on the Trail of the Wind into Utah. It was dark now, and the shale mesa shone above him in the moonlight.

The light in the back of her bungalow was on, and he accelerated over the hill, watching the light grow nearer and brighter. He hoped she was still in her nurse's uniform—the prim, clean white dress and blouse, the whitish stockings, sturdy white shoes. He liked her black hair and bronze skin against the white.

She had changed to jeans and a thin shirt, but he wasn't disappointed. She gave him a lingering kiss.

"I've been waiting," she said.

"I don't have much time. I've been in Chipeta all day."

"You're always busy," she said.

"Not always."

"Come on, then." She took his hand and they went into the living room.

The next thing he knew, he was on the tightrope. She curled above him in the dark, raised herself so that her small breasts were outlined against the wall and her black hair fell toward him over her face. She pushed her hair back so he could see her move.

She moved slowly. He thought of her as a cat lying in wait. If she barely moved, he would come closer to her. All she had to do was wait, do no more than breathe. He concentrated on her breathing, on the streak of light that shone through the window in her hair.

Finally he lifted his hands to her breasts. This touch seemed to be what she wanted, and she pressed down on him harder, turned, sprang at him as if she were pursuing now instead of hiding. He pinched her breasts harder, then slid his hands to her hips, holding on tightly. Suddenly she stopped. He heard her brief cry in the dark, listened to her sharp breathing, held on as hard as he could.

5

Ed hadn't been more than ten minutes on the road from Paula Esquebel's when a call came over the police band from Sharon at the dispatcher's desk. He'd just passed the intersection where there was a Texaco station and the Little Italy Restaurant, and the spur highway cut west toward the Utah line. As soon as he heard her voice, he remembered he was supposed to have called her from Chipeta Springs.

"Where've you been?" she asked. "I've been trying to get you for an hour. I called the Little Italy—"

"Meetings," he said. "I stopped at the Cubs' Lounge with Brannon."

"All this time?"

"What's happened?" he asked. "Anything big?"

"Some calls about John Meeker. Everyone wants to know whether he was the one who blew up the pools. I've been noncommittal. You'll probably have to make a statement. Jerilyn's been here twice."

The radio crackled, and Ed waited for it to clear. "That bitch," he said. "Where's Meeker now?"

"No idea. Home, I guess. He turned in his tickets."

"And?"

"He got Finn again. Let me see what for."

There was a pause on the other end while Sharon looked through the tickets. She was his best help, knew where things were, made the office hum. He didn't know what he'd do without her.

He watched the odometer roll past eighty-four thousand in the green dash light, then glanced up again at the road. Out ahead the highway raced between barbed wire fences on both sides. Spindly willows lined the shadowy ditch on his left. On his right was pastureland.

The white picket fence of the cemetery came into view a few hundred yards ahead, and in a minute he was easing past the fence and the gravestones. He didn't want to talk to Jerilyn. He never did. He didn't like to make statements. And why couldn't she give him some peace and quiet? Not that it was only him. She'd just as soon take on the county assessor or the zoning board. Whoever made news was the one Jerilyn had for breakfast.

He had nothing to say about Meeker. The Commission had hired him over Ed's objection, and they weren't going to back off for a little destruction of property in the name of a higher good. That was how politics worked these days. Of course, the easy way out would be to say Neil Shanks made a mistake. He couldn't have seen John Meeker on the River Road. But Shanks was his friend, and Shanks had enough troubles already in town.

On the other hand, Ed didn't want to put himself in a bad light with the election coming up. There wasn't any opposition yet—who would want the job?—but if he let a controversy get started, if Jerilyn got out of hand, someone might challenge him. The truth was he'd told Meeker to tear the pools apart. Ed hadn't thought he'd do it with dynamite.

Sharon came back on. "Parked with a horse trailer in a no-parking zone, parked in a handicapped space, expired registration, second offense."

"Not life threatening," Ed said. "Not ten to fifteen in the slammer."

"But you know Finn."

"I'll remind Meeker it's a peacetime job."

Static snapped over the radio as Ed came into the low foothills before the canyon.

"You coming home?" Sharon asked.

"Right. Do you need something at Matheson's?"

"You should talk to Louise."

"I should talk to Louise. What's she done now?"

"I found beer cans in her room."

"Empty or full?"

"Empty or full? She's fifteen years old."

"I know how old she is."

He stared into the sweeping arc of the headlights. He knew this road by heart, the way it curved away from the river just beyond the first low rise of the canyon by the trailer park, the way it tilted slightly along the juniper hill-side before it climbed more steeply through the sandstone breaks. He'd always thought Louise and Jerry would turn out differently from the way they had. Camping at the reservoir, fishing on weekends, school events—all the good things parents were supposed to do for their children hadn't helped them. Why hadn't that been enough? Sharon was even making a quilt for Louise's sixteenth birthday. And Louise had beer cans in her room.

"I'll talk to her," he said.

"She says she doesn't know how they got there," Sharon went on. "Someone's playing a joke, she says."

"I said I'd talk to her."

He steered into the curve, through the long line, and the shadows of junipers raced away out the window. The static of the radio got on his nerves.

"Ed?"

"I'll sign off," he said. "Too much interference in the canyon."

He clicked off the radio and hooked the receiver under the dash. That was all he needed, for Christ's sake, his daughter drinking. Let Jerilyn get hold of that. Louise had been hanging around the hot springs after school, though she said she wasn't. She denied everything. She didn't know how the car got dented or who'd stolen her homework at school. How was he going to handle the drinking?

He wondered whether Paula's scent was still on him. He always worried about that. You got used to the smells of things—smoke in a bar, say, or the reek of a stall. You didn't notice it anymore, but someone else might. Sharon might.

Sharon was still a handsome woman, a step slower, maybe, a little more makeup than ten years ago, an extra pound or two in the hips. But she had aged better than he had. He loved her. He thought he did, anyway, and they had kept a pretty solid balance over the years. Until now.

The red sandstone whirled past through the headlights, and he came out into a brushy bend where the river curved back on itself. Suddenly a deer jumped out from the patch of willows beside the road and landed gently on the pavement in two or three feathery steps. It was a small, big-eared doe, and instead of continuing on across the road, she stopped abruptly and stared into the headlights.

His first impulse was to drive right through her. That was the rule of safety: hit the animal. It was lighter than the car. Keep the wheel steady and take the shock straight on. But he swerved. He aimed the Blazer into the dark unbroken space in the other lane and, as if in slow motion, skidded past the tawny doe, literally right past her eyes. Then he spun the wheel back again so the Blazer veered across the road again toward the river. The car fishtailed, caught the momentum of its own immense weight, and tipped sideways. He thought it would flip, but the tires hit a patch of sand at the edge of the road. It slid, and he steered through the slide and braked gently.

The Blazer slowed, hit dry road, and jerked back into the right lane as if he'd never avoided the deer at all. He'd never seen it. He checked the rearview, but the doe had disappeared into the sandstone spires on the far side of the road.

6

At dawn Saturday the first shots rang out from the trees beneath Twin Peaks just above town—two sharp cracks answered in muffled echo across in the Amphitheater. More shots fell across the slopes of Mt. Hayden and Brown Mountain and down through the steep ravine of Cutler Creek. There was a pause then of ten minutes or more, and then more shots, muted by distance, caromed from Twin Peaks and Oak Creek Canyon and from the Ute Chief Mine Trail which skirted the ridge on the south side of the Amphitheater.

Shanks woke in his room in Tin Pan Alley. At first he couldn't remember where he was—what noise was it that woke him? Light was seeping into the kitchen. Furniture sifted into consciousness. Books. Then he saw the hawk Wendell Blythe had stuffed for him, hanging from a piece of fishline, its wings spread wide. It seemed to drift in the room on an invisible current of air.

He listened for the stream which ran in the cement flume beside his apartment, but he didn't hear anything—not the water or a bird or even traffic on Main Street a block away.

In the spring or after a rain the water was so loud in the flume, it sounded like a train barreling right through his room. But that morning, nothing. He got up and looked at the thermometer outside the kitchen window. That explained it: twenty-two degrees. He looked up the flume and saw ice had formed in a slick glaze, a jagged white line which looked like a scar.

He stoked the coals in the woodstove, laid in some thin kindling and a piece of pine, and blew gently on the embers. After the flame broke he got back into bed and waited for the room to heat.

He had only a general memory of the night before. The jukebox in the Golddigger had played an endless succession of country songs, and voices and laughter lilted in the smoky room. He remembered that part. He'd been drinking beer and shooting eight-ball partners with Weedy Garcia and Charlie Fernsten and Flash Toomey. Flash hadn't ever liked him much after Shanks had sold him the fast-food window and it went broke, and the game had more pressure than usual. Once when he'd scratched on the eight, Flash had been so angry, Shanks had gone across the street to the Outlaw for a while. The Outlaw had been busy too. He'd watched one hunter pass out at the bar and the other one go on talking and drinking. He'd had a beer with Jerry Wainwright, who was a good kid who had no more idea what to do with himself than a rabbit in a trap. Jerry liked working on cars, doing tune-ups and repairs and resurrecting old junk heaps for friends, but Ed wanted him in college or in the army. "Not that he says anything," Jerry confided, "but I know."

They'd had a couple more beers, and then they'd gone back to the Golddigger, which was cheaper. He should have gone home to bed, but Jerry wanted to drink. There he was listening to the same music, the slap of the same pool balls. It had slowed down a little, but the hard-core drinkers were still there—the ones who wouldn't leave until the bar closed. Even Flash and Weedy and Fernsten had gone home.

Earlene was behind the bar. Shanks had had a kind of endless conversation with her over the time he'd been in town—a few words when he had a beer in the afternoons— *Hi, Neil, what's going on?*—or late at night when she was making last calls and drinking herself. She was a willowy woman with very long brown hair which she wore in a barrette and let fall down her back nearly to her waist. She had crooked teeth, wide-set eyes, smooth swarthy skin. She'd offered Jerry and him a shot of tequila on the house. "Old times," she'd said.

He hadn't wanted tequila, but he'd taken it. He was in the bar, and the point of being in the bar was to drink, so he took it. Jerry had felt a little queasy after that. He'd spent a long time in the back room, and when he came out he said good night. Shanks stayed until the bar closed, and when Earlene had asked him to go home with her, he wasn't in a state to refuse. It wasn't the first time, and it probably wouldn't be the last.

At least he'd had sense enough to come home in the middle of the night. When his room was warm he got up again to measure the day. The sun rose later now and farther south, and each morning he could see it a little differently on the summit of Whitehouse Peak across the valley. The cornice on the peak emerged from the deep blue dark, a monolith of granite and snow that seemed to him possessed of its own light. It brightened to pink, then pink-yellow, and then the first sun hit it with an eerie glow.

The sun would work its way down the mountain against the shadow, through the dark spruce and the gray-white aspens and across the red sandstone to the river. It would get to the river about ten o'clock. He watched it every day.

His apartment was in a converted garage halfway down the alley and a half block from Main, between Placer and Mineral streets. A row of chinked-log prospectors' cabins lined both sides of the track. In the old days miners and millmen lived there, but over the years the cabins had become the outbuildings of the Victorian houses on Fourth

Street or the storage sheds for the shops on Main. Now the alley had degenerated into a conglomeration of broken fences, garages in disrepair, woodpiles, telephone poles, and a few run-down apartments.

Opposite his room was the back side of the newly remodeled Mother Lode Hotel and the Centennial Restaurant, which, in the evenings, billowed out the smoke of flame-broiled steaks or shish kebab through a huge fan. But traffic in the alley was scarce. An old woman who waitressed in the summers and didn't have a car lived two cabins down, and sometimes cars filtered through to the county building at the end of the block at Placer. Most of the trucks came in the mornings—food service trucks for the restaurant, repair vans, the laundry service for the hotel.

It looked like a good-weather day, a day to take care of a few things he had let slide. He had been waiting for the hunting season because the town began to wind down, and the one person he wanted to see—Aurey Vallejos—came down from his mining claim to get out of the way of the madmen who roamed the hills. So that was on the agenda, and he wanted to get up to the Xanadu Spring, and in the afternoon he meant to keep shop. But right then he wanted to assemble the information he had gathered on Thomas Shanks.

He had come west to find out about his great-grandfather. Thomas Shanks had spent four years in Gold Hill between 1880 and 1884, and the trail Neil had followed had led him down dozens of blind alleys, one-way streets that went nowhere, cul-de-sacs. It had taken him two years of patient work poking around the archives, exploring mining claims, asking questions. And still he wasn't certain what he had.

It hadn't been his fault it had taken so long. He'd put off making some inquiries in order to earn money. That was necessity. And there was no doubt he'd been hampered by the way he'd got started when he'd first arrived in town.

He'd got started on the wrong foot. He admitted that. He'd got his first job as a stringer for the *Chipeta Daily*

Pilot, covering events in Gold Hill. It had been just what he'd wanted—a way to learn about the town, a way to meet people. The first few pieces he'd done well enough. He'd put together an enthusiastic account of the Fourth of July parade and fire-hose water fight on Main Street and a straightforward feature on the town's public hot-springs swimming pool. But when he'd been assigned more controversial topics, he'd alienated, or at least polarized, a good portion of the town. He'd done a story on property reassessments which got the county commissioners mad at him, and then two articles about a proposed sign ordinance which had stirred up every business owner with a sign too high, too wide, or too bright.

Everyone wrote letters to the weekly *Gold Hill Chronicle,* not only protesting the proposed ordinance, but also vilifying the journalist who reported on it. He was variously called a scurrilous outsider, an ignorant newcomer, and a rabble-rouser.

He wrote a rebuttal which was never published: he'd meant no harm. Didn't people understand he was only doing his job?

Then in the midst of that controversy he was arrested for trespassing.

All he'd done was climb up a public trail to get a view of the town. He'd wanted to put himself in the mind's eye of Thomas Shanks—to look out over the bowl which held the history of the last hundred years, to imagine what his great-grandfather had seen. The letters Thomas Shanks had written home had been haunting, doughty, mysterious. He'd described the way the towering mountains rose into the sky, how gold fever corrupted men, the ways in which the climate determined character. He discussed books he'd read, philosophized about government policy. He was amused that the Indians still cherished their land as a hunting preserve when millions in gold were right beneath the surface of the earth.

No one else in his family had ever stood on that sandstone edge, and he had felt that summer afternoon as if he were looking straight down into the past. The governor of Colorado had stayed in the Mother Lode Hotel in 1876 during the town's charter celebration. Houses were being constructed, one after another on the sunny eastern hillside —frame houses with towers and gables and porches which afforded a view of Whitehouse Peak and Mt. Abrams. The opera house hosted *The Marriage of Figaro,* a variety of vaudeville troupes, readings of Shakespeare, and costume balls. Gold had made possible the singing of the human soul.

But Shanks had seen another town too. It was the shadowed land in the river bottom from which the sun disappeared at three in the afternoon. It was the back-alley cabins and the saloons and cribs and squalid clapboard houses on the lower side of Main. He imagined the men and women who had lived in rooming houses and in tents and shelters, whose chance it was at that moment of history to transform their lives and the lives of their children—as Thomas Shanks had done—if only they were the ones to find gold.

Shanks did not know how many had become rich. They were the lucky ones, the minority, he was sure. How many others had failed, had sunk into the forgotten lore of the city, he of course could never know.

Shanks had intended to write his own letters home. He had phrased in his own words his observations—even that very afternoon he had made notes—but he was afraid of being compared to Thomas. He had been formulating such notions when he'd heard a bird singing higher up the trail. He had ventured a little higher into the hill, following the source of the reedy whistle. But the bird kept receding. It called from a stand of tall pines, then from an aspen glen higher up, then from the next bench higher.

He spent a half hour in this vain pursuit, nervous of the altitude, strangely apprehensive of going on. Then he'd come upon an abandoned mine. All that remained of it was a few boards where a prospector's hut had been and a collapsed tunnel sunk into the side of the hill. There was no name on the claim, no sign for private property.

He'd poked around in the wreckage for a few minutes, found some newspaper insulation dated 1894, together with a few shards of blue glass and a barrel that had stamped on it Mount Holly Molasses. Then he'd looked into the plugged tunnel to see how far the darkness went into the mountain.

"Stop it right there."

Shanks turned slowly. On the rise above him was an old man dressed in plain leather, a big man with a head of wild gray hair and a full beard, holding a shotgun in one hand and the reins of two horses in the other.

"I got you," the old man said.

The man had marched him down the trail, riding one horse, leading the other, making Shanks walk. He'd kept the gun on him all the way through town, past dozens of people standing on the sidewalk, to the sheriff's office.

Technically he was guilty. He'd said that to Ed Wainwright straight out. If that was the old man's property, he'd been on it without permission. On the other hand, there wasn't a fence or a sign warning against trespassing. He hadn't been able to distinguish the mine from the national forest property surrounding it or from any of the other dead holes that honeycombed the hills. "I've been to a half dozen other claims," he said, "and no one ever pointed a shotgun at me."

"Nobody ever caught you before," the old man said.

"Now, Pop, it's severe to point a gun at someone, isn't it? I know this young man here, and he's not that bad a character. Writes for some newspaper, I think. I'll do a check on him, if you think that'll ease your mind any. But do you think we ought to discourage a man from curiosity?"

"The gun wasn't loaded," the old man said. "I don't want him at the mine."

"Did he do any damage?"

"I didn't give him a chance."

Ed nodded patiently and smiled. "How'll it be if I keep him in jail here for a day or two and give him some advice?"

Pop wasn't sure, but he consented in the end. They all shook hands, and when Pop left, the sheriff challenged Shanks to a game of pinochle, and they talked almost all night long.

That had been the start of a friendship with Ed, and it would have been the end to most of his troubles in town except that two days later the *Chronicle* printed its issue with the headline CHIPETA PILOT WRITER NABBED ON CLAIM.

The fallout had been swift and sure: he was fired from his job. The sign ordinance was defeated, and he was relegated to acquaintances on the fringe of town. No one would hire him. If he'd trespass, what might he do next? And few people would answer questions. The people who knew the history of the town wouldn't speak to him, and the ones who would—Weedy, Charlie Fernsten, Earlene—knew only a certain side of the present.

The exceptions were Ed Wainwright and Aurelio Vallejos. Shanks had told Ed what he was doing in town, what he needed, and Ed had put him in touch with Aurey.

"Aurey won't know about the sign ordinance or the article in the *Chronicle*," Ed said. "He's a loner, about your age, maybe twenty-eight. I could figure it out. He lives on a claim up in Gold Ring Gulch. You know his dad, Ernesto, down at the Nugget Café. They been in Gold Hill longer than I have. Raised five children. A good family. I want to know how they did it. All the kids turned out. Two of the boys are lawyers in Denver, one's a priest in Chama, New Mexico, and Tony is a graduate student at CU. Aurey's the only one who came home, though. Can you imagine that? He came home to look for gold."

"You think he can tell me about Thomas Shanks?"

"I think he knows as much as anyone else around here. Your biggest problem will be finding him, and then after that, getting him to talk."

Ed had been right about that. Aurey lived three miles up

a nearly impassable Jeep road, and he rarely came to town. When he did it was to get supplies, and even when Shanks was able to locate him, it wasn't easy to get information from him. He had no grudge. And he wasn't hostile to questions. It was just that Aurey was different. Shanks had never met anyone else like him. They'd sit across from one another and Shanks would ask a question, and Aurey would look at him, not coldly or cruelly, but placidly, as though Shanks had spoken in a different language. He wouldn't answer.

"What was the town of Uncompahgre Forks like before it was abandoned?"

"Who ran the Phoenix Mine?"

"Did Pop Krause help his father up at the Black Owl?"

Aurey would consider the questions for a long time, perhaps thinking what to answer. Shanks didn't know. He might have a system for remembering. Sometimes Aurey shrugged; sometimes he answered. Shanks never quite knew on what principle Aurey managed to speak, how he chose what to say. When he answered he was invariably correct. Shanks tested him occasionally with obscure questions and corroborated the answers in the records at the county clerk's office.

"Who operated the One-Foot Mine before Major Walcott?"

"Tess Steinberg from New York owned it for eighteen days," Aurey said, "but she didn't run it. It was run by a man named Crawford Tway, who married Tess later. Tess sold it for forty-two thousand dollars and it never paid Major Walcott more than three thousand in the six years he had it."

Whatever Shanks read, Aurey knew more. Whatever research Shanks did in books and records, Aurey understood from having explored the land. He had heard of Thomas Shanks.

"He owned the Sonja Claim in Dexter Creek and the Dusty Dan on Twin Peaks, but they were worthless pieces of ground."

"Then where did Thomas Shanks's money come from?"
Aurey stared at him for a long time and shrugged his shoulders.

It was cold outside that Saturday morning. Shanks dug his hands into his pockets as he walked down the alley toward Placer. Smoke from the woodstoves hung above the town like a layer of fog in the still air, and his breath feathered above his head. The sun line had fallen through the aspens and onto the red sandstone cliff, but it had not yet reached the river.

He had taken longer than he meant to in reading over his notes, but it couldn't be helped. He had been trying to unravel the idea that Thomas Shanks had been a silent partner in one of the mines. Thomas had known a man named Glen Wesley from St. Louis—he'd mentioned him in a letter, and Wesley had done well at Heaven's Hole. Perhaps Thomas had invested in the mine without being named in the board of directors. What he couldn't understand, though, was why Thomas was so secretive. It was true that in those days record-keeping was erratic. The registration of thousands of claims must have been particularly chaotic, despite the fact that the procedure protected the miner as much as it benefited the tax office. But why hadn't Thomas Shanks been clearer in his letters?

He had resigned himself to never knowing. Almost. That was what Becky kept telling him to do: either find out or forget it. Why do you keep postponing? But he wasn't postponing. He was thinking. He wanted to clarify the facts, dismantle myths. He had checked hundreds of claims in the records and had come up with the Sonja claim and the Dusty Dan. Where had the money come from?

That morning he meant to try a new tack with Aurey. Sometimes what a man didn't know could be as useful as what he did. And now he wanted to find Aurey and see what new turn lay ahead.

He reached Placer and jogged down to Main, heading for the Nugget Café. Cars were lined up in the diagonal spaces in front of Rita's and the pharmacy and Furze's Sporting Goods. The sky was a tentative blue he had not seen often—paler than usual because of the smoke or from the high misty clouds. Four-wheel-drives full of hunters drifted past the closed bars and the unlit windows of dress shops and arcades shut down for the season. The air was tight, exhilarating, and Shanks quickened his step. Sporadic shots echoed again from the direction of Ptarmigan Pass and from the trees on the lower slope of Whitehouse.

A volley of rifle fire burst from the Bridge to Heaven high up behind him. The people still in town were late, eager to catch up to whatever they had already missed. Shanks took everything in because hunting season was the closest thing to what Thomas Shanks must have seen in the gold rush days. It was a time of action, when men were driven into the hills by the hope of riches and so many otherwise normal men howled at the moon.

7

Shanks had been restocking two-by-fours on the catwalk when the flash fire had run through the sawdust in the air. A spark had jumped from a machine and exploded around him like a bomb. It had happened so suddenly that he'd been thrown backward from his narrow perch into nothing.

He had always imagined such a fall or an impending collision when there would be an instant of recognition, a second when he'd have time to regain his balance or steer to avoid the impact. But when he'd been thrown free by the concussion of ignited dust—when it had actually happened —he'd had no chance to do anything. His arms were wide open like a backdiver's, but he didn't soar or float. He fell. He hadn't had a moment to cover his head with his hands or to turn his shoulder. He'd fallen and struck the edge of the forklift which jerked his body in midair into another contortion before he'd hit the cement floor.

Three men had been badly burned. A woman's collarbone had been broken by flying debris. A lathe operator, escaping the flames, was crushed to death by a sheaf of plywood which toppled from the bin onto the deck. Shanks himself had been taken by ambulance to the emergency room in

Grayling, pained, bruised, in shock. But he had suffered no visible injury.

That had been nearly three years before, but it came back to him all the time. He still thought of it at odd moments, still dreamed of it, still relived it as part of what had brought him west.

After the accident he had taken time off: a week that lasted two. He lay in bed in his mother's house. He was twenty-six, and with the exception of a year's traveling, he'd worked in the family mill since college. The notion of the business had been ingrained in him, and it was as much a part of his life as the air or the jack pines or the low sky. He couldn't say he'd resisted it or chosen it. In small ways he'd been uncertain. Instead of studying forestry at Michigan State, as his brother and sister had, he'd majored in English at Michigan. And he hadn't gone right to work out of school. He'd used his savings and spent the year after graduation in Mexico and Costa Rica and Belize, fishing and reading and loafing in the sun.

But there had never been a question in his mind about going back. Belize was a postponement. He had a life's work staked out ahead of him, and travel was a luxury he indulged before settling in. After all, he'd spent every summer since he was fifteen working in one family mill or another, learning how lumber was cured, where it came from, what difference the weather and the soil made on hardwoods and softwoods, what grades of lumber could be cut for plywood or two-by-fours or four-by-fours. He'd visited lumber outlets all over Michigan, met loggers, tree-farm owners, timber brokers.

And he meant to go on after the accident. His mother and sister encouraged him to rest, but Roland needled him. "A business doesn't run itself," he said. "Someone has to do it."

"He could come back to a job in the office," his mother said. "He knows the mill operations. He can get experience in marketing and strategy."

"Let him take his time," his sister said.

Sylvia took long walks with him along the snowy, sandy

roads. They listened to the wind sigh through the trees. They talked. She told him not to hurry. "Don't listen to Roland," she said.

Roland tried to whet his interest. "It's hard work where I am," he said, "but we can make more money than we are now. We ought to consider developing the land we have. Maybe you could do research on that, Neil. You're good at that. I was thinking if we open up a little, say, to the potential of vacation homes or condominiums on some of the lakes, we can increase our cash position without sacrificing our timber resources."

"We have choices, then?" Shanks asked.

"We have a million choices."

Two weeks turned into a month. He couldn't describe the pain in words. He had no symptoms. He went ice fishing on Higgins Lake, sat in the cold shelter, listened.

His father had taught him how to cut bait, thread the hooks, sink the line into the deep water. One had to be patient. The fish were slower, more lethargic in winter, taking their body temperature from the water. They fed erratically, as if by mood.

The shelter was his father's—a loosely made frame of wood with a tarp slung over it. He had a small propane stove. Ice fishing was a long vigil he had shared with his father—Roland and Sylvia never came. His father pointed out winter birds: finches, grosbeaks, jays, an occasional owl. They talked baseball and hockey, about the smell of the mill which his father had never liked, about books and the rituals of the family.

When Shanks was there alone it had not seemed lonely. He watched for birds along the shore, nodded over the heat of the stove, read books which he held with his gloves on.

In the evenings at home he had taken to reading Thomas Shanks's letters. He had read many of them before, when his father was alive, when he was twelve or thirteen, and he remembered thinking of Thomas Shanks as a pioneer, standing in the middle of a brilliantly lit street filled with horses and gold.

He had heard the family stories too—how through his own sheer energy and will Thomas Shanks had made his fortune and had become as great as any president or army general. There was a photograph of him on the day of his departure west which showed a man of exceptional alertness, a high forehead gleaming in the sun, a luxuriant moustache and sideburns neatly kept. His dark eyes stared into the lens as if he meant to see into the soul of the camera. He was willing to take any risk, and almost single-handedly he had changed himself and his family from paupers to kings.

The letters were collected in scrapbooks according to whom they had been sent to, and arranged by date, each letter in its original envelope addressed to his parents, his brother George in Boston, his wife Sonja and their children, or to a variety of aunts and uncles. Nearly all the letters were written on coarse gray stationery in ink sometimes smudged.

Shanks did not read the letters by books, but rather in chronological order.

July 30, 1880

Dear Brother George,

So much has happened in the two weeks since I arrived in Gold Hill that I cannot begin to make sense of the events. It's a land of great opportunity, and it's good one of us had the good fortune to take advantage while the other is there in civilization to maintain sanity. The mountains are of such spectacular beauty that I cannot bear to see them stripped and gouged as men are hell-bound to do as quickly as possible. There will be more destruction before there will be any healing. And there will be more wealth before there's an end to this wild ride.

I am living in a rooming house with twenty other men jammed in and smelly. The owners, a man in his twenties and his wife, have recognized I am not of the class of most others, and have given me the liberty of using their sitting room. . . . They have made a strike in the area near here known as Plutarch's Folly, and they are intending to set up a mill there. Everyone had such dreams here. I have them myself. It's hard to find a man who doesn't believe that in a matter of hours he will be rich. . . .

September 19, 1881

Dear Mother and Father,

The weather in this forsaken land has chilled so that now the leaves of the quaking aspens are an exquisite yellow, rushing like flames up the sides of the mountains. You would be surprised how brilliant these banks of leaves are, even accustomed as you are to the countryside of Ohio and Michigan. The leaves are set fire by the crystalline air even from a distance of many miles.

As you might imagine, there is hearty competition for territory here, and no one is more aware than I of this hard fact of existence. The mountains are literally overrun with men intent on getting there first—wherever it is —and by contrast Michigan seems the more idyllic to me now. . . . As I've written to you before, I intend to come home one day, but not until I have played out my options, which, as you see from the enclosed sum of money, have already begun to pay dividends.

I have determined that what I mean to reap by the sweat of my brow shall not be spread along the saloon-keepers or wasted in risky enterprises which, as soon as this rush is past, will be themselves driven from memory forever. To that end, and in some measure as an expression of gratitude, I send this small token. . . .

December 15, 1881

Dear George,

After a hiatus of nearly three weeks, during which time I traveled to the capital of the State, I am returned to Gold Hill in a most healthy frame of mind. If you care for my opinion, there is more to the business of gold rushes than meets the common eye. . . .

The woman who lets me my room is a charitable sort

who came here from Toronto. I believe I told you her husband is starting a mill, but I suspect he won't make a go of it. He's found less ore than warrants a mill, and as yet it can't be profitable to process low-grade ore when such high-grade is still being turned up everywhere. . . . At least his charming wife had the presence of mind to buy up this house with the first proceeds. . . .

I haven't told anyone much about this woman, but I trust you, dear brother, who have always been close to me. Mrs. Trevor is her name, and she is a subject worthy of poetry, or at least one of the bright gaslights which are just now being placed in service here for the opera. The fact is I am in love with her and she with me. Her husband is frequently away (I felt it politic to retire to Denver when he was home), so we are able to relax together without undue fear, particularly since I have use of their sitting room. It is quite easy to be discreet about such a liaison in a town in which a hundred girls are openly selling their favors every night. I rely on your keeping a confidence in this, since I am only telling you because of my own excess of emotion. I love Sonja, too, of course, as I always have and always will. It is said a man cannot serve two mistresses equally well, but I intend to try. . . .

December 24, 1881

My darling Sonja,

It is with a heart of such mixed emotion that I address this note to you on Christmas Eve. How I wish to be with you and the children on the morrow. Man has yet to devise a means of travel that would bring me to you quickly enough and back again, were I able to escape this wretched town.

I hesitate to say it, luck's being a capricious and ill-tempered sprite, but I believe I am near at hand to a strike—not such as made Frederick Huntington a rich man overnight (I wrote to you of him), but one that will allow me to send you and the children and my dear parents in the coming months more money than I have sent in all the months before combined. I cannot speak too openly about it now, however, for fear that it will not happen.

I have been reading a great deal in my long hours and can give unqualified praise to certain English writers, including Charlotte Brontë, and to an American poet, Walt Whitman, who would make of these mountains greater songs of praise than my own poor images.

The town is ablaze with candles in every window, and as I walked earlier in the street, I prayed that you were well and happy and waiting for my return, which cannot be too many months away. . . .

March 15, 1882

Dear George,

Though it is not spring yet in this country there is a chinook, as the Indians call it, a warm wind, which is at present melting the tons of snow in the mountains and causing flooding in the lower reaches of the valley where the Indians are encamped. An avalanche had closed the railroad to the mines to the south of here, as well as the toll road. No one knows how or when they might be opened again. The toll keepers are busy with shovels and picks, just like the miners, and the owner of the toll road, B. J. Bright and Co., is losing great sums of money daily. Such is the precarious balance the economic system here teeters in. . . .

It has been some months since I've written you, I fear, but I think I have been correct in advising you not to come out just yet. Your offer of assistance is most appreciated, and I can think of no soul I trust more than you. It is indeed a great stroke of Good Fortune which has befallen me on my Western adventure. I cannot now take the time to explain it all to you, but suffice it to say I am making progress in the work, and I am currently able to send to the dear Sonja, who inspires everything I do, and to our beloved parents, a sum of money which will leave them well off should anything happen to me here. I am instructing Sonja and father to invest in land which at present is cheap in Michigan and which later on may provide an income from timber, which will be necessary for the growth of the Nation. Timber, at least, is a resource we can see, and, unlike a man's dreams, cannot be taken from him. . . .

June 1882

My darling Sonja,

Michigan looms before me in my daily thoughts, and I am anxious to return. How strange it is to feel one's heart in one place and one's body in another! Despite the beauty of this mountain land, which certainly you would adore if you were here, the cold air of the Lakes is in my blood, and the mundane panorama of jack pine and meadow grass would excite me as much as a thousand white mountain peaks.

Isn't it odd how things are named? And why do we do it? Now, I can grasp as well as the next the reasons for naming things. I'm a pragmatist, after all. A man must have a name in order to know when he's being shouted at. And where would he meet up with another man without the names of Placer Street and First Avenue? But must we call a mountain by a name merely because we can see it? Col. Walcott, or is it Major? a Civil War pirate and a man of inconsummate greed, will forever be honored by a mountain peak bearing his name, while I will fade from the minds of all souls, except perhaps those of my family.

Perhaps I am more conscious of names here where so much is new and yet to be labeled for our convenience. And perhaps the mixture of the past intrigues me, too, for the Spanish have left a legacy of their exploration—Escalante Canyon, Dominguez Peak, the San Miguel River— more powerful than the Indians.

Of course the Indians remain, though not for long. The river which runs through Gold Hill is called for them— the people of warm water, or Uncompahgre, and Chipeta

Springs to the north is named for the wife of Broken Nose. Whites are not good with Indian words, however, and prefer to name the mountains and the rivers to suit themselves. . . .

The mines have the most amusing names, and they fascinate me for their endless combinations of memory and invention. One claim high in the escarpment is called the Swamp Fox; another whose owner hails from Ohio is the Cumberland. (This man, Glen Wesley, is a friend of mine, and he has done well.) But it is thus that the small incursions of the past are echoed in this new land. Some mines have ordinary names: the Gray Jay, after an avian species known for its temerity; the Iron Spike, the Lone Pine. Dozens are variations on the same sad theme: the Last Gasp, the Strike-it-Rich, Heaven's Hole. Others are mysteries to unravel: the Broken Heart, the One-Foot, or the Battlefield. How many, like my own, are called for loved ones? The Lady Belle, Silver Sadie, the Guinevere, the Sonja . . . to whom I am deeply indebted for allegiance. . . .

September 1, 1882

Dear Mother,

The anguish I feel at Father's passing is all the greater for not having learned of it until now, and for being unable to travel myself in order to impart to you personally my solace in an hour already past. The mail was delayed several weeks for reasons which only God knows (we are in this isolated land never given the courtesy of explanations). In the meantime I have contracted a malady which has kept me in bed for a week. . . .

The Indians are still fighting skirmishes in the Dakotas and Montana to the north of us, but it has been some time since we have been troubled here in these mountains by the Uncompahgres. These Indians have understood the exigency of our mission to settle the country and reap the benefits of the gold and silver. But the White population has been afraid of turmoil. My own view is that the situation can be adequately resolved, and perhaps once the gold and silver is extracted the land will return to its natural state and the Indians may once again have it to themselves. . . .

The letters went on sporadically until 1884, when Thomas Shanks returned to Michigan, settled in Grayling where his father and his wife had purchased land, and began the timber business. He died in 1919.

Thomas's two sons, Jason and Frank, operated the company for thirty years, acquiring more land to the north and west of Grayling and further expanding the sawmills into Indiana and Illinois. When Jason's two sons took over in the mid-forties, the company had survived the Depression and was coming back strongly. "There is no such thing as being land poor," Thomas Shanks had once written to George. "So long as we hold our land we have an everlasting resource and shall not have to rely on Luck, that odious Deceiver."

Shanks had hoped, when he reread these letters after the accident, to be inspired by their vibrancy and the echoes of the grandeur they had invoked in him as a child. But he was not inspired. He was further troubled. When he was younger, of course, he had not been privy to the letters Thomas had written George. These had either been hidden from him or had come later to the family albums. It did not shock him that Thomas had had a mistress. That was common enough when men and women were lonely. Nor did it distress him to feel in Thomas's tone of voice the self-satisfied smugness of his own achievements. It was natural for an ambitious and enthusiastic man to embellish his own reputation and to make himself, in his family's eyes, at least, the object of envy. He no longer saw Thomas as a hero. But he knew his own vision was as subject to exaggeration as Thomas's florid prose. It was more than all of these things. A nagging question took root in him, a doubt which, he understood, would not go away no matter how often he read the letters or how many questions he might ask of his relatives.

Had he glimpsed Thomas as simply a different man, revised according to his own more critical appreciation, Shanks could have accepted his forebear as merely human. He could have tolerated a frailer man, less certain of himself, who compensated for what he perceived as weaknesses of the flesh or spirit. Neil Shanks was not a man who cared to judge the decisions others made. Rather, what troubled him was more than the details of a life story. He wanted a clearer version of events, a precise history, not simply to establish his own place within the family, but because any man's footing in the world depended upon the truth.

And the truth was what Thomas Shanks's letters did not tell. In the dozens of letters written to a wide assortment of relatives, Thomas had never recounted the one event that must have been to such a man the most astonishing and profound: the discovery of gold.

What experience could be stronger in a man than to realize he had found what he sought? That he was rich? Why had Thomas not shared the elation of that moment?

And it was all the more curious because he tiptoed around it. He spoke of the Sonja claim. He referred to being near at hand to a strike. He wrote George about his good fortune. For a man given to describing the countryside and the glory of the yellow aspens, who rambled about names and articulated banal emotions and predictable thoughts calculated to endear him to the reader, it was a unfathomable omission.

He contemplated these ideas, and after a few more weeks, he had importuned his mother and Roland and Sylvia for a leave of absence from the company to go west. He wanted his three months of ordinary disability. That time would be sufficient. If it wasn't he would make do.

Not even Sylvia understood, and he could not explain it. It was more a physical feeling than an intellectual quest. Three generations of Shankses had extrapolated Thomas Shanks's fortune into land, stock holdings, three large

houses, a camp on Crystal Lake, the educations of many
children. The company they worked for was founded with
his money. In essence, then, everything the family enjoyed
had derived from Thomas Shanks, a man about whom they
knew nearly nothing.

8

The sheriff spent most of Saturday morning in his office in the cellar of the county building. He had ventured out once to serve subpoenas in a divorce case, and another time to replenish his supply of Skoal, and again at ten-thirty to check the mail. He answered one call out on Dexter Creek Road where Layton Ferguson had heard "more shooting than in the World War." Layton said that every year, and every year Ed went out to make certain it wasn't true.

The office was called the Steam Room or, sometimes, Hades, depending on his frame of mind. He wore short-sleeved shirts year round, had a ceiling fan on, and still he sweated. The heating ducts and hot water pipes for the whole building, and for the firehouse next door, crisscrossed the ceiling above him, and he was certain the hot water that filled the swimming pool percolated under the floor. He'd asked the commissioners for a new office with a thermostat, but they laughed and told him to write more tickets. "It won't hurt you to sweat off a few pounds," they said.

He had talked to Louise the night before, but it wasn't a satisfactory conversation. She denied knowing anything about the beer, as he knew she would. She had never seen them before her mother set them on the dinner table. And what was her mother doing snooping in her room?

That was how Louise was. She didn't believe what was right in front of her eyes. It wasn't her fault. Whatever she did couldn't possibly matter to anyone else.

And what could he do? If he punished her, she would say it wasn't fair since she'd done nothing wrong. It was her word against his. And if he didn't punish her, she would think she could get away with anything. He couldn't lock her in the house. He couldn't brand her as they did in the old days. He could ground her, but what if she refused to obey the edict? What then? Punishment was only useful if the child agreed to it.

So he had been left with saying, "If what you say turns out to be false . . ." as if he didn't trust her. And, "Next time . . ." as if the next time would be different.

The telephone in the office rang constantly. Sharon screened some of the calls, but most of the people wanted to talk to Ed. Elvie McGrew, who was eighty-two, wanted Ed to check on Dottie Gingrich, who hadn't answered her telephone. ("I'll stop by," Ed said.) Barney Westin heard two shots over at the Van Zandt place and was afraid Wick had shot himself. ("A man doesn't shoot himself twice, Barney. Did you call him?") Alice Teague called to complain that Ignacio Krause was letting the junk from his yard spill out again onto River Road. ("I'll have a chat with him," Ed told her.)

He got along with nearly everyone in the county because his method of law enforcement was simple and direct: in every case short of physical injury, he gave everyone the benefit of the doubt. The broken muffler on Neil Shanks's Subaru or Artie Freeman's burning on a no-fire day were worth a little warning and a slap on the back. He'd talk to Pop Krause about his junk. ("Pop, do me and Alice Teague a little favor, will you?") And if Maria Leone, a sixty-six-year-old with twenty grandchildren, sat out on the fire escape of the Windsor Hotel in her slip on a sunny day, nobody suffered. ("I know it may not look the best," Ed told the Chamber of Commerce, "but the law deals with people, not dollar bills.") If Weedy Garcia drove his Camaro down Main with one drink too many, or even two, he could get out and walk home. No problem.

He had to draw certain lines, of course. If Maria Leone took off her slip, or Pop Krause dropped a TV set in the middle of the River Road, then he'd have to do more than talk. And he couldn't allow Finn Carlsson to drag-race with his friends down Main. But as a rule it was easier getting your friends to obey the law than it was getting your enemies to. And he'd be damned if he was going to set himself up as God in a small town where he lived and worked and was trying to raise a decent family.

There were only two windows in his office, both of them right up near the ceiling at just below ground level. Sitting at his desk he could see through the right-hand window directly into the redbrick wall of the fire station across the alley. The left one gave him a view of pure sky. That one he kept clean as the high lakes so he could judge the shades of blue the sky took on or the way the clouds streaked his small glimpse of the firmament.

Just before noon Ed was gazing up through the clean window at the rectangle full of blue, half dreaming of Paula Esquebel, when Sharon buzzed him from the dispatcher's desk outside the office. "Jerilyn McCrady," she said. "Do you want to give her a statement?"

"I'll give her a statement," he said. "You bet your ass. Tell her she's a piece of beef jerky."

"She's standing right here," Sharon said. "I'll send her in, and you can tell her."

A moment later Jerilyn burst in.

"So I'm a piece of beef jerky," she said. "Oh, Ed, you should know better."

"Better than what?"

"Alienating the press."

"Snake, then," he said. "More like a cobra." He took out his new can of Skoal and pinched a little into his cheek. "What can I do you for?"

Jerilyn was a small woman, fiftyish, and she did look a little like a snake—sinewy, weathered, tough—a woman not to be taken lightly, especially in high grass. That morning she had on a blue beret cocked to one side over a mass of short curls, a puffy down jacket, and lipstick too red for the human mind to comprehend.

"Have you been down to the hot springs?" she asked.

"I swung by on the way to the office. Why?"

"Did you order the devastation?"

"Oh, it doesn't look too bad," Ed said. "I wouldn't call it devastation. He only got five or six of them right along the edge of the river."

Jerilyn wrote something down on her pad, then strolled over and examined one of the zoning maps the sheriff had on his wall. The walls were covered with maps of all sorts—aerial photographs of the high country, road maps, topographical quads, blowups of Gold Hill proper, which was the only real town in the county. There were master plans for land use and zoning, mostly in the foothills where developers had begun to press for permission to build more houses, as well as climatic schema from the farmland to the north to the alpine tundra in the southeast and west.

She pulled her glasses down to the tip of her nose and looked over them. "John Meeker is a Lancelot to some people in town," she said.

"He's a West Texan to me," Ed said. "I told the man to close the hot springs. I didn't tell him to rearrange the landscape of the county."

"Did you expect him to put up a sign?"

"That would have been more helpful."

"No nudity, no loitering, no drugs?"

"Something like that." Ed leaned back, pulled out the third desk drawer on the right, and spat a stream of tobacco juice into a jar. Then he wiped his mouth with a handkerchief and patted the sweat off his forehead. "For a start he could have put up a sign. Area closed by order of the Sheriff's Department."

"Are you going to fire him?"

"If I thought it'd do any good, I'd slap his fanny and send him back to the Trans-Pecos. But you know how the commissioners are."

"They like him."

"It's a damn bunch of conservatives you got elected, Jerilyn," he said. "A troop of J. Edgar Hoovers." He leaned a little to his left so he could see the white buttress of Whitehouse Peak jutting into the rectangle of blue sky. "You know, when Sharon and I first came here we used to go to the hot springs. Not to the motel spas or the public pool. I was up at the mine then, and Saturdays when I was off, we'd lie around down by the river on the rocks, steep ourselves like tea bags in the water, maybe drink a beer or two. That's what we'd do on an afternoon. The Indians used to do that before the white man ever found gold in these mountains."

"We aren't Indians," Jerilyn said. "And I have a Sunday deadline."

"Make it an historical perspective. Sheriff used to bathe naked in the springs." Ed shook his head. "The land's not so different from the way it was. It's the town that's changed."

"There are economic reasons for the springs to stay closed," Jerilyn said. "Are you going to keep them closed?"

Ed shrugged.

"You know there's criminal activity going on there. Underage drinking, drugs . . ."

"Sex?"

"Yes."

"Mostly it's kids having a good time. Didn't you ever have a good time when you were young?"

"Not that kind."

"Well, I did. Being young is like shooting a hole-in-one. It doesn't last very long, but you remember it all your life."

"I'll quote you," Jerilyn said. "The sheriff's philosophy."

"Did I ever tell you about winning the Dijon Mustard Sweepstakes?"

"You've told everyone."

Ed smiled, and he ignored what Jerilyn said. "They sent me to France for two weeks. All expenses paid. *Tout compris.* I was just a farmboy from Gunnison, Colorado, and all of a sudden I was a celebrity in a four-star hotel in Paris. I went to Dijon and toured the mustard factory and had dinner with executives. When the two weeks were over I wanted to reenlist, and I stayed over there two more months on my own with French girls all around me. It was the best time of my life."

"That was twenty years ago, Ed."

"Twenty-seven. And I still speak French whenever I can."

"What I care about is yesterday, today, and tomorrow," Jerilyn said. "What are you going to say to the people of this town about John Meeker and the hot springs?"

"Shit," Ed said, "I don't know." He spat again into the jar in his drawer. "I'll tell you one thing. If this is the worst that happens this week, we'll all be lucky."

9

By midafternoon only four people had come into his shop, and Shanks was tired of sitting on his stool behind the cash register reading. He was about halfway through Rachel Elm's new novel, *A Woman of Impermanence,* whose topic, the slight allegiances a woman might suffer in the modern world, had not made him altogether comfortable. The writing was intense, and he liked the pace of the book, but it drained him. It made him feel he was far away from issues in New York and San Francisco, issues which somehow mattered.

He closed the book and laid it on the glass counter of the jewelry display and rubbed his eyes. Aurey had not come by. Shanks had looked for him that morning at the Nugget Café, but Ernesto said he hadn't been there.

"I opened at five-thirty, Neil," Ernesto said. "Tony went hunting. You think I keep track of Aurey too? Maybe he's sleeping."

"He's not sleeping."

"No, he wouldn't be sleeping. I joke with you. He probably went to Chipeta Springs already, or down to Grand Junction to get supplies. He doesn't tell me what he does."

"But he's around?"

Ernesto nodded, stirring home fries on the grill. "He's around. He's down from that worthless hole. You want some breakfast?"

"I'm opening the shop," Shanks said. "If you see him, tell him to stop by. I'll be there all afternoon."

"I'll tell him," Ernesto said. "But you know Aurey."

Shanks had never intended to own a souvenir shop in Gold Hill, Colorado. He had meant to stay only a few months and then go home. But when his disability ran out, he hadn't been ready to go. He'd lost the job as stringer and couldn't find another. No one wanted a discredited amateur journalist who'd been labeled trouble, and he didn't want anyone who didn't want him. Ed had suggested starting a business of his own, and Shanks had spent the last of his disability money scouting the terrain. That's when he got the idea for the fast-food window.

It was suited especially to the summer months when visitors were gouged $3.95 for an egg-salad sandwich and $2.75 for a slice of pizza. Tourists needed him. They scurried from the Jeep tour to the Chamber of Commerce slide show of wildflowers to the hot-springs pool, and they needed a place where they could get a quick meal. The summer help, too, barely had time to eat on their lunch breaks, and they couldn't afford the inflated prices most of the restaurants charged. The motel maids liked to sit in the sun on the sidewalk benches and hike their skirts for the midday sun, and they were a draw for business. The best thing about the window, though, was that nobody could tell him what to do, and he didn't owe anyone a favor.

He rented a window in the back of a store just off Main. In the first summer he made enough to get through the winter, and he spent a few months doing research in the archives. That was when he'd begun to discover that Thomas Shanks had been misleading his family. The Sonja claim existed: that was true. But it had produced no revenue at all since 1877. Shanks also had paid taxes on the Dusty Dan up on Twin Peaks. Shanks had never been up there, but in the records the Dusty Dan listed no improvements between 1881, when Thomas Shanks had acquired it, and 1884, when he'd gone home to Michigan.

These dead ends led him to speculate about other opportunities. He checked business receipts, real estate sales, the public records of the town meetings. The only mention he found of Thomas Shanks was of a lien against the rooming house, recorded pursuant to a loan to the Trevors in 1882. The lien was only for three thousand dollars, and it was discharged before Thomas left Gold Hill.

Summer rolled around again, and the fast-food window was more successful in the first two months than it had been the entire previous summer. The more he worked, the more money he made, but the less time he had to read or go to the hot springs or follow up his ideas about Thomas Shanks. The repetition of making hamburgers enervated him. There was nothing to learn standing over a grill or putting together a turkey sandwich.

At the height of the season in early August he sold out to Flash Toomey, who owned the theater in town. Shanks had no idea what Toomey wanted to do with a fast-food window, but Shanks hadn't asked. He was glad to be out.

For the rest of the month he puttered in the archives, talked to Ed Wainwright about the old mines and the characters in town, read novels. He loved novels. His father had read, and when they went ice fishing in Michigan his father recounted the stories of Dickens or Conrad or James. Nothing had given his father more pleasure than telling a long tale.

It was through novels, in fact, that he'd got to know Becky Carlsson. At least he thought it was through novels, though Pop Krause may have had a connection. It had been one night near the end of that summer. He'd taken a walk late, in the cool air, up Tin Pan Alley to Prosperity and then down Prosperity toward the river. The stars were out and a quarter moon rocked back. He'd forgotten a jacket and was half running down the hill toward the huge neon sign of the Panorama Motel when he'd seen what at first looked like a bear going through a garbage heap. Bud Saunders was extending the motel by four or five units, and there was a construction site in the trees. On closer look Shanks saw it was a man combing through the discarded lumber.

"Hey," the man called, "give me a hand."

Shanks's inclination was to keep running, but then the man straightened up, and he'd recognized the shaggy head of Pop Krause in the light of flashing neon.

Ed had told him the legends about Pop. He was a descendant of Rising Cloud, an Uncompahgre, and Arnulf Krause, a German who had owned the Black Owl Mine in the area called the Bridge to Heaven. Pop had been rich once, but he'd lost the money. No one knew where or how. Some said he'd gambled it away in Monte Carlo. Others claimed he'd burned it in a fit of rage one night on Main Street. Ed thought the money had never been as much as people thought, and over the years Pop had spent it trying to survive. Pop loved a woman dead fifty years. "He still loves her," Ed said. "Every afternoon he climbs that trail behind his shack. He rides one horse and leads another for the woman. That's what he was doing the afternoon he caught you trespassing."

Whatever happened to his money, Pop didn't have it now. Twice a week he swept and polished the floors in the county building on Placer and in the courthouse on Fourth Street. The rest of the time he scavenged. He collected cans and bottles and scrap metal. You could see him riding the highways on an old bicycle or rummaging through the trash cans in the park. People saved cans for him and dumped them on the side of the River Road by his tin shack.

So Shanks had stopped that night. Pop had been trying to load a broken TV set onto his cart, which was already half full of lumber.

"What are you going to do when you get it home?" Shanks asked.

"That's my business."

"I mean, how are you going to get it off?"

"If you won't help I can manage."

Shanks had followed Pop through the streets pulling the cart along himself. Pop stared straight ahead, his beard twitching now and then, his massive gray head lolling back and forth. They took detours down alleys Shanks had never seen, past Dumpsters and slash piles and discarded trash.

"What do you do with the lumber?" Shanks asked. "Is it firewood?"

"Ain't firewood," Pop said. "It's *nails.*"

When the cart was loaded, they descended the hill to the river and the narrow span which crossed at Placer to the River Road. Pop stopped on the bridge and stared down for a long time into the water, so Shanks looked too.

"What do you see?" Shanks asked.

Pop looked at him. "Light."

Shanks did not see any light. The river was high and fast from recent rain, roily, muddy, dark. The old man spat into the river and walked on. But Shanks had continued to look. He searched the eddies and the rooster tails, the small backwaters and the white cusps of waves rolling over rock. He listened to the rush of the river and the grumble of the stones rolling along the bottom. He smelled the sweet scent of pine and earth. And on the water's surface, in the eddies, was the faint glimmer of the reflection of stars.

It was another half mile to Pop's tin shack.

"Take it out back," Pop said. "You'll see."

Shanks pulled the cart around the house, while Pop went inside. Around the back was a pallet of neatly stacked lumber of all sizes, together with a mountain of TV sets—glassy eyed, lifeless, broken. There must have been fifty of them staring like cyclopses at the house.

He unloaded the wood and lifted off the television set.

"Pitch it," Pop said from the dark back door.

Shanks heaved the set into the pile, shattering the tube on the corner of another set. "What do you do with them?"

He turned around toward Pop, who held out a bottle.

"Save the world," Pop said. "Here, have a drink. Tomorrow you'll have a good day. Wait and see."

Shanks had taken a drink and held the bottle to the quarter moon.

The next day had been rainy, and he hadn't seen any prospect for anything good. His leads on Thomas Shanks had petered out, but he wasn't ready to go home to Michigan either. If the Sonja or the Dusty Dan hadn't produced gold, where had Thomas got his money? How long could he look through the archives and find nothing before he had to decide whether to give up?

He'd gone down to the Nugget to get out of his room and to feel the ebb and flow of people. But the rain hadn't helped Ernesto's business either. The tables were nearly empty, so he'd taken a corner table in the front window and ordered coffee.

He'd been reading for twenty minutes when Becky came in. Her hair was soaked, stringy, sticking to the back of her neck. Her shirt and shoes were drenched. She surveyed the tables quickly as if she were late to meet someone, but whoever it was wasn't there.

Then she spotted Shanks in the corner and came over. "You're Neil," she said. "You're the man with the hawk."

He nodded. "You're the one with the wedding dress."

She sat down across from him. "Have you seen Finn? You know him?"

"I haven't seen him."

"So he hasn't been here," she said. "The bastard."

Shanks shook his head. "I only said I hadn't seen him. I read the *Chronicle.* I thought you were living in Grand Junction."

"We are, or we were. Finn wants to move back here. He's tired of painting houses."

"I was tired of the fast-food window."

"I heard you sold it to Flash," Becky said. "What're you going to do now?"

"Read."

She twisted her damp hair in her fingers and wrung water

out on the floor. Then she set her two elbows on the table and leaned forward. "What are you reading?"

Shanks lifted the book and showed the cover.

"All the King's Men," she said. "What is that, a fairy tale?"

"Sort of."

"What's it about?"

"It's about politics in Louisiana."

Becky gave a little laugh. "You like to read? Is that what you do really?"

"Not always. Sometimes I sleep."

"That's what Earlene says."

The rain had eased a little out the window, but it was still coming down, splattering on the wet street. Ernesto came over to the table. "You want some coffee, Becky?" he asked, brandishing the pot. "Something to eat?"

"Nothing," she said. "I'm supposed to meet Finn."

"More coffee, Neil?"

"A little, thanks."

Ernesto poured the coffee and went back to the counter.

"Am I bothering you?" Becky asked. "Is that it?"

She knew she was not bothering him. She could sit with him or any other man in town whenever she wanted to. She just sat down. That was how she did things. Afterward she asked if she were interrupting.

"So how do you know about Earlene?" he asked.

"Everyone knows about Earlene."

"I mean Earlene and me."

Becky smiled again. "So what's the book about really? Is it about politics in Louisiana?"

"You aren't going to tell me about Earlene?"

"Tell me about the book first."

She looked at the cover, which showed an anguished woman up close, and in the background a man standing under a live-oak tree dripping with Spanish moss. Another man's face was superimposed in the branches of the tree.

"It's about the forms of love," he said.

"Forms of love?"

"You'd have to read it. A good woman wastes her life on a bad man."

"So you think I should read this book?" Becky said. She stared at the cover.

"I'd be glad to lend it to you."

All of a sudden she slapped the book down hard on the table. His coffee jumped.

"So what?" she hissed. "So damned *what*?"

He didn't understand what she meant.

"So what if I waste my life?"

"I didn't say you were wasting your life."

"Bullshit. That's what you were saying. I'll waste my life if I want to."

She pushed her chair back and got up and bolted for the door. As she passed the front window she stuck out her tongue at him.

After that he'd heard she and Finn had moved back to Gold Hill to a trailer a few miles north of town. He'd finished the book and sent it to her.

Two weeks later she'd sent the book back with an apology. The book was sad, she said, too sad to read to the end.

Toward the end of August he made an offer on a declining souvenir shop on Main Street next to the dress boutique. The shop had never done well, but Shanks thought it could become profitable by changing the hours. A tourist town didn't run nine-to-five. Two of the best restaurants in town —Diamond Lil's and the Centennial—were just up the street, and the Nugget, which was jammed every night, was a little farther along. If Shanks stayed open in the evening when the tourists browsed up Main toward the motel district, the business could double sales. After supper was when people had the time to seek out trinkets for friends and send postcards to the family back home in New Jersey.

The offer was accepted and he took over right away. He rearranged the shop and brought in crafts on consignment. He kept a cabinet of turquoise jewelry right by the cash register and a shelf of Swiss chalets made of pine bark and needles and birds made of round river stones where people could see them. The Hummels, laminated plastic place mats, T-shirts with Whitehouse Peak on them or GOLD HILL—SWITZERLAND OF AMERICA, hand-painted ashtrays, scarves made from the blue and white and yellow and red of the Colorado state flag, ceramic deer and porcupines and bears—all these he had on the long rows under the track lights.

What he wanted to sell most was books. He had hundreds of books in his apartment. *He* bought them. But he couldn't get people to buy them in his store. He kept a few best sellers on a rack, some mysteries and westerns. The money-maker books were histories and how-tos: *The Lure of Gold, Railroads in the Mountains, The Handbook of Rocks, How to Pan for Precious Minerals.*

The shop did better. He made his payments and had enough to get himself through another winter. But right away he had seen it was not an occupation he wanted to pursue. He was not a shopkeeper. As soon as he had the books in order, he put the store back on the market.

It was nearly three o'clock when he put down his book, and now clouds had come across heavily into the Amphitheater. Without the sun the red brick of the Elks Lodge across the street was pale salmon, and the sidewalk gray absorbed the yellow-and-green awning of Furze's Sporting Goods. Shanks went to the door and looked out. The clouds were moving lower, too, skimming the gray granite ridges and spilling over the rocks.

He supposed he should go to the library. That was where he was pursuing his current line of inquiry, and if Aurey weren't around, at least he could make some headway in reading the old newspapers. It was both fascinating and tiring—all the pages of the raw material of history jumbled together. Train wrecks, fires, marriages, gold strikes, news of the territories. Shanks was hoping for some clue to surface from the reports of mines and mining activities which the papers covered. He had read as far as the assassination of President Garfield by Charles Guiteau in July of 1881. Chester Arthur had assumed the Presidency.

Shanks closed the shop and walked up Placer to the courthouse and the library. The courthouse was redbrick with a blue onion dome bordered by gold leaf, and the library occupied one wing. Shanks knew where to go to find the newspapers, and he settled himself in a leather chair by one of the high windows where he would have good light.

The most interesting articles he'd discovered were about the Uncompahgres. After the gold strikes of 1870 they had been pushed down the valley toward Chipeta Springs, always with the promise that later on they could return. An encampment had been granted them by the territorial government in 1874 along the river and adjacent to White Mesa, where they had set up what the Indians considered a wintering territory. The government agency in Chipeta Springs supplied food and blankets.

But the Uncompahgres wanted back the mountain land. They had lived their entire history in the river valley, migrating up and down the river between the high peaks above where Gold Hill now stood to the hot springs along the river, and from the hot springs to the lower basin which collected the waters of the great rivers.

Thomas Shanks had mentioned the Uncompahgres several times in his letters, but only peripherally, as if they were no more than a swarm of gnats which would dissipate as soon as the wind blew. But the Denver paper made their plight seem more serious. Promises had been made and broken—not unusual in the government's policy toward the Indians—but the Uncompahgres, who had been peaceful, had made threats to recover their land by force.

The whites were fearful, naturally. They had built houses, stores, railroads. Millions of dollars were still in the earth to make them rich.

Shanks turned page after page. Now and then he looked out at the fading afternoon, watched the clouds descending into the spruce. A few snowflakes drifted across the scrub oak hillside up the street from where he sat.

Another page. December 10, 1881. On the front page was a blurry engraving of whites and Indians—four chieftains in ceremonial costume, together with a dozen whites, including Governor Pitkin. The Indians were Red Cloud, Broken Nose, Leg-like-a-Stick, and Lazy Bear, all chiefs of the Uncompahgres.

The article described an agreement that had been reached to transfer the Indians to lands in southeastern Utah territory. Several sites had been designated, each with land along a river, each with more land than the Indians had then by White Mesa. The Indian agency would supply what the Indians needed, on request.

Only a few of the whites in the photograph were listed by name: Governor Pitkin and the United States negotiators and a representative of the Territory of Utah. But Shanks recognized a face. The whiskers were longer, and the hair, too, but it was the same high forehead, the same intense eyes staring directly into the camera. The man was Thomas Shanks.

He looked out the window. It had begun to snow harder. Snow was sticking to the rooftops and on the gravel street, falling through the gray dusk.

10

In the boom days the Nugget Café had been a saloon and dance hall. It was a deep room from front to back, narrow, but with a twenty-foot ceiling bordered by ornamental molding and hung with chandeliers. A saloon made its money by darkness. The side walls were brick and the front windows had been painted black. When Ernesto Vallejos bought the building in 1950 to make it into a restaurant, he put in skylights and scraped the paint from the plate glass and wired the chandeliers for brighter light. He turned the saloon into a cheerful room with lots of air.

Over the years he'd replaced the bar with an L-shaped counter and swivel stools, installed booths along the brick wall, and filled the rest of the floor with tables of various sizes, covered with different-colored plastic tablecloths. His year-round business fluctuated with the price of metals, and fortunately for Ernesto, the mines hadn't closed completely until after his last son, Tony, was out of the house.

All the Vallejos boys had worked in the café. They'd put in their time before school, after school, on weekends. They washed dishes, served, and cooked. But they were all gone now. Only Ernesto was left, though his wife Vivien sometimes helped on the weekends.

That Sunday morning the café was quiet. Shanks had come in just after six, saying he couldn't sleep, and hunkered down in the corner by the window.

"Should be easy to sleep on a morning like this," Ernesto said.

"Worried," Shanks said.

"What do you have to worry about?"

"Nothing. That's just it."

A few hunters showed up—those who had stayed in motels and had thought better of trying to get out into the mountains in the snow. There was one table of old people from the Hotel Windsor up the street.

It was a big snow. It had snowed all night and all morning, piling up on the sidewalks and roads, and it was still snowing hard. A fierce wind from the pass drove the snow down Main Street, drifting it over cars and fireplugs and onto the sidewalks.

Shanks ordered waffles and coffee. "You have a Sunday paper?" he asked.

Ernesto shook his head. "Airport's closed down in Chipeta, so we didn't get a Denver paper. And the *Pilot* hasn't come in."

"I saw some snowplows."

"The boys were out all night," Ernesto said. He brought over the coffee, while the waffles were baking. "Aurey get hold of you?"

"No."

"He went to Junction yesterday to get something welded —some wheel he needs. He was back late."

"I'll see him."

Ernesto paused at the window.

An orange snowplow emerged through the snow with its yellow light flashing.

"Here comes the crew," Ernesto said. "I'll bet they've had a good time."

The truck swung slow-motion across Main and into a drift on the corner of Smelter Street. Weedy Garcia tumbled out, along with Charlie Fernsten and Ned Hatton, all of them with highway department bibs over their parkas.

They nearly tore the door down to get into the café.

"Motherfuck, it's cold," Weedy said.

"Winter ain't even started yet," Ned Hatton said, "and already the heat breaks on the truck."

They pulled off their gloves and coats and hung them on the rack by the cash register. Fernsten kept his parka on and stuffed his gloves into his pockets.

They took a table near Shanks at the window. Fernsten went to the men's room in back.

"You got hot coffee, Ernie?" Weedy said. "Just pour it over my hands."

Ernesto came over and set down three cups and poured coffee.

"We don't need no menu," Hatton said. "We know what you got."

"How is it on the pass?" Ernesto asked.

"Visibility zero," Weedy said. He rubbed his hands together hard. "That damn truck . . ."

Hatton blew his breath into his hands. "Nothing worse," he said. "But you should have seen Weedy up there. He was driving like it was on eggshells."

"That *was* eggshells. At the top it's a whiteout."

"Mr. Nerves of Steel," Hatton said. "It's the first snow of the year."

Fernsten came back and sat down and drank a swallow of coffee. "Oh, that's good," he said. "That's real good."

"You weren't up there looking for Carson Watson's body," Weedy said. "It took us five days to find the god-damn *truck.*"

"That was March," Hatton said. "That year we had two hundred inches."

Fernsten smiled, drifting a little. He had a peach-fuzz face, and his eyes floated around the café. "What happened to Carson Watson?" he asked.

"Shit, man. You weren't here. It was an avalanche right up where we were two hours ago. The guy was seven hundred yards down the canyon, not even in the cab of the truck. He was crushed like a soft-boiled egg."

"You got some food here or what?" Hatton said. "I want some fried eggs and hash browns and a doughnut."

"No doughnuts fresh," Ernesto said. "No deliveries today."

"Give me a stale one."

"That road gives me the willies," Weedy said. "You can drive off the edge too. You don't need an avalanche to help you."

"I'll have a short stack," Fernsten said. "A side of sausage."

"Has the chief been in?" Hatton asked. "I'm not feeling real good either. It's Weedy's driving."

Ernesto looked up from writing down the orders. "He called. He's coming up from the county line."

"So how's Tony?" Weedy asked. "He do any good Saturday?"

Ernesto stopped writing. "Nah. He was up on Brown Mountain and saw some cows. It was snowing like guano, he said, so he came down. For him it's got to be warm and sunny. You know how lawyers are. I told him to try Silver Shield this morning. The snow will push the elk down low, but he don't bother. He takes time off, then he won't go four steps out the door."

"It ought to be good once the snow stops," Hatton said.

"Finn'll be out," Weedy said. "I can goddamn guarantee it."

"Unless he hit opening day," said Fernsten.

"Won't matter. He'll be after more. I don't care how much snow there is. Give me a egg-and-ham plate," Weedy said. "And some syrup for the ham."

They settled down for a few minutes while Ernesto took the order back behind the counter. Snow was easy to watch, coming almost horizontally across the small stores on the other side of Main. They talked about the dope Fernsten had just smoked. Weedy gave Hatton flak for going out with Home Run Helen Howell, a waitress at the Outlaw, who,

Weedy said, had given her first blowjob in the bathroom of the café.

"I don't care where it was," Hatton said. "How good was it?"

"She was fourteen years old, man," Weedy said.

"How do you know how old she was?"

"I heard about it," Weedy said, smiling at Shanks and wobbling his eyes.

Then Fernsten craned over the back of his chair and looked out the window. "Is that Pop Krause?" he asked.

Weedy stood up and glanced down the sidewalk. "That's him. He's on his way to church."

"Right."

"No shit," Weedy said. "He's an Indian, and he goes up into the hills every Sunday and greets the spirits. Ask Ernesto."

The old man had just rounded the corner of Smelter Street and leaned forward into the grade of the sidewalk. His head was buried in a snarl of animal skins, and he tilted it down into the brunt of the wind and snow. He kept his mark through one slitted eye.

"He's half Indian," Ernesto called over. "Half German. His father had a claim up on the Bridge to Heaven."

"He has visions," Weedy said. "That's what people say. He speaks to the dead."

Fernsten slid back a little as Pop came closer. "He don't look German either. He looks Russian."

"Ask Neil over there," Weedy said. "He knows Pop. Hey, Neil, don't you know Pop?"

"A little," Shanks said.

"You ever talk to him?" Fernsten asked.

"Not much. He arrested me once for trespassing."

"Lead us not into temptation," Weedy said. "Listen, Pop does all kinds of miracles."

"The only miracle is the old fart hasn't been shot," Hatton said, "the way he goes around in hunting season with those skins on his head."

Pop came even with the window, and Hatton's voice died

away, hissing and crackling like water thrown on the grill. Pop's long, unkempt gray hair and beard were shrouded in snow, and the snow fell across his face like shards of glass. Pop stared through the window as if he were confused by what he saw—the dozen or so people sitting and eating in a warm room. He nodded at Shanks—a glimmer of recognition—and then he moved on, out of the frame of the glass, and there was nothing more to watch except the snow blowing along the empty street.

Fernsten did not ask any more questions.

Ernesto brought the food to the table, the plates balanced along one arm, and handed them around. Then he went back for more coffee.

The hunters at the other tables started in again about how, once the snow stopped, they'd be able to track elk all over creation. The old people at a booth got up and paid and trudged on up the street to the Windsor.

When the crew finished eating, they sat back and smoked cigarettes and drank more coffee, spinning out their break as long as they could until the chief came. Ernesto cleaned the grill, and when the hunters got up, he rang up their tab and took their money.

Now and then a Jeep or a four-wheel-drive slid past, some intrepid soul on his way to hear Father Shonnard preach on the wretched condition of the human soul. And then the street was blank again, white and gray, with only a faded pastel giving any color at all to the day.

Ernesto brought the coffeepot over and sat down with the plow crew.

"Aurey found any gold yet?" Weedy asked.

"If he has, he hasn't told me."

"The man's an engineer. I guess he has as good a chance as anybody," Weedy said.

"He wants to be rich," Hatton said. "That'll keep you in the hills."

"He doesn't want to be rich," Ernesto said. "If that were true, I could understand it. I could see it." Ernesto shook his head. "He gives up the Denver job for a hole in the ground."

He looked over at Shanks in the corner. "You all right, Neil? More coffee?"

"I'm okay."

Then a slow pickup truck came down the street from the direction of the pass. It moved heavily, weighted down by snow, as if it were feeling the road under it. The windshield and the hood were white, but as it approached, Weedy rose up in his seat. There was a broom handle sticking up from behind the cab.

"Finn must have got one already," Hatton said.

But no one else said anything.

The truck came on and pulled even with the café. It braked, slid a little, as if the driver were deciding something. Then it signaled and turned, coming too fast into the curb. The tires slammed into the raised cement of the sidewalk, and the front right wheel popped up over the curb, then dropped back again. The engine died. The truck jerked to a stop, but the windshield wipers swayed back and forth over the iced-up glass.

"He's hurt," Weedy said.

Finn slumped over the wheel for a minute, then swung open the door of the cab. But he still didn't get out. He stared straight ahead, looking at nothing, looking through the windshield wiper's steady motion at the snow falling on the hood. He looked like a man who had been shot in the stomach and did not comprehend what had happened to him.

"What the hell?" Fernsten said.

Weedy was up and moving from his chair. "I don't like this," he said. "I don't like this a lot."

Finn stirred from the cab, edged from the seat, and slid out. He leaned against the fender as though to gain some strength there. But his body sank. It was as if the snow falling on his shoulders and on his orange hunting hat were heavy as sand.

Weedy reached him, though, before he fell.

11

Ned Hatton and Fernsten were right behind Weedy, and together they got Finn into the warm café and to a chair at the table by the window. Weedy pulled off Finn's snow-crusted hat and unzipped his parka. "Undo the boots," Weedy said. "See about his feet."

Shanks came over to the fringe of the group and pushed his way in for a look.

Finn slouched in the chair with his eyes closed, holding on to the edge of the seat to steady himself, while Hatton and Fernsten loosened the icy laces of his boots. His face was red from the wind and cold, and a line creased his forehead where his hat had been. Snow was already melting from his hair and his scruffy blond beard.

"Coffee!" Weedy called out. "How about some coffee?"

Finn opened his eyes wide, as if Weedy's voice had startled him. "It's not me. It's not me."

"What's not you?" Weedy said.

"Not me," Finn said, and he closed his eyes again.

Ernesto brought over a cup of coffee already poured and handed it to Weedy.

"What's not you, man?" Weedy asked. He tilted the coffee to Finn's mouth.

"Becky," Finn said. He opened his eyes again, but stared blankly, as if he couldn't remember where he was or what he'd said. The usual tightness of his mouth was gone, and his lips were slack.

"What's Becky?"

"I don't know. Lost."

"Lost. What do you mean, lost?"

"Where is she lost?" Ernesto asked.

"In Bear Creek?" Weedy said. "She's lost in Bear Creek?"

Finn nodded, drifted, closed his eyes halfway.

"Whereabouts?" Weedy asked. "Up the mountain?"

"Way up."

"So what happened?" Hatton asked.

Finn drank a little more coffee and opened his eyes. His eyes were blue, but dull now, tired. Weedy wiped Finn's face with a napkin.

"I don't know. Maybe she's home. Is she home?"

"Ernie, call down there to the trailer," Weedy said. "If she's not there, call the sheriff."

"What's the number?"

"Five five five, four nine eight eight."

Ernesto moved, and Shanks moved into Ernesto's place beside Finn. "When was this?" he asked. "When?"

"Today." Finn tried to think. "No, yesterday." He took another sip of the coffee. His eyes seemed not to register on any of the faces bent toward him.

"You came out all the way just now?" Weedy asked. "Down the trail?"

Finn nodded and sat up a little. "With Bo Jack."

"You rode Bo Jack?"

"Followed him," Finn said. "Held his tail. If he went off . . ." He looked around slowly. "What time is it? Where's my watch? Becky has my watch." He paused a moment. "She didn't meet me. Goddamn it, she didn't meet me."

Finn sank back into the chair, and Weedy shook him. "Where?"

"The Depot."

"That far up?"

"I waited," Finn said. "I waited a long time. A long time."

Weedy suddenly remembered Finn's feet. "How're the feet?" he asked. "What about something to eat? Something to eat. Are you hungry?"

Finn shook his head.

"No answer at the trailer," Ernesto said. "I'll call Ed."

"What about some whiskey?" Ned Hatton said. "Ernesto, you have a bottle?"

Ernesto was dialing, and he motioned Hatton toward a cupboard under the microwave.

"This was when?" Weedy asked Finn. "When?"

"Yesterday."

Hatton got the bottle of whiskey and brought it back. He emptied water from one of the glasses on the table and poured a shot. Finn took a sip and winced with the burn.

"Ed wants to know what kind of shape Finn is in," Ernesto called over. "Should he go to the clinic?"

"No," Finn said.

"How're his hands and feet, the sheriff says."

"They look like they're all right," Weedy said. "Red. Not white. That's good. He's more tired than frostbitten." He turned back to Finn. "How're the hands?"

Finn splayed his fingers.

Ernesto nodded and listened again on the phone, getting instructions. "All right," he said. "I'll send them up. Yes, right away. Yes, I'll get Aurey."

Finn drifted again and then seemed to recognize Shanks. "I haven't got the ten bucks," he said. "Fuck you."

"Forget the ten bucks," said Weedy. "We need to think about Becky."

"I waited," Finn said. "I don't know how long. A long time. Maybe an hour or two at the Depot and then in camp. I waited and waited all night."

Ernesto came over. "Ed says to get on up to his office. He'll meet you right now, and Sharon will start calling around for people to go back up there."

"It was snowing," Finn said. "I thought . . . I waited all that time. It was snowing. . . ." He looked at Shanks. "Get away from me. I don't have the money."

"Move off, Neil," Fernsten said.

But Shanks didn't move. He looked at Weedy, then at Finn.

"She's probably holed up somewhere," Weedy said to no one. "There are lots of places in those mountains."

"I kept thinking it would stop," Finn said. "Snow like that . . . What time is it?"

"A little after eleven."

"Ed says right away," Ernesto said. "I'll get hold of Aurey."

Weedy and Ned Hatton got Finn to his feet, and Fernsten threw his parka around him. Weedy grabbed up a couple of dry napkins from a nearby table and dried off Finn's forehead.

"So much snow," Finn said. "I waited. . . ."

Ten minutes later there was a motley collection of men in Ed Wainwright's office. Hatton and Fernsten had had to stay with the snowplow, but Weedy and Finn were there, along with Neil Shanks and Jock Martin, the bartender at the Outlaw, and Bud Saunders, who ran the Panorama Motel. John Meeker, in uniform, stood against one wall, along with two ranchers who knew Wendell and Martha Blythe and were able to get themselves out of their driveways. Ed had wanted his son Jerry to help out, too, but Sharon wouldn't let him go up into the mountains in a blizzard. "There's no sense having more people stranded," she said. "He can help down here on the switchboard."

Aurey would be there for certain, Ed thought, and they might pick up one or two others along the way. He'd let Meeker go up as liaison for the sheriff's department, and he'd keep Neil Shanks down in town to help him with the logistics and errands. Neil didn't like the mountains anyway, though it wasn't laziness like Jerry's. It had something to do with his family, or some injury—Neil had never been that specific about it. It was like a fear of heights, though that was not exactly it either. Ed knew he'd explored some mining claims and he hiked around in the foothills. But he didn't like the high country.

Many of the men who might have contributed were already out hunting. They were probably snowed in themselves up in Cutler Creek or Ebeneezer Gulch or on the slopes of Mt. Abrams or Hayden or Brown Mountain. Some people Sharon had reached couldn't get their cars out, and others had more immediate tasks of their own. Cattle couldn't be left in drifts, and horses had to be fed. Luther Simon couldn't leave his service station because people needed tows and jump starts and gasoline. Sharon was still on the telephone, though, trying to find volunteers.

Neil had brought up from the Nugget two hamburgers and French fries and hot tea in a white plastic cup, and the food had revived Finn. He had regained his natural contempt for law in general and John Meeker in particular, and he leaned back in the metal chair and seemed to take personal affront at having to be cooperative.

"It's hot as hell in here, Sheriff," he said. "Why can't we get moving or turn down the heat? It's not getting any better for Becky."

"Ernesto said Aurey would be here," Ed said. "No sense in telling it twice, and there may be some others coming in. I'm sorry about the heat. You can complain to the county commissioners."

"The sheriff says wait, you wait," Meeker said.

Finn glared. "Why don't you go corkscrew yourself, Pork?"

Ed stood up and tucked his short-sleeved shirt back into his trousers. The ceiling fan blew a cool draft down over his forehead, and he sighed audibly. "Listen, John, I'd like you to drive on out to the trailer and make certain Becky isn't there. Just take a quick look and come right back. Call on the CB, and I'll give you instructions from here."

"I was just trying to help," Meeker said.

"That's the way you can help most right now. Go down and see whether she checked in like Finn suggested."

"Ernesto already called."

Ed smiled without showing his teeth. "Maybe she didn't want to answer the phone just then," he said. "Go on, now."

Meeker put on his coat and the khaki cap with brown fur earflaps. Ed nodded to him when Meeker went out the door.

Then Ed sat down and spit into the jar in his desk drawer and looked at his watch. "We might as well get started," he said. "No sense sitting around in this Florida heat." He got up again and scanned the wall maps for the quadrant he wanted. "I want you all to pay attention because when you get up there it might save your asses to know where you are. We don't want to have to send out anyone else to look for any of you, so come over here and get a place for yourselves around the map."

The men gathered around at the desk.

"Finn, you get in here close."

The map was the Red Cloud Peak quadrant. Most of it was closely knitted isobars of brown, which represented treeless terrain. The closer together the lines were, the steeper the territory. There were a few patches of green where the land was timbered, and blue where there were ponds or tarns.

"Show us where you started and where you were going to meet up," Ed said. "Here's a pencil."

Finn took the pencil and looked at the map for a moment to get his bearings. Then he pointed to a series of brown isobars close together. "This here is the Depot," he said. "That's where Becky and I were going to meet up and Becky never showed."

"Becky knows the place?" Ed asked.

"Sure she knows it. It's a group of big boulders me and my dad and Hank Tobuk named for trains. There's the Illinois Central and the D and R G and the Rock Island Line. Becky knows it. She was up there last year. Damn right she knows it." He traced the brown isobars back along the contour to an area of green. "The idea was for us to split up right here, which we did. I was going to come down quiet along the lower edge of this timber, and Becky was supposed to be up on the ridge, right here, moving across real slow. Elk scare out soft sometimes, and there was a little breeze coming upslope. We were taking it easy. She climbed to the ridge right about here."

Finn made a mark on the map.

"What time was this?" Ed asked.

"Nine-thirty."

"Saturday?"

"Yes, Saturday."

"And what was the weather then?"

"Mostly sunny. A few clouds far off. It wasn't all that cold either. Maybe thirty-five or forty. We were disappointed it hadn't dusted the night before because it clouded up a little, and we thought the front might be coming in early."

"Isn't that kind of late starting out opening morning?" Bud Saunders asked.

"We weren't just starting out. We'd been climbing for two hours. It's steeper than the price of shit up there. Even in the meadows you can hold out your arm horizontal and touch the grass on the upslope." Finn held his arm straight out from his shoulder. "That's how steep it is. Isn't that right, Weed?"

"Exactly," Weedy said.

"So you were down in the trees," Ed said, studying the map. "Could you see Becky from where you were?"

"I saw her start up the meadow," Finn said, "but once I got off a hundred yards or so, no, I couldn't see her after that. That was the last time I saw her, right there in the meadow."

A door banged in the outer room where the dispatcher's switchboard was, and Finn stopped. Ed listened with the others to the noise in the other room. It was Aurey, Ed knew. Finally.

"I got the message," the voice said, gasping and out of breath. "My father said it was Becky Blythe."

"They're in there," Sharon said.

In a moment Aurelio Vallejos rushed into the room. "I came as soon as I could," he said, yanking off his snow-covered lumberjack's cap. "What happened? Where is she?"

"Becky Carlsson," Ed said. "She's up in Bear Creek. Finn was just telling us what happened."

"This is up by the Depot," Finn said. "You know where that is? Becky was supposed to rendezvous with me yesterday afternoon."

"Up there near the Divide?" Aurey said. "I know the place. It's that ravine with the big rocks in it." He slid off his parka and dropped it on the floor and came forward, moving quickly as if there were no time to lose. His eyes fixed on Finn, then on Ed, then on the map.

The room with Aurey in it seemed to Ed like a different place—tighter, on edge. The whirr of the ceiling fan was louder than before, the air brighter. Everyone pressed in closer to the map.

"She didn't show up," Finn said again. "I came through these trees here, and she went over the ridge. She was supposed to meet me at the Depot at one o'clock."

"Here?" Aurey said, pressing his thin finger to the map. "Yes."

"What happened after you went into the trees?" Ed asked.

"I came around through here, through the spruce. There was lots of fallen timber. You have to climb over it. And fight through the brush too. It isn't easy to go quiet." Finn looked at Ed. "She was supposed to come around the other side like pliers. We were going to catch the elk between us, or one of us would drive them out to the other."

"You hear any shots?" Bud Saunders asked.

"Not then. There'd been lots of shots earlier in the morning over on Brown Mountain and Engineer Peak, but nobody else but us was in Bear Creek because of the trail. It's hard to get in there, and if you do get in, it's hard to get an elk out."

Ed took the pencil from Finn and circled the Depot. "So this is the search area—this ravine and this ridge here." ·

Aurey nodded. "Except that she could have tracked an elk," he said. "She could have come off this ridge and circled back over here." He slid his finger along the map in the opposite direction from the Depot. "When did it start snowing?"

"I don't know exactly. I didn't have my watch, and when it clouded up . . ."

"Did you look for her?" Aurey said. "You check back along this ridge?"

"No. I waited at the Depot a long time. It was snowing by then, and I figured she'd probably gone back to camp."

"What about signals? I assume you had signals."

"We had signals. Ones we've always used. If you had an elk down, it was three quick shots."

"And if you're hurt?"

"If you're hurt, more than three. Isn't that right, Weed? More than three. But I didn't hear any shots."

Weedy nodded. "I remember the time you fired a dozen shots at a fucking cow elk, and I ran up the mountain thinking you'd broken your neck." Weedy smiled broadly. "Maybe she didn't stay on the ridge like Aurey says. If you kicked out some elk from down below, they might've gone over the ridge in front of her and she didn't get a shot off."

"Possible," Finn said.

Ed tapped the pencil on the map. "Let's keep together on this," he said. "Finn, when did you get to the Depot? Approximately?"

"Before one."

"And you sure you didn't hear any shots?"

"I would've heard a thirty-ought-six," Finn said, "unless it was way off over the ridge. Sometimes in snow you can't hear so well, especially in a wind."

"And it started snowing when you were in the trees?"

"Just kind of sifting through. I never saw it coming. Up

there you're right behind the Amphitheater, and you can't see when the weather moves in. It's on you before you know it's changed." He looked over at Weedy. "Hey, you got a cigarette?"

Weedy took a cigarette from his pack and tossed it to Finn.

"At first it was just corn snow," Finn said. "Like a squall. You get that up high, though it's usually in the spring. I was glad because an elk's senses get scrambled in that kind of weather."

"So do people's," Aurey said.

"Mine don't." Finn tapped the cigarette on the corner of Ed's desk. Weedy held a match for him, and Finn took a long pull into his lungs. "Anyway, I've had elk come right at me in rain and snow. And I've seen them stay put and not get a scent so you could walk up on them as close as thirty yards."

"You need to be that close," Weedy said, grinning.

There was a moment's pause as Finn took another drag on his cigarette. Ed watched the smoke rise from Finn's mouth straight up along the plane of his face.

"You didn't think she was lost?" Shanks asked suddenly. "You just went back down to camp?"

Finn blinked through the smoke. "No, man, I didn't think she was lost. What was I supposed to do? It was a snow squall and good for hunting, and then all of a sudden it really starts coming down. Big flakes, hard, like a god-damn curtain. Who knows what the fucking weather's going to do? By the time I got up to the Depot I couldn't see ten feet, and there were maybe three or four inches on the ground. The Rock Island right across the ravine was gone. *Nothing*, man. But I didn't think she was lost."

"You didn't fire off any rounds?" Bud Saunders asked. "Let her know where you were?"

"I thought about it," Finn said, "but I figured it might confuse her. What with that wind and snow swirling around, you can't tell directions up there. Besides, what if she was all right and headed down, and she thought *I* was hurt or had an elk? What if she was somewhere about to walk off a cliff and came toward me? I waited up there a long time. I don't know how long. And for all I knew she was back in camp drinking hot chocolate. That's what I really figured. Nobody in her right mind should have been climbing around in that snow."

Finn took another long pull on the cigarette. "Besides," he went on, "there's no way to *get* lost. If she had any brains she'd just go downhill into a streambed and follow it until she came out in Bear Creek."

"Unless she was hurt," Aurey said.

"Or holed up somewhere," Weedy put in. "That's what I'd do in a whiteout."

The sheriff walked to the side of his desk, pulled open the drawer, and spat. "We don't need to be analyzing what Finn should or shouldn't have done," he said. "She might've tracked an elk away from the ridge or she might have taken shelter somewhere. Or maybe she's lost. The point is we should get up there and find her *tout de suite,* if you know what I mean."

"Wait," Shanks said. "So Finn went back to the camp. Then what?"

Finn looked at Shanks. "Why are you so curious, Neil? What's it to you?"

"I'm just worried is all."

"We're all worried," Ed said. "All of us." Ed came back to the map. "So you went back down to camp, and she wasn't there."

"I followed this gully down," Finn said. "This one starts right at the Depot. Normally we would have headed east from the Depot and dropped down in some other trees across from Wounded Knee, but with all the snow, I had no idea when it was going to stop."

"So are we ready?" Aurey asked Ed.

Ed nodded. "We have some idea what's what."

Aurey pulled his knit cap back on his head. "What kind of gear did Becky have with her? She had a rifle. Did she have any food? What kind of clothes did she have on?"

"Her orange parka," Finn said. "An orange hat she'd just bought at Matheson's. A red day pack."

"Matches?"

"I don't know. She had ammunition. A knife. We both had a sandwich for lunch and some trail feed and chocolate bars. If she's smart, she'll have matches."

"What about a flashlight?"

Finn shrugged.

Ed waited a moment, and when there were no more questions, he tucked in his shirt again and wiped the sweat from his forehead. "I'm putting Aurey in charge," he said. "He knows the terrain as well as anybody except maybe Finn, and Finn's not going to be the most objective man in this situation. Besides, I want him to go down to the clinic."

"Bullshit I am," Finn said.

"Just precautionary. If they say you can go, all right. Weedy, you take him down there. This is rugged territory and nothing to fool with." Ed looked around. "You're under my orders to do what Aurey tells you. That's the main thing. There has to be discipline. We can't have individuals making their own decisions about where to go and what to do. Is that clear?"

Everyone nodded.

"Now, the trail in there is steep, and when you get in, it'll be cold. Is there anyone who feels he can't handle it?"

Shanks was the only one to raise his hand. "I'd rather help in town."

"All right. Anyone else?"

No one else stirred.

"John Meeker, bless his soul, will be the voice of the county, so to speak, insofar as the authority of the county needs to extend. He'll be up there with you at the trailhead, and he better keep his politics to himself. I'll let him know. Finn and Weedy, you get along with him."

"As long as he keeps his mouth shut," Weedy said.

"I'll get word to the Colorado Search and Rescue personnel. Its being hunting season and all, they're probably standing by, especially in this weather. But send me down word as soon as you can. Tonight, if you can, Aurey. The CSR won't want to bring in their helicopter and dogs and whatever else if she's safe and sound in camp."

"A helicopter won't be worth shit in this weather," Weedy said.

"Right. But tomorrow it might help. Finn, you have anything else?"

"No."

"Aurey?"

Aurey picked up his parka from the floor. "Just that we should be at the trailhead in forty-five minutes. I'll start up to break the snow and get to the camp as quickly as I can. She might have come down since Finn was there."

"All right."

"What should we bring?" Bud Saunders asked. "Not everyone has spent time camped in snow."

"Down sleeping bag, food, small Thermos of hot water for tea or chocolate. Binoculars might help. It'll probably be best to camp down in the trees."

"Bring ski goggles," Finn said.

"I'll have the county rescue gear," Aurey said. "Medical stuff, flares. If you have skis or snowshoes, bring those too."

"You have topo maps?" Ed asked.

Aurey nodded. "The faster we move, the better it'll be for Becky."

The men all broke from around the desk and put on their coats and hats and gloves, all except Ed and Shanks. Ed spat tobacco juice into his desk drawer. Then he looked at Aurey. "Tonight," he said. "Let me know. Neil and I and Sharon will keep things together down here. Meeker should be checking back in pretty soon."

"I'll be in touch on the CB," Aurey said. "Let's hope we find her."

"Amen," Ed said.

12

Aurey Vallejos revved his Jeep over the snowpack and up Placer Street toward the courthouse where the rescue gear was stored. He gunned the engine to keep up momentum on the hill, slid a little, gave more gas. Finn Carlsson made him angry. He was stupid. That was the trouble. He steamrolled people without a thought to consequences, and there were always consequences. But Finn didn't care. For him there was no tomorrow.

Becky wasn't so smart, either, apparently, at least not so smart as he'd thought from listening to Lorraine years ago. Lorraine used to say Becky was the brightest one of the Blythes—smarter than the youngest one, Toby, or Lorraine. Becky didn't work so hard in school though. "Someday she'll catch fire," Lorraine said, "and then look out." But so far as Aurey knew, she hadn't ever caught fire. She married Finn, which was bad enough, and then she went hunting with him, which was worse. Anyone who was supposed to be that smart should know not to go out into the mountains with a madman.

What Finn did in the mountains wasn't hunting. It was drinking with guns. He and his father and his friends had been coming to Gold Hill for a long time. They came down

from Grand Junction and raced around the tundra meadows and shot as many elk with elephant rifles as they could.

He was not against hunting if it was done right. He'd
hunted once himself, though not with a weapon. He'd never
talked about it except to Raymond, who was dead now. He
might have told Lorraine about it—she'd have understood.
But he hadn't seen much of Lorraine lately.

It was hard to comprehend that Raymond was dead.
Raymond would have been a help now, of course, on a day
like today. For him snow and cold were the essential ele-
ments of a good time. Aurey had seen Raymond laugh,
holding himself upside down under a rock like a spider,
using only his fingertips and the edges of his boots, inside
edge or outside. And once he'd seen him shouting gleefully,
walking up the icefall above the newspaper office with only
crampons on his feet and an ice ax in his hand.

He couldn't think of Raymond anymore. It was no good
remembering what had happened in the past.

The courthouse loomed ahead on the right, the brick and
blue dome muted by snow. When he was younger Aurey
had wanted to be a judge and hold court in the huge room
on the second floor opposite the library. He'd wanted to sit
on the high bench, gowned in black, looking out over the
lawyers and spectators.

His father had taken him to the courtroom once, after Ed
Wainwright had given his father a summons for speeding.
His father had explained to him how the trial would proceed. Ed would tell one side of the story, and his father
would tell another, and the judge would decide which version to believe. If he believed Ed Wainwright, then the judge
would determine how much money would satisfy the
county.

Aurey had sat at the back of the courtroom by himself,
watching the judge and feeling the weight of the air in the
huge room. Ed Wainwright said he had clocked his father
with a radar gun going twenty miles over the speed limit.
Then his father had taken the witness box. The judge in the

black robe had questioned him, and his father had said, "Yes, sir," and "No, sir," in a way Aurey had never heard him speak before. His father explained he had been taking his wife's mother to the airport in Chipeta Springs, which Aurey knew was true because he had been in the car. His grandmother had needed to use the bathroom, just as his father said, and she wouldn't go at the Texaco station down the valley, so they'd had to drive all the way back to Gold Hill. The judge had smiled at that, and Aurey had felt relieved that his father was telling the truth. Then they had all been afraid they'd miss the plane, so his father had driven faster because his mother-in-law had been there for two weeks. That was all true, every word, and when his father finished telling his side, the judge had looked at him and smiled again and said, "Guilty," as if nothing his father said had made any difference.

Aurey pulled around to the back of the courthouse, where the rescue equipment was kept. Most of the gear had been donated by businesses in town—the portable stretcher, medicines, flares, ropes. He loaded the gear into the Jeep as quickly as he could.

Then he headed home to get his own pack and his skis.

His father's house was one of the better ones on the downside of Main. Most of the houses were miner's shacks and rooming houses, flaking their paint. The Garcias lived downside. So did the plumber, Pete Green, and Max Zendowski, who'd been the watchman at the Molly Kathleen, and Pop Krause. Some of the young carpenters and hangers-on had moved in lately, even since Aurey had come back to town.

Years ago Ernesto had blown insulation in through the clapboard of their house and had painted the siding himself. There was always some touch his mother added—a flower box in the window in summer, or a specially painted gingerbread around the porch. She had already shoveled the walk once when he got home.

"Your father called again," she said. "He says he'll pray for you."

"Thank him for me."

"I've put out food in the kitchen."

He nodded and went back to his room. His brother had come from Denver for the opening weekend and had left his two children in the house. Aurey could hear them arguing in another room.

"You want anything special?" his mother asked.

"No, thanks," Aurey said.

"Apples, oranges, salami, cheese. Will that be enough? You want *salchichas*?"

"I want the children to be quiet."

"Ignore them," his mother said.

"I will, but they could be quieter."

His mother almost never came into his room. Even when all five of the children were growing up and three of them slept there, she said it was up to them to keep the room neat. Aurey was usually the one to do it. But now she followed him, as if she needed to talk to him.

Aurey unlocked the closet where he kept his mountaineering gear.

The room was small, barren except for a cross hung on the wall above the bed. Besides the equipment piled on the floor, there were three suits hanging on hangers and still in their plastic cleaning bags. He hadn't worn them since he'd come back from Denver.

He pulled the gear out—a pack, tent, sleeping bag, snowshoes, a cardboard box full of food packets and cooking gear.

His mother sat on the bed. She was a short woman, round in the arms and legs, and when she sank into the soft bed, her feet didn't reach the floor. "You have to be patient," she said, "especially with children."

"I am patient."

"Your father said it's Becky Carlsson who's lost. Isn't that the Blythe girl who was in a class with Tony?"

"Yes."

"Lorraine's sister?"

"You know that," Aurey said. "Why are you asking me?"

"I'm old. I forget things."

Aurey spread the supplies from the cardboard box out on the floor and checked them against a list taped to the inside of the closet door. When he was satisfied he had everything, he began stowing things in his rucksack.

"Has anyone told Lorraine?" his mother asked.

"I don't know. Ed will call her if he thinks she should know."

"Of course she should know. Why shouldn't she? You might call her yourself before you go."

He packed his Primus stove, a set of aluminum pots, flashlight and extra batteries. He coiled his soft yellow climbing rope between the palm of his hand and his elbow, looped the last three feet around the middle of the coil, and cinched it onto his pack.

They argued in silence over Lorraine. His mother gazed at the cross over the bed, and Aurey listened to the children running from one room to another, laughing hysterically about something.

"I'm not calling her," Aurey said finally.

"You shouldn't be so critical of people," his mother said. "How can you be happy if you're so critical?"

Aurey didn't answer.

"You aren't happy. I know that. You think happiness isn't important."

"I'm happy."

"I wish there were something I could do," his mother said. She looked at him sadly.

"You could keep the children quieter," he said. "That would be a start."

His mother got up from the bed and called out to the children to be quieter when they were running around the house. Then she came back and watched Aurey. "I heard a rumor the other day," she said. "It was *chisme*, but just the same, it might be true."

"I'm not interested in rumors."

"I know you're not, and that's good. You believe what you see. But I was in the café the other day when Jerilyn

was there. She hears things, you know, she and Homer
both. They listen for things."

"The wrong things."

"Not always the wrong things. Yes, sometimes the wrong
things." His mother stared at him. Aurey was packing and
not listening. "Don't forget the food on the kitchen table."

He packed the medicines in the side pockets of his pack
where he could get at them easily if he had to. Then he
braced the pack against the wall and lashed the tent and the
snowshoes to it with a sturdy cord.

"How long will you be gone?" his mother asked.

"A day, maybe two days. It depends." He stood up. "If
we don't find her today or tomorrow, we won't be in such a
hurry."

"And her mother, that poor woman. I hope Ed won't call
Martha and Wendell. They've had a terrible time."

"You've had a terrible time too."

"Nothing like them. In a different way. Not like them."
She looked at the cross and made a sign. Then she looked
back at Aurey. "You don't want to hear the rumor?"

"No."

Aurey put back the things he was not taking and locked
the closet again. Then he picked up the rucksack and carried it past his mother and out to the kitchen.

He packed the apples and oranges and sausage which his
mother had laid out. They were too heavy for their value,
but he could eat them on the way or leave them later in the
Jeep. But now he packed them in his rucksack.

"Finn hits her," his mother said. "That's what Jerilyn
said. Finn hits Becky."

"That sounds about right for Finn."

"I don't know that it's true." his mother said.

Aurey closed the drawstrings on his pack and strapped
the flap. Then he kissed his mother and shouldered the pack
and edged sideways out the door, which his mother held
open for him.

13

Elk had been plains animals, but when the land had shrunk with the advance of settlers, and the prairie habitat diminished, elk moved west into the mountains. They could live at high altitudes, migrate for hundreds of miles according to the seasons and the weather, endure the steep terrain.

They were natural animals for men to hunt—animals of great strength and grace, beautiful animals—massive, canny, skittish. The buffalo had been easy prey for Indians and for whites, slow footed, prone to the mentality of the herd. Deer were plentiful and stayed in one place, circling the few acres of their territory in fits and starts, hiding and testing the air again and again. They were no match for a bow and arrow or a rifle.

A man who wanted to prove himself, a brave seeking the glory of the hunt, sought the elk. A bull elk might weigh a thousand pounds and carry a rack of antlers six feet across. He could start quickly and run for miles without tiring. Even on the plains a horse was useless in tracking an elk, especially saddled with the weight of a man. But a man on foot might follow. An Indian brave might tire an elk.

Aurey trained all one summer for the hunt. He rose at

dawn and ran from town at 7,700 feet all the way to the top of Ptarmigan Pass at 11,105. Or he zigzagged up the footpath to the Jay Bird Mine. Or he ran the precipitous scree to the summit of Whitehouse Peak, which was over 13,000 feet. Twice he ran the twenty-eight-mile loop up Bear Creek Trail, over the top of the Amphitheater, and down into Cutler Creek Basin.

In September, before the bow season started, he backpacked into American Flats, above Bear Creek and to the northeast of Engineer Mountain. The Flats was level tundra, pockmarked with small ponds and springs, carpeted with lush green and yellow grass. The willows and berry bushes had already turned red from the cold nights, but the days were warm when the sun burned through the thin air.

He set his camp at timberline above the Flats, just off the wind line of the Divide. On the first afternoon he'd scouted a herd of fifteen elk browsing the grass on the flank of Treasure Peak two miles across the tundra. Another dozen or so had crossed the lip of the Divide and headed into the timber to bed down for the night. Stars came out everywhere, and he knew when he went to sleep that he'd find elk in the morning.

That night he had dreamed of climbing with Raymond. He rarely recalled his dreams, but that dream was vivid and clear to him, and he remembered it still, long afterward, whenever he thought of the hunt itself. They were climbing a nameless rock in a nameless place, practicing, it seemed, though any climb was real enough. This time they were climbing blindfolded. Raymond was close above him, Aurey remembered, because he could feel the tension of the rope strung between them, and he could hear the jingle of Raymond's chain of carabiners and his clothing scraping the rock. Now and then pebbles burst down the rockface, glancing from Aurey's helmet or off his back and shoulders. He called to Raymond because with the pebbles came the threat of a larger stone or a boulder which might dislodge from above them. Could Raymond see?

Raymond didn't answer.

Aurey had no perception of how far they were from the ground or what was above them. They could not go back. Raymond had somehow made that clear. They had to go up.

In the beginning the blindfold had frustrated more than terrified him. There was the difficulty in finding holds, feeling where the rope was snagged, measuring distances. But once he became accustomed to the dark, he was surprised how adept he was at discovering what the rock offered. He scanned the surface at the radius of his reach, sensed with his fingers the topography of the stone, chose without second-guessing the strongest and most solid handholds. Footholds barely an inch wide seemed more comfortable and secure than he had ever imagined. His muscles flowed. His body seemed to fire in such high efficiency that he could have climbed on and on. It was as though, without the sky or the sensation of the earth, he had nothing to fear at all. Everything he needed and wanted was right there within him.

Yet there was, at the same time, another emotion, impossible to describe, which began to insinuate itself into his body. It was like a mist which, in the night, changed the composition of the air. He could feel the difference but could not see it, and he could only feel it after it had accumulated enough power.

It was like fatigue, but he was not tired. It was as if the higher they climbed the more the air resisted them, pressed against them like wind. Each handhold had to be gripped tighter and held longer. The pebbles stopped, but their absence made Aurey more nervous than their presence. Were they coming to the top? Was there nothing above them? He wanted to shake off his blindfold, but he couldn't let go of the rock. . . .

That was all he remembered. He felt there was more to the dream, that it had gone on longer, extended itself to some conclusion, but he could not recall anything more, except waking in the cold and shivering, and smelling the musk of elk on the cool breeze across the tundra.

That was how he still remembered it. He had awakened before dawn and had watched the stars fade into the early blue. When he could see well enough, he'd got up and put on a T-shirt and shorts and his running shoes. He had no fire. He ate a few pieces of bread, drank cold water. Then he stretched his legs, whirled his arms in circles, did several windmills. Finally he caked himself with cold mud from the edge of a stream.

Before the sun was up, he was striding along a game trail through the willows and berry bushes.

A half mile across the Flats he picked out tracks of elk which had moved through. He stayed downwind not because he meant to catch them unaware, but because he meant to get a glimpse of the herd in order to choose the animal he would hunt. The tracks led up a slight rise, and he hurried to stay warm.

From the rise he had spotted the herd several hundred yards ahead. They were grazing the low shrubs and grass, and he walked straight at them. When the elk saw him, they ran. They bolted from the swale and ran uphill toward the Divide, clattering over the talus. Aurey ran too. He jumped across a stream, broke through scrub, kept a line across the bumpy grass toward the point where the elk had disappeared over the ridge.

He kept a steady pace, trying to measure his gait against the hill. He knew the elk were in full retreat, far ahead of him. He would not catch them in seconds or minutes, but in hours.

He stretched his legs and loped up the grassy slope onto the talus, bending his body into the angle of the hill. He gained a rhythm of arms and legs.

At the top of the Divide he saw the elk again, traversing the shoulder of the ridge, easing down into the Flats again toward Engineer. He followed them along the shore of a shallow tarn, skipped after them over lichened rock, keeping all the time an eye on the tracks. The bull he wanted was still with the herd. He gained when the elk slowed, and gave up ground when they sprinted. He lost sight of them in the trees, found them again on the flank of Brown Mountain, lost them again in another valley.

That was how it went for three hours, when the bull finally split off from the herd. He veered away at the crest of a saddle, and Aurey followed the new track. It was a huge cloven hoofprint, deeper than the others in the soft scree. He did not know why the bull separated itself, whether to protect the others of the herd or to save itself.

Aurey kept after it, always trying to keep the animal moving uphill so it would tire faster. He circled under it, chased it up the scree where its massive body sank into the loose gravel, skittered after it on the downslope and into the trees.

He sensed it slow down. The elk lingered longer in cover, and when it climbed its hoofprints were closer together. It staggered sometimes now, and Aurey closed the distance.

Finally on an uphill pitch, the elk stopped abruptly and turned back into a glen of aspens. It stumbled, wheezed, crashed through the trees into a barren gully where a trickle of water gave sustenance to a patch of thin grass. It was browsing this grass when Aurey stopped running.

He came down the slope slowly, each step sliding a little in the soft earth. The elk saw him and lurched away, but stopped again a few yards higher up. Aurey came on, holding out his hand.

The elk's back was black with sweat, its pulse visible in its neck. It reeled away again, then again.

"Come on, boy. I'm not going to hurt you. Come on."

Aurey kept his hand out. The elk backed away.

Aurey came on, and the elk lowered its huge antlered head as though to charge. But it was too exhausted even for that. Aurey circled and edged closer and closer until he laid his hand on the elk's shoulder.

Then he turned away and walked slowly back down the streambed.

14

By the time Aurey reached the Bear Creek trailhead it had snowed more than a foot and a half. He pulled his Jeep into a drift not far from where Bo Jack was tied up to a spruce tree. The horse faced downwind, but the snow still stuck to its back and mane. It was snowing so hard, Aurey could barely read the trail sign across the road.

BEARCREEK TRAIL

NOT MAINTAINED

BEAR CREEK	4
YELLOW JACKET MINE	7
AMERICAN FLATS	11

There was no way to figure the weather. Sometimes the mountains held in a storm for days, forcing the air to curl back under the high peaks, stalling the clouds. But that didn't always happen. And it could be snowing in Gold Hill when it was sunny in the mountains east of Chipeta Springs. Or sometimes a blast of air would come out of Utah and knock the clouds right on through the high peaks. All Aurey knew was that it was snowing hard now.

He called the sheriff's office on the CB and got Sharon to

put him through to Ed. "I'm up at the trailhead," he said. "No one's here yet, but I'll go ahead. Can you get someone to bring up a vehicle with a trailer hitch? This horse here looks beat."

"Will do," Ed said. "And we have a couple more men coming. Granny Watson will be some help to you. What's it like up there?"

"Snow. You may need a shovel to get the trailer out." He paused a moment. "Meeker didn't find Becky, did he?"

"No luck."

"Has anybody called Lorraine?"

"I sent Neil down to tell her," Ed said. "Why don't you leave your Jeep open in case someone needs to use the CB when you're up there?"

"All right. We'll have a man back down sometime to-night."

"Good luck, then."

"We'll need it. Over."

He hung up the receiver and got out into the swirling snow. In another few minutes he had put on his pack and crossed the road to the start of the trail.

Visibility was poor, especially after he got out of the trees. In the trees he could judge from the angle of the hill and the spaces between the trees, but when he reached the shale blowout, all the landmarks disappeared. He could feel the shale underfoot, slippery even in deep snow, but the incline was white as space, without any markings or distance. Even Finn's track had been blown clean.

He knew, though, the general configuration of the terrain, knew roughly where the trail was supposed to go. He headed uphill at forty-five degrees, making for a place he hoped would be there if he took enough steps. What he had to find, eventually, was the opening through the rocks where the trail led onto the cliff above the gorge.

He made four tight switchbacks through the deep snow, retraced his steps so the others following could not miss the zigzags—at least if they came within the half hour—and then climbed two hundred paces straight up. From there he could see the gray shape of the shale slash on the cliff, the place from which, over the millennia, the loose rock had broken off and slid. He aimed to the right of the slash until he spotted a sandstone spire looming up from the gray, then circled the spire and climbed ten more minutes into the opening onto the cliff.

The snow slacked a little there because the outcropping was in the lee of Brown Mountain, and the wind was not so strong. Beneath him the highway wound up the pass. A snowplow with its headlights on and its yellow flasher whirling crept around a curve, drifting in and out of the sheets of snow.

He was glad to be alone. He liked Granny Watson, whom he knew a little, and Meeker was all right. He could even take Bud Saunders on occasion, though Bud had barely made it through high school. Bud wouldn't be any help, though, because he was out of shape. He'd married Vicky Bragga right out of school, and they'd had three children without blinking, which was a mistake Aurey couldn't fathom. Bud was all right, but someone would have to carry him back down the trail.

It was Weedy and Finn Aurey couldn't stand. They spent half their waking hours working so they could spend the other half in bars. They said absurd things, too, about animals especially. Aurey remembered one time at the Witches' Brew he'd heard Finn say that elk weren't as smart as deer.

"They're dumb compared to deer," Finn said. "They give off that musk."

"When they get mad, they're like tanks," Weedy said.

Aurey hadn't been able to believe what he heard. "What does the emission of musk have to do with intelligence?" he asked Finn. "That's the stupidest thing I ever heard."

"Who asked you?" Finn said. "Butt out."

"The emission of musk is a fear-oriented response," Aurey went on. "It also functions to attract females for the purpose of propagation."

"What's propagation?" Weedy wanted to know.

"Breeding," Aurey said, rolling his eyes. "To you and Finn, fucking, though with a higher purpose."

"What does rolling your eyes mean?" Finn asked, standing up naked from the hot pool.

"It means you don't know your ass from a hole in the ground."

Weedy laughed, but Finn clambered out onto the rock beside the pool. "I'll propagate your ass," Finn said, clenching a fist.

Aurey had rolled his eyes again and started up the trail with his usual quick stride, while Finn was left calling names.

No, he didn't mind being alone, though it was eerie looking out from the cliff. Across the gorge were the remnants of mines—cables, cogwheels, tunnels, a few boards, arsenic burn on the rocks—all behind the gauze of snow.

He didn't linger long. Becky was waiting.

Part of the trail along the cliff was wide enough to accommodate machinery. That had been the original purpose—to supply the mines up higher in the gorge with the necessary equipment to operate. But over the years sections of the trail had been eroded by waterfalls and avalanches and ice. That Finn had made it down in that weather with the horse was a tribute to the horse, because a slip would have meant a straight drop of a thousand feet. So it was slow going, even for Aurey. He had to test his steps, plow through drifts which accumulated in the hollows, make certain he was leaving the best track for the others coming along.

It was two-thirty when he got off the cliff and back into the higher trees. In three miles he had gained twenty-five hundred feet of elevation, and where he was then a good two feet of snow had come down. And it was still snowing hard. A wind spiraled down the creek bottom and he had to stop and put on snowshoes in order to make better time.

Time was a factor. Becky had already spent one night out, wherever she was, and surviving one night was easier than surviving two. He knew that from his own experience with Raymond. They had spent some perilous times roped in storms to some mountain, waiting for the weather to break. That was all they had been able to do: wait. But they'd been prepared. They'd had warm down sleeping bags and hammocks and burner-stoves.

The wind funneling down the creek sifted snow from the trees. This was a lighter snow which slithered through the sides of his goggles and down the pack of his parka. He had to stop and clear his glasses. And the snowshoes rubbed the backs of his heels.

But these small discomforts didn't trouble him. The wind and the snow were what he expected. What disturbed him more was that he didn't smell any smoke on the wind. He'd wanted that for Becky's sake. He'd hoped she'd have a fire at the camp, that she'd be sitting in the tent sipping tea or bourbon even, warming her feet, drying her boots and socks. He'd sit down with her and find out where she'd spent the night, how Lorraine was doing, how her parents were. He hadn't seen Martha and Wendell in a long time. Then he'd either take her down with him on the other horse or, if she were all right, he'd leave her there and head down himself to tell the others.

But there was no smoke. It was still snowing in the trees, and the air was cold and filled with snow. If she was not at the camp, he hoped she had the sense to stay put. The smart thing to do when you were lost in the mountains was to let someone else find you. That was the way people survived, and it took good sense. There were two parts to making it through any bad time. It was like climbing a mountain: there was a physical part and a mental part. For the physical part you lifted weights, ran in the gym, practiced the small gestures of holding on to stone. You did curls and bench presses and sprints. But that was not enough. It was good, but it was not preparation for the sudden demand of a rain-slick piece of granite when you were eight hundred feet from the floor of a canyon. For that you needed to get beyond the muscles. You needed to be separate from maps and geochemistry and formulas of physics. You had to be mentally sound. You had to have the flame. That's what Ray-

mond called it. Real strength did not come from the muscles, it came from the head. When you had to do the right
thing, you needed the flame. And some people didn't have
it. When the weather turned, some people panicked, lost
touch, gave up. Maybe Becky had it. Aurey hoped she did,
but it was hard to tell until the moment was upon you.

15

Lorraine's yellow Volkswagen was parked in the driveway under a smooth arc of snow, and Shanks pulled in behind it and sat for a minute in his warm car. Snow was falling through the cottonwoods in the river bottom and over the river and over the small A-frame, which looked deserted. The cabin was two miles down the River Road where the land smoothed out from the mountains and opened into the ranchland to the north. Where the A-frame stood had been the original homestead of the Jepson Ranch, though all that remained now was the brick chimney covered with snow.

Lorraine was an enigma to him. He'd learned a little about her, the way one learned anything in a small town— by bits and pieces over time. He'd asked a question or two of Weedy Garcia, heard a scrap from Ed Wainwright, read "Around the County" in the *Chronicle,* which detailed the whereabouts and activities of every relative of everyone in the county. But still he didn't know very much. She'd studied Spanish at the University of Colorado, had a son, Christopher, whom he'd seen at Pinnacle Ridge and once or twice around town. She'd been divorced and taught high school. It was her first year.

Now and then he encountered her in the Outlaw or at the post office. She looked thinner than he remembered her from Pinnacle Ridge when he'd taken the hawk to Wendell. Her hair was cut shorter, too, dark hair that curled just below her ears. She never noticed him, or if she did, she didn't seem to know who he was. She floated, he thought, and yet, though he couldn't explain it, she seemed aware of everything around her, just as Becky was, but in a different way. Becky was earnest and eager, while Lorraine was composed.

The one time he'd talked to her hadn't been pleasant. That had been right after Labor Day, after most of the tourists had cleared out and the town was taking stock of itself after the hectic summer. He'd been answering a question of a retiree from Illinois, a man who wanted to know about columbines. Did they bloom in July or August? Could he still find one now at lower altitude? Lorraine had come into the store and had paid no attention to him, though at the same time, she hadn't ignored him either. That was Shanks's impression. She listened to what he said to the man while she strolled through the store. She studied the turquoise jewelry for a while, flipped through the wildlife photographs he had in large folios near the window. Once she went outside to look at the crystal display in the window—a collection he had borrowed from Ed Wainwright.

When she came back in, the man had gone, and he knew by the set of her mouth she had come to see him. She did resemble Becky. Becky was blond and rougher, more used to Finn Carlsson and his friends, but Lorraine's eyes had the same steadiness in them. She walked straight up to the counter where he was standing.

"Can I help you?" he asked.

"You're seeing my sister," she said.

That was the first thing she said, straight out, and he'd been surprised by the hard tone of her voice.

"Not in that way," he said. "It's not what you think."

"You don't know what I think," she said. "All I know is that Becky's reading books."

"Do you object to books?"

"I do if they upset her."

"I don't mean to upset her."

"I didn't say it was you," Lorraine said. "Becky is old enough to make up her own mind about whom she sees and what she reads. But she's not so strong sometimes as she seems. I don't want to have things be worse for her."

"Worse in what way?"

Lorraine hadn't answered. She'd stared at him a moment as if deciding what to say next. He'd been seized with a sudden pang of guilt. Certainly he had never meant to do anything more than be kind to Becky. He had run into her around town from time to time and lent her books he liked —a Hemingway novel, a book of poetry, collections of stories. Sometimes they talked about the books and sometimes they didn't. She came to see him once in a while at the shop, or when something affected her, she might stop by his place in Tin Pan Alley.

Becky often said she didn't understand the books he gave her, but it was his view she did. "You understand exactly," he told her once. "You simply aren't used to the ideas. You haven't ever talked about books so you don't have the words."

"I'd rather walk a trail than read about it."

"Yes, but can you walk the streets of Dublin?"

"Where's Dublin?" she asked. She'd looked through the window of his shop as if Dublin were across the street.

"Ireland. Dublin is in Ireland. It's a city. If you read books you can know Dublin in some fashion the way you know Gold Hill."

"Not the way I know Gold Hill."

"Better," he said.

Becky had stared at him for a long time. Then she asked, "What are you running from, Neil?"

He'd smiled at her. "I'm not running from, I'm running *to.*"

"You and this relative of yours you've told me about?"

"Yes."

"Is that what you're doing here in this junk shop? *Running to?*"

"Yes."

He had given her more books.

But he had meant only to teach her what she might want to know. He hadn't meant to unsettle her.

Or maybe he had.

Lorraine had kept staring at him for a long time.

"I'll do whatever I can," he said. "Whatever I can do. . . ."

He had thought Lorraine would say not to see Becky anymore. That was what her expression seemed to tell him. But instead she said, "Give me the names of the books you think Becky might like."

"The ones she hasn't read?"

"Yes."

He had given her more names.

"Is it her birthday?" he asked.

Lorraine gave no sign. "Just don't tell Becky," she said.

He rolled down the window and let the cool air and snow into the Subaru. He had wanted to talk to Lorraine again under circumstances different from these, but Ed had asked him to tell her about Becky's being lost. "A personal visit is the kindest," Ed said. "And see whether she thinks we should tell Martha and Wendell. I'll let Lorraine decide."

He sat until the cold had taken over the car, imagined Lorraine's watching him from the window of the A-frame, her face indistinct and faint behind the snow and the misted glass. He rehearsed what he would say to her—"I'm sorry to be the one to say this. . . . Ed asked me to come around. . . ."—but nothing would sound right. How could he tell her what he knew?

Then he saw Lorraine come out onto the deck of the A-frame and wave to him. "Are you going to sit out there forever?" she called. "What do you want?"

He got out and ducked into the snow. The walk was unshoveled, and when he reached the door, he kicked the snow from his shoes.

"Never mind that," she said. "Come in."

She led the way into an entryway separate from the house where Christopher's boots and sled were kept, along with two pairs of cross-country skis. Then she opened the door, and the rush of smells rose around him—apple, fresh bread, cinnamon.

"I've been baking," she said. "Excuse the mess."

She had an apron over her jeans and a red plaid shirt, and her hair was pinned back from her face. She brushed a blemish of flour from her cheek.

He was barely conscious of the room. It had a roof-high ceiling, a loft, a free standing fireplace with the embers of a fire in it. School papers were spread out on the table in front of the sofa.

"It's about Becky," he said.

"Becky?"

"Finn came down this morning from the camp—"

"She's not dead?" Lorraine turned suddenly toward him.

"No, she's lost. She and Finn were supposed to meet somewhere called the Depot, and Becky didn't show up. This was yesterday in the snow."

Christopher's small face appeared like a moon above the back of the sofa, a round face framed by wispy brown hair. "Is Aunt Becky dead?" he asked.

"Lost," Shanks said. "She was hunting with your uncle."

"Are they going to find her?"

"I'm sure they will. People are going up right now to look for her."

"Aurey?"

Shanks nodded. "Aurey and Finn and Weedy and some others. I just came from the sheriff's office. They're meeting at the trailhead in half an hour."

"I'm going up too," Lorraine said. "Oh, shit, Becky. Jesus."

Christopher climbed over the back of the sofa and padded

across in his socks to where Lorraine was standing at the kitchen counter. He waited beside her for a minute, until Lorraine picked him up and hugged him.

"Will you stay with Aunt Vicky?" she asked.

"No."

"You get along with Jason. Doesn't he have video games? I can't think where else to take you."

"I'd rather go to Gammie's."

"Gammie's is too far. We don't have the time. Anyway, Gammie and Papa would be sad if they knew about Aunt Becky right now."

"I wouldn't tell them."

"I know, sweetheart, but if you were there, they'd know." She put Christopher down. "Now I want you to go pack your clothes."

Christopher didn't move.

"If you want I can give you a ride up in the Subaru," Shanks said. "I've got four-wheel."

"All right."

"What else can I do?"

"You can put out the fire in the fireplace. And get the bread out of the oven. Come on, Christopher, we have to go."

Lorraine pushed Christopher gently and then threw off her apron.

Shanks went to the sink to get water in a pan. "Aurey said to bring skis, goggles, a camp stove."

"I know what I need," Lorraine said. "Are you going up too?"

"Ed wants me to stay in town and help run errands. I'd like to, but I'm not sure I'd do any good up there where she is. What about your parents?"

"God, let's not tell them. They'd both go crazy. She's lost, you said, not dead."

Shanks doused the fire, watched briefly while the embers boiled and cracked. There was no use in his going up. He knew that. He didn't know the country and high places scared him and he didn't like the snow. It was snowing so hard now. Even watching from indoors, he could feel it all around him.

When the fire was soaked, he went to the kitchen and took the bread from the oven and turned the oven off. He put the two pans of bread on the rack on the counter, inhaled the sweet smell.

Lorraine was up in the loft, and she tossed her gear down over the rail—sleeping bag, gaiters, a pair of down boots.

"Let me know what I can do," Shanks called.

"Would you look in on Christopher?"

He could hear Christopher singing to himself in his room in the back of the A-frame. It was colder in that part of the house away from the fire, and the smells from the kitchen diminished. He passed a bookcase in the hall—a thin table, really, with books stacked on it. He happened to see the library numbers on the spines of some of them, and he turned one into the light. It was *Too Late the Phalarope* by Alan Paton.

Christopher was in his room stuffing clothes helter-skelter into a satchel.

"How're you coming?" Shanks asked.

"I don't like Jason," Christopher said.

"No?"

"He beats me up. And he thinks he's great because his mom and dad own a motel. I'd rather see my grandmother, but mom never takes me there."

"It's pretty far," Shanks said. "Maybe you should think of going to Jason's as helping your Aunt Becky."

"And getting beat up?" Christopher stopped shoving his clothes into the satchel and looked at Shanks. "Do you know Aunt Becky?"

"I'm a friend of hers. My name's Neil."

"I'm Christopher."

"I know."

"Do you know my mother too?"

"I've met her before. I came over because the sheriff asked me to." Shanks surveyed the room, which had on the walls posters of motorcycles. "You like bikes?"

"My father sent me those," Christopher said. "I think he races them."

"That sounds exciting."

Christopher shrugged.

"I'll tell your mother you're almost ready."

He'd heard Lorraine come back down the stairs, and she was in the kitchen now, putting together some food to take up the mountain.

"Is Christopher moving?"

"He's making headway. Look, if he's unhappy at Jason's, I can take him out to your parents' place."

"He'll be fine with Vicky."

Lorraine had got down macaroni and spaghetti from the cupboard and put them together with packets of soup and a jar of peanut butter she had on the counter. "Can you wrap that bread?" she asked. "I'll take a loaf to Vicky, and you can keep one too."

But Shanks didn't wrap the bread. He walked through the kitchen to the window. The windshield of the Subaru was covered with snow, and beyond the car the sandstone cliff across the road was glazed with white. The forecast had been for rain to nine thousand feet with flurries in the higher mountains, but a forecast only filled a void. In the absence of anything else it was what you believed in.

He remembered the time in Michigan when his father had told him to wait in the shelter on Higgins Lake. "Wait," his father said. "Don't move."

His father had gone out of the flap of the shelter and headed for the car. It had been snowing then, the white gauze sliding over the summer houses on the shore. The houses seemed to recede behind the snow, and the docks which spider-legged out into the lake looked like giant insects. And his father had moved away, diminishing into the snow.

Shanks turned around and looked at Lorraine. "Can I ask you something?"

"You can try."

She sat down on a chair and laced up her hiking boots, crossing the strings, pulling them tight.

"Has Becky ever said anything to you about how she feels?"

"About you?"

"Not about me. No, not about me."

"What, then?" She looked up. "What are you asking?"

"Doesn't she talk to you?"

"She used to," Lorraine said. "She talks to you now."

Lorraine tied her boot and stood up. She stuffed her red gaiters into her pack.

"Christopher, we're going. Did you pack your pajamas?"

"Yes."

"We're not coming back here."

"I can't find my shoes."

"They're by the fireplace."

Christopher came out of his room dragging his satchel across the bare floor, but halfway across to the fireplace he detoured to the bathroom.

Lorraine turned to Shanks. "I came to your shop that day because I was worried about Becky. I used to think I knew her, but lately she's been different. That's why I wanted to read the books you were giving her."

"You think the books made her different?"

"They're beautiful books, Neil. I don't know."

"Where are my shoes?" Christopher asked.

"By the fireplace."

"I don't see why I can't go to Gammie's," he said, slouching down onto the floor and grabbing his shoes. "You never take me."

"Come on, Christopher, we're in a hurry."

Lorraine wrapped the bread in tinfoil and set it on the edge of the counter.

Shanks watched the snow. It swirled down the canyon and through the cottonwoods, and across the road. He didn't know how to tell Lorraine about what he knew, or what else to ask her. Maybe Becky would be down at the camp when Aurey got there, and he wouldn't have to tell her anything. That was how he hoped it would turn out. But the snow kept falling as if it would never stop, over the yellow VW and the Subaru, over the cottonwoods and the river, over anything and everything, as if it were filling the world.

16

Neil was right: she did know Becky. She knew her temper and how stubborn she was and about the time she'd socked Finn. She knew about the time Becky had run away. She knew a lot about Becky. She knew how hard Becky had worked on the ranch after Toby had died, how hard she practiced the things she was good at—horseback riding, roping, softball, shooting a .22. If Becky had spent half the time on school as she'd spent on 4-H, she'd have been a straight-A student.

Even so, Lorraine had always thought of her as the smartest one in the family. Becky picked up details quickly, entertained ideas more easily, *listened.* She also got what she wanted on her own terms.

That was why Lorraine had been surprised about the reading. It wasn't something Becky would normally do. Not that Becky never read. But her taste wasn't to the books that Neil Shanks picked out for her. She'd never read good books or studied words. What did *diaphanous* mean? Becky had asked once. Or *plunder*? Wasn't it surprising, Becky had asked recently, how you could get feelings from words?

For the most part Lorraine admitted that Becky was changed for the better. What harm could come of knowing more about words? But the subtler hazards were there too. Every change in a river resulted in a change in the shore. Who knew whether it was good or bad? But Becky had, after all, constructed her own life with Finn. She had a way of doing things that got her through the days. It wasn't easy living with any man. Lorraine knew that herself.

Becky had told her early on she wasn't going to tell Finn about Neil Shanks. "He wouldn't get it" was the way Becky put it. "You know Finn."

She knew Finn well enough to understand how Becky might feel that way.

Lorraine had seen him once in the Golddigger arguing over whose quarter was up next for a game of eight-ball. "It's my quarter," Finn had said in a cool voice.

"Mine, friend," said the other man, who was four inches taller and fifty pounds heavier than Finn.

The man pushed Finn away from the table, and as he leaned down to fit the quarter into the slot, Finn ducked under and gave him an uppercut. The big man reeled backward with blood spurting from his nose.

No, Lorraine thought, Finn wasn't the type to understand a conversation about books.

Finn wasn't Lorraine's favorite person in the world, but Becky had seemed fairly happy in the first two years. Lately, though, Finn was spending his time after work in the Golddigger with Weedy and Flash Toomey and Charlie Fernsten. Becky had even punched Finn once when he came home drunk one night, and he'd punched her back so that she had a black eye for a week. But he was still her husband, and that was enough reason to be cautious about spending much time with Neil.

Besides, what was the point of asking too many questions? Neil knows this, and Neil knows that, Becky said. Neil seemed smooth. That's what Lorraine thought. His manner was different from other people's. He was not from there.

She thought these things while they were riding up the River Road toward the Panorama Motel to deliver Christopher. The road was plowed and packed down, but more snow had fallen, and no car had passed in the new snow. Neil drove painfully slowly past Pop Krause's shack, past the Placer Street bridge, as if they had nowhere they had to be. Lorraine wanted to get to the trailhead and talk to Ed and Aurey and Finn to find out what had really happened.

She looked over the back of the seat and managed a weak smile at Christoper. He was a sad child, she thought, but she didn't know what to do about it. It was true that some children could be sad anywhere, even around other children they knew. Christopher seemed that kind. When she'd been at school in Boulder he'd played alone in the day care, preferring to look at pictures in books to playing with the others. He was too controlled, she thought, too introspective, too much the way she was.

She supposed Becky was the other extreme. Growing up, she'd never accepted the limitations others imposed on her. Even after Toby died, and there was so much more to do on the ranch, Becky had fought against whatever strictures she felt were unreasonable. Like against their mother.

Their mother's craziness was an agony no one could have predicted, the kind which happened only to other people or in the movies. Grief could do that. Martha would go for weeks being lucid, cheerful, her old self. Then she'd have days when she thought Toby was still at the dinner table.

"Toby, you look so nice tonight," she might say. Or, "I like that shirt on you."

One week Martha would tell them to wear sweaters to school to keep from getting a chill, and the next she'd worry they were dressing too warmly. One semester she drove fifteen miles each way to school and back because she didn't trust the school bus, which stopped right at their mailbox on the county road.

One of the bitterest times had been the fight over the Youth Rodeo. Becky had set up a barrel course in the pasture and had practiced for weeks, steering Toots, the pinto she'd raised, through the loops. And she'd trained Toots to jerk-stop for calf-roping. Becky let Toots out full tilt, whirling a lariat overhead, roping everything from posts to cows in the feed lot to squirmy calves. She had geared herself and her horse to the rodeo the first week in August.

One night they were all sitting on the porch in the evening, watching Becky go through her drills. Wendell had timed her barrel race and was shouting numbers. Martha and Lorraine were playing cribbage. At the end of the practice Becky walked Toots over to cool her down.

"I think I'm ready," she'd said. "Don't you think, Dad?"

Martha had looked at the pinto. "Ready for what?"

"Saturday, Mom, the rodeo."

"Well," Martha said, "you can't."

"What do you mean, I can't?"

"You might get thrown off. I won't let you take that chance."

"I've been thrown off before."

Martha had furrowed her brow. "It's too dangerous," she said. "You can't ride."

"Dad says I can," Becky said.

Becky had looked at Wendell, who'd been looking out at the ridge. "What?" he said, as if he hadn't heard.

"You said I could ride in the rodeo."

"I thought you were," he said, nodding.

"See?" Becky lifted her head at her mother.

"He doesn't know anything about it," Martha said. "If he did, he wouldn't let you."

"Well, it doesn't matter," Becky said, "because I'm going to ride."

"You're not going to ride, and that's final."

Lorraine had felt sorry for Becky. She'd consoled her, talked to her. What difference did it make, anyway, compared to the satisfaction their mother got from not worrying?

"Lots," Becky said in the darkness of the room they shared.

"But there isn't anything you can do unless Dad lets you."

"Dad's out there drinking."

"I know it doesn't make sense. The world doesn't always."

"Well, it should."

Becky had not said anything after that, and Lorraine had fallen off to sleep. In the morning, early, when she woke, Becky was gone.

"Gone where?" Wendell said. "Her horse is here, and the car's out back."

"For a walk, maybe?"

Lorraine had taken Toots out on the logging roads behind the house to look, and Wendell drove the car down Pinnacle Ridge Road. When they got back, Martha had called Ed Wainwright and said Becky had been kidnapped.

Ed had come right over. "Now, Martha, she hasn't been kidnapped. She's run away. That's what I'd have done too. About the only thing you can do is wait for her to call."

She had called too. Two days later. She'd hitched over to Dove Creek on the Utah-Colorado border and spent one night in an alfalfa field. Then she'd got a ride up to Green River, Utah, the next day. She slept in a motel that night, and the morning after she called and said she'd come back if she could ride in the rodeo.

How could she be lost? That was what Lorraine wanted to know. She might have tracked an elk the way Neil said, and she might have taken shelter somewhere in a mine, but she wouldn't be lost. Lost was when you didn't know where you were, not when other people didn't. Becky knew exactly where she was.

That didn't mean she wasn't in trouble, though. There was an awful lot of snow coming down awfully fast. But Aurey would find her. Even in all the snow Aurey would know what to do and where to look. If Neil would only drive a little faster.

17

There were already several trucks and Jeeps parked in the turnout at the Bear Creek trailhead. Bud Saunders was digging out the horse trailer, though with the snow coming down so fast around him, he looked like a man doing nothing. As fast as he dug, the snow filled in the space.

"There's Vicky in the Bronco," Lorraine said. "Drive over and I'll tell her we left Christopher with her mother."

Shanks inched forward through the deep snow. The sheriff had brought up Granny Watson and Jock Martin, who were organizing their gear on the wet hood of the police Blazer. The snow coming down was still melting from the engine heat. Meeker was directing traffic—a rancher and his wife and Neil.

Shanks pulled the Subaru alongside the Bronco, and Vicky got out and came over to Lorraine's window. She was chewing gum, and had on a pink parka and calf-high mukluks.

"Goddamn hunters," Vicky said. "How're you doing, Lorraine? Aren't hunters a bunch of assholes?"

"I'm all right," Lorraine said. "Listen, I left Christopher—"

"Fine. Jason will be glad. Me and my mom will take care of him. Will you look at Bud? He thinks he's going on a search expedition when he can barely walk across the living room to change the channel. I told him he'd be worse than more snow." Vicky looked in the window at Shanks. "What're you doing with *him*?"

"He gave me a ride."

Lorraine got out and let Shanks pull up near to where Bo Jack was tied.

Bud stopped digging. "Hey, Neil, you got a trailer hitch on that piece of Jap tin?"

"What?"

"A trailer hitch! We're trying to get Bo Jack back down to Becky and Finn's."

"No."

"Why don't you come shovel, then? The Bronco has a hitch, but I don't trust Vicky to drive the rig down."

"I can drive it," Vicky said. "Fuck you."

"Anyway, she'll need help getting the trailer off at the corral."

"Shut your mouth," Vicky said. "I can get the trailer off too."

Shanks got out and Ed Wainwright called to him. "Neil, you see Finn?"

"We came by the River Road. Isn't he at the clinic?"

"No. Is Lorraine going?"

"She says she is."

"Good."

"She can sleep in my tent," Bud said. "Come here, Neil, and give me a hand."

Shanks shoveled a few minutes while Bud rested. Then Jock Martin and Meeker came over, and together they pushed the trailer up onto the flat of the turnout where the Bronco was waiting.

"Here's Finn!" someone called.

A car was coming up the grade from town, and everyone turned. The engine whined and the car surged on the snowpack as if it were a pool ball caroming from the cushion. But it wasn't Finn. It was a light green station wagon.

"Goddamn," Vicky said. "The vultures already know."

The driver's head appeared above the steering wheel like a frizzed doll, and the station wagon slid through a snowbank into the turnout. Bud and John Meeker scattered like fat cattle, and Granny Watson jumped up onto the hood of the Blazer. When the car stopped, Jerilyn McCrady snapped open the door and uncoiled from the seat. She wore sunglasses, and had on a beret and a puffy blue down coat.

"Ed, Ed, Ed," she said. "Why do you try to keep secrets from us?" she wailed. "You know how left out we feel?"

"I don't try," Ed said. "If I tried, I'd do a better job."

"Why don't we get a *min*imum of cooperation? Well, what happened? Will you *please* start at the beginning?" Jerilyn tugged off her sunglasses and looked around at the assembled people. "Is this the search team?"

"Where's the Mongoose?" Ed asked.

"He's right there," Jerilyn said.

Homer was slower to emerge. He spent some moments adjusting the earflaps on his hat, and then had to disengage himself from the seat belt. He was an older man, late fifties, balding. A small, neatly trimmed moustache flecked his upper lip.

"Hello, boys," he said. "Hello, Ed. How's everybody?" He nodded in the general direction of Lorraine. "Ladies too."

"How'd she get lost?" Jerilyn asked. "That's what we want to know."

"Snow," Ed said. "How do people get lost in snow? All we know is that Finn came down this morning and said he hadn't seen Becky since yesterday afternoon. Yesterday morning. We formed a search group immediately, and we're going to find her."

"These men?"

"Aurey's started up already. We're waiting for Finn and Weedy Garcia. I guess Lorraine's joining up too."

"You're not going?"

"I'm sending Meeker. That's what deputies are for. I'm staying in town to keep the lid on things."

"Where's she supposed to be?" Homer asked. He lifted an earflap to hear.

"If I knew that, Homer, I wouldn't be assembling this search team."

"I meant, where'd she get lost?"

"Bear Creek drainage," Ed said. "I know that's a little general, but it's the best I can do. Finn said he saw her last way up in the meadows. You could ask Finn if he ever gets here."

"Finn won't tell us anything," Jerilyn said. "You know that."

Ed surveyed the empty road down the pass. Snow was still falling along the canyon walls and in isolated patches of spruce. "You print the news," he said. "That's not my business. I don't care what you put in your paper, but this is a small town, and when you publish a story someone doesn't like, you have to live with it."

"You gave us the details," Homer said.

"I gave you the police record."

Lorraine had got down her skis from the top of Shank's car and had strapped them onto her pack. "I'm going up," she said. "I'm not waiting for Finn and Weedy."

"Me either," Granny said. "Let's get the horse in the trailer."

Bud and Jock had hooked the trailer to the Bronco and had pulled out the ramp, but they were having trouble convincing Bo Jack he wanted to climb up. Bud yanked on the bridle. "Git on," he said. "Come on, you piece of glue meat. Git up there."

Bo Jack kicked out, slipped, jerked the bridle out of Bud's grasp.

Then Meeker came over. "Let me," he said. He took Bud's place and ran a hand through Bo Jack's forelock and along his cheek. He gathered the bridle and whispered in the horse's ear. Then he led Bo Jack forward to the ramp.

"You have to be nice," Meeker said. "A horse isn't a human being."

Bo Jack went up easily.

Jock Martin was ready. He had his pack on and his heavy mittens and his yellow goggles snapped around a wool hat with reindeer on it. Shanks took Lorraine's pack out of the back of the Subaru and held it for her while she slipped her arms through the straps. Granny Watson and John Meeker had rucksacks without frames. Granny wore an army fatigue jacket and army boots, tinted wire-rimmed glasses, and a blue scarf across his forehead to keep his long hair back. Meeker had on his winter police uniform and the fur hat with the badge in front.

Bud's pack was a monster which he balanced on the hood of the Bronco. "It's the beer," he said, "and too many cans of pork and beans."

"How're you going to climb in cowboy boots?" Ed asked him.

"I'll make it," Bud said. "Don't worry. We'll find her."

Granny was the first out across the road toward the trailhead. Jock Martin was right behind him, then a rancher who'd volunteered at the last minute. Lorraine looped the leather thongs of her ski poles around her wrists and followed.

"You find her," Vicky called. "I'll be praying."

"Wait for me," Bud said.

They climbed in single file through the snow—Granny in his army jacket, Jock Martin with the reindeer hat, the rancher in jeans and red parka. Lorraine waved from the first rise and then climbed up the snow-filled gully and into the trees.

18

Vicky maneuvered the Bronco and horse trailer ten miles an hour down the pass, and Shanks kept his distance in the Subaru. He wasn't going to take any chances with Vicky. During the controversy over the sign ordinance she and Bud had written one of the letters to the *Chronicle* about him, calling him "a troublemaker of the Communist sort," and he had stayed clear of them ever since. Bud had loosened up a little, especially when he got out of the house and into a bar, which was where Neil saw him most often, but Vicky hadn't mellowed much. In the bars the men called her the Geiger Counter. No matter what time of day or night it was, she knew exactly where Bud was hiding. Her talent was so uncanny it was as though Bud had a piece of metal in him. Once when he'd skipped an Elks meeting, she'd appeared in her nightgown at the door of the Gold-digger yelling, "Come on, fuckstick, take me home!" And another time he was supposed to be playing poker at Harry Matuszek's trailer, but she caught him in the lobby of the Mother Lode Hotel with a secretary from Teaneck, New Jersey. That time she'd brought an aluminum baseball bat and had smashed the chandelier in the lobby. The night clerk, at whom she'd screamed obscenities, wondered every

time he told the story why she hadn't bothered to bash
Bud's head in and end his misery.

Anyway, Shanks wasn't going to press his luck with
Vicky. He stayed well back on the snowy road, and when
she turned off Main and past the huge flashing neon sign for
the Panorama Motel, he kept a reasonable three car lengths
behind.

He assumed she was stopping to see about the children,
and Shanks idled the Subaru while she went in. He was
surprised when she brought out Jason and Christopher and
ordered Shanks to leave his car and get into the Bronco too.

"My mother's a wreck," she said. "You might as well
save the gas and ride with us."

Shanks got into the backseat, and the two children rode
in front. Vicky drove like a semi-truck driver, both hands
high on the wheel, chewing gum a mile a minute, as if the
road were an enemy. Jason jumped around the seat, pester-
ing Christopher, and now and then Vicky reached across
and slapped Jason. "You be still," she said. "We'll have a
wreck." Once she grabbed his arm, and the Bronco veered
suddenly. "Goddamn it, Jason, I said *behave*. You want us
to crack up? Is that what you want? You want to hurt Bo
Jack back there?"

When the road left the upper canyon, it curled east away
from the river. The immense white V of the lower valley
opened toward the low hills and mesas in the distance,
which they could see through the ebbing snow. There were
only flurries in the lower valley, and the blanket of clouds
was lifting gradually through the scrub oak and juniper. A
brighter light shone out of the west. For a moment the
feathery line of cottonwoods along the river caught a wedge
of sun.

Finn and Becky's trailer was in the Paradise Mobile
Home Park eight miles out. The main highway had been
plowed, but not the trailer park, and the turn-in was a leap
of faith which Vicky took without hesitation. "Got to keep
momentum," she said through her gum.

She accelerated and slid around a car someone had abandoned on the edge of the road. At the second driveway she made a fast right and coasted down a short hill toward a huge turquoise satellite dish.

"This is Bo Jack's house," she said. "End of the line. We have to feed Bo Jack and give him lots of water."

They all got out. The two children ran off toward the corral, while Shanks went around to the back of the horse trailer and pulled open the metal gate. The ramp was heavy, but slid on a wheel.

"I'll get the horse," Vicky said. "You unhitch the trailer. Becky keeps the trailer tongue on a cinder block. And brace the wheels while you're at it."

Vicky climbed the ramp in her suede boots and sweet-talked Bo Jack down the incline. "Chris, open the gate there, will you?"

She led the horse through the gate and into the corral, where she unhooked the bridle.

"There any oats, Jason? Go look."

"There ain't no oats," Jason said. He was already in the shed. "There's hay."

"Bring some hay, then."

"It's in bales."

"Well, bring a bale."

"I can't *lift* a bale."

Shanks had swung the neck of the trailer hitch onto the cinder block. There was no reason to brace the wheels on level ground and in deep snow, but he fetched two logs from the woodpile and tossed them under the back wheels. "You want me to bring a bale?" he called over.

"We're taking care of the horse," Vicky said. "Chris, what about water? Is there water?"

Christopher tried the spigot near the shed. "It's frozen," he said.

"He's got snow, Momma," Jason said.

"Snow's cold," Vicky said. "We'll get water from the house."

Shanks had already climbed part of the way up the steps

to the house, sweeping the snow off as he went. Meeker's tracks, dusted with new snow, led up to the door.

Shanks had never seen where Becky lived. He knew where the trailer was, but he'd imagined it as a double-wide, a spacious place with big windows and a view out over the valley. But it was an old silver Airstream that resembled a salvaged airplane. The windows were small and looked out on one side into the snowy hillside. On the other, she could at least see the river.

He shaded his eyes and looked in through one of the windows. Against one wall was a big-screen TV and in front of it, two chairs, one of them a La-Z-Boy recliner. Above the TV was a poster of a silver Coors can.

Christopher startled him, coming up behind. "We're getting some water," he said. "And I have to go to the bathroom."

"I think it's locked," Shanks said.

"Aunt Vicky knows how to break in."

Vicky treaded gingerly up the steps, wielding an emery board. Shanks made way, and in twenty seconds she had the door unlocked.

It seemed colder inside the trailer than out, though perhaps, Shanks thought, it was the smell of grease and cigarette smoke or the grimness of the room that gave him that impression. There was a sofa he hadn't seen through the window and another poster above it: a bull elk with the cross hairs of a scope superimposed on the animal's shoulder. A rifle was lying on the sofa, along with a couple of blaze-orange vests, a box of shells, and a note.

Vicky went into the kitchen where Jason had the water blasting from the spigot. "If you spray me, Mr. Smart-ass, I'll break your knuckles. Turn on the hot. We'll give Bo Jack a treat."

Shanks went over and read the scrawled note.

Hank—
There's a stash in the sugarbowl.
If you want to use my Dad's 30.06,

bring it, and don't shoot yourself.

See you Monday.

Finn

P.S. Becky is pissed.

"Who's Hank?" Shanks asked. "Do you know Hank?"

"I can't hear with the water on," Vicky said. She turned it off. "What?"

Shanks held up the note. "It's a note from Finn to Hank."

"Bring it here."

Shanks brought the note over, and Vicky turned the water back on and finished filling the pot for Jason to carry out. "Don't spill it," she said. "Where's Chris? I have a pot for him too."

"In the bathroom."

She let the water run into a big canning pot and read the note. "Hank Tobuk," she said. "He's a creep."

Christopher came down the hall, and Shanks went past him into the bathroom. He closed the door and dropped the toilet seat loudly. Then he opened the medicine cabinet. He didn't know what he expected to find. Just evidence. Just something more to worry about. But there wasn't much: Alka-Seltzer, aspirin, Kaopectate, Sleep-Eze, shaving soap, plastic razors, a mangled tube of toothpaste.

Under the sink were cleansers, a couple of extra bars of Ivory soap, a yellow plastic pail to catch the leak from the gooseneck. There was nothing he might not have had in his own bathroom.

He waited for Vicky to fill the canning pot and go back outside. When the water stopped, he listened.

"Come on, Neil," she said.

"You go ahead. I'll be a minute."

He thought she might wait for him, but Jason came back up the steps and in the door. "I spilled mine," he said.

"Goddamn it, Jason." She smacked him. "You know where the water is. I'll be outside."

Shanks flushed the toilet and opened the bathroom door

and turned right down the hallway to the bedroom. It was a cramped space, pastel green, with a double bed in it and two dressers. A yellow wool blanket and the bedspread had slipped off onto the floor, and Shanks pulled them up to make room to walk.

On Finn's side were *Penthouse*s and *Field and Stream*s. He had to climb over the bed to get to Becky's side where her dresser was. He was surprised how neatly she kept things. Unmatched socks were stacked on one corner and unpaid bills on the other. He looked through them quickly —$172 owed to the dentist, overdue rent on the trailer space, an electric bill from San Miguel Power. A small ceramic dish held some loose change, bobbie pins, and a small locket. Her few bottles of lotions and scents were arranged in the center, next to a photograph stuck in the mirror.

The photograph was a yellowing black-and-white of Wendell and Martha standing beside a vintage Allis-Chalmers tractor. Lorraine and Becky were up on the tractor seat looking into the camera, but Toby was squinting into the sun. He guessed Becky was about nine, which made Lorraine twelve and Toby seven. The picture reminded him of the old tintypes of Thomas Shanks's family, the way everyone looked so posed and proper.

He wasn't looking for anything in particular—Becky's watch, maybe, or the books of his Becky still had. The magazines scattered on her side of the bed on the floor were mostly *People, Family Circle,* and *4-H News.* There weren't any books.

The alarm clock by the bed read two-eleven. Where was Becky at that very moment? It was strange to imagine her. He could envision her face clearly enough—the freckles, the wide-open blue eyes, the way her hair puffed out under the orange hunting cap. But he couldn't see where she was. She had described Bear Creek to him a dozen times in various ways—the meadows and the mountain peaks, the grass and the dark spruce, the glades of aspen with their tattering leaves—but the place was only what her voice had made it. He could imagine her face, which he had seen before, but not the world of wind and moving leaves or the sounds she might hear.

How different words were from the pictures he conjured in his mind of the things he had seen! Becky had given him the barest images. A voice only, not even a photograph. Not a letter, like Thomas Shanks had written, which he could refer to again and again. Not a book to read over with words that sounded true.

There weren't many clothes on the rack in the closet. There was a Western shirt with mother-of-pearl buttons which he knew she liked, and blouses, and one blue dress. He pulled the dress from its hanger. It was a short-sleeved shift with scalloped white lace around the collar, and he held it up to the dim light at the window. The stitching looked hand done. Had Becky danced in it? He swirled the dress out onto the bed and imagined Becky in it moving across the dance floor, half smiling at the man who held her. Her expression was happy, as if she were dreaming of the music far away.

He had hung up the dress again when he heard Vicky coming down the hall.

"What are you snooping for?" Vicky said. She stood in the doorway chewing her gum.

"Just waiting for you."

"This is waiting? Going through people's things?"

"It's using time well," Shanks said. "What did you think about the note?"

"Nothing."

"She told me before she was angry about Hank. Do you think that's all?"

Vicky stared back. "If I knew," she said, "I wouldn't tell you."

One of the boys in the other room turned on the television set, and the crowd noise of a football game sifted down the hallway.

"Let's get out of here," Vicky said.

"Hold on a second. Please."

"I don't want to hold on a second."

"I guess Becky told you about me. Is that it?"

"Is what what?"

Shanks nodded. "It doesn't matter what you think of me. So I wrote something about your goddamn sign. . . ."

"The sign! You think I give a shit about the *sign*?"

"So she told you something."

"No."

"No or maybe?"

"Finn is a creep," Vicky said. "You're a creep."

Vicky turned away, but Shanks leapt across the bed and grabbed hold of her arm. "Finn and Becky were arguing when they left town Friday afternoon. Now, listen. If you know something else, you've got to say."

Vicky pulled away. "I don't have to say anything."

"Don't tell me," Shanks said. "Tell Ed. If you know something that would help Becky, tell Ed."

Vicky stared at him for a moment, and then she started crying without sound, the tears running down through the powder on her cheeks. "Poor Becky," she said. "Jesus God, I'm so worried."

19

The sheriff had not been able to reach Hugh Menotti at the Colorado Search and Rescue that afternoon. He assumed Menotti would get back to him. In the meantime Sharon was still calling around for volunteers who might be able to come in the following morning.

The new message service had also been busy. Relatives all over the country were inquiring about men and women out in the storm. There were two calls from wives who had delivered babies while their husbands were hunting, and another three from people reporting emergencies at home—an aunt who had died, a fire, an auto accident with injuries. Ed relayed the names of the hunters involved to the radio and TV stations for broadcast.

There were several local calls, too, about Meeker's blowing up the hot springs, but after the second one, Ed instructed Sharon not to put these calls through. "I don't want to talk to anyone about that," he said. *"Tu comprendes?"*

"Speak in English, Ed."

"Tell them we have an emergency on our hands," Ed said. "I don't want to be bothered, period."

"You're in a fine mood," Sharon said. "What'd I do?"

"Nothing. I'm not in a fine mood. I want to talk to Menotti." He paused a moment. "Maybe you can make up a list of people you haven't reached so I can send Neil after them in person."

"Whatever you say," Sharon said in her sweet voice.

He hated it when she said that. *Whatever you say.* He didn't like it because first, he was always messing something up and trying to cover his ass, and second, he didn't like it, second, because it sounded as if he wasn't right about anything. Sharon had a way of making it sound both ways.

But Sharon didn't move. "You don't trust Aurey?" she asked.

"Of course I trust Aurey. I think he'll find her. But what if he doesn't? It's a blizzard up there. We don't know what'll happen."

"And you don't want to call Wendell?"

"No. I agree with Lorraine on that. No sense getting them all stung by bees."

He was looking into the whirring gray ceiling fan and the pipes which ran all over the ceiling. The metal ducts cracked and ticked as they expanded and contracted, and he closed his eyes for a moment, feeling the sweat ooze from his pores. Wendell was a friend of his, and he didn't want to betray a friendship. On the other hand, what could Wendell do? He tried to think whether he'd want to know something like that himself. Would he want to know something he couldn't do anything about, like if Louise were in surgery, say, or Jerry were missing in action somewhere in a war? It was the modern condition to know too much. In the old days, before radio and TV and daily newspapers and jet flights and satellite communications, you came by your information much later in more or less final form. Someone was either dead or alive. You didn't know all the variations in between, the gray areas. Everything had happened at least last week, if not last month or last year.

"You don't think she ran away again, do you?" Sharon asked.

Ed shook his head. "It isn't exactly the kind of weather to run away in."

"She did it before."

"That was six years ago," Ed said, "and she had some cause, too, as I remember it. Martha wanted to lock those girls in a vault."

"Where was it you got her?"

"Green River. Kidnapped, Martha said. Kidnapped, my ass, and I made a joke of it. I said I'd kidnap her myself. Remember that? 'You sure she's not out on a date?' I asked Martha. She wanted me to put out an all-points."

"It's hard to blame Martha," Sharon said.

Ed agreed with that. He'd have been like Martha, too, if Jerry had been the one who'd drowned instead of Toby. He didn't know what he would have done. But Martha had made the girls pay. They were always carrying around some special charm or a piece of colored cloth Martha thought was lucky or wearing a bracelet that would save them from harm.

He smiled grimly at Sharon. "I don't think she's run away this time," he said. "I think she's up there in a lot of snow, and I hope to hell Aurey can find her. You better keep trying Menotti."

"Whatever you say."

Sharon went back out to the switchboard, and Ed spat out tobacco juice into his jar. He swiveled his chair around toward the window, where there was now a brighter sky. Whitehouse was covered with clouds still, but the snow had ebbed some and the sky was higher. That was a good sign. Becky might come down in better weather. On the other hand, if she was hurt and cold, the clouds were an advantage. Clouds kept in the earth's own heat.

He didn't blame Martha, though. And he certainly wasn't going to tell her about Becky.

Who knew what Becky would do? She could be stubborn as a cold car in January. There was no doubt about that. But she was tough too. She backed up being stubborn by being tough. He still remembered the calf-roping event—the same one she'd almost missed by running away to Utah. He and Wendell had been in the bleachers when Becky had taken a spectacular spill headfirst over her horse's neck. The horse had stopped on a franc, and Becky had hurtled forward in a half somersault. The medics had carried her off, but ten minutes later she was back in the barrel race. Afterward they found out she'd broken her wrist and had cracked some ribs. "It hurt," Becky said, "but you don't need ribs to ride a barrel race."

She'd been stubborn about Finn too. Wendell still claimed she'd never have married Finn if he and Martha had been for it instead of against it. She'd been eighteen when she'd met him. It was the summer after she graduated from high school because Ed still remembered how Wendell wanted her to go to college. She'd been accepted at the University of Colorado, but she'd wanted to go to Mesa in Grand Junction to be able to help out at the ranch. Then Finn had arrived. He'd been driving a Jeep for Will Hawthorne's summer tours.

Wendell had thought Finn was a college boy, which was a mistake that was easy enough to make. Most of the summer help—the motel maids and shopkeepers and waiters and waitresses—were hired from colleges because they were polite and cheerful and good with tourists. Every noon the Jeep drivers sat out on the curb at the livery barn waiting for their afternoon groups to assemble, drinking Cokes and maybe smoking dope, for all he knew. And the maids and waitresses would walk by or drive by, depending on where they worked in town and how much time they had. That was the ritual.

Becky hadn't worked in town, but Wendell sometimes sent her in to the post office to pick up skins for his taxidermy business. She and Vicky cruised Main Street, which was how she'd met Finn.

Which was too bad because no one trusted Finn. One time Finn had broken the window of a parked car for no reason except he was mad, and he'd done it right in front of

Ed. That was about par for Finn, and it made Ed furious whenever he thought of it.

A shadow broke across the cellar window, and Ed looked up quickly enough to see Neil Shanks pass in front of the sky. He was back from taking Bo Jack to Becky's, and Ed wanted him to round up some volunteers for the search and to sound out a few motel owners about rooms for the Colorado Search and Rescue team if they had to be called in.

There was a lot to think about, but at least Shanks was competent. He'd be some help, and Ed liked him. A lot of people in the world gave up at whatever they did, but Neil wasn't one of them. He didn't want more of everything, like most people. But he was a hard one to figure. That's what Ed thought. Two years ago, when Pop Krause had first brought Neil in, Ed had considered Neil a transient, though not the garden variety you saw most often in a tourist town. He wasn't a hustler or a vagrant or an adventurer on skis. He spoke too well, and he wrote some fine articles for the *Chipeta Daily Pilot,* and after a night playing pinochle, they'd become pretty good friends. Neil had had the sense to take his advice about going into business for himself, though for the life of him, Ed couldn't understand why he'd sold the fast-food place, which he could have unloaded anytime, and had got himself mixed up in a trinket shop. It all had something to do with that relative Neil didn't want to find. That's how Ed saw it anyway. For a man who claimed he wanted to know something about somebody, Neil spent a lot of time avoiding the subject. But Neil kept himself out of trouble and paid his taxes, and managed a business that kept him clothed and fed. That was all any man needed.

The door opened at the head of the stairs, and Neil came into the dispatcher's office. "Come on in," Ed called. "I was just thinking of you, Neil. Get in here. We have work to do."

Shanks took off his coat in the warm room and came over to Ed's desk.

"What's the weather?" Ed asked.

"Clearing. There was sun down the valley, and it looks better in town too. They say it'll clear off tonight."

"They said it wasn't supposed to snow either," Ed said. "If it clears, it'll be colder."

"I guess." Shanks said.

"You get the horse put up?"

"Vicky did."

There was a strained moment, when neither of them said anything. Ed stood up, rolling his desk chair backward, and tucked in his shirt. His glance fell over the map on the wall, the Red Cloud Peak quadrant with the pencil marks on it, and then he turned to look at Shanks. "I've got a call in to Hugh Menotti at the Colorado Search and Rescue," he said, pressing his thumb, enumerating. "I've got Sharon making calls for volunteers. I've got the best man in the county up in the mountains right now. Why is it that something's not right?"

"We haven't found her. That's what's not right."

Ed shook his head and dropped his hands to his belt.

"You're doing everything you can," Shanks said.

"I know. That's what I'm saying. I *think* I'm doing everything I can, but something still doesn't make sense. You know what I mean? Something . . ." He pinched a little tobacco from the can on his desk and slipped the wad into his cheek.

It was a feeling, that was all. Nothing substantial. But it didn't sound right that Becky was lost. He'd known her too long, maybe. Or maybe he didn't want to think of the worst. "You know Becky some, don't you, Neil?"

"A little."

"Maybe it's Finn," Ed said. "Maybe I don't trust Finn."

"You think Finn's not telling the truth?"

"I don't know. Why wouldn't he?"

Shanks backed away from the desk. He didn't have an answer. "You know Finn and Becky," he said. "You know them better than I do. They fought. Everybody knows that. They were arguing before they went up the mountain too, after Pork gave Finn a ticket. Finn blamed Becky for taking too much time in Matheson's. She was mad because she was shopping for things Finn was supposed to have got last week."

"How do you know that?"

"She told me. I saw her in the store. She was buying freeze-dried dinners. And she was mad that Finn had invited Hank Tobuk up to hunt. She didn't want Weedy and Hank and Finn to get drunk up there."

"Sounds about like what they'd do. I locked Hank up once for being drunk and disorderly."

"We found a note," Shanks said. "Vicky and I. I guess Hank is stopping off at Finn's to pick up a gun or maybe spend Sunday night. It didn't say much, but the PS was that Becky was pissed."

"About what?"

"It didn't say about what. That Hank was coming up, I guess."

"What else do you know about this hunting trip, Neil?"

Shanks shook his head. "Not much." He came over to the map and located the trail and the Bear Creek Gorge and the place where he thought the camp was. "I know Becky went up there Wednesday to take hay for the horses," he said. "That's about all. I know Weedy and Finn have a bet on who gets the first elk."

Ed thought about that. "Alone? She go up on Wednesday alone?"

"I guess alone. Yes. Finn didn't go."

Sharon buzzed from the dispatcher's switchboard. "I've got Brannon on one," she said.

"Okay." Ed picked up the receiver, pressed one, and sat back down in his chair.

"Ed, how're you coming in all this snow?"

"Well, all right. We got that girl lost up in Bear Creek. You might keep an eye out for her on your side. What about you?"

"Real good. I swear the snow keeps the lid on 'em. They can't get back into town to raise hell. Who's the girl?"

Name's Becky Carlsson. She's about five four and weighs

maybe one twenty. Blond. She was hunting this side of the
Flats, but you never know. I've called Menotti, and we'll
make a sweep tomorrow if our people don't turn something
up by tonight. We think she's probably up in a mine somewhere. It's Wendell Blythe's kid."

"We'll keep a lookout over here."

"I'll be in touch," Ed said, and he hung up the phone.

Shanks had been studying the map, trying to make sense
out of how Becky might make it to Lakeland County. From
the looks of it, Lakeland as twenty-five or twenty-six miles
cross-country. That wasn't possible, though he'd have been
glad to have her found in Lake City or anywhere else.

"What about other hunting camps?" Shanks asked.
"Could she have wandered into someone else's camp up
there?"

"Could have," Ed said, "but the only camps I know of
are in Cutler Creek on the other side of the Divide and then
on the back side of Brown Mountain, where you can get in
with a four-wheel-drive."

"Then she might have."

"It'd take some doing to get over the mountains in either
direction," Ed said. "I don't think we're talking about that.
What we need to think about are the possibilities. And we
don't want to think about them too soon."

Shanks nodded, drifted, lapsed into silence. "I know a
possibility," he said. "I don't know whether it's too soon to
think about."

"Like what?"

Shanks pulled up a chair by the sheriff's desk and sat
down. "I don't know if it's anything," he said. "It may not
mean anything at all. I don't want you to have the wrong
idea."

"So far I haven't got *any* idea."

"There ought to be a way to explain this so it sounds
right."

Ed nodded and let Shanks take his time. He pushed his
swivel chair around toward the window where the sun was
trying to make an appearance among the riffled clouds.

"We didn't do anything," Shanks said. "That's the start of it. We didn't do anything."

"All right. Who?"

"Becky and I. She used to borrow books. That's all. Most of the time she came to the store, but sometimes she came to my room in the Tin Pan Alley. We talked. I don't want you to think—"

Ed whistled, but made no sound. "You and Becky. Jesus H. Christ. Is that what you're saying?"

Shanks leaned forward. "I never touched her," he said.

Ed put his head into his hands and then looked up again. "So why are you telling me this, Neil?"

"We were talking about possibilities," Shanks said.

"Did Finn know?"

"Becky didn't want to tell Finn. She even hid the books I lent her so he wouldn't find them and ask questions. It didn't matter that nothing was going on. Finn would be furious."

"I can see that," Ed said. "Finn wouldn't like it. Did anyone else know?"

"Lorraine. Maybe Vicky Saunders."

"Vicky wouldn't have told Finn anything, would she?"

Shanks shook his head. "Vicky isn't a great fan of Finn's. But Becky . . ."

The telephone buzzed again, and Ed pressed the lever. "If it's Brannon I don't want to talk to him."

"It's Wendell," Sharon said. "He knows."

"How come?" Then Ed knew right away. "Oh, *Jesus.*"

"Will you talk to him?"

Ed took a deep breath. "I'll talk to him."

He picked up the receiver but kept a hand over it. "Can you go out there, Neil? If I need you . . . wait."

"Ed? Is that you? If you think . . ." Wendell's voice scratched over the wire.

"Wendell? I hear you."

"I'm coming in, Ed. The McCradys are out here now and they have some tale about Becky being lost up there in Bear Creek."

That was all he needed. He rolled his eyes at Neil and listened to Wendell spin out a string of epithets about the McCradys and being kept in the dark and how he was going to pack up his gear and come into town.

Ed motioned for Shanks to get going. "Head him off," Ed whispered. "I don't want Wendell in here. Stop him."

To Wendell he said, "Yes, right, Wendell, but we're doing everything we can think of. We've sent out a search team with Aurey Vallejos. Lorraine went up too. We didn't call you because there was no sense getting Martha wrought up. You know what I mean? I'm sure Aurey'll find her, and we'll have some word down here by this evening."

Shanks was out the door, and Ed turned his attention up to the window, which showed patches of high gray clouds and misty white-blue sky. Shanks appeared again across the window, running, and passed the other window in front of the fire station.

Wendell was still yelling into the phone, and Ed had no defense except to listen as long as he could and to make Wendell stay on the line.

20

Instead of heading north out of town toward Pinnacle Ridge, Shanks swung around past his shop. It was clear that Ed didn't need Wendell Blythe going up the mountain after Becky. He didn't need him in town either, and Shanks had an idea that he hoped would keep Wendell at bay. He made a phone call to Vicky.

It wasn't dark yet, only three-thirty, but the lights of the houses were already on, glimmering through the snow. The sun, which had glanced briefly through the clouds a half hour earlier, had gone down now behind Whitehouse Peak, leaving the town colder, starker. Whitehouse looked to Shanks all the more forbidding now with the new snow on it and the sun behind. The granite headwall was laced with gray-white, and the summit might as well have been K-2 or Everest. No one could scale such a mountain, though he knew many climbers had done it, and Aurey Vallejos had accomplished the feat alone in winter.

The town looked immaculate. The littered vacant lots and construction slash heaps were buried under a foot of new snow, and the roofs of the houses shone like white glass in the air. The cliffs above the river were darker, too, maroon outlined in white, and the black spruce lifted in waves up to the bald white head of Mr. Mears.

He followed a snowplow for a couple of blocks up Main, then cut down impatiently to the River Road. He turned left at the end of the street and raced up to Prosperity.

Vicky was waiting for him with the motel office door open. She had wet hair up in curlers and didn't seem to mind the least bit standing in the cold in her pink bathrobe. Shanks rolled down the window of the Subaru.

"He's ready to go," she said. "Listen, I'm sorry about this afternoon."

"It's all right."

"You're not a creep. This whole thing has me crawling the walls."

"We're all on edge," Shanks said.

"Christopher! Come *on*!"

Christopher appeared from behind the office counter with his satchel.

"You got everything, honey?" Vicky asked. "You get those Oreos?"

"Everything except my truck," Christopher said. "Jason took my truck."

"I'll get it back for you next time," Vicky said. She put her arm around Christopher's shoulder and turned back to Shanks. "Becky did tell me something," she said. "That's what has me so worried. She made me promise not to tell anybody. I mean *no*body. Not even Bud. She was ice water on that."

"Promise not to tell what?" Christopher asked.

"Never you mind, Mr. Noseypants. You go around and get in the car. Run. It's cold standing here."

Christopher stayed put. "I don't see why you can't tell me."

Vicky pointed, and Christopher walked around the back of the Subaru, where exhaust was billowing in the cold air.

"The thing is," Vicky said, "what if she's all right? If I said something to Ed, she'd kill me. For all we know they've found her already. If they don't find her . . . God, I don't know what then. It's awful. All of it is so awful. You men. You're all fucking goddamn hunters."

"Ed wouldn't tell anyone."

"God, Neil, what if they don't find her?"

"They'll find her."

"See? They'll find her, so I can't tell anybody. When are they coming back?

"Someone is coming down tonight," Shanks said.

"You go ahead and see Wendell now. Go on. Give him a kiss for me. The dear man." She pulled her pink robe tighter around her throat. "You men, though. It's your fault these things happen. Becky wouldn't be up there if Finn took care of her. Go on, now. Hurry. Bye, Chris!" Vicky waved and touched her hair, which was frozen solid on her head.

The highway out of town was still slick, and now that it was colder, Shanks drove more cautiously. Snow was banked up under the telephone wires at the edge of the road, and beyond the near hills the arc lights of ranches burned through the dusky air. The white hills and mesas in the distance looked like dreamlike islands in a white sea.

"Have you ever seen this much snow?" Christopher asked. He looked out the side window and then out the windshield.

"Yes. I used to live in Michigan."

"Is that in Alaska?"

"That's in the Midwest. The heartland of the country. Farms and forests, Big Ten football, the automobile industry. Lake Michigan is one of the Great Lakes."

"I've never seen this much snow."

"It snowed more than this last winter," Shanks said. "Where were you?"

"In Boulder. Why does Aunt Vicky always wear pink clothes?"

"I don't know. Why don't you ask her sometime?"

"I wouldn't want her to hit me."

"She wouldn't hit you."

"She hits Jason."

"But she wouldn't hit you."

Shanks slowed and held the Subaru through the last banked turn of the canyon, and then he eased off the gas on the straightaway. They passed the Paradise Mobile Home Park, where Becky and Finn lived, and Christopher followed the trailers out the back window of the Subaru.

"What do you think she's doing?" he asked.

"Who?"

"Aunt Becky."

"What do *you* think?"

"I think she's walking around. That's what I'd do if I were cold. I bet she's walking across a huge field of snow that is bigger than you can see across."

"That sounds nice," Shanks said.

"She can see just snow and the sky."

Shanks nodded. Out ahead of them the first stars were sifting from the evening sky over White Mesa in the distance. He slowed and turned right onto Pinnacle Ridge Road. "Do you know where we are?" Shanks asked.

"We're on the road to my Gammie's."

"Why doesn't your mother like to take you out here?"

"She says Gammie and Papa are sad. We go for birthdays sometimes."

"And are they sad then?"

Christopher shrugged.

"Where is your father now?" Shanks asked. "You said he liked motorcycles."

"He's in California or Nevada."

"Do you see him?"

"Not really. Once in a while he sends me a poster or a badge he won. He sent me a little motorcycle once that wasn't plastic." He looked at Shanks. "Where is your father?"

"He's dead."

"Your grandfather too?"

"Yes."

"I think my father makes a lot of money," Christopher

said. "He works in a mine somewhere. I think it's Nevada, but I'm not sure."

Headlights appeared ahead of them on the crest of a rise and shimmered through the gray air. She slowed and pulled over, and in a minute the McCradys' green Chevrolet lipped the hill. It plunged into the swale, gained speed, and accelerated up the hill. Jerilyn was driving, and she stared straight ahead when she passed.

Shanks gave them the finger.

"Sorry," he said to Christopher. Then he downshifted to first and started up the hill.

Wendell was untangling his climbing ropes when Shanks and Christopher came through the back door. Bert Parks barked once but did not get up from his bed in the corner. "Oh, it's you," Wendell said to Christopher. "What are you doing here?"

"What's this stuff for, Papa?" Christopher asked.

"I'm going up to look for Becky." Wendell looked out over the sea of army gear which littered the floor from the sink to the kitchen table.

Christopher picked up a ring of metal spikes. "What are these?"

"Those are pitons."

"Were you in the army?"

"You bet I was in the army. On the American side too. Camp Hale Ski Troop, 1945 to 1947. We were ready, but they never called us." He lifted a dusty ski and showed it to Christopher. "This is the old binding we used to use. It's a bear trap. You get your foot in that, and the ski won't ever come loose."

"Didn't you break your leg?"

"You're supposed to ski, not break your leg." He pushed back a swath of gray hair from his forehead. "See that scar? That's where I got a ski pole once. Thirty stitches in my head, but I never broke my leg." He looked over at Shanks and shook hands. "Hello. Did the sheriff send you?"

"Lorraine went up with the search team," Shanks said. "I thought you'd like some company."

"Martha would," Wendell said. "I'm going up."

"What are these?" Christopher asked. He held up what looked like pitons welded together.

"Those are crampons. You wear them on the bottoms of your boots when you're walking on ice."

"They're heavy."

"You have to have strong legs," Wendell said.

Footsteps echoed through the house, and they all looked toward the door. "Whose voice is that?" Martha said. "Is that who I think it is? Is that you, Toby?"

"It's me," Christopher said.

Martha appeared in the doorway and paused for a moment as if she were not certain who was there.

Shanks had never seen her before. He had expected a big-boned woman, stocky like Becky, with gray hair. Old. But she wasn't like that at all. She was slight and tall and her face showed barely a crow's-foot at the corners of her eyes. Her hair was reddish brown, streaked with only a bit of gray.

"My goodness, it *is*!" she said. She got down on her knees and held out her arms.

Christopher looked at Wendell, who nodded at him. Then he went forward and gave Martha a long hug. Martha rocked him back and forth with her eyes closed.

"Why don't you two play some games or trade stories?" Wendell said. "Let me get packed in here."

Martha opened her eyes and pulled away from Christopher. "All right," she said. "Why don't you come into the other room with me? I haven't seen you in a long time. You can tell me some stories."

"I can tell you about Michigan," Christopher said. "And how Jason stole my truck."

Martha stood up and took Christopher's hand, and they went into the other room.

Shanks drifted through the kitchen, not sure he had done

the right thing bringing Christopher out there. "Is she all right?"

"She's fine," Wendell said. "Take off your coat and stay a minute. You know Lorraine doesn't bring Christopher out here much."

Shanks nodded.

"Sometimes I think Martha starves for him. But I never could tell either one of those girls anything. They do what they want to. And that's a fact."

Shanks looked over the equipment Wendell had assembled—the bear trap skis, the pitons that went out of style thirty years before, the iron mess kit. Wendell had cans of hash and Campbell's soup on the counter, along with a bottle of Jim Beam. "You going to carry all this?" Shanks asked.

"In the ski troop we used to go out a week at a time," Wendell said. "Fraser, Colorado. It was the coldest post in the United States. They closed it down, finally, a few years ago."

"Cold, huh?"

"Some nights it was fifty below."

"It won't be that bad tonight," Shanks said. "Not even up the mountain."

"Let's not talk about that," Wendell said. "Has anyone questioned Finn?"

"Ed had Finn in his office right after he came down. I was there. They pretty much went over everything."

Wendell worked the cables on the bindings back and forth, oiled them, made sure they were loose. He levered the release two or three times, then tugged at the leather strap, which broke off in his hand. "Well, fuck a duck."

"You need new skis," Shanks said. He walked over to the door and listened to Christopher in the other room telling Martha how in Michigan it snowed all the time because it was in a great lake.

"Why aren't you up there?" Wendell asked. "Don't you want to find her?"

"I'm not a mountain man," Shanks said. "I'd have been a liability."

"What kind of liability? You just hike around and keep your eyes open."

Shanks came away from the door. "It's been a long day," he said. "You mind if I have a sip of Jim Beam?"

"Help yourself."

Shanks found a glass in the cupboard. "You? I'm going to put some snow in mine."

"A pinch," Wendell said. "Snow's fine."

Shanks took the two glasses outside. It had got colder, he thought. The clouds had cleared from over Pinnacle Ridge, and the granite spires shone black against the pale sky. Water was dripping from the eaves of the house, especially over the low warm roof of the kitchen. Shanks walked out a short distance and scooped fresh snow into the glasses.

He stood for a moment longer in the cool air. Becky was up there somewhere. He preferred to think of her the way Christopher did, walking across a field of snow she couldn't see across, and maybe it was true. He had to believe it was. What he had wanted to tell Ed back in the office was only an idea he had, not something that had happened. What Becky had said had been only a part of their conversation. But there was no hurry to say anything now.

He turned around and watched Wendell inside the kitchen, still fiddling with the bindings of his skis. Water dropped off quickly from the low roof.

Shanks went back inside and poured the bourbon. "Water?" Shanks asked. He held up the bourbon and snow.

"Snow will melt fast enough," Wendell said. "Thanks."

He took the glass and sipped it, then looked at Shanks. "Here's to Becky." And he drank again.

Shanks sat at the table. "It's cleared off," he said. "Visibility will be good. You going to go up by yourself?"

"I guess I will." He paused and looked at Shanks. "The thing about it is, she knows the mountains."

"That's what Finn says."

"And she's a damn good hunter too. We used to go up

Winchester Gulch, which is as rugged a country as you'll ever see. She knew what she was doing."

In the other room Martha laughed at something, a high titter that made the air tingle. Wendell went over to the door and looked.

"They're playing Parcheesi," he said.

"What's Parcheesi?" Shanks asked.

"It's a dice game. I haven't seen Martha play Parcheesi since Toby died."

Shanks got up and looked and, on his way back to the table, got the bottle of Jim Beam from the counter. He held the bottle, ready to pour, out to Wendell. Wendell stuck his glass under.

Shanks poured the glass full, and splashed a little more in his own.

It was hard to figure out what made Wendell think he could do that night what he hadn't done for forty years. Shanks studied Wendell's face, which seemed resolute and confident. How could he believe these skis on which the leather thongs were rotten could do the same as they had done in 1947? Or that his legs could take the strain? Shanks thought of himself as having the same weakness, thinking the past could determine the future. Why else was he so concerned about Thomas Shanks? But perhaps there was no correlation, nothing to point to with smug confidence and say, "There!" as if something important had been revealed.

He drank and felt the whiskey take hold in his throat. When the burn eased, he drank again.

Outside the window Pinnacle Ridge had dissipated into the dark sky. The pasture was gray, barely perceptible now beyond the pale golden light the kitchen threw onto the snow in the yard. Icicles were forming at the edge of the roof, gathering in slow accretion, one drop at a time, the way the alcohol was absorbing into his blood.

Wendell swallowed loudly half his glass of bourbon, then knelt down beside his pack and set his glass on the floor. He stuffed some wool knickers into the back pocket of his pack, then looked up at Shanks.

"If we still had Toby, we'd be all right," he said softly. "It was an accident." He stared at the floor.

"What happened?" Shanks asked.

Wendell picked up his glass and drank. "Toby and Jerry Wainwright were tubing the river," Wendell said. "They got down to the cross-valley canal where the irrigation water gets taken off for the lower basin. There's a culvert there, and Toby wanted to run it. Jerry said no. So Toby did it alone. He went in laughing and waving to Jerry, and when the tube popped out the other end of the pipe, Toby wasn't in it." Wendell stared as if he were seeing it. "There wasn't any air. Sid Towe, the sheriff over in Chipeta Springs, found his body a half mile down the canal snagged on some willows."

Shanks looked up at the doorway, and Wendell followed his gaze. Christopher was standing there.

"What happened to Parcheesi?" Wendell asked.

"Gammie didn't want to play anymore."

They heard Martha in the back part of the house, rummaging, it sounded like, through boxes.

"Is she crying?" Wendell asked.

"She heard what you said about the accident," Christopher said. "I don't know. She just stopped playing."

Wendell nodded. "Come over here," he said. He drank the rest of his bourbon and reached his glass out to Shanks for more. When Christopher came over, Wendell pulled him onto his lap. "Do you remember the time you came to my studio?" he asked. "I was working on a kestrel."

"No."

Wendell drank.

"You asked me why some trees lost their leaves and Christmas trees didn't. You were just four, I think. And you asked why the rocks of Pinnacle Ridge turned red when the sun went down. You asked what bird I was working on."

"I don't remember what you said," Christopher said.

"I didn't answer you."

"Then how can I remember?"

Christopher looked up at Wendell, and Wendell tilted his

glass back again and sipped his bourbon. Shanks knew Wendell was not packing anymore to go up the mountain.

Shanks took a drink of his own.

"Why didn't you answer?" Christopher asked.

"Because sometimes the answers to questions change the way you see things. You stop seeing the colors of a bird when you know its name. Or maybe you stop wondering what happens to the leaves."

"Maybe knowing the names of things helps you to learn more," Shanks said.

Wendell smiled and ran his hand over Christopher's hair. "A kestrel is a bird with colorful feathers," he said. "Blue and orange and black and tan. Each feather is patterned in such a way that it fits into the one next to it. I'm supposed to make it look lifelike. That's what I do."

Christopher leaned back again and looked at Wendell. "Are you drunk, Papa?"

"Yes, oh, yes," he said. "I am drunk."

21

The hunting camp looked to Aurey as though it had been deserted for weeks. It was in a flat stand of Engelmann spruce, protected on the east by a large boulder, and on the south by the steep timbered slope of Brown Mountain. Snow had drifted into the fire pit from up the creek and had inundated the food cache and the woodpile. It covered the logs around the fire pit and the cross poles on which Becky and Finn had intended to hang their elk. The creek beside the camp was slow moving, clear, its amber bottom etched with ice at the edges. There were no tracks anywhere, and it was still snowing.

Aurey shook the snow from the tent and tightened the ropes, made slack by the wind and the accumulation of snow. He left his own pack inside the tent and hiked up the creek trail another two hundred yards to where the willows and brush started and the meadow opened out. He could not see very far up the meadow, though, because the snow and clouds were down so low. In the lower flats a few husks of cow parsnips stuck up through the snow, along with the thin heads of grasses gone to seed. Here and there boulders protruded too—snowy-crowned gray rocks in the midst of the vast white. Beyond the lower meadow he could make out the dark timber through which the trail continued on up toward the Yellow Jacket Mine.

Becky and Finn had hunted the terrain higher and to his left where the meadow angled into the clouds. He knew the meadow leveled off higher up onto a plateau. The plateau broke into a long ravine on the west. That was the gully Finn had followed back to camp in the storm. There were more meadows still higher, a quilting of slopes and angles, but all of that country was in the clouds.

It did not matter to Aurey who he was looking for. He wanted to get moving. Someone was up in that vast territory where no one belonged, and he didn't want to wait for help. He could cover more terrain by himself than all the others put together, and do it well too. But he knew that even for him, there were too many ravines and slopes and streambeds and cliff bottoms. It was an expanse of hundreds of square miles, and Becky could have walked in almost any direction except west, which was over the Amphitheater. She could have gone southeast over Engineer in Mineral Creek or north across the western flank of Red Cloud Peak and come out into the Cutler Creek drainage. Or she could have walked east, the path of least resistance. If she stayed up high at eleven thousand feet she could have walked right across American Flats and downhill on the long gentle escarpment into Lakeland.

If she weren't hurt.

If in the snow she weren't walking in circles.

If she weren't holed up somewhere in the timber or in the shaft of an old mine.

He backtracked toward camp by way of the makeshift corral at the edge of the trees where Becky and Finn had kept their horses. The corral was built from aspen poles nailed to the spruce trees on one side and aspen poles fitted into X's of cut and braced aspens on the meadow side where there were no trees to nail to. An opened bale of hay and a sack of oats were buried under the snow at the gate.

But there were no horses or traces of horses. Aurey did a circle of the corral and the lower meadow, thinking Finn might have tied Becky's horse somewhere else so it wouldn't be exposed so much to the snow. But he couldn't find it.

Back at camp he set up his own one-man tent a little way off from the fire pit, beneath a spruce bough which sheltered the ground. It wasn't a level spot, but he hadn't come for his own comfort. He stowed his sleeping bag and some of his gear in the tent and rearranged the rescue equipment in his pack so he would be ready to go as soon as the others arrived.

Then he cleared the snow from the fire pit, broke twigs and dry needles from the low branches of a tree, and set them into the pit. A fire in camp was good for morale. To have a place to sit and dry your boots and get warm encouraged everyone—at least for a few minutes.

He lighted the kindling and with his body shielded the flame from the wind and snow until the fire had an inertia of its own. After that the wind helped the fire take hold. When it was burning fast, he laid in larger twigs and some wet wood and laid the sooty grate over the top.

When he'd put some water on, he poked into Finn and Becky's tent. Finn's Remington 30.06 lay on his sleeping bag on his cot, along with a half bottle of Yukon Jack. Becky's cot was a mess of Finn's frozen clothes—underwear, socks, a shirt. Becky's big backpack was at the end of the cot with her clothes hanging out of it, as if someone had searched through it. There was a box of matches on the floor, but that didn't tell him much one way or the other about what Becky had with her.

He unfolded his topo map and spread it over over the rifle on Finn's bunk. He had Finn and Weedy and Jock Martin and John Meeker and Bud and Granny Watson, who would be a help, and he hoped for some others. That still wouldn't be enough people in the weather they had. He sketched across the wavy lines of the map. About all they could hope to do was to search the area where Finn had last seen her— the ridge and the line toward the Depot and then the ravine to the east and the trees on the far side of the ravine. That would take the rest of the afternoon. They'd make a pass through the trees where Finn had come through on the lower slope in case Becky had come down that way to look for Finn and had taken shelter there. And then they ought to search the ravine Finn had gone down—maybe he'd send Bud on that errand, since it would take him back to camp first and get him out of the way.

The rest of them would sweep the canyon on the other side of the ridge from the Depot. The map didn't show all the mines. There were two or three in the timber and scree east of the canyon, and if she'd tracked an elk that way, she could have holed up in any one of them. The problem was, the ridges and the cliffs and ravines all ran at varying angles to one another and even in good weather it was easy to misjudge where you were. Then, too, he didn't know how familiar Becky was with the terrain. The Yellow Jacket farther up was another alternative, and she might have headed there.

The possibilities were endless. He knew that. He couldn't consider everything. The main thing was to have a plan to follow and cover the ground systematically. And one thing was certain: snow or no snow, they had to work fast.

Granny and Lorraine and Jock were the first to reach the camp, and Aurey was surprised to see Lorraine. But it was no reunion. They said hello to one another, and that was all. They had work to do.

Lorraine set up her tent and stashed her food. The mood was serious and somber, and when they were ready to go they waited by the fire warming their hands and feet. Snow was still coming down hard.

Finn and Weedy showed up next. "We passed Bud and Pork on the cliff," Weedy said. "They're hanging on. No sign of Becky, huh? We smelled the smoke and thought she was here."

"We wish she were," Lorraine said.

Weedy shed his pack and sank down onto the log beside the fire. "Goddamn, man, where the hell is she? She hasn't been here at all?"

"Everything was covered with snow," Aurey said. "The only thing is the horse. Weren't there two horses?"

"Bo Jack and Toots," Finn said. He propped his ski goggles up on his orange cap. "Why? Where's Toots?"

"She isn't in the corral," Aurey said. "There aren't any tracks."

"So what are you saying?" Lorraine interrupted. "Does Becky have Toots?"

"Was Toots here this morning?" Weedy asked. "That's the question, Finn. Was she here when you went down?"

Finn tried to think. "I don't know."

"How can you not know?" Weedy asked. "A horse is a big animal. And we could save ourselves a lot of pain in the ass if we knew Becky had Toots."

"I said I don't know," Finn said. "It was snowing like shit. When we came up I didn't put Bo Jack in the corral. I kept him down in the trees because he doesn't always get along with Toots. All I remember is Toots was in the corral opening morning. I saw her from the top of the meadow."

"But not when you came down?" Lorraine wanted to know.

"Down where? From the Depot? I came down the ravine."

"Maybe you were drinking that Yukon Jack," Aurey said.

"Fuck you, man. What were you doing in my tent?"

"Wait a minute, Finn," Weedy said. "Maybe Becky got her elk, and you owe me fifty bucks. She came down and got Toots to pack the elk out."

"So where is she?" Finn asked.

Bud Saunders and John Meeker appeared through the trees down the trail—two dark, cumbersome figures advancing like weary soldiers shrouded in snow. Bud's pack slid from side to side as he walked, the way a loose load might swing on a camel.

"It's about time," Lorraine said. "Let's get up the mountain."

"We're going to find Becky with the biggest damn elk," Weedy said. "And I'm going to be rich."

The snow had let up a little by the time they reached the
first false summit on the plateau at the top of the lower
meadow, but it was hard to tell whether the storm was
moving past or whether it was simply getting too cold to
snow. The flakes were smaller, more brittle, like thin slivers
of glass brushing against the skin. The hills above them rose
in misty series, one after another. To the left, off the edge of
the meadow, they could see down into the ravine which
skirted the back of the Amphitheater. But ahead the white
hills were always rising into the milky air.

Each step was painful. They sank down, slid on the slick
grass beneath the snow, caught balance, lifted the snow
which caked on their boots.

Aurey led. It would have been easier had he been able to
see the animal trails because deer and elk and coyote always
traveled by instinct the simplest line of a slope. But the
snow had kept the animals in the trees. Aurey traversed at a
long angle across the meadow, and the group strung out
behind him. Then he reversed direction and climbed higher
on a new pitch. Lorraine and Granny kept a good pace,
then Finn carrying his Remington, and Weedy. The other
followed at intervals down the zigzag of the broken trail.

They had not brought much gear—just the necessities for
their own use and a few sticks of dry wood in case they
needed a fire. Aurey carried the rescue equipment and his
skis. Lorraine had her skis and an extra down jacket for
Becky. Weedy and Granny had brought camp stoves and
ropes. Finn carried his rifle, he said, for emergencies.

It was nearly three o'clock, and though the snow had
eased a little by the time they reached the fourth rise, there
was already the pressure of evening coming. The wind had
died a little, too, but snow still blew across the rise and
down from the ridge above them.

Aurey stopped and waited for everyone else to catch up.
The sky was gray still, and the Amphitheater was in clouds,
but he could see now the ridge and the downhill slope toward the patch of dark spruce in the distance. Granny and

Lorraine joined him on the rise and stood catching their breath in the thinner air.

"Are those the trees?" Lorraine asked.

"I think so. We'll ask Finn."

Finn and Weedy had slowed down, especially Finn. Finn was coughing and rested every hundred steps. But he was still ahead of Bud Saunders, who was well back down the hill.

"This it?" Aurey called down.

Finn nodded, out of breath, and leaned for a moment against Weedy. "That's the ridge," Finn said, pointing with a ski pole. "She was going to the top, and I went straight ahead here and kept in the trees."

Finn recouped his energy and started climbing again, and in another few minutes he was on the rise with them.

"Becky was going to hold the top," he said. "I was coming around through the trees down low."

"Why did you send Becky up?" Lorraine asked.

"I didn't send her. She wanted the top. Besides, elk move uphill. She had the better chance unless I got to them bedded down in the trees."

"What's on the other side of the ridge?"

"It drops off into a basin," Weedy said. "It's a side canyon we call Wounded Knee because one year Finn's father shot an elk in the knee."

"It's a steep drop," Finn said. "Steeper than here and mostly scree. Not much grass for elk. If you followed the ridge north, you'd come right out at the Depot."

Meeker struggled up, and then Jock Martin. Bud was still zigzagging on the trail down below.

Meeker bent over, coughed, and spat.

"Fun, huh, Pork?" Weedy asked.

"So where are we?" Meeker wanted to know. "I didn't see any horse tracks. Where's this Depot with all the trains?"

"We're way up," Aurey said, "but not far enough yet. We'll split up here."

"If the weather were clear," Weedy said, "we could see

five or six fourteeners from here, Pork. It's the top of the world. And you could see Bear Creek too."

"If it were clear, spick-o, we wouldn't be up here."

Bud labored up the last few yards, putting one foot in front of the other. When he was on level ground, he knelt in the snow and retched.

"Morning sickness," Weedy said. "You shouldn't have let the Geiger Counter get on top."

"You all right?" Aurey asked.

Bud nodded. He scooped snow with his glove and washed out his mouth.

"Listen up, now," Aurey went on. "Come on, Bud, get over here."

Aurey laid out his map in the lee of a gnarled stump, and they all huddled around.

"Each of us will stay about a hundred yards from the next person through the trees. The bottom man will be Bud, so he won't have to climb so much, and then Jock. When you two get through the trees I want you to peel off from the rest of us and follow the ravine back to camp. If Becky headed out that way, you might run across her in a boulder cave. It's a piece of ground we'll have to check."

"She won't be in the trees," Finn said. "If she were in the trees, she'd have made it back to camp."

"She could be hurt," Weedy said. "She could be hurt anywhere."

"Our job is to cover the territory thoroughly," Aurey said. "Try to move in a line at a medium to fast pace. We don't want to pass her by under any circumstances, but we don't have a lot of light left either. We have to move. The rest of us besides Bud and Jock will bear north when we get into the trees and we'll head toward the Depot. Then we'll circle around to the east to the top of the side canyon beyond this ridge." He lifted his head toward the Amphitheater, where clouds swirled and rose like birds soaring over the rocky crags. "It looks as though we're going to get some better visibility, which is a help."

"If we can see her, she can see us," Meeker said. "Why

don't we fire off a couple of shots? If she hears us she can try to get out into the open."

He drew his pistol from the holster on his belt.

"The Remington would make more noise," Weedy said.

Finn stepped off to the edge of the group and fired three rounds into the air. He paused, loaded three more shells, and fired again. The shots echoed from the back of the Amphitheater, faintly, the sound absorbed by the clouds.

"Maybe she'll answer," Lorraine said.

They listened for a moment, but all they could hear was the hiss of snow over the lip of the rise.

"I'll take the top," Aurey said. "We should stay close enough together to call back and forth. Granny, you stay below me down the slope, and then Weedy and Lorraine. Every man is as important as every other. Keep a lookout for anything unusual." He paused again. "What about it, Bud? You think you're all right enough to make it through the trees?"

"Easy," Bud said. "There's nothing wrong with me that being home watching *Miami Vice* wouldn't cure."

"You, Finn?"

"Fine," Finn said. He loaded three more shells and put the safety on. "Let's get moving."

Finn started off, breaking through the deep snow, holding the rifle across his body as he walked.

"Any questions?" Aurey asked.

No one had a question. Weedy and Granny and Lorraine angled up from the line Finn chose, gradually splitting farther and farther apart as they climbed. Bud and Jock rested until Aurey had taken a last glance at the map and had folded it back into the zippered pocket of his parka. Then they headed out, too, downhill toward the lower section of trees.

Meeker stayed behind a minute until Aurey was ready. "I'll watch Finn," he said. "I'll keep a good eye on him."

Aurey shook his head. "You worry about your own job," he said. "Let me worry about Finn."

"I don't trust him," Meeker said.

Meeker started off in Finn's track and broke off a little way down the slope. Aurey watched the others fan out across the slope for a moment. Then he started off, too, climbing almost straight up the meadow toward the crest of the ridge. The white line of the ridge knifed across the backdrop of gray.

If the clouds lifted, he thought, they'd have a good hour of daylight left, maybe an hour and half to see color and distance. Maybe, like Meeker said, if she were holed up, she'd come out into the open. Even if she were hurt she might make the effort. It was colder, though. Clearing meant it would get colder still. That was what he worried about most. She might have made it through one night. But it would be hard to live through another.

22

The top of the headwall of Wounded Knee was only a few paces across, and Lorraine did not see how they could get down it. From where they stood the ravine widened as it fell away, like a spearhead pointed at them from Bear Creek, which was a good mile below them. The snowy ridge where Finn had last seen Becky was on their right now, and from her perspective it dropped almost perpendicularly into the rocky bottom. If Becky had slipped off the ridge, she would have fallen two hundred feet.

"Becky. Beck-ee. Beck-ee!"

Becky, Beck-ee.

Her voice came back more shrilly in echo, as though it were the breeze itself speaking. Beck-ee. The snow had stopped now, and the air was clearer. Clouds still lingered along the granite and scree of Brown Mountain across Bear Creek, and Engineer Peak was in clouds. But over the Amphitheater and the peaks to the west—Potosi, Whitehouse, and Abrams—the clouds rose fast into mist in the waning sunlight.

The cold numbed their fingers and their faces, so that even when they were standing and looking, they had to move constantly from one foot to another and tuck their hands under their armpits or inside their shirts.

"You think she could have crossed this?" Meeker asked Aurey.

"She could have. We have to think of what might have happened. If it hadn't started snowing yet, she could have skirted this headwall and gone across into the trees on the other side. Or she might have had an elk go down into the ravine."

"There's a falls down lower," Finn said. "She knew about that. She'd have had to go up top in the trees or else take it on the right along the aspens where the ridge starts to peter out."

"We should check the ravine anyway," Weedy said. "Aurey's right. She might not have seen where she was."

"We have to check everywhere," Aurey said. "We'll go down the headwall slowly on the rope. When we get to the bottom, John, you and Finn scout the boulder caves. Granny and Weedy can take the cliff bottom and the hill. Spread out a bit and check out the lumps under the snow. Lorraine can take the east side, up along the rim where she can see out. I don't think she's going to be in the stubby trees, but maybe you can pick out a color or a strange shape."

"You make it sound like she's dead," Lorraine said. "She's not dead."

"We have to consider everything," Meeker said. "It's a job."

Weedy descended the headwall first, sliding a little, holding the rope, scrabbling with his feet. The others followed one by one. They wasted fifteen precious minutes of light getting everyone down. Lorraine was the last one, before Aurey.

Lorraine was not conscious of the cold. Sweat rose on her forehead and beneath her arms as soon as she got back into stride. The upslope where she was was mostly subalpine fir, scruffy small trees which gave way higher up on a different pitch to the taller and darker Engelmann spruce. She felt as though she were walking in a dream. The hillside was a moving landscape, more gray in the evening light than white, defined briefly by the mound of a tree stump, then by Aurey's swift body above her, then by the drift of snow over rock. *If she will just be all right. Please, God, let her be all right. Just this once. She never hurt anyone else in her life. She couldn't be dead. She'll be all right. Yes, she's safe.*

Why hadn't Finn come down earlier so they'd have had more light to work with? That was what she wondered. There wasn't enough time now. It was already getting dark. *God, let it stay light. Becky will be all right. Please let it stay light. Let it stay light for days.*

It was strange to her how sometimes uphill was indistinguishable from downhill, as if the images were reversed. Even when she climbed against the slope, it seemed she was floating downhill. The snow made the world subtle and immense, and she was surprised each time she stepped out into the soft powder that her foot fell onto such solid ground.

The scree was not so slippery underfoot as the grass. She angled across the slope, and every hundred feet or so she stopped and scanned with binoculars the rocky bottom and the back side of the cliff.

Finn stumbled along the bottom of the draw with his rifle, looking neither right nor left, as if there were nothing to see, no one to look for. He rested often and drank from his canteen, leaning against the boulders which had rolled into the bottom from higher up. Meeker was more careful, slip-sliding on the rocky bottom. There was no water now in the ravine, but over eons the snowmelt had washed out a combination of smooth rock and loose debris. Meeker checked every crevice, every hole in every pile of boulders.

Weedy and Granny were higher up near the base of the cliff, where they pushed their ski poles into the lumps of snow. Clouds continued to rise from nothing, from the warmer earth, pouring upward and outward into the expanding sky. An eerie light diffused through the mist, as if through a curtain of lace. It was a snow-gray light, and in the ravine there was no wind. There were no noises of airplanes and no voices.

There was an explanation for everything, Lorraine thought, some reasonable accounting for how things happened. Why was Aurey so certain of the worst? She watched him angling away from her, higher and higher toward the dark trees. His stride was graceful, deerlike, a marvel of coordination. The snow powdered up softly around him. He balanced himself perfectly, holding his ski poles outstretched, just touching them to the snow.

In high school he had been her first boyfriend. Her mother had objected, as she did about everything, though not because Aurey was Hispanic. Martha didn't like him because he was dangerous. He would make her unhappy.

All they had done was go hiking in the afternoons after school. On weekends and evenings he worked in the café, but afternoons were free to do homework, and they took advantage of the time. Aurey was high-strung and nervous and awkward around people, but she liked his shyness. Ernesto said he was so shy and aloof that he couldn't wait tables. He was impolite. But Lorraine assumed it was only that he asked of everyone else what he did of himself. With her he was gentle. They walked to the top of Mt. Meers or to the Ute Chief Mine or along the shaded trail in Oak Creek Canyon. He showed her arnica and vervain and alp lilies, though often he did not do more than point to the flower.

He saw everything. He picked out the nests of birds, or bighorn sheep camouflaged across the valley on the gray cliffs of the Amphitheater, or a blue grouse frozen in fear in a barren of kinnikinnick. He recognized deer he had seen before—one had a split ear, another a mark on its face she would never have noticed. He knew when the wild berries were ripe on which exposure—huckleberries or buffalo berries or currants or chokecherries. He could track animals, too, better than any hunter, better than her father.

But he was not a man for love. She was sensible enough to bide her time and not push him, but she grew impatient too. There were other boys who wanted her to go out with them, though Martha objected to them all and often hung up when they called. The most persistent was Teddy Karabin, who'd quit school to go to work in the mine. He'd asked her three times to the senior dance, but she'd rather have gone with Aurey.

The day they'd broken up she had meant to have him ask her. They'd hiked up toward the Bridge to Heaven. It was nearly May and some early flowers were out in the high meadows. A chinook had fanned from the south, and the wind fluttered through the aspen benches. She'd flirted with him more than usual, glanced at him the way she'd seen Becky glance at boys, tried to hold his hand. He seemed distant that day, though she thought later that it had been her own desire which had made him seem that way. When he went ahead on the trail, as he usually did, she found herself angry when she caught up. And when he pointed out a sharp-shinned hawk weaving through the spruce trees in pursuit of a junco, she refused to look at it.

How was she supposed to know he cared for her if he never kissed her? Was he going to go through high school without attending a single dance?

When they were in the open, climbing the last pitch to the narrow backbone of the Bridge, the wind had shifted. Clouds drove over the valley, burgeoning high, gray cumulus which promised rain. Aurey wanted to turn back; she wanted to go up.

"There'll be lightning," he said. "This isn't a place to be in a storm."

"Then you go down."

"I can't go back without you."

She had for an instant admired this sentiment until she realized its ambiguity. "Why can't you?"

"Because I'm responsible for you."

"Since when? Since when are you responsible for me?"

He had stared at her, dumbfounded by her anger.

A sliver of lightning wavered above them, and thunder rolled through the clouds.

"I'm going up," she said.

She had climbed higher, and he had stayed in the trees. When the storm broke, she had thrown herself facedown in the flowers and the lush grass. The earth shook with the thunder, and the lightning flashed around her, and she cried out, swearing at Aurey while the rain and hail stung her arms and the backs of her hands, with which she'd protected her head.

She watched Aurey a moment longer, still striding away from her up the slope. He saw everything, yes, but he wouldn't ever understand what Becky might do. Not the way Neil Shanks could have. Neil would have grasped Becky's state of mind after an argument with Finn. He'd have known how she felt. That had to be considered too.

The time Becky had socked Finn she'd been angry. "He said I was a bitch," she said, "so I punched him. Then he punched me. I can't blame him for that."

And there had been the time not too long ago when Becky had tried to keep Finn from driving away by holding on to the side mirror of the truck. She'd had slippers on, but when Finn took off up the gravel drive, they'd come off and Becky had braced against the gravel with her bare feet, rubbing them blood-raw on the bottoms.

What would Aurey say about that? He didn't know people, living as he did up by himself in Gold Ring Gulch.

What else had Becky put up with? Lorraine remembered when Finn's father had rammed a rifle butt through the wall of the place they'd lived in in Grand Junction. They'd had a trailer over by the interstate, and when a semi went past on the highway, all the dishes clattered in the cupboards. Finn's father was mad about something—maybe Becky's cooking. Something. Lorraine couldn't remember. There was a man next door who worked at Freddy's Taco Bakery, and Becky baby-sat for his two children while Finn painted houses with his father. The man was always after her, but she couldn't tell Finn because she was afraid Finn would kill him, and she couldn't quit because that was her only money.

Aurey didn't know anything.

Becky took all of it as just what it was—life with Finn. So what if she didn't have that much money? She'd never had money before. The problems were just situations she had to deal with or accept. There were good things, too, to compensate.

"Like what?" Lorraine had asked once.

"Like the other," Becky said.

"Sex?"

Becky nodded. "Finn's better than you'd think. He's good. He can do things I didn't know enough about before to dream about."

That had been in the beginning, though. Lorraine knew about beginnings and endings. Things changed over time. What Becky might have thought when she'd first gone up to Grand Junction she might not think now. Ask Neil Shanks. Then was then, and now was now.

The last time she'd seen Becky was the week before out at Pinnacle Ridge for their father's sixty-sixth birthday. Lorraine had got a baby-sitter for Christopher because family birthdays had a way of turning sour. Finn had brought a six-pack of Coors and some marijuana, and every little while he'd gone outside to smoke. Becky drank beer for a while, and when she'd already had enough, she helped herself to the Jim Beam that Wendell had been drinking.

The trouble had begun in the usual way. Martha had cooked Toby's favorite meal, not Wendell's, and that had set Becky off kilter. Instead of letting it pass, Becky had to right a wrong.

"It's Dad's birthday," she said. "Why can't you cook for him?"

"I cook lamb on birthdays," Martha'd said.

"Dad doesn't like lamb."

"I can eat lamb," Wendell said. He'd slugged on his Jim Beam. "It doesn't matter. I can eat lamb."

"I know you can eat lamb, but you like beef better. Why doesn't she cook you a steak on your birthday?"

Wendell poured more bourbon.

They settled in around the table, and Finn was whistling. Becky didn't like that. He whistled until Wendell gave the blessing.

That was the trigger. The blessing. He omitted saying a prayer for Toby.

"How could you forget Toby?" Martha asked. "How could you leave him out?"

"He left him out because he's dead," Becky said.

Martha had sat utterly still.

That infuriated Becky even more.

"Go ahead and make us all feel bad," Becky screamed. "Give us that expression. Go on, show us. Look! Look! There." Becky leapt up and threw her napkin into the gravy bowl and pointed at Martha.

Martha had turned her eyes down, helpless and hurt.

"Sit down," Finn said. He'd tried to grab Becky's arm and pull her back into her chair, but Becky had the better purchase.

"You shut up," she said, and she yanked her arm free. Her chair flew backward into the wall and toppled over. Then she leaned forward, both hands on the table, and looked at each of them. "What kind of family is this," she whispered, "that celebrates the dead?"

A moment later she was out the door, running.

Running. What if she had been doing that when Finn last saw her in the meadow?

Aurey disappeared beyond the dwarf fir trees at the edge of the ravine, and Lorraine felt suddenly deserted, as if Aurey were going off without her. He knew what he was doing, knew he could cover the trees more quickly than they could work the ravine, but it still troubled her. He couldn't do everything himself.

She scanned again with the glasses. They were nearly to the falls, or at least to the point where they would have to climb around the falls. Wounded Knee was wider here, but the slopes on both sides were steep. The ridge above Weedy and Granny had begun to curve downward over the shoulder of the meadows they had climbed earlier. That was a way out.

But if Becky had escaped the ravine over that curve and into the aspens, she wouldn't be lost. She'd have known where she was. Aurey was right to say they could exclude the theories that assumed Becky was all right. If she was all right, she'd come down. They had to operate on the notion that she was hurt, that she couldn't move, that she was somewhere waiting to be found.

The sky brightened suddenly as the sun burst into the clouds high above them. It was a cleaner light, high up, a light which itself seemed to rise into the air. It did not reach to the ravine, but passed over them like a wraith.

Lorraine felt lonely. They were all headed into the soft edge of night, and the abrupt infusion of the last sun made her feel more keenly Becky's predicament. It was not a loneliness which could be solved by a drink with a friend or by a telephone call to Christopher or by a man who might hold her in the night. It was the separation any woman felt in a moment of despair, and she did not know how to stop it. All she could think of was Becky out in that immense, cold, silent space.

"I got something," Meeker called. "Right here! I got a track!"

Meeker's voice seemed to reverberate from everywhere at once out of the bottom of the ravine. It stopped Granny Watson in mid-stride. Finn looked over from where he was urinating behind a rock. Weedy was punching his ski pole down into the snow.

"What kind of track?" Granny called down.

"I don't know. Shit, I'm from West Texas."

Weedy scrambled down the steep scree, arms and legs flailing through the white. Finn zipped up and started down the wash toward Meeker.

Lorraine scanned and found the continuation of the

track. It cut upward in a smooth arc toward a patch of brush and rocks a few hundred yards ahead, where the ravine broke away into the aspens.

Weedy reached Meeker before Finn.

"Coyote," Weedy called out. "Looks like a coyote."

Coyote, came the softer echo.

"You sure?" Lorraine called.

Sure?

"It's a pad track. Not an elk or a deer. Not Becky's."

Becky's. The echo of Weedy's voice faded away into the quiet.

Granny pushed ahead through the drifts in the direction where the track curved, still poking in the snow. Meeker continued lower, apparently determined to go all the way to the drop-off of the falls. Weedy climbed toward the shoulder, along with Finn.

A minute passed. Quiet, until the coyote jumped from the brush. Their voices had perhaps made it lie low, Lorraine thought, but when Weedy and Finn started up around the upper part of the falls, they pushed it out. It made a run for it across the hill.

It puffed up billows of snow so that its gray body seemed without shape, without legs or head, just a gray blur flourishing a bushy, white-dusted tail.

Then Finn shot. The shot was an ear-bursting blast amplified by the canyon wall. Weedy toppled sideways from the force of the sound, and Lorraine froze. The coyote leapt high, as if the bullet had given it a momentary spurt of energy. Then it crumpled into the powder, rolled once, and stopped. The tail twitched a few times, and then it stopped too.

Finn lowered the rifle slowly.

"What the fuck?" Weedy shouted. "What was that for? What're you doing, man? You're crazy."

Finn didn't answer. He stood for a moment without moving a muscle—confused, it seemed.

Weedy struggled to his feet, balancing himself with his ski poles. "That fucker wasn't going to hurt anybody."

Finn snapped the bolt and ejected the spent shell. He looked at Weedy as if he hadn't heard.

"Jesus Christ, man."

Lorraine focused the binoculars on Finn, who looked dazed, more stupid than angry.

"In the neck," Granny called down. He'd run forward to where the coyote had fallen, lifted the body by the scruff of its neck, then let it drop again.

They all stood still for a few moments. Finn had shocked them into a weariness they couldn't shake. A dull light filled the ravine now, not strong enough even for shadows.

"We should keep on," Lorraine said finally. "We don't have much daylight left. We have to keep moving."

23

So far there was nothing. Aurey had come down through the trees calling out Becky's name, but had got no answer. He'd found a mine called the Long Lost Home, but she hadn't been there. There were no tracks anywhere except one deer and some wing-prints of grouse.

He'd heard the shot, but just one, which couldn't have been a signal. He didn't know what it meant, either. Meeker or Finn—he couldn't tell the calibers of guns. Maybe one of them had shot the other, and he didn't care which. What mattered now was getting over to the Yellow Jacket Mine.

He stayed on the traverse along the flank of the main valley, keeping down in the trees until they became sparser in the upper end of the valley. The hill bulged out and around like the white belly of a bird, and when the snow was smooth, he snapped on his skis to make better time.

He knew the country. He knew this terrain better than anyone else, including Finn, who had hunted in it for years, because he knew how one valley fit into another, how all the ridges fed into the peaks, where the water flowed. He'd hiked and skied every one of these bowls and high valleys. He'd climbed every peak.

As a boy Aurey had climbed with his brothers who had

often dared him to perform feats of strength. At fourteen he had free-climbed the Amphitheater, which even his brothers said was madness, and in winter he'd done Abrams and Whitehouse on successive days. But it was not until college that he'd really begun to take the mountains seriously. That was when he'd met Raymond.

Raymond was older by six years and already a veteran of Half Dome and El Capitan in Yosemite and the toughest ascents in the Cascades. He'd done the Eiger North Face and the Wetterhorn and the Blümlisalphorn, and he was putting together an expedition to McKinley in the winter.

"I want you to go with us," Raymond said. "It's the chance of a lifetime."

"I can't. I have a job in Denver."

"Quit."

"I can't quit. I haven't started yet. It'll be the first money I'll have earned. I owe people."

"I'll lend you what you need," Raymond said. "I have plenty."

Aurey'd refused.

"So it's not the money," Raymond said.

Aurey hadn't understood. Of course it was the money. He wanted to pay off the debts he had to his father and to the School of Mines. There would be other expeditions to McKinley.

The job was with a mining exploration company headquartered in Denver, and he'd had an office job to start. He hadn't minded the work so much as the city. He ran the seven miles to work, showered in the company's health spa, put in a full day's work, then ran home again. Now and then he went bouldering behind Flagstaff Mountain northwest of the city, and sometimes he did rockwork on the side of a church down the block from his apartment. But these were exercises only, not real climbing.

Real climbing was what Raymond did.

One morning Raymond called him from Talkeetna, Alaska, where he was waiting out the weather for the attempt on McKinley. "You could still make it," Raymond said. "Get a plane to Anchorage. We're going to be here for a couple more days at least." He sounded so far away.

"Some of us have to keep the country going," Aurey said.

"It's all a matter of definition."

"Maybe next time."

Raymond told him about the team, how they were planning to use sled dogs to go into the base camp. They were going to try the southwest ridge.

When they hung up, Aurey had considered what Raymond said. Raymond was right: there wouldn't be another time. He had to go then or never. There was never a next time.

He didn't go, but he began making plans to quit his job. He ought to be doing what he loved most, which was not working in an office. What he wanted to do most was mine gold. That was what he knew about and why he had gone to engineering school. That was what he had spent his days in the mountains for. He wanted to mine because that was what the country where he grew up had imparted to him.

And that was what he'd done. When Raymond came back from Alaska, Aurey had suggested a partnership in a mining claim in the mountains near Gold Hill.

It was near dark and stars were multiplying in the sky when Aurey approached the last contour before the Yellow Jacket. A thin strip of light still lingered in the west, but the glimmer was too pale to illuminate specific landmarks where he was. The snow emitted its own pale glow, and he could make out the broad outline of gently rising hills which ascended toward American Flats and Engineer Peak.

He skied easily under the curl of the wind drifts and rounded the bend above the mine. But there was no light below. From the crest he had hoped to see a fire or a light, but the mine buildings were dark—a still life in a background of white. The tailings pile was a smooth gray cone, the wheelhouse black. The ore shed and the mine office were dark.

The main trail split here, one branch curving southeast

toward Engineer Mountain, and the other east up to the Flats. There were pitches of timber up both creekbeds, though the slopes here weren't so steep as in the lower canyon. He could see the indentation of the drainages spreading upward toward the Divide.

He skied down to take a closer look at the mine. His weight carried him down through the powder, gently, smoothly. Snow kissed under him. What he hoped for now was to find a horse track. Becky might have come up this way with Toots.

But there were no tracks. He searched both streambeds and the trails, but couldn't find a sign. It was possible the snow had blown the tracks clean. But certainly with a flashlight he'd make out some sign—an indentation, a snapped branch, some clue in the lee of a building or under a tree where the snow wasn't so deep.

He searched the buildings. He shined his flashlight into the tunnel where the timbers braced the earth. He beamed it into the wheelhouse, which had once been used to bring ore down from the secondary mine over on Brown Mountain. He checked the ore shed and the office. She wasn't there, and there was no sign that she ever had been.

Aurey knew the others would be back in camp, warming themselves around the fire, waiting for news. But he couldn't hurry. The snow light was barely enough to make out where he was in the trees, and he had to estimate the trail by listening to the creek on his left. A coyote called from the cliff somewhere across the creek—a shrill bark and yap and howl so familiar to him from Gold Ring Gulch. The call never sounded to him so mournful as other people said it was. It was simply the way one animal communicated to others in the pack, and there was no point in attaching to it human sadness or joy.

One night was gone and another was starting, and unless Becky had got down some way on her own, he had to consider the facts. He could feel the cold in the hollows and in the ravines he crossed—an unmoving cold like darkness.

The wind had stopped, and the cold burned his skin as he moved through the air. It did not bother him. He was used to such cold. He had endured much worse and did not think of it. Except that it was not the same for Becky. Cold and time—those were the natural enemies. Two nights were more than twice as long as one.

He skirted the creek and dropped down through the last stand of aspens into the lower meadow where the snow lay smooth in the starlight. He could see sporadic flashes of the campfire leaping up among the trees. He had never been one to sit around a fire, and the idea of going down now to be with the rest of them did not interest him. But that was his task.

A movement startled him from off to his right, a glide out of the darkness. For a moment he thought it was Becky, for even in silhouette against the snow the figure appeared more frail than a man. It wasn't until she spoke that he realized it was Lorraine.

"I've been waiting for you," she said. "Did you find anything?"

"Nothing." He could not see Lorraine's face, but he knew her voice. "She's not back?"

"No."

"And nothing up in Wounded Knee?"

"We searched all the way down past the falls. Then we split up and combed the bottom of the ravine on both sides."

"I was up at the Yellow Jacket. She hasn't been there either. There weren't any tracks." He leaned forward on his skis and braced his weight on his poles. "I heard a shot. What was that about?"

"Finn shot a coyote."

"For what?"

"For no reason. We jumped it from some brush. No reason at all."

"I thought it might be a signal."

"It wasn't a signal."

"What about the others?" Aurey asked. "How's Bud?"

"He's tired. He and Jock had the fire stoked up, and they had on hot water for the rest of us."

"Good."

"He isn't going to be much help tomorrow."

"I'll send him down to the sheriff," Aurey said. "What about Finn?"

"Finn's sleeping."

"You don't know why he shot the coyote?"

"No. He looked confused afterward. Even before that he wasn't really looking. He was just following along in the bottom of the ravine."

"He's been through a hard day."

"So have the rest of us."

Aurey knew the tone of her voice, even without seeing her eyes. Lorraine was frustrated and angry. At Finn, at him, probably at Becky too. There was no use arguing with her. There never had been, and there wasn't now.

He lifted his ski poles and glided across the meadow toward the corral. Lorraine walked along in the snow, so he didn't go quickly. He let her keep up. "Have you eaten anything?"

"I'm not hungry."

"We should both eat something to keep up our strength," he said. "It's no good not to eat." Aurey stopped near the corral. "What about Toots?" he asked. "What could have happened to her?"

Lorraine opened the gate which was held by a piece of aspen slotted between the gate and the post. "She could have been spooked."

"And jumped the rail?"

Lorraine measured herself against one of the sagging limbs on the meadow side. "She could have jumped this. Or maybe she wasn't in the corral. Maybe Becky tied her in the trees and she got loose. You don't think Becky came down for her."

"No."

"She could have shot her elk and dressed it out. That

would have taken some time, especially by herself. Then she could have come down for the horse."

"Today or yesterday?"

"Either one."

"Then where are the tracks?" Aurey tapped the gate with his ski pole. "Bo Jack's tracks were snowed in, but they were still visible. Anyway, why would she come down the mountain in that blizzard and go back up? A dressed-out elk would keep."

"Becky might."

The coyote howled again, farther away now. Or perhaps it only seemed farther because a light wind had risen.

"Do you think she wouldn't leave some message in camp? She'd come down and not tell Finn?"

"I think she did," Lorraine said. "I think she was arguing with Finn, and she didn't want to talk to him."

Aurey did a kick turn and climbed back to the trail. All of what Lorraine said was conceivable, but he didn't believe it. He would have found some sign of Toots or Becky somewhere on the trail.

"Let's get down to camp," he said. "We should get word to Ed as soon as we can."

The camp was a welter of tents scattered through the spruce trees. An arrhythmic light fluttered into the low branches from the fire, cast shadows across the snow, illuminated the faces of the men who sat huddled in a small circle around it.

Finn and Becky's tent was the largest one, a white canvas A-roofed tarp arranged over poles. Weedy's was a red dome he was going to share with Hank Tobuk. Granny had a small yellow Caddis fly, Lorraine a blue cocoon.

Granny gave his spot by the fire to Lorraine, and Aurey edged in beside Bud. From among the boots and socks drying near the fire, he extracted a pot of water and poured a cup of hot chocolate for Lorraine.

"Everyone get something to eat?" he asked. "You, Bud?"

"You bet I did."

"Good. We'll have to send someone down. You too tired to go out?"

"Out where, sweetie? To a movie?" Bud flapped a limp wrist.

"Down to town."

Bud's face folded up. "You mean in the dark?"

"We have to report to Ed." Aurey looked around the fire at the men. "Anyone else want to go out with Bud? We need two people. Granny?"

"I'd just as soon stay up with you," Granny said.

"It might be that Becky went out some other way too," Lorraine said. "Maybe over Cutler Creek. She might be in town right now."

"Right," Meeker said. "We're freezing our butts off up here, and she's at the hot springs."

"What hot springs, Pork?" Weedy asked.

"What about you, Weedy?" Lorraine said. "You're in pretty good shape. You go with Bud."

Weedy looked around and shrugged. "Sure, I'll volunteer. But if I go, I'll be back first thing in the morning."

Weedy got up from his seat near the fire and fetched some dry socks from his tent. "Come on, Bud. No sense wasting time up here when we could be drinking a beer in town."

"I could be drinking a beer here," Bud said, "if I weren't so tired."

"You won't have to check in with Vicky," Weedy said.

That got Bud stirring.

Aurey got up and found two freeze-dried dinners in his pack and used someone else's dirty pot. He poured the two dinners together and mixed in water and set them on the grate over the fire. "I'm making some for you," he told Lorraine. "You have to eat."

Weedy laced up his wet boots at the edge of the fire. "You know, Aurey, there's one other place I was thinking Becky might be."

"Yeah?"

"It's a place she and Finn knew. We were looking downhill today, but what if she went *up*? What if she climbed up from the Depot?"

"It's just scree," Aurey said.

"But elk move up. And maybe she wasn't tracking anything. There's a mine up there. Finn and I discovered it a couple of years ago when we came up for the sheep season. We saw this bighorn ram go into this mine, like for shade, or the cool air. Finn went crazy. It was a big ram, and we were a good half mile below the hole, and he was shooting round after round. The shots whacked off the rocks and ricocheted all over. I was thinking if Becky got up near there when the snow started she might have found that mine."

"How would she know this mine was there," Meeker asked, "if you and Finn found it?"

"Because, Pork, she did. Finn took her up there last hunting season."

"For what?"

"For what? He told me for what. It's none of your business. Let's just say Becky called it the Love Mine."

"Becky did?" Lorraine said.

"It wasn't *me,*" Weedy said. He smiled, and his eyes wobbled. "Don't get mad at me. Becky and Finn came around real high last year, trying to drop from above into those trees we came through today."

"Show me on the map," Aurey said.

He got out the topo map and spread it out near the fire on the slushy snow. Weedy limped over with one boot untied.

"The idea was to sneak *down,*" Weedy said. "Get the drop on them. Elk don't think much about danger from above."

Finn appeared just then in the doorway to the tent. "You talking about that mine way up?" he asked. "She wouldn't have gone up there."

"She knew about it, though," Weedy said. "What if she saw an elk go in there before the snow started?"

"Elk wouldn't do that," Finn said. He came out of the tent in his long underwear and down boots and stood beside the fire. "It's still a long way up there."

Weedy knelt down with Aurey over the map and traced the isobars to get his bearings. "Let's see. . . . Dylan Peak, Red Cloud, Treasure Peak. . . . The Divide runs along here, and here's the Depot. The mine is up here somewhere between the Depot and the Divide. Maybe this black square. It doesn't have a name on it. This it, Finn?"

Finn came over and looked. "Somewhere there," he said. "It's about that altitude."

"Over twelve thousand," Weedy said.

Aurey fixed the point in his mind. "You're sure that's it?"

Weedy nodded. "I think."

Aurey folded the map and put it into his pack.

The dinners were ready, and he pulled the pot off the fire and poured some stew into a tin plate for Lorraine. "Plate's hot," he said. He used Bud's dirty mess-kit for his own.

They ate while Weedy finished getting ready to go down the trail.

Bud emptied most of the canned food from his pack and left his tent, too, which he'd never set up. There was no sense in carrying down weight, especially when someone else might use it. He left the two six-packs of beer by the fire. "Drink one now, and save one for Becky," he said.

Weedy shouldered his pack. "I guess we know what to tell Ed," he said. "We didn't have any luck. We'll have some volunteers up here in the morning real early."

"If the weather holds, we could use a helicopter," Aurey said. "And the more men the better."

"Right."

"Tell him about Toots," Lorraine said.

Weedy tested the flashlight, while Bud pulled on his soggy cowboy boots. "I hope we make it," Bud said. "I hope Vicky's saying her prayers."

"One more thing," Aurey said. "Tell Ed I'm going up to the Love Mine."

"Now?" Weedy asked.

"As soon as you go," Aurey said. "If Becky's up there, she'll need some help."

Weedy nodded. "Good luck."

"You too," Aurey said.

"Come on, Weedy," Bud said. "I'll race you down."

Aurey watched the flashlight beam move down through the trees, but before Bud and Weedy had turned the first bend, he went to his tent to collect a few things for his pack. He replenished his supply of tea and made certain he had the medicines he might need.

When he had zipped his pack and secured his tent, he stood up again. Lorraine was waiting for him. "I'm going too," she said.

"You should get some sleep. Tomorrow we'll start early."

"I won't sleep," she said. "Are you going to take skis?"

"Yes. It should be light enough when the moon comes up."

She took this answer as assent and went to her tent to get her ski boots and some dry socks.

"You're going to leave me with this crowd?" Meeker asked.

"Nobody will make trouble," Aurey said. "Finn's too tired, and Weedy's gone."

"Why are you taking Lorraine?"

"I can't stop her," he said.

"It's a long shot, though, don't you think?"

"Oh, it's a long shot, all right. But we're to that point."

Lorraine gathered her skis leaning against a tree and cradled them against her neck while she put on her pack. Aurey did not help her or say anything. There was no reason to argue. Besides, he knew what she meant: it was better to keep the legs moving, to keep looking. It was better to keep the rhythm of arms and legs and heart so there wasn't time to think. If you started thinking, too many things could go wrong.

24

When it got dark in town right around five-thirty, the sky was clear and Whitehouse Peak shone like a crystal through the window in Ed's office. He often thought of the mountains as crystals. When he'd worked in the mine he'd collected them, even though it was forbidden to carry them out of the hole. He found a way—in his lunch box, wrapped under his shirt, even hidden in his underwear. He had smuggled out quartz and galena and pyrite, geodes and amethysts. Like crystals, the mountains had been wrought of the same fires of earth and lava, the same forces of upheaval that still ran close to the surface in town.

He didn't like the office at night. It was bad enough in the daytime when he could see out, but at night he had to turn out the lights if he wanted to see anything at all besides the reflections of maps. And it was hard to get work done with the lights off.

The heat seemed worse at night too. The other offices above him and the firehouse turned their thermostats down, so all the leftover heat stayed in his room. That was his theory. He swore the room was fifteen degrees hotter after the people with normal jobs went home.

The worst thing right then, though, worse than the dark

or the heat, was that he didn't know what was going on. In this modern age of gadgets and technology he was supposed to *act*. He was supposed to do something, and he couldn't do anything if he didn't know the facts. He needed facts.

Menotti had called and was willing to help, but Ed hadn't known what to tell him. All he could do was explain the circumstances. The storm had blown out, but he hadn't heard from Aurey Vallejos, who was the search leader in the field. When he got word, he'd call back. Menotti had promised to stand by.

Nor had he heard from Neil Shanks. Wendell hadn't come into town, so Ed assumed Shanks had been able to educate Wendell to the folly of trying to find Becky on his own. On the other hand, Neil hadn't come back, and there were still some details Ed wanted to hear about. Everything was significant in an ordeal like this. He remembered the time Sean Latson went moto-crossing down in Chipeta Springs on a Saturday afternoon and didn't come home for a week. He was only sixteen. It turned out he had known this woman who was twenty-four, and they'd gone off camping in the Gunnison basin. But for several days they'd thought a cult had plucked him off the street. Knowing about the woman would have explained it, even if it wouldn't have made it all right with Sean's father. Jesus, the father was mad. But details were important, and Ed wanted to know everything relevant and irrelevant he could find out about Becky Carlsson.

He was in the midst of these thoughts when Sharon appeared in the doorway. "I'm going home to cook dinner," she said. "You interested in some chicken?"

"I'll get something later," Ed said.

"You could use a break."

He nodded. "There ain't no rest for *les épuisés*," he said. "Do you have that list of potential volunteers? I'll make a few calls."

"Jerry and Louise would like to see you," Sharon said.

"Since when?"

"*I'd* like to see you."

Ed got up and tucked in his shirt and gave Sharon a hug. "Someone has to stay here. There's too much to do. And Neil's coming back."

"Neil knows where to find you. We'll put the telephone on call-advance."

"You don't think Jerry and Louise can get their own dinner?"

They kept the impasse alive for a few seconds more, and then Sharon gave up. "Whatever you say," she said. "I'll keep something warm for you."

When Sharon left, the office seemed quieter. Even the clanking pipes over his head and the clicking metal of the ducts didn't bother him. He didn't like the office, but he didn't mind the peace.

He contemplated the idea of Becky and Neil Shanks. Nothing had happened. That's what Neil said. *Nothing happened.* What did that mean? Ninety-nine times out of a hundred that was a lie. *It didn't happen. I didn't do it. You're making that up.* How many times had he heard that? That's what he would have said to Sharon if she'd asked him about Paula Esquebel. He'd lie, and if he were caught in the lie, he'd lie some more. That was how you got away with things. Was Neil Shanks that one time out of a hundred when nothing really did happen?

Ed doubted it. From what he gathered around town, Becky wasn't exactly a Puritan princess. She'd spent some time at the hot springs, and her friends, Dixie Garcia and Vicky Saunders, he wouldn't have described as role models for *Christian Life.* On the other hand, stranger things had happened. If Becky decided something, it stayed decided, and if she'd decided to be faithful to Finn, for whatever obscure reason, then that was it. That was one side of the prism.

The other side was Shanks. And what did Ed really know about him? He had always thought Neil was smart, maybe too smart. If he was so smart, in fact, where was he now?

Ed picked up the telephone and dialed the Blythes. Wendell answered on the third ring.

"He's here. Yes, right here," Wendell said. "Can't you hear?"

Ed could hear some music in the background—someone picking badly at a guitar.

"You want to talk to him?"

"If he isn't too busy."

"Well, he is busy. How'd you know he was here anyway?"

"I asked around," Ed said. "Have you two been drinking?"

"We been taking care of Martha and Christopher." Wendell's voice faded from the line, and he could hear Wendell say something to Shanks.

"*Ed*. It's *Ed*," Wendell said. Then Wendell came back on the line. "He's drunker than I am, Ed. It's Jim Beam."

"Well, shit," said Ed.

The guitar made a racket, and someone was singing.

"You know how to play Parcheesi?" Wendell asked.

"Parcheesi? No."

"Christopher's pretty damned good. He had Martha playing for a while, till she got in a funk. Lorraine's up the mountain, I guess. What's going on?"

"I haven't heard anything yet, Wendell. I expect to hear any minute."

"We're drinking some Jim Beam," Wendell said.

"I guess you are."

"We're singing," Wendell said. "Neil and Christopher wanted to hear some songs."

"Good. Is Martha all right?"

"She's all right," Wendell said. "You want to talk to Neil?"

"No, I guess not."

"He says he'll see you tomorrow."

"Early," Shanks said in the background.

"Right. Okay. Good-bye, Wendell."

Wendell hung up without saying good-bye, and Ed was left with the hot room. He turned off the light and looked out the window at Whitehouse Peak.

Shanks: he was smart, all right. But he didn't do any good if he was drunk. It wasn't late—something after six, Ed guessed—but it seemed as if it had been dark for a long time. Whitehouse was bright up against the sky, caught in the first light of the moon.

"That's enough," Ed said. "Please, stop."

He touched Paula's arm, and she stopped.

"It's only been once," she said.

"And once Friday."

"Friday was the day before yesterday," she said. "You don't want to, Eddie?"

He was too old for this, he thought. He was too old to burn the candle at both ends and in the middle too. "Don't call me Eddie," he said.

Paula touched him again. It had been ten minutes since they'd made love the first time, and now as he lay in her bed on his back all he wanted to do was go to sleep. He was too old to do it again. He'd have liked to sleep holding her. That would be fine.

But Paula continued to touch him.

"It worked before," she said. "It ought to work again. I bet I can make it work again."

She slid down beside him in the bed, kissed the hair on his chest and the curved hump of his stomach. Then she laid her head on the inside of his thigh.

"I can smell me on you," she said. "Do you want to smell you on me?"

He didn't answer. He didn't want to do that now. He didn't want her to do what she was doing, either, which was touching him with her fingers. He leaned up in the bed and opened his eyes. He could see her head on his leg, her long black hair flowing backward across the sheet. Snow light filtered into the room through the window, over her sleek shoulder and her back.

"I shouldn't be here," he said. "I should be in town."

She stopped what she was doing and smiled at him. "But you aren't. And if you aren't you might as well be with me."

"I am with you."

She kneaded his soft skin with her hand. "You have to relax," she said. "If you don't relax, it'll never work."

She kissed the pliant skin, and he leaned back in the bed. Relax, he said to himself. Relax, when Sharon would be wondering where he was? How had he ever called Paula when he had so much to do? And why, beyond calling her, had he driven the twenty-three miles to her house? Relax, when God knew where Becky Carlsson was.

She got up onto her knees over him. "Do you like that?" she asked.

"Paula, listen."

"Just another minute," she said. "Think about the next time, not the last time. Think about what you'd like to do to me."

He stared at the ceiling. He'd like to sleep a little and then go back to town. He didn't want to think about doing anything else. But he felt the touch of her tongue on him, her mouth moving. He stirred faintly, felt himself begin to open like a spring flower behind the lens of a camera, opening the way the petals did in time lapse, so slowly. Colors opened. Colors and more colors as the flower expanded— orange, red, yellow, red again, blue. The colors swam before his eyes, more flowers, all opening and opening.

"See?" Paula said. "See?" She smiled and slid her hand over his wet skin.

He was afraid she would stop now, and he pressed her head down.

She took him into her mouth again, deeper than before. Deeper. The colors came back, and he felt his whole body pushing through orange and red and yellow, opening and opening.

Ed thought of the Little Italy Restaurant as his unofficial headquarters. He often stopped there when he was touring the county because it was at the intersection of the state spur west and about halfway between Chipeta Springs and Gold Hill. It was a red wooden building with a white sign on the peak of the roof, a comfortable place that usually fit in with Ed's mood, whatever it was. And Rico Bonnano, who was there day and night, knew how to listen and not talk.

Rico brought him a draft before Ed had even stepped up to the bar. "You want pizza too?" Rico asked. He half looked at Ed and half watched the TV. *60 Minutes* was on, and Morley Safer was doing a segment on a Central American dictator who was skimming millions from cocaine.

"Pepperoni," Ed said. "A couple of slices."

Rico took the pizza from the freezer and put two slices in the microwave. "What gets me," Rico said, "is that these guys all end up on the Riviera with a dozen broads."

The dictator was speaking from a balcony to a cheering crowd. Ed couldn't tell whether it was last week or in some former, happier time.

When a commercial came on, Rico filled Ed's glass. "You got two phone calls," he said, bringing the glass over from the tap. He wiped the counter and set the glass down.

"Thanks for telling me."

Rico lifted the telephone from behind the bar. "Hey, I'm not an answering service."

"Let me guess," Ed said. "One was my wife."

"The other was Bud Saunders," Rico said. "Here's the number. He said it was important."

Ed dialed Bud's number and backed away from the bar. *60 Minutes* came back on—a plastic Diane Sawyer. Ed looked at her, then turned away. There were a couple of hunters in the bar, and three ranch hands at a table drinking beer.

Bud finally answered. "I was asleep," he said. "Where are you?"

"Tell me what happened," Ed said.

"Me and Weedy came over to the office," Bud said. "We called Sharon, and she didn't know where you went. She said you might stop at the Little Italy. We didn't turn up anything, Ed. Not a thing."

Ed stared at the TV, where some Jeeps were running

through rubble and gunfire. It was a place with white buildings—maybe Syria, Ed thought, or Pakistan.

"How much ground did you cover?"

"A whole lot of ground. The Depot. All the meadows. Jock and me came down one ravine, and Meeker and Lorraine and the rest of them went down another. Aurey got up as far as the Yellow Jacket, and he's going up to some other mine tonight."

"She wasn't at the Yellow Jacket?"

"Weedy thinks she could be at this other place, real high up. But so far we got zero. We thought she might come down when the weather cleared."

"*Merde,*" Ed said. "Where's Weedy now? Did he go home?"

"I guess. Listen, Lorraine wanted me to tell you about Toots."

"What about Toots?"

"We don't know what happened to her. She wasn't in the corral. I guess Lorraine thinks Becky must have come down for her or something."

"What'd Finn say?"

"He doesn't know anything. He couldn't remember."

"Couldn't remember what?"

"Whether Toots was there this morning. He got mad too. Defensive. Then he shot this coyote. I wasn't there, but that's what Meeker said. Shot a coyote for the hell of it."

Rico pulled the pizza from the microwave and slid the two slices onto a plate. The pizza steamed in the air beside Ed's glass of beer.

"Sounds like Finn," Ed said. "What are the conditions up there? I want to tell the Search and Rescue people."

"Snow's real deep. Maybe two feet, three feet. We were lucky to get up and down in one piece. It's drifted some too."

"Cold?"

"Damn, it's cold."

Ed tested the pizza and washed it down with a swig of beer. "I'll need your help tomorrow," he said. "Can you come over to the office early? We'll have people in here from all over."

"You bet."

"Bring Vicky, too, if you can. We'll need all the help we can get."

"Will do," Bud said. "But hold on a minute, Ed. Listen. I mean, this next thing will blow your mind." Bud paused on the other end of the line. "Guess who came to see Vicky?"

"Shit, Bud, I don't know. The pope."

"The McCradys," Bud said. "They had a story they wanted Vicky to collaborate."

"Corroborate."

"About Neil Shanks and Becky. When I got down here, Vicky was crying and yelling crazy things about how someone saw Neil and Becky fucking up at the Xanadu."

"Who?"

"Neil and Becky. That's what the McCradys said."

"I mean who saw them?"

"I don't know who saw them. Can you believe that? Up at the Xanadu. This was something like two weeks ago."

"Bud."

"Huh?"

"Listen to me. If there's one thing I've learned from being sheriff it's not to count too much on hearsay. You know what hearsay is?"

"More or less."

"Hearsay is what someone else says. It might be true, but it might not be true too. You get me?"

"Vicky said Jerilyn had a witness."

"Then let's hear it from the witness. See what I mean? Who was the witness?"

"I don't know. You don't sound so surprised."

"Nothing surprises me anymore."

"I mean, can you see Becky with that bastard Shanks?"

Ed sipped his beer. "Now, you hear me real good, Bud. Are you listening?"

"Sure."

Ed watched Diane Sawyer talking to some man dressed

in a white robe. He had a turban wrapped around his head and a blue jewel holding it together.

"It won't help anybody to spread something like that around town. It won't help Wendell and Martha. It won't help me. And it sure as hell won't help Becky."

"I'm not the one spreading it," Bud said.

"You hear me?"

"Yes, sir. It's the McCradys."

Ed watched tanks rolling through the piles of rubble.

"Now let me get off this line and call the Colorado Search and Rescue. I want to check with Weedy, too, about that mine."

"There's one more thing," Bud said. "Are you in town?"

"I'm at the Little Italy," Ed said. "Tell me."

Bud lowered his voice to a whisper. "Vicky told me not to say anything about this, but I think I should. I mean, I think you ought to know. What do you think?"

"It depends what it is," Ed said. "I don't want to hear rumors from the McCradys."

"It's not a rumor."

Bud paused, and Ed had the image of Vicky standing right there.

"Becky was going to leave Finn," Bud whispered. "You understand? That's what Becky told Vicky."

"When?"

"I guess this was a while ago," Bud said, still in a soft voice. "When Vicky and Becky went down to Chipeta together. I can't talk," Bud said.

"What about Vicky?" Ed asked. "Will she speak to me?"

"Maybe," Bud said. "She told me because the McCradys upset her and we hadn't found Becky. She doesn't know what to do. If she knew I told you, she'd kill me."

"I'll send flowers to your grave," Ed said. "I'll be over in a little while. Let me handle it."

"I'm dead meat," Bud said.

"Thanks, Bud."

Ed hung up the telephone and pushed it across the bar.

Andy Rooney was on the TV, slouching behind his eye-brows. Ed took a bite of lukewarm pizza.

"So did they find her?" Rico asked.

"No."

"You get hold of Sharon? She must think you work here."

"It was busy," Ed said. "Thanks for the pizza." Ed took another bite and dropped the rest on the plate. He put a five on the bar. "Can I have change for cigarettes?"

Rico made change. "I didn't know you smoked."

"I just started," Ed said. "If Sharon calls again, tell her I'm looking for someone."

"But I saw you?"

"Of course you saw me."

Rico smiled and nodded. "Okay, Chief," he said, and he turned back to the TV set.

25

The police Blazer was three years old and had eighty-four thousand hard-earned miles on it, but it still did what Ed wanted it to and when. The big engine could crank up to a hundred if he needed speed or acceleration, and with four-wheel drive he could navigate the steepest terrain or the worst road conditions. It had the usual police extras—flashers and siren, police-band and CB radio—and some options for rural duty like blaze spotlights off both doors and twenty-inch clearance. The only thing he didn't like was the siren. He'd meant to get a French donkey horn installed—that *ee-aw, ee-aw* which cleaned your ears out in a hurry—but he'd never got around to it. There were lots of things he never got around to, and the hard fact of it was he probably never would. Time seemed to spin away into thin air—the minutes, hours, days, disappearing into air. Time was invisible like a gas and faded away. But could a person?

He knocked a cigarette from the pack of Vantages and lit it from the lighter in the dash. In the dark he smelled more than saw the smoke around him. He hadn't smoked in years, not since Sharon had made him quit and he'd switched over to smokeless. Cigarettes and chewing tobacco

were nasty habits, but it was all right to have a couple of
things to be forgiven for.

So *nothing happened*. He smiled at that. Make it a hundred out of a hundred. That didn't trouble him so much,
really. It didn't matter to him if Neil and Becky were fucking their brains out at the Xanadu. He didn't care one way
or the other, except that he liked Becky and Neil and didn't
want either of them to get hurt. What bothered him more
was that somebody else knew about it. Whoever had told
the McCradys might have told Finn, and Ed didn't like to
think about the consequences of that.

Or suppose Finn didn't know yet. Instead suppose what
Becky told Vicky was true, that she was going to leave Finn.
That put another light into the cave.

He slowed for the turnoff to Pinnacle Ridge and made a
left onto the snowy road. There was no sense in calling
Wendell again at that hour when he was so close, and besides, it was a clear night, a stark and peaceful night with
the snow deep and clean, and the stars out. He wanted to
sort things out in his own mind too. Paula Esquebel: he
wasn't going to do anything stupid. What he didn't want
was to have a heart attack in the middle of it. He could
explain away a few hours here and there, and he knew it
wasn't going to last forever, but it would be hard to explain
a heart attack.

He knew he had to face the McCradys too. That was first.
He couldn't let a story like that get out in the newspaper,
even as gossip. There wasn't such a thing as gossip in Gold
Hill. Everyone believed everything that was said. Gold Hill
wasn't Hollywood. Shanks wasn't going to be much use to
him drunk, but against the McCradys it would be better to
have a drunk's story than no story at all.

The house was dark when he got to the Blythes' driveway. A thin ribbon of smoke twirled into the moonlight,
and the single arc light in the yard spread over the barns
and sheds. He didn't want to drive in all the way and risk
waking anyone, so he parked just past the mailbox. Somewhere down the road a dog barked, but it wasn't Bert Parks.

The tire tracks in the snow didn't tell him much except that a couple of cars had come and gone. He knew the McCradys and Shanks had been there, and maybe some neighbors too. Neil should have had the sense to stay put if he was drunk. He walked halfway down the drive, and didn't see the Subaru. The yard was empty. So Shanks obviously wasn't there. But there was a light on at the window. He stopped where he was, conscious suddenly of the quiet and the cold. Martha was at the window staring out at the fields and the unencumbered darkness. What was she doing, he wondered, keeping watch?

Ed backtracked to the Blazer and drove slowly back to town.

Shanks was not at his apartment either. The alley hadn't been plowed, and the place where he usually parked his car was a blanket of fresh snow. Ed idled the Blazer and got out to check the door, thinking Shanks might have left his car on Main and walked home.

The snow was unbroken to the door, but Ed went up and knocked anyway. No one answered, so he tried the knob. The door was unlocked, and he turned the handle and stepped inside.

Right away—the first instant—he sensed the threat, and he jerked his left arm up and ducked at the same time, curling his hand instinctively for his pistol. He pulled the gun and braced himself, feet apart, with his left hand still shielding his face.

But there was nothing.

His eyes adjusted to the dim light. It was a hawk he'd seen, floating out of nowhere in the darkness, its wings outstretched above the table. A shard of light from the moon glinted in its eye.

Ed stood up slowly and took a deep breath. Goddamn, he was on edge. He hadn't drawn his pistol in five months, not since LaRue Sturgis shot the noon whistle off the top of the county building with a .357 Magnum. He holstered the pistol and tapped the hawk's wing with his finger so that it spun around slowly in the air.

Shanks's apartment was full of books—books on the table by the bed, books on the kitchen counter, books on the desk, books packed in boxes. He had a suitcase of clothes on the floor, too, but Ed couldn't tell whether he was packing or unpacking. There was no dresser in the room.

Ed had a mind to search the place right then for whatever clue he might glean about Becky, but he'd rather have Neil tell whatever there was to explain than to find out by snooping. That's how he had always handled things.

But where was Neil?

Ed took a prowl around town, past the darkened shops and the bars on Main, down Prosperity Street to the Panorama Motel, and to the corner where people parked when they used the hot springs at the river. He drove down the River Road to Pop Krause's shack and back up to the Nugget. No beige Subaru.

He stopped in at the Golddigger to see whether Neil had been there. Earlene said she hadn't seen him, but she'd like to. "It's one of those nights," she said. "We could use a few customers."

"Tell him I'm looking for him," Ed said. "I'll either be at the office or up at the *Chronicle.*"

"I'll tell him. Any word on Becky?"

Ed shook his head no.

He might have called Sharon then, but he knew she'd have questions about where he'd been. He'd covered himself a little by stopping at the Little Italy, and some of the time he'd been out to Wendell's and around town looking for Neil, which would be close enough to the truth to account for where he'd been in the Blazer. But he still had a couple of hours to explain. Anyway, he needed to see Vicky and the McCradys, and those tasks would complicate his alibi, if Sharon asked him anything.

He decided to try the McCradys first. They'd be pasting up the newspaper to get it to the printer's in the morning, and if they'd let him, he wanted to see what they intended to run. That was a big if.

The *Chronicle* office was at the top of Tincup Street beneath the falls. In summer the kids used the falls for a shower, and they climbed on the rocks. In winter it was training for ice climbs. Now, as Ed did a U-turn at the top of Tincup and the headlights swung around, he could see the falls were a trickle and already icing over.

The office was in a Victorian house which had once belonged to the owner of the Taylor Mine. Homer had bought it during one of Gold Hill's down cycles in 1962, the same year Ed and Sharon had bought their place on First Street. In those days Jerilyn had run the *Chronicle* from the back of a real estate office, and when Homer married her—a decision no one in town understood—they'd moved the paper to his house, where it had been ever since.

The lights were on in the back, and Ed got out and stomped down the walk. He could see Jerilyn's shadow moving on the snow outside the window—talking, no doubt. *Bullshitting,* that's what she did best. He barged through the door without knocking.

"Goddamn it, you're holding out on me," Ed said. He peeled off his gloves and smacked them down on the cutting table where Homer was piecing together an advertisement. "I won't have it. I'll tell you right now, I won't tolerate any interference in the investigation."

Homer jumped off his stool and backed away, but Jerilyn looked over calmly from the typewriter where she'd sat down. "So it's an investigation now?" she asked. She smiled, but her mouth was nasty as a barbed-wire cut.

"I need every bit of information I can get," Ed said. "It's not an investigation exactly. Not yet."

"What information do you think we have?" Jerilyn asked.

"If we held out something," Homer said, "it would only be the same as what you do to us."

Ed took a menacing step forward. "Except, Homer, you aren't the legal authority in the county."

"People have a right to know," Homer said, backing away further. "The first amendment—"

"Homer, be quiet. Let Ed make his point."

Ed glanced around the office. There were memory typewriters, computer screens, graphic design charts, drawing tables. It was a cozy place where important work looked to be in progress. "All right," he said, "why did you go after Vicky Saunders?"

"We didn't go after her," Jerilyn said. "We asked her a few questions is all. She got hysterical."

"She didn't even answer," Homer said. "She wouldn't talk."

Ed milled around, looked at some copy that was lying on a table nearby. He read a little of it quickly, mumbling as he did.

Rebecca Blythe Carlsson 1965–1988

Rebecca Blythe Carlsson, daughter of Wendell and Martha Blythe of Pinnacle Ridge, died the weekend of October 20 of exposure and internal injuries suffered in a fall in the area known as Bear Creek Valley, northeast of Gold Hill, in the rugged San Juan Mountains. The body was discovered Monday by a volunteer search team headed by Aurelio Vallejos of Gold Hill and Becky's husband, Arthur A. "Finn" Carlsson of Grand Junction. . . .

"What's this?" Ed asked.

"That's a sample," Jerilyn said.

"You already have her buried too?"

"We're prepared," Homer said.

Jerilyn got up from her typewriter and snatched the article away from Ed.

"How'd you know enough to ask Vicky anything?" Ed asked. "That's what I'm curious about." He addressed his question to Homer.

"She's a friend of Becky's," Jerilyn said. "Why shouldn't we ask her?"

"I wasn't talking to you."

"She was a friend of Becky's," Homer said.

Ed walked over to the cutting table where Homer had been working and picked up the copy ad for a hunter's special, accompanied by a photograph of an ancient Cadillac with a huge rack of elk's antlers as a hood ornament. "I thought you were against hunting," Ed said. "As I recall, there were some editorials about it."

"We are against hunting," Homer said.

"But you're going to print this?"

"Businesses have a right to advertise," Jerilyn said.

"You know, Homer, Bud Saunders called me this evening. He said you asked Vicky about Neil Shanks and Becky Carlsson up at the Xanadu Spring. Is that right?"

"Yes," Homer said.

"Homer, you keep quiet," Jerilyn said. "Let me handle this." She clicked across the floor. "The people of the county want a story. They deserve a story, and we're going to give them one."

"But not about Becky and Neil."

"About Becky," Homer said. "We got information from Wendell and Martha."

Ed sighed. "And you couldn't leave those two poor people alone," he said, keeping his voice calm now. He pulled a cigarette from the pack in his pocket and lit it. Then he measured Homer, pointing the smoking cigarette at him. "The people of the county want Becky found," he said. "That's what they want most."

Homer looked over at Jerilyn. "Maybe we should tell him, Jay. What do you think?"

"I think Ed's working you over," Jerilyn said.

"You're damn right I am, Homer. Let me tell you something. We have some people up there tonight on the mountain who are freezing their tails off because this woman is lost. We don't have the first idea where she is or what's happened to her, and I need to find out. Do you understand what I'm saying? I want to get her out of danger."

"Becky was seeing Neil Shanks," Homer said, letting his voice trail away.

"Shit, Homer, I know that. Be a hero and tell me something I don't know."

Homer shot a quick glance at Jerilyn, then looked back at Ed. "Becky may not be up there."

"Not up where?"

"Not in Bear Creek."

"Oh, yeah? Where is she, then?"

Homer was shaking. A few strands of gray hair stuck to his forehead and his eyes wavered. "We don't know where she is. That's the truth."

"And you weren't going to tell me this until later?" Ed asked. "You weren't going to tell me she wasn't up there? I have the Colorado Search and Rescue Team coming in here at six o'clock in the morning, and you were going to let me risk their lives and waste the taxpayers' dollars on a wild goose chase?"

"We don't know she's not up there, Ed," Jerilyn broke in. "It's a theory."

"Oh, a theory?" Ed took a quick puff on his cigarette and slitted his eyes through the smoke. "A theory or a guess?"

"An hypothesis," Jerilyn said.

"We're trying to find out what was what," Homer said. "That's why we went over to Vicky's, to see what she knew."

Ed took another drag on his cigarette. "And then you were going to tell me?"

"We wouldn't want to interfere in an investigation," Jerilyn said.

"Who told you Becky wasn't up there?"

"Nobody," Homer said.

"Okay, then, who told you about Neil and Becky at the Xanadu?"

"Our source," Jerilyn said, "who shall remain anonymous."

"Naturally," Ed said. "All right, I can live with that for

the next minute or two. What exactly did this UFO tell you?"

"Confidential."

"It said Becky was going to meet up with Neil Shanks," Homer said. "They had it arranged. She had gone up last week to hide extra food to carry out. Neil was selling his store. They were going to meet up somewhere and take off together."

Ed thought for a minute. "But you don't know whether it's true."

"Our source said it was," Homer said. "He wanted us to publish the story."

"We know Neil and Becky were seeing each other," Jerilyn said. "Even Vicky said that."

"There's a difference between seeing and running off," Ed said. "If they were going to run off, why do it in the mountains?"

"Diversion," Jerilyn said. "Becky and Neil didn't count on the snow."

"Have you got a better idea?" Homer asked.

"She's lost," Ed said. "I don't have any better idea than that."

"Have you talked to Neil Shanks?"

"Of course I've talked to Neil Shanks."

"And?"

Ed shrugged.

"We went by his place after we talked to Vicky," Homer said. "We couldn't find him."

"That's because he was out at Pinnacle Ridge. I had to send him out to keep Wendell Blythe from coming in to look for Becky. That was all I needed."

"You couldn't have asked Neil about a rendezvous," Jerilyn said, "because you didn't know."

"*Rendezvous* is a French word," Ed said. "Neil doesn't know French."

"If I were you, I'd try to talk to him again," Jerilyn said.

"You ain't me," Ed said. *"Tant pis."*

* * *

That was the way the matter was left. Ed had tried to get Homer to tell him where the information had come from and had even mildly hinted at obstruction of justice. But Jerilyn had argued just as vehemently about the need to protect sources of information. He didn't get the name of the UFO, but he did extract a promise not to mention Neil Shanks in any article about Becky. That was the best he could hope for.

Ed left the *Chronicle* after ten o'clock and drove around Tin Pan Alley again past Shanks's place. Still not there. That made Ed a little worried. It wasn't so much that he believed the McCradys or their source, though he could imagine worse things than Becky and Neil riding off into the sunset in a beige Subaru. In the French part of his soul he liked the idea. But he dismissed it as improbable, if not impossible. That was where it fit on the spectrum.

He didn't stop at Shanks's this time, but continued on up the alley in second. What he could not understand was who would have made up such a false story and why. Becky's friends had no reason to lie, and Finn's wouldn't have confessed anything to Jerilyn and Homer McCrady if it meant eternal redemption.

He swung down Placer Street by his office and crossed Main. He paused in the middle of Main to see if the Subaru was parked in front of one of the bars. It wasn't, but Ed recognized Weedy's Camaro, which hadn't been there before. He ought to talk to Weedy too. But he coasted on across the street and down Placer to the alley in back of the theater. He stuck the Blazer into four-wheel-drive and churned up through the snow to the Panorama Motel.

He rang the night bell and stood out from under the eaves to look at the night sky. The moon had risen above the rim of the Amphitheater and its white light filled the basin of the town. It was cold, or maybe the moon made it seem that way. It shone like a stone from its deep hollow among the stars.

"What do *you* want?" Vicky asked from behind him. "Don't you know what time it is?"

Ed glanced at his watch and tilted it into the moonlight. "Ten twenty-seven," he said. "Don't you watch Johnny Carson?"

"Bud's asleep," Vicky said. "Not me. I'm too worried."

"Me too," Ed said. "Can I come in?"

"Help yourself."

Vicky backed away from the door so Ed could get through. She had her hair rolled up under a pink plastic sack and was dressed in a pink sweatsuit.

"Buddy Boy was so tired he just about couldn't make it to bed," Vicky said. "You want some coffee, Ed? All I got to do is turn on the machine."

"I'll have some. Thanks."

Vicky turned on the Perkomatic on the little table in the waiting room.

"So what is this," she asked, "a social call?"

"I was wondering how you were holding up," Ed said, "being such a good friend of Becky's."

"I'm a mess," Vicky said. "I was up at the church twice. The last time I stayed two hours. I haven't stayed in church two hours since we sanded the floor in the Sunday school. Not dressed like this. I sure wish to hell they'd find Becky."

"She's got to be somewhere," Ed said, "and if she is, they'll find her."

"Amen," Vicky said. "But I hope she's okay."

The coffee machine started wheezing coffee, and Ed sank down on the sofa in the waiting room. Vicky disappeared behind the desk and into the apartment, and when she came back, she brought a plate of cookies. She'd taken the pink plastic sack off her hair, and her hair was combed out in long blond curls. She offered Ed a chocolate chip.

"No, thanks," Ed said. "I'm watching my weight."

"Since when?" Vicky said. She took a cookie and set the plate down on the stack of magazines on the coffee table.

"Since I started worrying about a heart attack," Ed said. He watched the coffee drain down into the beaker. "I'v been up to the McCradys," he said. "I hear they came to see you."

"Those assholes," Vicky said.

He nodded. "I know exactly what you mean," Ed went on, still nodding, though there was nothing to nod about. "They said they'd heard about Becky and Neil Shanks."

"I didn't tell them," Vicky said. "They already knew. They wanted me to rat on Becky. Well, I wasn't going to. Not to those SOBs."

Ed was still nodding. "I know," he said. "Yes, but let's consider for a moment what they might do if they give out Becky and Neil's little plan."

"What little plan? Becky hasn't got any little plan with Neil."

"That's what I mean," Ed said, backtracking. "If the Mc-Cradys get started with something like that, we're all in trouble."

"What I worry about is what Becky said to Finn," Vicky said. "That's the real disaster."

The coffee finished brewing, but Ed was afraid to make a move to pour himself any. "Like what, for instance?"

"Anything," Vicky said. "Finn gets mad at anything."

Ed risked pulling a foam cup from the stack on the tray. "What about the note down at the trailer?"

"What note?"

"Neil said Becky was mad at Finn. *Pissed,* I think was the word he used."

"She should be pissed," Vicky said. "All the things Finn does."

Ed poured his coffee. He'd hit the right nerve with Vicky, and now maybe she'd talk. "I don't know what all Finn does," he said.

"You're a man, aren't you?" Vicky asked. "You're all alike. Your names are just different. You think being married is like being in a free whorehouse. You want to *get* in, but you don't like *being* in. You'd rather be off drinking beer and chasing foreign poontang than being at home. I've had to scare the crap out of Bud to keep him home. But Becky couldn't scare Finn if she tried."

"Has she tried?"

"Not really. Well, maybe some." Vicky sat down and crossed her legs and uncrossed them again. "Once she asked Finn what he wanted to do, for example. She wanted to know whether he was ever going to be serious. What he *really* wanted to do, you know? Did he want to be a Sheet-rocker? A carpenter or what? She didn't care. She just wanted to know something. But Finn wouldn't answer. He just wanted to hang on to his construction job through the winter."

Ed sipped his coffee. "What do you think he wants to do?"

"Me? I think Finn wants to be ready to go to Mexico."

"Does he love Becky?"

"Probably. I don't know. He has a funny way of showing it."

"Maybe he doesn't know how," Ed said. "Does she love him?"

"That's what she says."

"So she'd never take off and leave him?"

Vicky eyed him. "Have you been talking to Bud?"

"Bud gave me the report from Aurey," Ed said. "Sure, I talked to him."

Vicky got up and walked around the table, talking to the ceiling. Finally she stopped. "Becky told me something in *confidence,*" Vicky said. "She didn't want me to tell anyone, but seeing as this has all happened like it has . . . God, I was up at the church trying to find out what to do."

Ed watched her carefully and decided not to say anything.

"Two weeks ago Becky and I were down in Chipeta Springs, driving around like we do sometimes, and we found Finn's truck over at the Black Canyon Motel parked in front of a room. This was an afternoon in broad daylight. He was supposed to be working. Well, Becky wanted to go right home then and get a gun, and there was no question she would've used it. I told her to calm down. She could castrate him later."

"So what'd she do?"

"That night she asked where he'd been, and he said working. When she gave him some talk, he slapped her around a little. He said he'd lent the truck to Flash Toomey."

"Did she ask Flash?"

"By the time she did, Finn had talked to him. Flash said his car was in the shop. Becky's too naive to know how to get a straight answer. You have to ask just right to get a man to hang himself."

"I'll remember that," Ed said.

"And Finn asked her to be nice to Hank Tobuk," Vicky said. She put her hands on the coffee table and leaned forward. "Can you believe that shit?"

"What do you mean, be nice to him?"

"You know, be *nice* to him. Don't be so dense, Ed."

"You mean sleep with him?"

"Isn't that sick?" Vicky asked. She stood up.

"She told you that?"

"That's what she's so angry about. Hank's been coming on to her ever since she lived in Junction, and Becky doesn't want any part of it. He scares her. And now Finn says this stuff about being nice to Hank. That's what I call perverted. Maybe Finn thinks if she does it, he'll be off the hook for what he's done. I don't know. All I know is that she didn't want Hank to come up to hunt. Weedy either. She wanted to have a week with Finn all by his lonesome to see whether she couldn't talk some sense into him."

"I see."

"Finn said he'd rather have Hank come up than her. Isn't that generous? So Becky had the weekend—Friday night, Saturday, Sunday."

"To talk to him."

"And then she got lost."

Just then Bud opened the door from the apartment and stepped out behind the desk. "That's not the way I see it," he said. "I don't see it like that at all."

"You been listening?" Vicky asked. "Goddamn you."

Bud limped around the desk in his pajamas. "I heard you in here yelling," he said. "Sure, I listened. Even with these blisters I couldn't miss a word."

"Let me remind you how tired you are," Vicky said.

"I'm not tired now," Bud said. "You just talk about Finn. What about Becky?"

"Becky didn't do anything."

"Becky and Neil at the Xanadu? That's nothing?"

"We don't know Becky and Neil were at the Xanadu."

"It takes two to tango. That's what I'm saying."

Ed got up and stepped between them. "There's no reason to get exercised about this," he said. "We don't know what happened exactly. That's the problem here. It's like the time I was in Marseilles and there was this man at the waterfront with a bucket of eels. He was taking bets you couldn't tell which head was attached to which tail."

"Well, your job is to find out," Vicky said. "Goddamn it, then, what are you doing here?"

Ed nodded. "Let me take Bud with me," he said. "We'll go find Neil and get some things straight."

"Right," Bud said. "Becky deserves some blame. And Neil too. The chicken-shit."

26

The headlights of the Subaru sprayed out to the pasture fences, but beyond the circle of artificial light, under the moonlight, the fields of snow stretched on and on. Shanks leaned in close to the windshield and eased off on the gas. The wires along the highway were silver threads, ice-covered in the night. There were no words to tell how he felt. He was drunk. He was sleepy, but not tired. He was drunk and clearheaded and had more energy than he'd ever had in his life. He could have driven for days. Momentum: that was the way to drive in the snow. That's what he had now. He could have driven to Arizona, maybe Mexico. He could have made a straight line for Belize.

He could barely focus on the road, it was so white. So bright white. He turned off the headlights, floated through the eerie blue air. Stars were out around the moon. The mountains rose clean and clear into the night sky.

God, he was drunk. Old Wendell and the Jim Beam blues. He'd left Wendell lying on the kitchen floor in all that climbing gear. Guitar on the chair. He turned out the lights and sneaked away.

Where was Becky now? He couldn't think of now. Now was too hard to keep fixed in his mind. The arc lights of

ranches flashed by him and across the landscape like mete-
ors skimming the sky. The stars wavered. *Slow down*, he
thought. *Slow down*. He took his foot off the gas, and the
Subaru drifted to the left across the road. There was no
traffic, though. Too late. Too dark for traffic. Too light.
Now: he didn't want to think of that.

He switched on the radio, scanned a minute through several stations with static, then turned it off. Maybe he'd turn
around and head back to Michigan right then. That was
what he should do. He'd go back and tell his mother and
Roland and Sylvia he was ready to take whatever job they'd
give him. Close his eyes. He wouldn't mention Thomas
Shanks. Not a breath.

Or Belize. He'd go back to Belize and lie on the beach
and read. That had been the best year, reading the books his
father had liked. Knowing what the man had thought when
he was alive. That was the link. Sunshine. He could feel the
heat right there in the Subaru, driving across ice.

Maybe he'd look up Earlene. He'd done that enough
times. Friday, after Becky had gone up the mountain. Every
time he thought of Earlene he remembered the first night
with her, how they'd been throwing darts in the Golddigger.
Late, rainy, no one there. Tequila shots. They'd bet tequila
shots, and Earlene had brought the bottle to the table in the
back. Not good to drink tequila and try to hit numbers. He
hadn't been able to drink tequila since, except a little.

They'd been playing cricket—three twenties, three
nineteens, and so on, to three bull's-eyes. A funny word.
Bull's-eyes. They couldn't hit any. Two o'clock, time to
close. Earlene wanted to finish the game.

"I forfeit," he'd said.

"Then I win."

She'd kissed him right there where anyone could have
seen them, if anyone had happened to be passing by in the
rain at two in the morning. The next thing he knew his shirt
was off and she was pulling down his pants.

"Lock the door!" he kept saying. "Lock the door!"

She kept pulling his pants down.

He laughed now, but then it hadn't seemed so funny. He'd been ashamed, and afterward, lonely. Earlene made him feel lonely still. Like now. Like Thomas Shanks must have felt in his rooming house years ago. The landlady had divorced her husband for him. He'd found that out. Thomas lent her money for the rooming house.

He didn't want to think of that either. Who cared what Thomas Shanks did? He'd rather think of Becky. God, where was she? Up there somewhere in the mountains. Maybe in someone's camp around a fire. Or maybe alone. She was reading one of the books he'd lent her. He couldn't even remember the names.

Books. He had never thought of books as something to hide from anyone else. Finn was a crazy man to make her feel she had to hide things. What harm could books do? Finn drank in bars and squandered money on dope. But hiding books? He didn't know. Maybe. She culled out minutes from her days to read. Wasn't that cheating too? Never letting him know what she was reading, how the words struck her, what she thought about the story. That was a kind of betrayal too. He imagined the words wedged between Finn and Becky, every sentence insinuating itself through the wall of their marriage like a vine growing into cement, opening up space for water and ice to seep in. Every page pushing them apart.

Ahead of him an orange light whirled out of the darkness. He braked instinctively, though he was a good half mile from the light. Hard to judge distance in the clear air. It looked so close. Was it coming toward him or moving away?

Ed wouldn't give him a ticket. He'd done him a favor keeping Wendell out of town. But he shouldn't be driving. All the way to Arizona. Belize. He braked and turned onto the first road he saw, which was the spur to the River Road. He crossed the steel bridge and crept into the cottonwoods, where he stopped and waited. The light was coming down the valley toward him.

It was a snowplow, not the police. Orange, not blue.

The snow was deeper on the River Road. The plow had

only come through once, earlier in the day, and the road had filled again. He concentrated on staying in the tire tracks of the people who'd gone before. Bright. Even in the trees the moon was out, slithering down through the branches. This was not the road to Arizona, though. He was shit faced, and Wendell too. Wendell wasn't going anywhere.

Twenty miles an hour. Faster. Keep up the momentum in the snow. He peered through the windshield and saw Lorraine's yellow VW in her driveway, deep in snow, snowed in. Beyond it the A-frame was dark.

He swung around into the driveway, and the headlights flashed across the windowpanes of the house. No one had been there since the afternoon. Snow had consumed the track to the door.

He stopped and shut off the engine and leaned his head for a moment on the steering wheel. Wheel. The car spun around, a scary vortex, and he opened his eyes again. *Don't sink,* he told himself. He looked up through the webbed branches of the trees into the moon. Cold had already started to seep into the car.

Spinning. He couldn't drive. He got out of the car and listened to nothing. It was quiet. Cold. He could hear the cold coming down into the river bottom, hear the soft rush of the river. Sink. The river was dark through the trees, unmoving, it seemed, caught in the moonlight.

He reeled away from the car, urinated into the snow, covered the hole with powder. Then he continued walking around the A-frame to the back porch, where he sat down on a snow-covered chair.

He imagined Becky, saw her climbing up the meadow carrying her rifle, leaving Finn behind. Once it had begun to snow, where had she been? She put down her rifle and watched the snow cover it, lay down in the snow, letting it fall over her. No, Christopher was right. She'd be walking. She walked away from the Depot somewhere higher and higher where it would be colder and exposed to wind. She'd keep walking and walking.

Snow melted through the backs of his jeans. He was so cold. He got up from the chair and looked through the windowpanes of the door. The sofa was still littered with Lorraine's papers. A piece of moonlight gleamed from the spigot in the kitchen.

The door was locked, but he pushed gently at one of the small panes. The glass snapped in a silver arc, and he tapped out a space large enough to put his hand through. He unlocked the door from the inside.

It was warmer in the room. Still air. He'd not been conscious of the breeze off the river until he was inside. He walked unsteadily to the kitchen, where the smell of bread still lingered in the air. They'd forgotten to take the bread to Vicky that afternoon—one loaf for Vicky, one for him. He broke a piece and stood at the window, chewing the bread. Sweet in his mouth. He was hungry. Snow light moved through the window like a breeze.

He wished he weren't drunk. He wished Becky weren't lost up in the high country and he had never heard of Thomas Shanks. He wished Lorraine were there with him. The moonlight was so bright, it made shadows of the trees on the snow.

He turned away and circled through the kitchen back into the living room. At the back of the A-frame he looked into Christopher's room, still with the same clothes and toys on the floor. Then he stumbled back into the hallway and climbed the ladder to the loft.

Some of Lorraine's clothes were on the down quilt on the bed, the drawers of the bureau pulled open. He folded a shirtsleeve back into the drawer and closed it. He smelled Lorraine in the room, her clothes, her sweat, cedar wood. All he wanted was peace. All he ever wanted. Not Becky, though. He smiled and pulled back the quilt. He lay down without undressing on Lorraine's unmade bed and pulled the comforter over him.

27

The noise came from such a distance, through such confusing signs and memories, that Shanks could not move. He was reading an immense book, a very large, heavy book which he could barely lift and hold in his hands. To reach the edge of a page he had to extend his arm full-length and pull the page across in front of his eyes and flatten it out.

On one page was a leafy black tree, slightly asymmetrical, rooted in what he assumed was the ground. Its branches intersected intricately, like blood vessels descending to the heart. On the next was the outline of a cat, a large cat, he thought, with sturdy legs, spikes of fur around its face, ear tufts, and a short tail. On the next page, turned with great effort, was a woman's body distorted in the angle of the light. Her head was smallish and one shoulder was canted upward. Her hips were full, and she was holding something he could not see. He exhausted himself by the lifting and pulling, and each page made him fade little by little into a background he could not resist, as if he, too, were a shadow.

"Neil! Hey, Neil! Where are you? It's me, Ed. Come out of there."

Shanks turned over in the bed and sat up. It was dark,

and he reached for the familiar light on the bedside table. His head ached.

"Neil, we know you're in there!"

That was a different voice. Someone was banging on the door.

There was no light. He scrabbled along the table, knocked something off.

"Neil Shanks. Jesus H. Christ. It's me, Ed!"

Ed. That was the first connection he made. Then he remembered where he was. *They found Becky.*

"Around here, Ed," the other voice called. "He's broken in the back way."

Shanks heard the door open, and a flashlight beam zoomed erratically around the ceiling. Footsteps crossed the living room to the front door, where the banging was still going on.

The banging stopped. "Where is he?" Ed asked.

"I haven't looked. The place isn't that big."

Shanks recognized the lower voice as Bud Saunders's. Bud had gone up the mountain, so they were back. But where was Lorraine?

"Where's the goddamn light?" Ed asked.

Shanks found the lamp by the bed and then the switch, and Lorraine's loft burst into full view around him.

"He's upstairs," Bud said. "You want me to get him?"

"He'll come down. Neil, is that you?"

"Barely," Shanks said.

"You alone?"

"Yes."

Shanks peered over the edge of the loft down to where Ed and Bud were in the living room. "What about Becky?"

"No word," Ed said. "Come down here."

Shanks backed away, fumbled into Lorraine's bathroom for some aspirin, splashed water on his face. He came out dripping water on the floor. Then he climbed down the ladder.

In the hallway he passed Bud, who gave him a push toward the living room.

"You didn't find her?" Shanks asked.

"You son of a bitch," Bud said.

"Take it easy, Bud," said Ed.

Bud climbed up to the loft, while Shanks went into the living room. He rubbed his eyes and dried his face on his shirtsleeve.

"I've been looking all over town for you," Ed said.

"I was right here."

"How am I supposed to know that?"

"No one else here," Bud called down.

Ed nodded and turned back to Shanks. "You don't have a place of your own to sleep in?"

"I went out to Wendell's like you told me to," Shanks said, as if that explained something.

"I know. You two got drunk as two bees in a wine bottle. Martha said Wendell passed out on the floor. I had to call her finally from Bud's. You two did a number on each other."

"I took Christopher with me," Shanks said. "I figured he'd keep Wendell from coming into town, but Wendell was going to come anyway. I had to think of something."

"So you came around here after, looking for Lorraine?"

"I stopped by," Shanks said. "And then things started to spin around. I was afraid to get back into the car."

"I went by Tin Pan Alley three times," Ed said. "And to every bar in town. I was starting to get worried."

Bud came back down the ladder. "Nobody up there," he said again.

Shanks looked at Ed. "Who were you expecting to find?"

"Nobody," Ed said.

"We got some questions is all," Bud said. "Like about you and Becky at the Xanadu."

"What about it?"

"Bud, let me handle this." Ed waited a minute to gather his wits. "Someone told the McCradys you and Becky were up at the Xanadu together. You didn't tell me that."

"I was going to when Wendell called. I was about to say something."

"I don't care, really, except as it affects where Becky might be. What you and Becky do is up to you."

"I want to hear about it," Bud said. "Damn right."

"We didn't do anything."

"The McCradys have a witness," Bud said.

"A witness to what?" Shanks said, raising his voice. "There can't be a witness to something that didn't happen."

"Bud, you are not a deputy. Remember that. You're not asking the questions here." Ed turned back to Shanks. "I said I didn't care about that. The McCradys want a story. I'll settle for the truth."

"I've told the truth," Shanks said.

"All right," Ed said slowly, "why don't you tell me what you wanted to tell me before. Maybe we can piece this together."

"Who's this witness?" Shanks asked. "Who says he saw Becky and me?"

"We don't know," Ed said. "Maybe there isn't anyone. But you were at the Xanadu with Becky, right?" He started around the room, touching the corners of the chairs and the sofa with his index finger. "What I'm concerned about is Becky. I don't care about anything else. I have the Colorado Search and Rescue coming in here in five hours, and I want to give them the best information I can. We know the conditions on the mountain weren't very good. Becky got lost. Then Bud comes down and says Becky's horse is missing too. We don't know what to make of that." Ed paused with his fingertip on the edge of the cold fireplace. "Are we looking for Becky or are we looking for Becky and the horse together, in which case she might be twice as far away. You see what I mean?"

"I don't know anything about the horse," Shanks said.

"But you know something about Becky. You know Becky and Finn weren't getting along. She might have been leaving him."

"You're damn right he knew," Bud said.

Shanks shot Bud a glance. "Not because of me."

"Because of who, then?" Bud asked.

"Lots of people knew Becky and Finn didn't get along. Why does she have to leave for someone else?"

"Because she's a woman."

"Oh, Jesus, Bud. Did Vicky say that?"

Ed stopped pacing and measured Shanks. "You didn't know she was leaving Finn?"

"No."

"Bullshit, Ed," Bud said. "That's bullshit."

"I'd call it progress," Ed said. "Why is it bullshit?"

"Because how can he be up there at the Xanadu fucking Becky and *not* know?"

Ed nodded slowly as if he understood what Bud was saying. Then he took his car keys out of his pocket. "I got an idea, Bud. Why don't you go get us a pizza."

"A pizza? There's no pizza. The pizza place closed Labor Day."

"Then go out to the Blazer and listen to the World Series."

Bud didn't get it. "The World Series is over, Ed."

Ed smiled without showing any teeth. "Then get the hell out of here and *sit* in the goddamn Blazer and listen to music. Turn on the heater. Go to sleep. Just get the hell out of here so I can talk to Neil."

"I'll be quiet," Bud said.

"Get out!"

Bud shuffled across the room and into the vestibule where Christopher's winter gear was hung up. He paused there and looked back.

Ed pointed outside, and Bud finally went out the door.

"So where were we?" Ed asked. He sat on the low brick firewall in front of the stove.

"Becky never told me she was leaving Finn," Shanks said. "There was no reason she should have. Like I said before, we talked mostly about books."

"But not all the time."

"Most of the time. I'd lend her something to read, and she'd bring it back."

"You were educating her, is that it? A handbag from a cow's ear. A guru, sort of. Is that what you were?"

"Nothing like that. We'd talk. I considered it mutual."

"But not romantic?" Ed said. "I like the romantic parts."

"I never touched her. I told you that before."

"Lots of people tell me things that aren't true," Ed said. "But you were at the Xanadu."

"Yes. But it wasn't arranged. It just happened to happen." Shanks tested Ed, who seemed to be holding judgment on the matter. "Do you believe me?"

"I don't know, Neil." Ed got up from the brick hearth. "Let me tell you something first. There's lots of talk that flies around when something like this happens. Somebody says Becky and Finn are trying to get insurance money. Or that one or the other of them had a lover. I'd be a fool if I didn't listen to the gossip and check out the stories that seem at least remotely plausible. You see what I'm getting at? I'd be in the hot grease. Someone says that you and Becky were up at the Xanadu, and someone else says that the two of you were going to meet up in goddamn Florida or somewhere. Personally, I don't care, see? I don't give two monkey fucks for all that. My job is to find Becky."

"You have to know whom to believe," Shanks said.

"I can check on certain facts. I'd bet a handful of magic beans that Becky hasn't got any insurance, for example. But for the rest of it, you're right. Somewhere along the line I have to know whom to believe. Like I believe Vicky. When Vicky tells me what Becky said to her, I think it's pretty accurate. I think Becky did say she might leave Finn. But that doesn't mean she'd do it when they were climbing around at eleven thousand feet."

"Will you believe me?" Shanks asked. "There's no point in saying anything if you aren't going to listen."

"Oh, I'll listen, all right."

"More than listen."

"You haven't lied to me before," Ed said. "I guess you could have. You looked all right that time Pop brought you down for trespassing, and you look all right to me now. Any man who can drink with Wendell Blythe can't be all bad."

"That's a start," Shanks said. "At least that's a start." He sat down at the small table just in front of the kitchen counter. The aspirin he'd taken hadn't started to work, but he felt surprisingly alert. He'd slept four hours, almost five. It wasn't a time to be tired. How much to tell? That was the difference between a lie and the truth. He could omit details, certain nuances, certain things that happened. He had to. He couldn't tell everything, even if he remembered it.

"We haven't got all night, Neil," Ed said. "Bud's going to start honking the horn."

Shanks sat up. "We hadn't planned to meet at the Xanadu," he said. "It was a day, I guess ten days ago now, when I'd closed my shop early. I go up to the springs every once in a while—like yesterday, Saturday, I was up there. The Xanadu is a little farther than the ones Pork took out, and it's harder to get down into the gorge. But not many people go there, so it's quiet."

"And private."

"Yes."

"And Becky happened to be there?"

"Becky was at the Panorama visiting Vicky. The trail goes right by there, and she saw me go past out the window."

He had been naked in the pool, watching the tendrils of moonlight in the river. The river water was cold beside the hot water of the spring, and he'd let the cold water flow into the hot to cool it. He'd thought of it as letting silver light flow into the dark. The water burned, it was so hot.

He'd been composing a letter home, one of many he'd made up in his mind and never committed to paper, about why he'd stayed away so long, why he hadn't written. He described it as necessity—he'd had to take the time to absorb the place in order to understand what Thomas Shanks had written about it. There was history, after all, as alluring as any gold, and as powerful. It had been for him not merely an exercise in finding out what had happened. That was perhaps

*what it seemed. Rather, he had been intent on assimilating
the days, reconstructing an era of memory in which Thomas
Shanks had lived, and which, finally, had given some meaning to his own life. Could he name it?*

*He had tried to put the idea into words his family would
understand. They saw only the accident at the mill as a cata-
lyst for his going away. They had made it clear he ought to
come home to resume his normal life, as if this interim had
been a moratorium of some kind, a phase.*

*The water was so hot. He'd felt the cold silver swirl into the
pool.*

Then he'd heard his name. "Neil?"

It came from the air.

"At first I thought it was Earlene," he said. "She was the
only person I could think of who might come looking for
me. But then I realized it was Becky." He stopped and
looked at Ed. "Then she called again. 'Neil, are you down
there?' So what was I supposed to say? No?"

"You could have kept quiet," Ed said.

"I did. That's just what I did. Nothing. I didn't say anything, and then the next thing I know she's right there. I
could hear her coming down the trail in the dark, dislodging
stones, sliding on the steep gravel. 'Can I come down?' she
said."

*Then she was on the flat rock beside the pool. It was so
dark and quiet, he wasn't certain she was there. He could
hear the river sliding quietly through the gorge like a huge
bird flying down through the canyon, just a hushed sound,
water running over rock.*

*She knelt down beside the pool. "I can barely see you," she
said.*

"I can barely see you."

*"I wanted to say hello," she said. "I saw you go by the
motel."*

"Hello."

*"Hello," she said. A little nervous laugh came from the
darkness where she was. She stood up and turned away.*

He could see her only dimly through the dark. She kicked

off her shoes, kept her back to him as she lifted her shirt over her head. She peeled down her jeans slowly. Her naked back was luminous then, the curve of her waist and hips cream-colored against the rocks. She folded her clothes and laid them on a ledge away from the pool.

Then she came toward him and sat down on the edge of the pool not more than five feet from him. She seemed in no hurry to get into the water. Dark-tipped breasts, small breasts, wide shoulders. She splashed water with her hand, looked at the half moon rocked on its back. It was her manner that struck him, as if her nakedness were the natural condition of the moment as much as listening to the river or watching the stars.

Then he laughed.

"What's so funny?" she asked.

All his desire faded. "Finn," he said.

"Finn is funny?"

"Yes."

"What's Finn done that's so funny?"

"He hasn't done anything. What if he saw us now?" He stopped laughing and caught his breath. "I don't mean to laugh."

He looked up at the stars, at Orion tilted on its side above the Amphitheater. There were three bright stars at his belt, lesser stars at an angle for his sword. Two first-magnitude stars were a shoulder and a foot. He found Taurus, whose red star, Aldebaran, he'd admired every winter. And the Pleiades —seven dim stars in a cluster. All of these were myths, appearing in fall, lasting through the winter, disappearing in spring.

Becky lowered herself into the pool. He was separated from her by water as heavy as steel. His hand would not reach out to her. His leg would not move. He wanted to touch her, but he was afraid, not of Finn, but of what he knew was only the moment. Even if she consented, and she'd never given any indication she would, he was afraid the touch would be an end to something he wanted, and the beginning of something

*else. So he had done nothing, except watch her body sink into
the pool.*

*"I wonder if—" He had meant to ponder the long chain of
cause and effect which explained how each of them arrived at
that place and time.*

But Becky stopped him. "Wait a minute. Be quiet."

"What?"

"Quiet."

*He thought he heard something, too, a pebble loosened on
the cliff above them. Something fell. But no one came down
the path, and he could not see anyone between the silhouette
of the cliff and the stars. It might have been a deer or the
wind or some burrowing animal whose country was the night.*

Then it was still again, with just the river behind them.

Shanks opened his eyes. He hadn't realized he'd closed
them until he opened them and saw Ed Wainwright standing in front of him.

"And then what?" Ed asked.

"Then we talked. We talked about my going back to
Michigan, and what I'd found out about Thomas Shanks,
and my accident at the mill back home. We were looking up
at the stars and sitting in the hot pool, and I could feel the
cool wind come down the canyon. Then Becky said, 'Stars
make me think about dying.' "

"Dying?"

Shanks nodded. "And the way she said it scared me. She
said she thought about it all the time."

Ed backed away into the center of the room. "I see what
you mean," Ed said.

"I don't know what I mean."

"But you think it's conceivable she's done something
drastic. Maybe purposely."

"I think it's not certain she's lost," Shanks said.

Ed thought a moment. "Except Becky wouldn't do that.
No, it's something she might think about, but not something she'd do. I know her better than that. I've known her
all her life, and she wouldn't do that."

"I don't think she would either," Shanks said.

He had been surprised when she'd said it. He remembered the way the moon had slipped behind the cliff and the stars seemed to expand into a bridge over them. He stirred his hand through the hot water, feeling the heat more keenly when he moved than when he was still. "You mean dying," he asked, "or what it would be like to die?"

"I used to think of drowning," she said. "Because of Toby it was hard not to. My father said you stop fighting for air, and you don't want to breathe. You feel good."

"Fire would be terrible," he said. It hadn't occurred to him to keep quiet. "It'd be hotter than this water, and you'd breathe in the flames. You'd feel every nerve ending burn."

"A car accident seems a waste," Becky said.

"Don't think of it."

"But freezing to death wouldn't be so bad. Pop Krause said the Indians believed it was the best way to die. If you could not die in battle, you went up into the mountains in the winter. When the cold comes on you, you feel weary and peaceful. Under me peaceful, over me peaceful, all around me peaceful."

They had been silent then for a long time. He had not wanted to think of death or the world without him in it. It made him feel so small. He loved everything in the world. He loved the wind and the hot water and the stars which made him sing for joy. He didn't want to leave it.

Becky went under into the pool and came up again, barely making a sound. "What would you want," she asked, "if you could have anything you wanted?"

"What if?" He'd smiled at the question.

"Yes."

He'd tried to think of something he wanted more than anything else, but the words that came to mind were silly, child's words. What he wanted he couldn't think of the word for. "I don't know," he said finally. "What would you want?"

"Wings," she said. "I would want wings."

28

For the first two miles above camp, Aurey and Lorraine climbed without skis. The track was the same one Aurey had made earlier in the evening, so the snow was packed down, and even in the trees it was easy to see where the trail was. Aurey had one snowshoe slung across his backpack in case they needed an emergency litter, and he carried an unlighted lantern in one hand and his skis shouldered in the other. Even with the load he moved at a good pace. He went out ahead by a hundred yards or so, then stopped and waited, then went ahead again.

Lorraine struggled in this way for an hour, keeping in Aurey's track. The moon threaded through the thin clouds and gave enough light to see the indentation of the trail. But it was hard to follow so far behind.

Once, when she couldn't see Aurey or hear the swishing of his step, she'd turned on her flashlight to pick out where the trail zigzagged up through the trees. The mosaic pattern of the waffle treads were clearly defined in the light, but a coyote had crossed, too, and recently an elk. The deep cloven hoofprint had melted the snow, and feces still steamed in the air.

"We should keep the lights out," Aurey said from the trees above her. His voice was so loud it startled her.

She stopped abruptly and took a breath and turned off the light. "You scared me."

"It's better to walk in the dark," he said, "so we can look around."

"But Becky won't see us."

"She's not looking for us. We're looking for her."

He waited for her to catch up to where he was in the trees before he spoke again. "I thought from here we'd head southeast toward Engineer," he said. "Then we can curl around on the Divide. It'll be longer, but when we swing back, we can cover both sides of the ridge in case she's gone over to the other side."

"How far?"

"Three miles to the top. Maybe a little less. We'll be able to see Engineer when we get out of the trees."

"Where's the Love Mine?"

"From Engineer? Maybe six or seven miles. But we'll ski it. We'll be level most of the way."

He let her rest for a minute and adjusted the strap of his pack. She leaned against a tree to get the weight off her legs.

"You all right?" he asked.

"Yes, I'm all right."

He nodded and started away again up the hill. His stride was effortless, and in no time he had established the distance between them.

For her the uphill climb was dreamlike pain. She was not in bad shape. She jogged a few miles a week and helped coach basketball at the school. But it was not like climbing in snow. The muscles of her upper legs pulled hard against gravity, against the curve of the hill. When her foot sank, she had to lift it to take the next step. Snow fell out of the trees, floated down through the air, melted against her sweaty skin. She took fifty steps, stopped to rest, fifty more and stopped. Aurey kept moving away ahead of her.

When they came out of the trees, they put on their skis.

She laid hers in packed-down snow and dug her toes into
the metal fittings. Then she clamped the toes down and
fastened a leather thong from her ski onto each boot. Aurey
stayed with her long enough to make certain her skis were
tight.

With the skis on it was harder to climb. Though she
didn't sink in so far, the skis were awkward to handle on the
hill, and she had to use more arm strength. She her-
ringboned the gentler slopes, sidestepped up the steeper
ones. Even in Aurey's track her balance was precarious. She
held too much of her weight over her poles, not enough over
the hill. She was afraid to fall, not for fear of being hurt, but
because it was so hard to get up again in deep powder, and
Aurey was so far away.

The moon cast a wonderful light. Without a tree or a
jagged edge, the country seemed soft, a place to sleep. All
she could think of was that this was where Becky had died.
No other light shone here but the moon and the stars. There
was no flashlight, no fire. Nor was there sound, either, except the swish of skis through powder and the occasional
sweep of wind over the snow. And her heartbeat, which was
loud in her ears.

Aurey kept climbing, a moving dark figure.

Sometimes he had no thoughts at all. His body moved,
responded to the shift of his own weight, to the movement
of one leg and then another. One set of muscles made the
adjustments necessary to go forward, and another set per-
formed an equivalent countertask, correcting, measuring,
balancing. He did not think of Lorraine behind him, or how
far back she was, or what she might be thinking. It was as
though he did not know she was with him.

But sometimes he felt her presence in a strange way, the
way one understood the lessons of parents who were not
there, who had loved you and taught you and then set you
out in the world with what appeared to be nothing. Lorraine was like a subtle pressure on him, a memory which,

for the moment, was not in the surface of thought, a current in the river of who he was.

He remembered the day he and Raymond had been practicing on the icefall above the newspaper office—two hours in twenty degrees, wind chill zero—and then afterward they'd lifted weights in the basement of the house Raymond had bought in town. "You don't think," Raymond had said in an off moment. "You don't think, you just climb."

Aurey had nodded, doing reverse curls, feeling his forearms tighten and relax. "So when the time is right—"

"No, no. So it's in you. Do you see? In you. The mountain must be in your muscles and your eyes and your fingernails." He tapped his head too.

Aurey had been too young to see it then. But he understood now what Raymond had meant. He understood it not from climbing but from having lived alone. It was being in the mountains so long that the weather was always what you expected and never what you wanted. It was never other than right. Everything was only what it was, and anything you encountered as an obstacle was simply an extension of yourself, like the mountain, like the weather, like the night he and Lorraine were confronting now, climbing to the Divide. The land was yours because you had made it that way by countless hours.

He did not feel tired. Ahead of him was the whitish gray outline of Engineer Mountain. There was plenty of light. The moonlight on the hill refracted outward in the billows of gray hills set off from one another by distance and shadow. The hills were all grayness and lightness, as he expected them to be.

He moved across a frozen creek and up the other side of the ravine, which was darker in the lee of the moonlight. It was smoother terrain now, this high up, and he poled and glided with an easy rhythm of arms and legs, step and reach out, turn the shoulders, reach and pull. The exertion made him sweat, but he did not think of it.

"Wait! Aurey, please!"

He was surprised by the voice behind him.

"Can you please wait?"

The wind had scoured the saddle of Engineer Mountain so clean they could walk on the rocks. Lorraine took off her skis at the edge of the talus and found Aurey in a niche where he had the Primus stoked up. Water was already boiling. He poured her tea, and she wrapped her hands around the hot metal cup. Her breath and the tea and the sweat on her forehead evaporated into the cold air.

It was a brittle cold even out of the wind. They were at 11,500 on the backbone of the continent. Beneath them was snow and more snow, and above them the white drift of the summit of Engineer. And the moon. Nothing between them and the moon.

Far away to the north the lights of ranches moved through the clean air. These were on the plateau above the river, and in the lower valley toward Chipeta Springs. To the east was Lakeland, which they could not see behind thirty miles of cliffs and ravines and dark trees which fell away into ravines and river canyons.

Aurey scanned with binoculars, while Lorraine finished her tea. She pressed her back against the rock, smoothed the ache of her shoulders. Where Aurey was looking was the long slow curve of the Divide: dark talus, drifted snow, outcroppings of rocks. It looked to Lorraine like a necklace of stones and snow.

Aurey came back and crouched down into the sheltered niche where the Primus was still glowing with blue gas. "Nothing," he said. "If she's in a mine it'll be hard to see a light unless we hit the right angle."

"And the Love Mine's over there?" Lorraine pointed toward the far bend in the necklace, where the gray line of the Amphitheater cut across the horizon.

"Yes. Are you cold?"

"A little."

"From here it'll be easier going. We should keep moving if we can."

She drank down the rest of her tea quickly, and Aurey made her another cup before he packed the stove away.

"We'll have to ski off the ridge," he said, "off the wind line. Every mile or so I'll climb back up to the top and look over."

"We could split up."

"Let's stay together. It's too easy to miss something."

She was glad he was willing to give that consolation, though she doubted it was for her. He didn't want her lost, too, or falling behind so far he had to go look for her.

"We're aiming for some point maybe a mile southwest of Red Cloud Peak," he said. "We'll watch for Becky every step."

They descended the talus to the snow line, where they clipped on their skis. Aurey tested the line where the snow was deep enough to glide without hitting rocks.

It was smoother going on the contour of the ridge. Aurey went out ahead, as always, but not so quickly now. He paused to scan with binoculars every hundred yards or so. The snow was not so deep, not so heavy, and Lorraine stayed in the running lines of Aurey's skis.

29

The ridge of the Divide curved north-northwest almost perpendicular to the back of the Amphitheater. Red Cloud Peak loomed ahead of them, a silky white pyramid broken off on the east face by a plane of darkness. The snow flowed around them in the long fields that descended to the trees. The snow radiated a clean translucent light, surreal as shimmering air.

Sometime around nine o'clock, the wind began to blow harder. It came up the illumined slopes, through the glistening ravines and ephemeral canyons. It was not a gale wind, but it pressed them to keep moving. They poled past Red Cloud Peak on their right, sideslipped down lower around a rocky tor. Aurey strode evenly, as though he were unaffected by wind or cold or moonlight.

Lorraine called to him several times when he got too far ahead, but he did not hear or, if he heard, did not answer. She knew he was trying to save time. He stopped and shed his skis and ran quickly up the talus to look over the ridge into the Cutler Creek Basin on the other side. Each time she caught up and waited for him where he had taken off his skis.

The stars were brighter than she had ever seen them, a

white mist across the darkness of space. She had not prayed often and was not good at it, but once, when Aurey was on the Divide, she got down onto her knees in the snow. She knew Becky was either alive or not and that no prayer could change that. No prayer or hope or word would alter what had at that moment already happened. But still she spoke aloud. "God, let her be alive. Let her be safe. Let her be in town or ready for us to find her. Or let her be somewhere else where she's warm and safe and in someone's arms."

She got up and set up the Bleuet stove she'd brought, balancing it against Aurey's ski. She poured water from a plastic jug into a small pot, set the pot on the flame, and shielded it with her body. Once she thought she saw Aurey at the top of the ridge, or a shadow which passed over the rocks. It was a moving shape, but so light it seemed to float in the air. It passed through a swale, where the snow was ribbed by wind, and she recognized it as an owl. It glided without sound, a shadow as well as a bird, and it sailed down into the canyon.

She had not chosen to be alone. That was simply what had happened to her after she left Teddy Karabin. She hadn't wanted to live by herself, especially with a baby, but given the circumstances, it was the only thing to do. Everyone thought she'd left him because of the drinking, and it was easy for people to forgive her. She hated that. People thought he must have done something awful to her when he was drunk, but he hadn't. She tried to tell them not to blame Teddy. He was a hard worker and a fine man. But people believed what they wanted to no matter what she said.

Becky was one of the few people who understood, and that was because she'd lived in the same house with their mother and father. Becky knew what dreams Lorraine had had.

Teddy had taken her to the senior dance, and afterward he'd continued to ask her out. They dated a few times, usually to movies in Chipeta Springs or Gold Hill. Aurey didn't call. He was gone that summer, off climbing somewhere in

Wyoming, and Teddy filled her time. They played softball, watched the rodeos Becky was in, went on hikes in the mountains.

Teddy had quit school to go to work as a mechanic in the Molly Kathleen, which was the last mine operating in town. He knew about machines. Anything with an engine. He could take apart cars, lawn mowers, dump trucks, water pumps, furnaces. At the mine he repaired the drills and the conveyors and the pumps and the various company trucks. He made good money too. He had a King Cab truck, and he always brought small presents when he came to see her—candy and flowers.

But her mother still objected. To see him, sometimes she'd say she was spending the night with a friend, though she didn't have many girlfriends, and sometimes she sneaked out. She waited till her parents were sleeping and then meet Teddy down at the road where he'd be waiting with the headlights off. They'd drive up the last mile of the Pinnacle Ridge Road and park.

They'd made love in the cab of the truck with the motor on and the heat blowing in and the radio on—a strange, empty, physical love that surprised her more for its hurry than for its desire. She'd just begin to want more when he'd hold her tightly and say, "I can't stop."

Once they'd gone to a motel. She'd been embarrassed someone would recognize them, and even inside the room, she'd felt nervous, scared. In the truck cab, love had seemed so easy and without consequence, but in the motel room with a bed, it was different. Teddy had undressed her and wanted to look at her standing up naked. Then he'd taken off his turquoise shirt and kissed her, then his jeans, and kissed her again. She could feel him hard against her stomach.

"Okay?" he asked.

She'd nodded, unable to speak, not knowing what to say. She trembled, not for the reason she knew he imagined, not from love or what she wanted, but for what she didn't want. He took her nod as assent, kissed her again, stepped away to remove his underwear. It wasn't the lovemaking she trembled for, but what she knew was next, what she was allowing to go on and on.

He pushed her back onto the bed and pressed her legs apart with his knee. She ought to want him, she thought, and she shifted her weight slightly so he wouldn't hurt her, to make it easier. And once he was inside her, he moved blindly. Blind, blind, blind, and she pushed against him, too, wanting it over.

They were married in the early summer, after she finished high school. Becky was the bridesmaid. Her father gave her away. Her mother refused to attend. Teddy bought an A-frame cabin down in the cottonwoods along the river, and they lived there a year before Christopher was born.

The first time he got drunk it didn't particularly surprise her. She had seen her father drink, and why should Teddy be different? But it was the way he did it that made her wonder. He went to the Elks Club one night after he'd got paid and drank himself into a stupor.

Bud Saunders brought him home. "Payday," Bud said. "That's what he does. He drinks rum and says he's going to Jamaica, and then he passes out."

"He could take me," Lorraine said. She cleared a path for Bud to bring Teddy into the living room.

"Me too," Bud said. "Where to? Put him in bed?"

"No, there on the sofa."

Bud put him down gently. "That all?" Bud grinned at her.

"That's all until next payday."

She had stood in the living room after one of those paydays—she couldn't remember which one—and watched Teddy's face. She listened to his unimaginably long sighs. She wasn't angry at him. In the morning he would suffer. And yet she realized she didn't want to change him. He was good hearted, and he loved her and Christopher. But there was a half smile on his face that made her impossibly sad. It was a gentle smile. He breathed so slowly and easily, it frightened her, sleeping that way when she was awake, as if he were pulling from the room all the air. She leaned down over his face and felt the warmth of his breath against her neck and cheek and said to herself over and over in the cadence of his breathing, "What have you done? What have you done?"

Aurey had been gone half an hour over the lip of the Divide, though it seemed longer to her. There was no shelter where she was. It was the place he had left his pack, and she had hunkered down behind it as best she could out of the wind. The water had boiled, and she'd made hot chocolate, and when she was done she'd added snow to the hot water. But when Aurey didn't come, she turned the stove off to conserve fuel.

It seemed more like early morning than before midnight. The stars had inched farther to the west, and the moon had fallen over toward Potosi and Whitehouse beyond the Amphitheater. Maybe he had found something. That was what she hoped. That was all there was to hope for.

Then finally Aurey came out of the dark background of the talus several hundred yards ahead of her. He apparently saw there were no ski marks ahead, so he backtracked at the edge of the snow, walking quickly and running. He ran a little awkwardly in his boots, in slow motion, it seemed, and she imagined for a moment he was coming back to her. He had been away someplace where she could not reach him, and now he was back. He was different in a way, too, as if he had seen another country which had a language different from hers, and the words could not be translated, even for the most mundane objects. Hand, star, love. He was different and could not speak to her.

She knew he had not found anything. His eyes were shadows and his face angles of bone. He would have called to her from the ridge if he'd found something, but she wanted to hope.

She stood up as he approached, to welcome him, and her arms and legs were stiff from the cold. Aching. She got out the Bluet again to heat water.

"I'm all right," he said. "We have to keep moving. I wanted to search here thoroughly because it's the cut between Bear Creek and the Cutler drainage. It's the low point, where she might have come across."

"There wasn't any light?"

"No."

"You and I came up here once," she said. "I remember it. But it was in the autumn."

"This is the autumn."

She boiled water for him, though he wanted to move. Finally he sat down for a moment. She gave him the hot chocolate, and he blew across the surface of the cup with visible breath.

"Raymond and I were up here three winters ago," he said. "We climbed Red Cloud. The east face. It was January. There wasn't much snow, but it was colder than now."

"Now is cold enough."

"We were prepared for it," he said. He drank the hot chocolate before it chilled. "Raymond . . ." Aurey shook his head. He was going to tell her about Raymond, but he thought better of it.

Aurey handed the cup back to her. "The mine's not far now," he said. He stood up and stretched and gave her his hand to pull her to her feet.

The mine was beneath them and a little to the west in a small gully. The moon shadow darkened the plane of the ravine, but once they got over the lip, they could see the black rectangle of the adit, partially obscured by a drift of snow.

Aurey stopped once to scope the tunnel with his binoculars.

"You think that's the place Weedy meant?"

"It's the place," Aurey said, "but I don't see any sign."

"I don't either."

There was no light in the circle of her glasses, just the black hole with snow rising over it like a curving white wall.

"Let's check to make sure," Aurey said.

They skied the east flank in the moonlight, crossed the narrow V in the bottom of the gully, then traversed at an angle to the other slope.

When they reached the mine, Aurey started digging with the snowshoe.

"Becky!" Lorraine called. "Becky!" She shone the flashlight into the top of the tunnel. The light did not carry far.

Aurey cleared a space and they climbed up and over the drift into the opening.

Lorraine shone the light. The tunnel only went back a few yards, then dropped off into blackness. The rock was an amber granite, shored up by a doorway of spruce beams. Far away was the trickling sound of water.

Aurey took the light and beamed it around. "They used to dig the mines this way high up," he said. "They'd blast in a few feet and then go down into the mountain for a cross section. It wasn't any different from going in straight, except you could have a small claim and mine it straight to hell."

He aimed the beam into the pit, down along the wet rock. Then he picked up a stone, dropped it, and counted the seconds until it hit bottom. "Two hundred feet," he said. "A little more. That's where the water is."

He handed the light back to Lorraine and took off his pack.

"What are you going to do?" she asked.

"Climb down. Shine over here."

He took out his yellow climbing rope and fastened one end to a vertical timber. He tested it by pulling and leaning backward. Then he played the rope out into the darkness.

With no wind in the tunnel the air was warmer. If Becky had found a mine she could have survived for days. That's what Lorraine thought. The earth was insulation, and in the windless air, maybe she would not have needed a fire to keep warm. She would be all right. God, let her be all right. Let Aurey not find her here.

Aurey backed over the edge of the pit and lowered himself slowly. He had looped a cord through the handle of his lantern and fastened the cord around his neck so the lantern dangled and his hands were free. There was not much space. His shoulders and back touched the wall behind him. He couldn't rappel, but instead had to pick his way gingerly down the wet rock.

Water percolated through seams and faults, trickled downward into the schist. He inched his way down.

Now and then he shone the lantern into the bottom to see whether he could see anything at all.

"Aurey?"

Aurey, Aurey.

"I'm right here."

Right here, right here.

"I can't see you."

"I'm here. I can't see the bottom yet."

Yet, yet.

"Be careful. Tell me what you see."

He worked his way lower and shined the light. She could see the light below her, hear the water. Way down she could see something pale.

"What is it?" she called. "What?"

What, what.

"Horns," he called back. "Bones of a bighorn sheep."

PART II

1

Monday morning, October twentieth, was the kind of morning people lived in the mountains for—clear and white and simple, with the promise of all-day sun. Above the town, snow lay on the ledges of the red sandstone cliffs and on the spruce trees and on the head of Mt. Meers. The high peaks—Abrams and Potosi and Whitehouse—glistened in the sharp blue sky.

The town emerged from what seemed like a week of sleep. People shoveled snow from the walks and roofs, dug out their cars, shouted to one another across streets and vacant lots.

"What a surprise, hey? Awfully early for this."

"It caught a lot of folks."

"Get out the skis."

"What a day! Great, huh?"

But there was talk about Becky Carlsson, too, at the post office and at the pharmacy where people waited for the shipment of the Denver newspapers.

"I hear she got tired of Finn and all his drugs," Scott Furze said.

"They never did get along," said Walt Cogswell. "Who could get along with that guy?"

"Anyway, they didn't find her yet."

"I guess not."

The children had taken to the towrope ski hill before the sun had cleared the Amphitheater, and early on someone had blocked off the top of Placer Street with barrels so cars wouldn't ruin the sledding. School was canceled because the buses couldn't run on all the county roads. It was a free day for almost everyone.

Shanks heard the children running past his window down Tin Pan Alley toward Placer, and he turned over. Daylight glimmered in the window, and he tried for a moment to hear water in the flume. Earlene was beside him in the bed.

It had been two in the morning when he'd come back from Lorraine's. He'd have liked to have spent the rest of the night there, to have waked to the smell of her cedar chest and her sweat in the sheets, but Ed had convinced him it wouldn't look right to leave the Subaru in the drive. It was bad enough he had been there at all.

So he had followed the Blazer back along the River Road, past Pop's shack, all the way up to the Panorama, where Bud had got out. Then they'd gone up the hill and turned on Main. After two blocks Ed had honked good-bye and had veered off toward his house, and Shanks had continued down Main, still a little woozy from the Jim Beam.

The bars were about to close, and the street was empty. He felt down. He cruised past the Golddigger to see whether anyone was still there and saw Earlene talking at the bar to the diehards. But he didn't stop. He turned up the next street, banking on the hill, and funneled up through the snow in Tin Pan Alley.

He hadn't started the stove. It was cold in his room, but he'd got undressed and got into bed and turned out the light. But he couldn't sleep. Thoughts blew around in his head. Images. He thought of Thomas Shanks in the photograph with the Indians—what was he doing there?

He thought of all the letters Thomas had written, all the time it had taken him to compose the sentences and the paragraphs. And yet he had never said much about the Uncompahgres. To be in such a picture at such a time had to mean something. Why hadn't he spoken of it? He had perhaps been careful not to lie—so far as Shanks knew, everything he had written about the Sonja claim and the rooming house had been true. But he had been careful not to tell the truth.

And where was the truth? The only place Shanks could think of going was to the Uncompahgre Indian Museum.

He turned on the light again. If he couldn't sleep, he could at least read, and he opened the book of stories he'd liked by Anna Haviland called *Mixed Blessings,* and turned to a random one. It was called "The Train to Lugano," and it was about a man who was riding a train to visit a woman he had known years before. The man was intrigued by what his old lover might look like now and imagined her old beauty as new—her skin as smooth and her eyes the same, full of the pure life she must have led in the intervening years. He compared her life to his own, which, despite good intentions, had been corrupted by divorce and failure. The countryside passed by him out the window, the Swiss landscape which he remembered in collages of color and memory. When the train pulled into the station at Lugano, there she was, almost as he had envisioned her, her beautiful face tilted up expectantly from the crowd toward the windows of the train cars that were passing her. He knew her instantly, but her gaze fell across the window where he stood without even a momentary flicker of recognition. He did not get off the train. That evening, as darkness fell, he rode on like a ghost across the border into Italy.

He had known Earlene would come. He turned off the light and lay in his bed and his first thought when she opened the door was *no*. Please, not tonight. He guessed she was lonely. Becky was her friend too. But he wanted to be by himself.

He pretended to be asleep, but that did not dissuade her. She undressed in the dark. She touched his bare shoulder, and when he didn't respond, she sat on the mattress, rolling him toward her.

"Neil?"

Even naked she smelled of cigarette smoke from the bar. She slipped into the bed beside him, and her long hair fell in wisps across his face. She curled into him like a cat. Why not? he thought. Just to sleep. Her skin was cold, and his warm. Just to sleep. And he reached for her as if in the dark nothing mattered.

Now, in the daylight, he thought of the man riding the train into Italy. Perhaps the woman in the station had inadvertently overlooked him. Maybe the angle of the light from the train window where he stood had hidden him. But how terrible to admit to himself he was of no use to someone else. And was that true? If the man had disembarked from the train . . .

He did not hear any water in the flume. He got out of bed and tried to find his clothes under Earlene's. She stirred in the bed.

"Where are you going?" she said, leaning up on one elbow. "What time is it?"

He was embarrassed by his nakedness in the light. It was not the first time she'd seen him, but that morning he wanted to dress quickly and get out. "It's after six," he said. "I'm going to help Ed."

"Can't you stay for a few minutes? Just keep me warm."

He looked at her for a moment. Her long hair fell over her bare shoulder, and she smiled a little, showing crooked teeth. "I can't," he said. "I could build you a fire in the stove."

"That's not what I meant."

He knew that wasn't what she meant. He pulled on his jeans and sat down in the chair in the kitchen and dug his feet into his crusty leather boots. He kicked the floor to settle them onto his feet.

"People are arriving," he said. "The Search and Rescue people, volunteers. And there's something I have to do first down the valley."

"What's that?"

"Something for myself," he said. He stood up and looked at her in the bed. He thought of getting back into bed with her—her skin looked smooth in the early light—but there was nothing, no feeling, no more than that glance he was in the midst of.

"Don't say it," Earlene said. "Don't say what you're thinking."

"All right."

"I'm sorry I came last night. You didn't ask me."

He didn't say anything to that, though it was true. He wanted to tell her the way it was between them, but she already knew. He wanted to say he was leaving town. When Becky was found and things settled down, he was going back to Michigan where he had a job waiting. When this was over, he'd go. But he didn't say anything.

Earlene slid down under the covers and pulled them over her shoulders.

"You sure you don't want a fire?" he asked.

"Yes."

He nodded slowly. "Sleep as long as you want," he said. Then he put on his coat and went out into the cold.

The Subaru turned over harshly without catching, and he pumped the gas hard and it shook to life. He let it idle for a minute, billowing exhaust into the clear air. The heater ran cold, and even before he'd shifted into gear and started off, his face and ears were chilly.

He was surprised how many people were already in town. The streetlamps were still burning through the dawn, and at the end of the alley the county building was aglow with lights. Ed's Blazer was parked out front to keep cars away from the steps, but even so, the street was jammed with an assortment of trucks and four-wheel-drives. Bud's Bronco was there too.

Ed might need help, Shanks thought, but for the moment, Bud could handle whatever it was. He slipped down the alley, past Ed's window, and turned down toward Main at the Nugget Café. He parked by the stop sign and went across the street.

Vivien was at the cash register, where she took his order for two blueberry muffins and a large coffee to go. Ernesto waved to him from the grill.

"No word?" he asked. "You hear anything at all?"

"Not since last night. They hadn't found her."

"Today they will. Aurey will."

Vivien took his money, and he went back across the street.

Everyone wanted to reckon the loss. It wasn't just Wendell and Martha who needed to know. Everyone needed an answer, a definite conclusion, an accounting. They wanted to fill out forms. But what if no one ever found her? What if she had simply disappeared of her own volition? Run from Finn, from the small town, from the life she'd led. She wouldn't be the first one who wanted to erase the past.

And all this time he was trying to *form* the past. He was trying to create the past out of a few letters Thomas Shanks had written home a hundred years before. He was trying to make things clear—no different from the people in town.

He passed the softball field and the empty swimming pool on the curve and headed into the river canyon. There were more cars on the highway coming toward town, their headlights blazing into the gray light.

Farther down the canyon he hit a stretch of no cars. The road twisted among the sandstone spires, hugged the slow river. His mind drifted. This mission he was on was for Becky too. He'd taken a lesson from her. She had urged him to finish, and he was going to now. He was going to the Indian Museum for her. That was how he thought of it. If it weren't for Becky, he'd have put it off again.

He knew Thomas Shanks had never made any money out of the Sonja claim or the Dusty Dan or any other mine. Aurey would have known if he had. Finally all these things that hadn't happened were adding up. Everything that Thomas Shanks had not done pointed toward what he had.

Not directly, of course. Thomas had been too cagey for that. His letters were made up, but the money was real.

He glimpsed ahead around a curve at a stream of headlights coming up the canyon. From a distance it looked as if a rancher hauling hay was blocking the traffic on the curving road. Shanks slowed, and when he got closer, he saw it was a tractor with Martha Blythe driving it. She had on a Purina feeds cap with a scarf tucked under it and over her ears and a heavy leather coat that he'd seen Wendell wear. She looked frozen to the wheel, grim faced, ramrod straight, chugging along in the John Deere.

He passed her and the fifteen or twenty cars she had backed up behind her. He thought of turning around, but there was no place to get off the road. And what could he do anyway? He could get Wendell drunk and keep him out of town, but he didn't know what he could do with Martha.

The road north of the county line was clear of snow and ran straight on through farmland. The fields here were a thousand feet lower than Gold Hill, and only two or three inches of snow had fallen. Snow still lay in the stubbled corn and in the alfalfa pastures, but in the feed pens the cattle had trampled the earth raw. The drafts of passing cars had blown the road clean.

From a distance the Uncompahgre Indian Museum appeared as a slab of stone in the middle of the desert. It was a low building faced with lichen-covered rock, and it blended into the gray mesa like a nighthawk perched and camouflaged on the curve of a boulder. It was a solitary structure out away from the surrounding ranch houses and trailers.

There were no other cars in the parking lot. Shanks had wanted to get there early when the sun was still spreading its long reach across the fields and dry hills. That was how Thomas Shanks would have known the place: without cars and traffic, without the noises of machines.

The museum was at the edge of what had been the Uncompahgre encampment. From what Shanks had read, he gathered it had been a broad flat field next to the river, and the narrow strip of territory that extended up along White Mesa. The museum was a tourist monument, run by the Department of the Interior as a commemoration. Shanks got out and walked the marked trail, which pointed out with numbered signs the desert plants and noteworthy information: the yucca from which the Indians made baskets, the red sandstone from which they derived colors for sand drawings. A replica of a kiva had been built, half buried in the earth, a cross section cut away to show the adobe construction. A plaque nearby explained the function of the kiva in the organization and life of the tribe.

The exhibits depressed him. They were mementos of a culture, pieces of a great urn which could never be resurrected to give a true account of history. The encampment had not been the site of a battle like the Little Big Horn or the place where a famous treaty had been signed or the birthplace of a warrior. It was a patch of ground maintained by the government, a barren field and a dry mesa from which the Uncompahgres had vanished forever.

2

The woman who opened the museum was fiftyish and walked with a slight limp. "We don't get many visitors," she said, "especially this time of year. School groups, mostly. What can I do for you?"

"I'm looking for a man named Thomas Shanks who had something to do with the Uncompahgres when they were moved out to Utah."

"Was he an agency employee?" the woman asked. "I know most of the names from that period."

"I don't think he worked for the agency," Shanks said. "Are there ledger accounts? He may have made some money. I'm making a kind of inquiry. . . ."

"For a book?"

"No. It's a personal matter."

The woman looked at him. "What makes you think this person . . ."

"Thomas Shanks."

". . . Thomas Shanks, was involved with the Uncompahgres?"

"Because he was photographed with them in Denver on December tenth, 1881."

"We have ledgers going all the way back to before that

time," the woman said. "And you're welcome to look through our photographs. The Indian agency here operated as a clearinghouse. The Indians were registered by number and received their allotments of food and so forth from the government."

She led the way to an adjacent room where there was a display of artifacts—leather leggings and shirts, bows and arrows, arrowheads, spears, axes, beaded moccasins, amulets. In one corner was a plaster Indian dressed up in ceremonial costume and wearing a feather bonnet.

The woman passed through this room and went into a small alcove lined with shelves. "The ledgers are marked," she said. "You can read the dates. And these are the photographs." She laid her hand on a stack of folios on a large table. "Go through as many of them as you like. I think you'll find there's no better record of history than photographs."

"Thank you," Shanks said.

The woman nodded. "I hope you find what you're looking for."

She went out, and Shanks listened to her hobbled step across the museum floor. When she was back at the curator's desk, he found himself alone in the quiet alcove.

It was peaceful there. A wedge of sunlight drifted from the high window and spread out over the table like white cloth.

He was afraid to look, though he did not know what he was looking for. Whatever it was—and he could not imagine what—Thomas Shanks had meant to keep hidden. He had meant to keep it secret from his wife and family, even from George, to whom he had confessed other sins. Why else would he have persuaded George not to come west?

Shanks scanned the shelves of ledgers and found the dates he wanted. The books were dusty, brittle. He turned the pages carefully. Most of the pages contained numbers, items of clothing or food, names of the agency personnel who had meted out the allotment. The names of the Indians appeared in the frontispiece: Dark Cloud, Me-ho-te, Joe Red Deer.

The perversion of the names had already begun. He did not find Thomas Shanks.

The salaries and expenses of the agency were detailed in the back of the book, but Thomas Shanks's name was not there, either, and the amounts, even in 1881, would not have made anyone rich.

Shanks had already given thought to the money. Thomas had mentioned gold all the time, but that was the regular subject of conversation. Everyone knew about gold. But there were other ways to make money quickly. Money was loose in such towns, very loose, and Shanks hadn't shirked from considering Thomas capable of any calling. It wasn't unusual for a man to travel from town to town and set up a big card game. And prostitution was rampant. Either career might have made Thomas loath to reveal to his wife or to his brother where his money was coming from.

But there was no mention of Thomas in the histories of Gold Hill or the nearby towns. Nor did the archives have records of scrapes with the law of any sort. Many other famous gamblers and madams had chapters written about them, and some entire books. A man who made such money as Thomas sent home would have been remembered.

Besides, the tone of Thomas's letters was too serious. He had been cognizant of the precarious economy, and far too anxious to stockpile for a secure future. He was a conservative man, capable perhaps of a sting, but not of running cathouses or operating a big game.

After half an hour Shanks gave up on the ledgers and turned to the photographs. He opened the first folio at random to a page of brown-tinted pictures dated April 12, 1881.

Most of them showed tepees set out in a dusty field with Indians and horses milling about. A dry corral bordered by wooden rails ran along the river in the background. He paged backward and came to a series of photographs of Uncompahgre families, taken not for posterity, but for the information of the agency. Each had as background the agency headquarters—a log cabin with a sign on it that read

UNITED STATES GOVERNMENT. The Indians were seated on a wooden bench. They looked to Shanks neither noble nor proud. They were not savages. They were people unable to choose—stubborn, bewildered, suspicious.

He studied the faces of Joe Running Deer and Dark Cloud. The names were written in hand beneath the picture. Even the moment of the photograph seemed for them an instant of confusion.

It was, Shanks thought, a familiar story with many chapters and verses. It didn't matter the tribe. Creeks, Seminoles, Utes, Sioux, Uncompahgre, Cheyenne. They had all endured the same hypocrisy. A millennia of habitation counted for nothing in the face of a white man's law. The law measured and remeasured the land according to some principle that seemed at the moment to make the most difference. That was how the government proceeded. The Indians were displaced to territories more remote, and when these new lands became valuable, whether as farmland or for gold or, later, for oil, the Indians were sent again to land still more remote.

There were other photographs of the Indians going about their life in camp, meeting with agency personnel or with state officials. These were dated and labeled with a short description of the event and the persons in attendance. These fragments were what the woman had called history, but Shanks considered them only as moments in a long continuum, no more true than that the stars he could see at night were the total universe.

Assembled tribe at Chipeta Agency on the occasion of the visit of Capt. Rafael Greenwood, Colorado Militia, April 25, 1882.

(The trees were still barren of leaves, Shanks noticed. Fifteen soldiers, twenty Indians.)

Chief Red Cloud with State Senator Alvin Roberts and William Benton, C.S. Agency, May 15, 1882.

Review of Indian camp by H. R. Smithworthy, June 3, 1882.

(Smithworthy, in U.S. Cavalry uniform, was on horseback, a saber hanging from his belt. Indians were sitting in the dust in the background in front of their teepees. A man resembling Thomas Shanks appeared in the distance beneath tattered cottonwood trees.)

Allotment of agency food, July 1882.

(There were two photographs. One showed Indians receiving caches of food tins and sacks, with soldiers standing near the agency building and agency personnel seated at a table out-of-doors. In the other a steer had been let go from a stockade, and Indians on horseback were pursuing it with spears at the ready.)

Assembled chiefs prior to trip to Denver, November 14, 1882. L. to R. Lazy Bear, Red Cloud, Broken Nose, Leg-like-a-Stick.

Assembled Chiefs with negotiators prior to Denver trip, November 14, 1882. L. to R. Abraham Cook, Red Cloud, Lazy Bear, Leg-like-a-Stick, Broken Nose, Darwin Owens.

Shanks pulled this picture closer. Right away he knew the man on the right: the muttonchop whiskers, the dark eyes, the high forehead. That was Thomas Shanks. Shanks looked at the face for a long time and then back at the name under the picture: Darwin Owens.

He turned to the next page.

Return from Denver, December 13, 1882. Darwin Owens, Broken Nose, Red Cloud, Leg-like-a-Stick, Lazy Bear.

(Thomas Shanks was sitting on the bench with the four chiefs in front of the log-cabin headquarters. Abraham Cook was not there.)

He studied this picture for a long time. Then he took the

folio out to the woman at the curator's desk and set it down in front of her.

"This man," he said, pointing to the picture, "what do you know about him?"

The woman studied the photograph, then took off her glasses. "Not very much. He was friendly with Broken Nose, who was the head chief of the tribe. He went to Denver to speak on the Indians' behalf."

"As interpreter?"

"I'm not sure his role was that limited. The Uncompahgres had never been belligerent like the Sioux or the Cheyenne. But they wanted to return to their ancestral lands, particularly to the hot springs, which had been of religious importance to them. Of course, by that time Gold Hill was already a thriving town with dozens of mines in operation. The problem was that the territorial governor had promised the mining would be only temporary."

"And this man interceded for them?" Shanks pointed to the picture in the book.

"He wasn't successful, I'm afraid. Have you looked on the next pages?"

The woman leafed through a few pages of the folios and laid it flat again.

Tribe in retreat before New Year's, 1882.

(The photograph showed the barren cottonwoods along the river. The teepees had been disassembled, and the camp was being packed on horses and travois.)

Assembled tribe before dispersal to Utah, December 29, 1882.

(The photograph was of a line of Uncompahgres that stretched several deep across the page.)

Chief Broken Nose and Darwin Owens in caravan to Utah, December 30, 1882.

(In the foreground Thomas Shanks stood beside Broken Nose. Behind them, in the distance, the Uncompahgres

were moving up the mesa in a procession that had no beginning or end. Some rode on horseback. Many walked with
their possessions. The horses were heavily loaded.)

The woman looked at Shanks. "The government at the
Denver hearing decided the Uncompahgres should be resettled in Utah. They were given four separate parcels of land
in the canyon lands and west. There wasn't a transcript of
what was said at the hearing, but the decision was written
down, if you would like to read that. That was the beginning of the Trail of the Wind."

"What did the Indians get?"

"More land. They had a piece on the Snake River, one on
the Colorado, another in the vicinity of Moab."

"But not hot springs or mountains," Shanks said.

"And separate. Though it was more land, none of the
pieces was particularly close to another. The families became divided. The tribe assimilated itself into the surrounding communities or left the land."

"What became of Darwin Owens?"

"I don't know," the woman said. "He's your relative, you
say? The agency closed after the Uncompahgres were dis-
persed and was moved over to Moab. For a time there was a
placer mine on the river not far from here. Isn't it strange
we remember institutions and not people?"

Shanks looked at the photograph again and picked up the
book and took it back to the alcove. The light angled differently now onto the table, and he set the folio down in the
direct sun. He studied the picture of Broken Nose and
Thomas Shanks for several minutes, trying to read into the
faces of the two men some emotion or camaraderie, some
meaning to their parting. Broken Nose's face was as it appeared in his other pictures—lips tightly set, nose askew
and shading part of his face, dark eyes unsmiling and for-
lorn, as if he knew what awaited him wherever he went.
Thomas Shanks's face revealed nothing at all. It was un-
yielding in its silence, though if Shanks had been able to
interpret anything, he would have said Thomas looked
tired.

He folded the sheath of photographs closed and stacked the folios one on another on the table where they had been. He picked up his jacket from the chair and went out.

"Done so soon?" the woman said.

"I think so."

"I'm glad the materials were of some help."

"Yes, thank you again."

He pushed open the door and walked down the sidewalk from the museum. The sun had risen now and had melted the snow from the parking lot and from the surrounding fields. White Mesa stretched away to the west where, miles away, the shale and moraine of the escarpment gave way to the canyon and the desert. It was, he supposed, a land beautiful in its own way—a country different from the mountains, with buttes and deep river canyons and few trees. But it was a place the Uncompahgres had no past.

Ed stood on a chair in front of the left-hand window in his office and gazed out at ground level at the snowplow skimming the sidewalk in front of the firehouse. There was nowhere to put so much snow, so Ned Hatton was pushing it into Ed's vacant parking place. At some point Ed knew he'd have to call the section chief to get the snow moved again, but for the moment, at nine in the morning, he was so overwhelmed by the turn of events, he couldn't do anything.

The helicopter was supposed to have been in the air an hour ago, but he hadn't heard from the airport in Chipeta. And he had just been through a harrowing few hours with Hugh Menotti. He had never seen anything like it, really. He was a small-time, small-town sheriff, born and raised on the Western Slope. The most memorable recollection of his youth was seeing a man electrocuted when the crane he was operating accidentally glanced into a high-tension wire. He'd been to France, of course, but that hadn't prepared him for life, as Sharon was fond of pointing out. He'd led an uncomplicated existence for the most part, rather dull, even for a sheriff.

What he'd expected that morning was a crack squad of

the CSR—ten to fifteen men equipped to the teeth with the latest in winter climbing gear, as knowledgeable as Aurey about the mountains and the weather, and more knowledgeable about human psychology. The Green Berets of rescue was what he'd hoped for. He'd wanted helicopter support with two pilots and some men with bloodhounds. But what he'd got was a mob of undetermined number—at least a hundred, but more like a hundred and fifty—of all ages and skills, ranging from the top-dog personnel of the CSR, including Hugh Menotti himself, to the Boy Scout troop of Chipeta Springs. A Rotary Club from Grand Junction had sent a contingent; some college students had driven all night from Alamosa; the women's cross-country ski team had flown down from the University of Colorado. Every halfway able-bodied person in the county who'd ever known Becky Carlsson had appeared at the doorstep of the county building. Even her second-grade teacher, Jeff Bishop, had braved Lizard Head Pass on a motorcycle to get there from Cortez. It was the biggest mess Ed had ever seen.

He watched Hatton solidify his parking spot with tons of wet snow, and then he got down from the chair and went to his desk for a cigarette. He had been up most of the night, and his eyes felt as though they were filled with ground glass. The smoke made them worse, but he sat on the edge of his desk and smoked anyway. The whole night whirled around his brain like the smoke, a gentle pungent haze beginning with the memory of Paula and ending with the nightmare of Louise.

Sharon had been waiting up for him at home. That had been the start of the downhill slide.

"I called the Little Italy," she said. "Didn't you get the message?"

"I got the message," he said. "I went to look for Neil Shanks."

"All this time?"

"He was out at Lorraine's. He broke in. It's a long story involving too many people—Jerilyn and Homer, Wendell

. . . what do you mean, where was I? I've been searching all over town for him."

Sharon had fixed him with a hard stare without saying anything. Then she reached up and turned off the light. "Where were you before that?"

"Before what?"

"Before you got the message at the Little Italy."

He had felt his heart jump tempo. "Out and around," he said. He started to undress. There was a long pause while he took off his shoes and trousers and unbuttoned his shirt.

"You're just like Louise," she said.

"Look, I want to get a shower and go to sleep," he said. "It's late. It's after midnight. I was thinking. Is that all right? I took a drive to think things over."

"You didn't answer the CB."

"That's right. I didn't answer the CB."

"What if there were an emergency?" she asked. "The deputy is gone, and the sheriff incommunicado. Thinking. What if they'd found Becky?"

"They didn't find Becky," he said. "What's like Louise?"

Sharon sighed and turned over in the dark. "Nothing."

He'd put on a robe over his pajamas and went down the hall to the bathroom. He stopped at Jerry's door and listened. The radio was playing, and he knocked. There was no answer so he opened the door. The light was off and Jerry was asleep. Ed listened a moment to the snoring.

What he wanted and what he got: that was the insidious thing about hoping children would turn out a certain way. It was his own fault, though. He'd hoped to give his children all the things he hadn't had himself, but in the end he hadn't given them the things he'd *had*. He'd wanted them to be superhuman, better versions of himself. No wonder he was disappointed.

He turned off the radio and went out again and down the hall. That disappointment didn't change his wishing Jerry and Louise had been different. It didn't stop the desire.

He washed his face, stared into the mirror. His eyes looked blank. He was too old to be chasing people around town at that hour of the night, too old for midlife crises, too old for Paula Esquebel. Too old to be sheriff maybe. He and Sharon could sell the house. They'd bought it for thirty-five thousand, and they could sell it for eighty, maybe ninety thousand. Live off the interest. Go to France. Aix-en-Provence, Juan-les-Pins. He wouldn't have to work.

He needed a shave. Small black whiskers tipped with gray stuck out from his chin like a porcupine. He opened the cabinet and got out his razor and the aerosol can of aloe shave cream. That was what Jerry wanted: not to work.

He lathered his face, under his chin, his neck, above his upper lip.

"What are you doing, Dad?"

It was Louise, looking through the slit where the door was ajar.

"Shaving. What's it look like?"

"At this time of night?"

"If I want to be elected," he said, "I have to look presentable to the public. It isn't like high school romance."

"It's almost two in the morning."

"Yes, and where've you been? Are you just coming in?"

Louise opened the door. She had on a long T-shirt which said on it SHIT HAPPENS. She'd been asleep. He could tell by the way her eyes slitted in the light. Her curly hair was mashed on one side, loose, too short, in his opinion.

"I heard you and Mom," she said.

"What's that mean?"

"I heard you arguing. You didn't answer the CB. Where were you?"

"Do I get cross-examined by you too?"

"Well?"

He looked back into the mirror and drew the razor down from his ear to his chin. He liked the first stroke of a sharp razor.

"What'd she mean you were like me?"

"She didn't mean anything." He curled the blade around his chin, then made three or four short strokes across his moustache.

"You avoid things," Louise said. "Like now. That's what she meant."

He glanced at Louise in the mirror. She was looking at his real face, not his reflection, so her eyes were averted. "You say someone must have put beer in your room?"

"And you blame other people," Louise said. "Have they found Becky yet?"

"Not yet. You might think about helping out in the morning. We're going to have a lot of visitors in town." He finished shaving the other side of his face, leaning in close to cut the short whiskers around his mouth. Then he ran the water.

"Dad?"

"What?"

"Are you having an affair?"

He was bent over in the midst of lifting water in his hands when she'd asked that question. He'd closed his eyes and splashed the water over his face. Then again. He remembered thinking he was glad she couldn't see him. But of course she could. He stood up and took down a towel from the shelf.

"Are you serious?" he asked.

"Yes."

"What makes you ask something like that?"

"You and Mom don't get along."

"We get along fine." He dried his face, muffling his voice. "We work together. A lot of people who work together don't get along."

Louise leaned against the doorjamb and stared at him as if she were only asking questions to get him to tell her what she already knew.

He turned the water on again and rinsed the whiskers from the sink. He had felt Louise watching him, and he looked at her. She looked away, and then backed out of the bathroom and went down the hall to her room.

That was like a dream now. He still tried to remember whether his voice had been as calm as he'd have liked, as convincing. He had gone downstairs to the den where he had his crystal collection and lay down on the sofa. All those rocks were such exact shapes, formed by pressure and evaporation, subtly colored, but precise. He'd dreamed of Paula.

He had slept only a few hours, and then he'd got up in the dark and had come down to the office.

Bud and Vicky had come in at six as they'd promised they would, and Ed had got Vicky to take the switchboard until Sharon arrived. He sent Bud out for coffee and sweet rolls. Then Menotti showed up at a quarter to seven.

Menotti had already dispatched an advance team of four or five men with walkie-talkies up to the camp, and by seven-thirty they were able to make a test call. The signal was too weak, so they had to set up the five-watt receiver on the roof of the county building. That would have to do. Ed could get a signal by having someone bang on a pipe from the roof.

Meeker had been the only one in camp when the men arrived. Aurey and the others had already headed up into Wounded Knee, Meeker said. They were going to push to the east through the trees. It was clear, but very cold.

"We need to talk to Aurey," Ed said.

"He's skiing back down at nine-thirty," Meeker said. "He wanted to make contact with the CSR. Him and Lorraine didn't find her last night at the mine."

"We assumed not. Okay, so he'll call?"

"We'll be in touch."

Ed went over the topographical maps with Menotti, who listened to everything very carefully. In real life he was a dentist, Ed knew, and it was no wonder he was glad to go off on rescues. Some thought of him as the Red Adair of mountain rescue, while others claimed he was a daredevil à la Knievel with a wolverine's appetite for press clippings. That didn't matter to Ed. To him Menotti was a calm-looking man, who might help him find Becky Carlsson.

Menotti figured one acre per man under normal conditions, but in the terrain of Bear Creek with so much snow, he was allowing a half acre per man. The Boy Scouts could run messages from field headquarters which they'd set up somewhere in the vicinity of Finn and Becky's camp to the field stations—one at the Divide where they'd establish a sender, and one at the Yellow Jacket Mine. The field stations were critical points, like pressure points of the body. Lose the flow of blood through one of them, and the body went numb. Information had to flow from the camp down to town.

"We've got skiers to work the tundra," Menotti said. "The CSR will be responsible for steep ravines and cliffs. There's a lot of territory that's just hiker's country."

"She was on foot, we think," Ed said.

"It's a big area, that's the thing."

"When's the helicopter due now?"

"Eight hundred hours. But an air search is limited in snow. If she's out there waving her arms, that's one thing. Or walking around. A pilot with good eyes can pick out a lot of details on the ground. But he can't see into mines or through trees or under the snow."

"Well, then, let me give you what we know about Becky."

"Roger."

Menotti had paid attention while Ed rambled on, pointing now and then to the map. He tried to sum up the events of the past two days in some kind of comprehensible fashion. Aurey and the others hadn't had any luck around the Depot or on the ridge where Becky had last been seen. And according to Meeker, Aurey and Lorraine hadn't found any sign from the Divide in the dark. The trouble was, nobody knew where she might be.

"The most plausible notion is that she tracked an elk away from the ridge," Ed said. "Right here where it's marked. Then she got caught in the whiteout. But her psychological state is in some question, though we don't know about that."

"You mean she's a weirdo?" Menotti said. "The psychos are the hardest ones to find."

"She's an experienced hunter," Ed said. "Born and raised

right here in this area. She knows the mountains. What I meant was, she's been having these marital problems with her husband."

"God, one of those."

"Then there's the horse. If she has the horse, she could be anywhere."

"What horse?"

"That's what I'm saying. We have to make a plan that fits all the contingencies."

"You know the girl," Menotti said. "You tell us what to do."

The helicopter had been delayed then, and it hadn't been hard to convince Menotti to go along with another idea Ed had. Aurey hadn't come up with anything, and now that they had some men, they had to explore a little, take some chances. Ed thought that the search team had gone past her. He didn't like to think that way, but the gorge was the most likely place to check out now. What if Becky had come down to camp? She'd have got there either before the snow started or after, it didn't matter. Finn wouldn't have been there either way. She'd taken Toots and had come down the trail. Then it had started to snow, or it had already been snowing. That was where she had to be. "It'll take two men with climbing skills," Ed said. "I want you to search the Bear Creek Gorge."

4

Bud met them at the falls turnout. It was just after eight when Ed and Menotti pulled to a stop beside the rock retaining wall and the chain link fence that kept the tourists from falling or jumping into the riverbed. The snowplow had cut a swath through the turnout.

The turnout was a quarter mile past the trailhead at the point where Bear Creek crossed under the state highway. In summer tourists stopped there to load their cameras and gooseneck over the fence at the tons of water which careened 330 feet into space. When the melt was on, it was a thunderous rush, and it seemed as if you were right beside a huge water slide that you could ride right down into the canyon. But it was nothing now, just a soundless dribble sliding over rock.

Bud had brought up Miller Greer, CSR captain, and right away when they got out of the Blazer, Miller lifted his pack from the back of Bud's car and slung it onto his back. He was a small, scraggly-bearded man who looked like a sherpa. His bandy legs seemed to bend under the load of his pack. He was ready and wanted to get going.

The sun was already streaming onto the high ridges of Potosi and Whitehouse, but in the canyon where they were, it was still dark and cold. They stood for a moment and looked up the narrow gorge.

"The trail runs up there," Ed said, pointing over Miller Greer's head and above the trees. "You can see part of it—that line that runs parallel with the layers of sediment."

Greer nodded.

"Right," Menotti said. "That where you think she fell from?"

"You'll go into the gorge here," Ed said. "See what you see."

The cliff was riffled with color—orange and red and white where the snow had caught the ledges. Different formations of rock blocked out the sun, and the face was sprinkled in shadow.

"How far up do we go?" Greer asked.

"It'll take you to the camp eventually," Ed said. "Go however far you need to."

From where they stood, the gorge seemed to dead-end a few hundred feet above the falls. The walls were nearly perpendicular, the soft stone eroded quickly by the swiftness of the water.

"And this is your man on the walkie-talkie?" Menotti asked, looking at Bud. "Does he know how to use one?"

"Halfway," Bud said.

"It doesn't work halfway," Menotti said. "Look, it's a modified telephone. You press the button to transmit. Then you wait for a second before you talk."

"Sort of like spitting and fucking at the same time," Bud said.

"It's a line-of-sight system," Greer said. "We have to get some lucky bounces off the cliff walls. It may not work too well in the gorge here."

"Then just shout," Bud said.

"I'm going to be in town," Ed said to Bud. "You're my link. Menotti's receiver will be on all the time in case I have something to tell him. Now, if they have something, you send it on down to me."

"To Dixie?"

"She'll get it first on the roof. Then she'll tap the pipe and I'll come upstairs."

"Roger," Bud said.

Greer and Menotti crossed the highway together and climbed the guardrail and the barricade to the top of the falls. Menotti looked like a parrot compared to Greer. He had on a green windbreaker and red vinyl pants and climbing gloves. His pack was festooned with lightweight silver—crampons, snap links, screws for rock and ice. Greer had on a brown anorak and carried the climbing ropes.

Greer led down a quick pitch of scree and snow into the creek, then turned upstream along the slow water. Menotti slipped once and dangled a boot in the cold water.

They stopped just before the first bend to test the walkie-talkie.

"You there?" Menotti called. "Over."

"Where do you think I am?" Bud said. "All the ox are in free."

"I think we'll climb above the creek," Menotti said. "It won't be so icy, and it'll be faster than figuring a way around every pool."

Bud fumbled with the apparatus, and Ed grabbed it. "Take the quickest route," he said. "This may be a waste of time."

Menotti waved a red-gloved hand. In another minute Greer and he had gone out of sight around the red sandstone wall of the gorge.

After he'd settled Bud, Ed headed straight back to his office. He issued a missing persons' bulletin over radio and television that morning, and already there had been a bundle of calls. Sharon had come in and handed him a sheaf of messages, saying nothing at all about the night before.

"These you might want to call on," she said. "Vicky and I are trying to screen the cranks. There's a group of people waiting in the all-purpose room upstairs. They want instructions about what to do. And the helicopter still has engine trouble and won't get here until eleven o'clock."

"Well, shit."

"Neil's here. Maybe he could deal with the crowd."

Ed took the messages and went into his office.

Shanks was staring at a map on the wall—not the topo of Red Cloud Peak quadrant, but an aerial map of the lower portion of the county.

"So how do you feel this morning?" Ed asked. "Where've you been?"

"All right, considering. I was at the Indian Museum."

"You get around." Ed swung into his chair. "We have people started."

"Sharon said there was a crowd."

"It's a circus. And they're still coming. I'd like you to go out front and keep them away from the office here. Will you do that?"

Shanks nodded. "I guess so."

"Tell them to go up to the trailhead and go up to the field headquarters in Bear Creek. Some of the late CSR people can ride up with the helicopter if it ever comes. Send them to the softball field."

Shanks looked back at the map. "What do you know about a placer mine down by White Mesa?"

"There isn't one."

"Not now," Shanks said. "In 1883 or thereabouts. It was somewhere near the old Uncompahgre encampment."

"Aurey would know," Ed said. "And there are some books upstairs you can get. Don't think of that now."

The phone buzzed, and Ed answered. "All right, yes." He turned to Shanks. "Someone thinks he's seen Becky in Pueblo." He motioned Shanks to move. "Take this topo map up with you. You should warn people it isn't a piece of cake to walk in there. We don't want tourists up there sightseeing."

Shanks waited until he was certain it wasn't Becky who'd been seen in Pueblo.

"Red hair, you say?" Ed asked. "She doesn't have red hair."

* * *

At nine-thirty Aurey called down from the camp. Dixie Garcia was monitoring the receiver on the roof, and she signaled to Ed in his office with five taps on a pipe.

Ed had to climb four flights of stairs to the roof.

Transmission was shaky. Even with the big-watt receiver Aurey's voice was intermittent. For a few moments it would nearly fade out, then there'd be a surge and he'd come in clear as the Amphitheater. Then it would fill up again with static.

"Where's Menotti?" Aurey wanted to know.

"Coming up the gorge," Ed shouted, as though shouting could make himself heard. "Wait for him there. Can you hear me?"

The receiver crackled and sputtered, and there was a delay in Aurey's voice. "I hear you. Where's the helicopter?"

"Engine trouble. It'll be here at eleven."

Aurey came on clear. "I'm going to start sending these people up and around. There's no sense waiting for Menotti. I'll make up a team to ski over to Lakeland. And the CSR people can lead a group into Cutler Creek basin. Becky might have gone over."

"I want you to stay in headquarters," Ed said. "You hear me? Once we get the helicopter, I want you there as a linkup with the air."

The receiver blew in static. "You want me to wait?" Aurey asked. "Is that what you said?"

"Wait for Menotti," Ed said. "And when you see Finn, send him down."

"Finn?"

"Send him down. I want him down here."

"He's up with Weedy and Hank Tobuk," Aurey said. "They came back up early this morning."

"The sooner the better," Ed said. "Don't tell him I'm asking." He paused a moment and looked over at Dixie Garcia, who, from the edge of the roof, was watching the children sled down Placer Street. "I have to talk to Finn."

"Okay. Anything else?"

Just then Homer McCrady poked his head through the doorway to the roof.

"That's all I have," Ed said. "As soon as you can. You hear me?"

The receiver crackled. "I hear you," Aurey said. "Over and out."

Ed handed the apparatus back to Dixie. "Keep me posted," he said, "And Bud Saunders might call. Signal down to me, will you?"

"I will."

Ed walked over to the door, where Homer was waiting.

"Any news?" Homer asked.

"Not yet. You look beat, Homer. I guess we all do. We all need to put in a couple of weeks in St. Tropez."

Homer's face was more pained than weary, though, and as Ed tried to push past, Homer stood in his way. "I wanted to say I'm not responsible," Homer said.

"Not responsible for what?"

Ed paused and took a pinch of chewing tobacco from his pocket.

"Jerilyn is taking the paper to Chipeta Springs to get it printed," he said. "She put it together."

"Good for her."

"I wanted to ask if there's anything I can do to help."

"You mean run an errand or something, give someone a bed?"

"I mean I want to do something. Any small thing. Please."

Ed measured Homer with one eye and pressed the chewing tobacco into his mouth. "You could tell me who's trying to set up Neil Shanks."

Homer looked into the sun and squinted. Then he looked over at Dixie Garcia, who had pulled her blouse up to get some sun on her stomach. "If I told you that, Ed, we'd never get another tip."

"Then don't tell me, Homer."

Ed pushed past him into the stairwell and went down to the landing.

"Name some names," Homer said, hurrying after him.

Ed stopped on the next step. The stairwell was dark compared to the roof, and he looked back up toward Homer. "Flash Toomey."

"No."

"Weedy Garcia. He was down here last night."

Homer came down a few steps. "No."

"A man?"

"Yes."

"Hank Tobuk."

Homer didn't say anything.

"Hank Tobuk?" Ed said. "He's the witness?"

"Not Hank per se."

"Per se. Don't per-say me, Homer. Was he the man or wasn't he?"

"He was the one who came to us," Homer said.

"I don't have time for question-and-answer games," Ed said. "I have work to do. You know how many telephone calls I have to make?"

"All right," Homer said. "Flash saw Becky and Neil at the Xanadu, but Hank was the one who came to us."

"Flash told Hank, and Hank told you."

"Yes. We tried to call Flash, but he won't talk. The story is that he was in the theater splicing film right about dusk one night, and he saw Neil go up the trail. A few minutes later Becky followed him. So he went up there himself to see what was going on."

"So what's Hank Tobuk have to do with it?" Ed asked. "What's he got against Neil?"

"I don't know that he's got anything against Neil."

Dixie Garcia appeared in the doorway above them, cutting off the light. She was a dark shape surrounded by blue. "Sheriff, it's Bud calling."

Ed stared at Homer for a second, then said nothing for a moment. "Okay."

He climbed the stairs again. The light was brilliant. The sky was a crucible of blue, and a silver airplane rode a vapor trail high above him in the heavens.

He followed Dixie over to the receiver.

"Yes, Bud? Come in. What?"

"It's me," Bud said. "Stay on, Ed. Will you?" Bud's voice was hoarse, and then the line was empty.

"Bud, are you okay?"

Ed looked around at the ring of white mountains.

"It's me," Bud said.

"For God's sake, I know who it is."

Bud was moaning. "They found Becky," he said. "Becky's dead."

"What?"

"Menotti . . ."

Ed felt his throat tighten up, but he took a deep breath and spoke calmly. "Get hold of yourself," he said. "Calm down and tell me."

"Menotti called down," Bud said. "Can you hear me?"

"I hear you." Ed looked at Dixie Garcia, who was already crying, then away again. "Tell me slowly."

"Menotti called from up above the gorge," Bud said. "He's seen Becky. He's roped off on the cliff where the trail's washed out. He can see her from there."

"I'm coming up," Ed said. "You stay there. Hear me? Stay there."

"Yes."

Ed handed the receiver back to Dixie. "Don't go anywhere," he said to her. "Don't tell anyone anything."

She nodded, still crying.

Then he took a long breath. The plane looked so clean and untouchable so high up like that. There was not any sound. It streamed through air, and the vapor trail just vanished.

5

"I don't believe it," Shanks said.

Ed was taking the switchbacks up the pass too fast, and the Blazer swung wide on the tight turns. Homer was clinging to the armrest on the suicide, and Shanks leaned forward over the back of the front seat.

"Keep quiet, Neil," Ed told him. "Just keep quiet."

Ed picked up speed where the highway straightened along the flank of the canyon, then slowed again when he came up on a line of slow-moving cars. The road was still shaded in the lee of the cliff.

The cars ahead pulled off at the Bear Creek trailhead, but there was no place to park except along the edge of the highway. The road narrowed to one lane. People were milling around, talking, getting on their packs, wandering across the highway to the trail.

Ed turned on the siren and they scattered.

Bud was waiting for them at the turnout for the falls.

Shanks was the first one out. He had a dozen questions he was trying to ask, a dozen answers he wouldn't believe. But he had just cleared the door when Bud grabbed him with two hands around the neck.

"You son of a bitch," Bud shouted. "You fucker."

Then Ed got out of the Blazer in a hurry. "Bud, leave him alone! Bud!"

Ed pulled Bud backward hard, and Bud let go. Shanks tumbled down headfirst into the snow.

"Bastard," Bud said.

"Stop it!" Ed slapped an open hand across Bud's shoulder. "He didn't do anything."

"If he hadn't been in this, it wouldn't have happened. Goddamn it, Ed. He screwed her."

Shanks picked himself up from the snow and brushed himself off.

"He didn't," Ed said.

"Then he's a faggot. What are you, a faggot?"

Bud made another lunge at Shanks, but Ed stepped in the way and whammed Bud in the chest with his fist. Bud stumbled and coughed and caught his breath.

"Jesus, Ed."

"I said leave him alone." Ed looked up the gorge where the sun was full on the cliff. "Did Menotti call again?"

"Not yet. He was climbing down."

Ed retrieved the walkie-talkie from the hood of Bud's Bronco. "This is Wainwright," he said. "Come in, Hugh. Can you hear me?"

The walkie-talkie crackled, and Menotti's voice dissolved into static and then came back. "I can barely hear," he said. "I'm on an overhang above the creek. Can you hear me? I can see the horse clearly now."

Ed jammed down the button. "What horse? What horse? Over."

"I don't know whose horse. It's a dappled mare. The coyotes have been on it."

"That's Toots," Bud said. "That's Toots."

They all crowded around Ed, who was leaning over the fender. "What do you see?" Ed asked. "Over."

"Just a minute," Menotti said.

The walkie-talkie went dead, and it seemed a long time before Menotti came back on.

"I see a bloody horse," he said. "Broken neck, it looks

like. Broken legs." The apparatus squawked and smoothed out. "It's a thousand-foot drop. There's blood all over. I could see the blood from way up top."

"Coyotes," Ed said to Homer and Shanks. "Coyotes! You see what I mean? Coyotes won't touch a person for days." He signaled back to Menotti. "Where's Becky?"

"I don't see her," Menotti said. The static scratched out the rest of what he said.

"What? Repeat."

"I told you," Shanks said in a whisper. "I told you she was alive."

Menotti came back on. "I said I saw blood."

"She's not around. Not anywhere there?"

"Not here. I can see maybe fifty yards upstream and down. If she'd fallen with the horse I'd see her. And she didn't wander down. We could see the creek all the way."

"Up, then?"

"I don't think she could have survived any fall," Menotti said. "I'm going on down to the creek now. It looks as though we can walk from here."

Ed lowered the walkie-talkie and stood for a minute with his arms at his sides. He stared up into the sky, into the blue.

"He said he found her," Bud said. "I swear. When he said he saw blood, I thought he meant . . ."

Ed bent his head down. "It's all right," he said.

"He said it," Bud said. "That's what Menotti said. Listen, Ed, it's Neil's fault, all of this."

"Thank God," Ed said. He was still trying to be calm. "Now, Bud, I want you to go back to town. Tell Dixie up on the roof that it wasn't Becky. Can you do that without screwing up?"

"Ed, listen—"

Ed snapped a fist into Bud's chest. "And after that, keep your mouth shut. That's an order."

6

The sound of the helicopter was a distant, continuous gunfire. It moved up the valley from the north a little after eleven that morning, the whirring blades and the dull green body and the transparent cockpit seeming to emerge from the noise itself. Ed and Homer and Shanks and half the children of Gold Hill watched it hover in the sun above the softball diamond and then descend slowly like an immense insect onto the spot where, in summer, second base was fixed.

The chopper was a Bell JetRanger, lent by the United States Army at Fort Carson. It could carry eight passengers at a time, and Ed had made up a list of CSR people who might get a ferry up to the field headquarters.

Ed had hoped, once the helicopter had arrived, that things would go more smoothly, but it turned out that the JetRanger had a military frequency radio which did not correspond with the emergency frequencies of the walkie-talkies. Ed had therefore devised a system of communications relays. The pilot would call the Chipeta Springs air controller, who would in turn telephone the sheriff's office in Chipeta Springs. The information would then be sent up via the police band to someone in Gold Hill, who would transmit it to the field station from the power-watt sender on the roof. Ed didn't like the potential glitches in the method. He'd already seen what had happened when Bud was in the middle of a message relay.

Ed had a short conference with the pilot, a lieutenant named April Higuera, and the navigator, Richard Bennett. Ed briefed them about the lay of the canyons and the various drainages along the Divide. Everyone figured Becky must have headed east or southwest—those were the lines of least resistance. But she could have gone up and over, straight north into Cutler Creek. It was also possible—anything was possible—she could have stumbled into, accidentally or otherwise, some other hunting camp. All hunting camps they saw should be marked on the aerial survey map and reported. As the day progressed, too, there might be a change in orientation, a wider arc. What might not be visible now under the snow might become visible by the afternoon when the snow melted. Anything out of the ordinary should be radioed immediately to the controller in Chipeta Springs.

"Is that clear, Lieutenant?" Ed asked.

"You betcha," April Higuera said.

"She's on foot," Ed said. "We know that much."

The news that Menotti had found Becky's horse in the gorge intensified speculation among the townspeople about what had happened. People out in the heat of the day—it was sixty in town out of the wind—talked in excited whispers. "She's not dead," Marcia Frankenthal said. "Not by a long shot. She ditched her husband and is probably halfway to Acapulco. I wish I'd have done that years ago."

"Some hunters have her, that's what I think. And if they do, she's been raped a dozen times and murdered."

"She's all right. God is watching out for her. He wouldn't let nothing happen to her when there's all these other bad people around."

"I heard she was in love with some rodeo man over in

Gunnison," one woman said. "She wanted to go with him on the circuit."

"What does the horse have to do with it anyway?" someone else asked. "I sure don't understand this at all. I don't. All of it just makes you shake your head."

Ed didn't have the answers either. He had never been good at picking the tail of an eel to match the head, and he'd spent a lot of money trying. He didn't know how Toots got out of the corral, or if she'd been in the corral in the first place. Not that it mattered now.

There were still dozens of telephone calls. Most of them were about the condition of the roads, particularly over Ptarmigan Pass, and a few were curious whether the body had been brought down yet. But most were from people who thought they'd seen Becky. One woman thought she'd seen her in Las Vegas, New Mexico, in a bus station. Another man was positive it was Becky buying a nightgown in May D & F in the Cherry Creek Mall in Denver.

One call was from Brannon over in Lakeland. "It's me, Ed. Jake. How're you holding up?"

"Fine. Good. We have things under control over here." Ed put his feet up on his desk, then swung them back down. "Of course, we haven't had any luck yet. We just got the helicopter in the air. We found her horse down in the gorge."

"But not Becky?"

"We have a team working their way over toward you," Ed said. "You might keep a lookout."

"Listen, we circulated word around here," Brannon said. "A woman called a few minutes ago. Her name's Esther O'Malley. She says she spotted a hunter Saturday on Sheep Mountain."

"I bet Sheep Mountain had a lot of hunters Saturday."

"A woman hunter. Why don't you call her?"

Brannon gave him the number, and Ed called.

Esther O'Malley wasn't sure what time it had been Saturday, but sometime after lunch. She was sure of that. She wasn't positive, though, that it was a woman, but it could have been. The person had on an orange hat, just like the missing persons report said. She was in thick oak brush.

"How far away?" Ed asked.

"Sheep Mountain is about half a mile from my window, Mr. Wainwright."

"In oak trees, then, a half mile away, through heavy snow."

"I had opera glasses," Esther O'Malley said.

"Merde."

"I beg your pardon?"

"Merde," Ed said. "That means thank you very much in French."

At noon he was hungry, but he had no time to eat. He sent Shanks out to Rita's diner for a ham and Swiss on white bread, a package of taco chips, and coffee black. And some cigarettes.

It had been a long morning, one he knew he'd never forget. He still had flashes of the doubt on Louise's face—or was it certainty? Then Sharon this morning: business as usual. He supposed Louise hadn't talked to her. Of course, the office wasn't the place to hold grudges from the night before.

In any event, he should cool off seeing Paula for a while.

He stood up when Shanks came back and tucked his uniform shirt into his trousers.

Shanks had brought the sandwiches, the coffee, and a newspaper which he held up as soon as he came through the door. The headline read, BECKY CARLSSON ALIVE!

"Jesus H. Christ," Ed said.

Shanks flapped the paper in the air. "Can you believe this? That's where Martha was going this morning. I saw her on the tractor coming into town. She went to Pop Krause's and then right to the newspaper."

"Give me that," Ed said.

Shanks threw the paper across Ed's desk. The subhead was "Krause Confirms Mother's Hopes."

Ed read it aloud. "Otis Ignacio 'Pop' Krause, a local psychic, has spoken to Becky Carlsson, according to a story furnished the *Chronicle* at press time Monday by Becky's mother, Martha Blythe of Pinnacle Ridge. Becky, who had become separated from her husband Finn Carlsson during a hunting trip (see related stories this page) had been lost since Saturday afternoon in the rugged mountains east of Gold Hill. A search team headed by Aurelio Vallejos has been in the area since Sunday afternoon, apparently without success in locating the girl.

"Mrs. Blythe, concerned about her daughter's fate, visited the psychic early Monday morning because she had strong visions. 'I knew Becky was alive,' Mrs. Blythe said. 'She was so close to me. I went to see Otis [Krause]because he had experience in these matters.' "

Ed stopped and put the newspaper down. He stared for a moment at the welter of pipes running across the ceiling. Then he looked at Shanks. "This is what got us Hank Tobuk," he said.

"What?"

"Hank Tobuk. Shit, Hank Tobuk. Aurey said he was up there with Finn."

"What's Hank Tobuk got to do with this?" Shanks asked. He picked up the paper and scanned for Hank Tobuk's name. The other articles on the front page were SHERIFF LEADS SEARCH EFFORT and BLAST CLOSES HOT SPRINGS.

He took the paper from Shanks.

"Maybe it's true," Shanks said. "I could go talk to Pop."

Ed was thinking of something else. "You do that. You go talk to Pop." Then he got furious. He tore the newspaper in half and then in half again. "Fantasy. That's what this is. Nothing. *Rien. Nada.*" He looked at a corner of the torn page. " 'I heard Becky's voice clearly,' she says. Oh, for God's sake." And he tore it again and again and threw the paper into the wastebasket.

7

Aurey was in the high meadow when Finn came down just before noon. Finn was still a half mile away, descending through the aspens with his rifle above his head. There were still leaves on the aspens and with the snow melting and the leaves falling, Finn looked as though he were a prisoner of war coming down in the rain.

Where Aurey was on the south-facing slope, the snow had melted nearly to the grass. The grass was dead, wet, trampled down with the boots of all the searchers who had come through the upper field station. Aurey had taken off his coat and was sitting on it, feeling anxious in the warm sun.

He had already heard from two of the search teams. The Alphas had headed southeast over Engineer Pass and down the Jeep road on the other side. These were mostly hikers, not climbers. They were to conduct a cursory sweep of the south ridge, and then to descend via the Jeep road through several of the hunting camps. When they called, they said they'd found a snowed-in camp at 10,500 feet, just off the saddle of the ridge, where four men from Arkansas were still sleeping off a drunk. The men had never seen so much snow before, and they'd been so scared, they'd stayed up the whole night, drinking all the liquor they had. No, they hadn't seen anyone else. Who'd be stupid enough to be out in that snow?

The largest search group was the Betas, going east toward Lakeland. This team included the ski team from Colorado University, together with ten volunteers and CSR personnel, plus some recreational skiers. They were going to comb the Flats. Some of the skiers would then curve back via the Divide, while the others would continue east, on into the canyons and gullies and trees that gradually filtered down into Lakeland and the Lanier Fork. Beta hadn't found anything, either, but they had barely got started across the Flats. Aurey advised them to spread out wide when they got across the tundra and into Horseshoe Basin and Henson Creek.

The temperature in the meadow had risen steadily all morning, and Aurey had stripped down to jeans and a plain white T-shirt. The melting snow had started a rivulet in the gully beside him, a murmuring rill that collected from the aspen glade and the higher meadows. It was fifty degrees, but at that altitude it felt like eighty.

He could see the main field headquarters below him next to a huge boulder and the helicopter landing zone. Through the binoculars he'd watched the people milling around, sunning themselves, lounging against their packs. Menotti was still shuffling volunteers out onto the trail. Most of these were being sent into the wide band of trees between the Depot and the Yellow Jacket, though the last time he'd talked to Menotti, Aurey had suggested expanding the area to include part of Brown Mountain. It was unlikely Becky would cross Bear Creek and go up the other side of the canyon, but if they had enough men, they could search even the places where she would probably never be.

The helicopter had made two ferry runs, bringing in CSR people. These men Menotti was dispersing to the tougher terrain along the Divide and to the long, more difficult ravines. The helicopter had also done four traverses of the area—twice lengthwise up the main drainage of Bear Creek, and twice across from Brown Mountain to Cutler Creek Basin. On its way back to town it had also done a pass over the Divide. He assumed the helicopter hadn't found anything.

The more he thought of it, the more it seemed to come down to Finn, and he was certain Ed had arrived at the same conclusion. It wasn't that he thought Finn had done anything wrong. Maybe small things like waiting too long at the Depot or not firing his rifle, but it was hard to judge those. But he wasn't coming clean on something.

Finn stopped in the meadow across the gully. He had lowered his rifle now to his waist, and he looked haggard and exhausted, as if he'd been out in the country for a week.

"You going down?" Aurey asked.

"I'm beat," Finn said. "It's the legs. They got enough people running all over here."

"Take a break," Aurey said. "Maybe you should head back to town."

"I am."

"The helicopter will be back in a few minutes. You can get a ride."

Finn seemed barely to hear. He stared down at the main field headquarters and then over at Aurey, but he didn't say anything.

"Did you hear Menotti found Toots?" Aurey said.

"No. Where?"

"In the gorge. I guess about halfway along the cliff at the blowout. He said coyotes were already on her."

"You think she followed me out partway?"

"Maybe."

"Well, goddamn," Finn said softly. He stepped down into the gully and crossed the rivulet on two rocks. Then he climbed the short, steep hill to where Aurey was. "Nothing from anyone else?" Finn asked.

"No. Did Weedy and Hank find you?"

Finn nodded and looked back up into the aspens. "I'll be glad to get down."

"Check in with Ed," Aurey said. "He may have some other news."

"Right."

Finn took off along the edge of the gully and went straight down for several hundred yards before he angled across the bottom of the hill. He was almost running on the slope, sliding, holding the rifle over his head. But he didn't check in with Menotti. He went on past the helicopter landing zone and headed into the trees where the trail led down to the camp.

An hour passed. Aurey hated sitting there, though he knew Menotti was right: they needed someone on the walkie-talkie at the upper station who knew the terrain. When the groups called in, someone had to know where they were and how they might proceed. But it was tedious.

Then he saw Lorraine. He thought at first she was covering the territory they'd already been over. She was combing through the aspen trees where Finn had been, coming down toward Bear Creek. Her pace was dogged as ever. She side-slipped on the steep slope, bent her weight downhill. Sometimes she used her ski poles to keep balance.

He was watching her when a voice came over the receiver. "Gamma team to field HQ. Can you read? Over."

"This is Aurey Vallejos. Go ahead."

"Gamma reporting. This is Greer. We're over the Divide into Cutler Creek. We just jumped twelve to fifteen elk bedded down in the trees. There's a lot of snow on this side." The voice was clear, and then it dissolved a moment and came back. "Not much melt. We haven't found anything. Over."

Aurey shielded his eyes and looked up toward the Divide. Higher up the snow hadn't melted so much, and the ridge glared white. "If she came over that way from the Depot, she'd have crossed a little to the west side of the saddle. Can you see the saddle? She might not have found the trail, so you should fan out into the trees."

"I can see the saddle. It looks from here as if everything

slides off into the creek. That's where the trail is. We'll send one man down the trail and the rest of us will work through the timber. The elk scared the shit out of some people. Over."

Lorraine had worked her way down through the trees to the gully, and she followed Finn's track into the bottom and up the side. She caught her breath for a minute and took off her parka and tied it by the arms around her waist.

"Any word?" she asked.

"Nothing."

"Not from town either?"

"They found Toots in the gorge. That's all. No sign of Becky."

"They found Toots?"

"Menotti did. Ed sent them up the gorge from the road. But they didn't find Becky. Toots must have tried to follow Finn and the other horse out, or else she spooked before and bolted down the trail."

"Maybe Becky was taking her down."

They were silent for a moment, and then, far off, they heard the helicopter droning behind the Amphitheater. It was a muffled sound that grew louder and louder, and when it broke over the ridge it became louder still.

"I thought you were going to check out some of the mines," Lorraine said.

"What?"

"The mines!"

"Menotti wanted me to stay here."

The helicopter passed over them and drowned out their voices. The pilot, dressed in a yellow flight suit, waved from the bubble, and Aurey waved back.

"I'm advising," Aurey said. "And I'm ready to go out if the helicopter finds something."

The helicopter descended the face of the meadow sideways, above its own shadow, receding in size and sound. The rotors whirred gray, and now and then the sun flashed from the cockpit.

"Where is Finn?" Lorraine asked. "Did he come through here?"

Aurey pointed down toward the trees. "He said he was going to town."

"Is the helicopter going back?"

Aurey held up one finger. "One more trip," he said. "That's what Meeker said from down below. I told Finn."

The helicopter hovered above the landing zone, then settled down, and the pilot shut off the engine. The blades slowed, and someone—it looked from a distance like Meeker in his uniform—ducked down under the wind draft of the propellers. The engine died out and the meadow was still.

Aurey looked through the binoculars. Meeker was helping several people out of the hatch, and one of them gave Meeker what appeared to be a newspaper.

"Hank said something to Finn," Lorraine said. "All of a sudden Finn had to get down to town. But Hank wouldn't tell me, and Weedy didn't know. That's why I came down. I thought somebody should keep track of Finn."

"Ed wanted to see him too," Aurey said. "I'll give a call."

Aurey picked up the walkie-talkie and pressed send. "Field HQ to Main Base. This is Aurey. Dixie, are you there? Come in. Over."

A voice that wasn't Dixie's came over loud and clear. "Dixie's off for lunch. This is Vicky. Hi, Aurey, whatcha up to? Over."

"Where's Ed?" Aurey said.

"Shit, I don't know. Why don't you ask nice? I thought he was in his office, but Sharon just came up here to the roof looking for him. I bet he's at the *Chronicle* breaking a few typewriters. Did you see the paper? All hell's got loose in a handbasket. The paper says Pop and Martha talked to Becky, and she's alive."

"Talked to Becky? What do you mean, talked to her?"

Lorraine came over to listen too.

"You heard me, mister. Some kind of telepathy or whatever it is. You know. All I can say is poor Becky. She's missing a real show."

"I want to talk to Ed," Aurey said.

"Well, wouldn't we all? What do you want me to do, pretend I'm him?"

Aurey pressed down send. "I want to find him."

"*You* find him. Who do you think you are?"

"Tell him Finn's coming down the trail," Aurey said. "And that I've had reports from three of the search teams. None of them has found anything. Over."

Lorraine reached for the walkie-talkie. "Let me ask her about my mother."

Vicky came on again. "Is that all, your highness? Over and *out.*"

The walkie-talkie clicked off.

"Damn it," Lorraine said. "Why'd you get her mad!"

Aurey was still steaming. "Her?"

"She said Becky was alive."

"That's what Pop said." Aurey looked at her. "There's a paper down at field headquarters," he said. "Why don't you go down and read it?"

Lorraine held Aurey's gaze for a split second, and then she looked down at the group of people huddling near the boulder near where the helicopter had landed. "I will," she said. And she started down.

She skied on her feet, slipping sideways, her bare arms and her ski poles flailing. Her blue parka kilted up around her waist as she jumped and slid.

What should he have said? Aurey wondered. Was he supposed to agree Becky was alive because Pop Krause had talked to her in the air? He followed Lorraine in the glasses, watching her through the heat shimmer. She appeared wavy, as if she were in a dreamscape and not the meadow. Slender threads of blue, the red-and-white of her shirt, her hair flying. She waved to John Meeker down at the landing zone and called out some word Aurey could not make out.

But his anger dissipated as Lorraine moved farther away.

Why hadn't she ever waited for him? Or was it he who hadn't asked her?

The engine of the helicopter startled him: that stark noise rising out of the stillness. The rotors turned through the air, slowly at first, then picking up speed so they were invisible again, a gray blur. The hatch was still open, and Meeker was waving to Lorraine to hurry.

Then Aurey dropped his binoculars onto his coat and stood up. He started running. The meadow dropped away in front of him, slippery, snow-patched, muddy. He cried out, "Wait! Wait!" But his voice was swallowed up by the noise of the chopper engine. The helicopter revved and subsided. Meeker helped Lorraine into the hatch.

Aurey was still yelling, but no one could hear him. He slipped and fell on the wet grass, banged his elbow on a stone. But he was up again quickly, still scrambling.

The helicopter rose straight into the air, the sun glinting from the plastic shell of the cockpit like the blinding reflection of a mirror. Aurey slid down in the wet snow in the middle of the meadow and watched the burst of light lift and climb away from him.

8

April Higuera made a sweep over the Divide on the way back to town. The country from the air looked so gray and white, Lorraine thought, and the yellow-brown aspens and dark spruce did little to relieve the monotony of snow and rock. And it stretched so many miles in every direction: mountain peak after mountain peak, ridges, valleys of snow, rock where the wind had blown it clean or it was too deep for snow to settle. They whirled past the west summit of Red Cloud Peak, down into Cutler Creek Basin. Below them she could see men on the ground, making their way through the dense trees—specks of red or yellow or orange.

Overhead the sky was brushed with cirrus drifts, smooth wisps of white. But to the west, far away, more gray clouds had banked up against the horizon.

"A new front?" Lorraine asked April Higuera.

"A weak one," April said. "It won't get here till nightfall, and we'll have Becky out of here by then."

The newspaper said Becky was alive. Her mother and Pop had talked to Becky, but that was not the same as seeing her. Lorraine had never known what to make of Pop. He was an eerie-looking man with bushy gray hair and a beard. His leathered face seemed to hide his eyes, which peered from beneath bushy gray eyebrows. He said he was descended from the daughter of an Uncompahgre medicine man. But she had never known whether to believe him.

Pop had always been kind to her mother. Lorraine remembered taking Martha in the truck to Pop's shack when Becky refused to do it. Lorraine sat outside in the cab and did her homework to country music. It was a cycle her mother went through—a slow sinking into quicksand that took weeks. At the end of the time, she'd get up at night and stand in the window and speak to Toby, and they'd know she wanted to go to see Pop. Pop made her feel better. That was what they all accepted. He would put her in touch with Toby, and she would come back home more cheerful, almost sane.

She'd read about Bridey Murphy. And there was another case of a woman who had never left her hometown of Yemassee, South Carolina, but who had, under hypnosis, spoken a dialect of German which a scholar identified as prevalent in eighteenth-century Austria. And there were the miracles of faith healing and religious conversion and tales of people whose hearts had stopped who talked of floating in the air, seeing themselves down below.

Lorraine had neither believed nor disbelieved. She had merely accepted the consequences. That was how she lived her own life still. She lived with the choices she had made and the consequences she could not control.

The helicopter came down over the Bridge to Heaven, a bare flank of snow, and across the red sandstone cliffs toward the softball field. Lorraine was surprised, watching the town come closer, how small it was, how arranged it seemed on the hillside. The streets and houses which seemed from the ground so haphazardly placed looked from the air like packages neatly wrapped.

She scanned for Christopher among the children near the field. There was a small knot of them throwing snowballs near the entrance to the park and another group of teenagers loitering at the pool house, which was closed. The children had built a dozen snowmen and snow forts, and someone had sculpted what looked like a Loch Ness monster surfacing from the field.

Second base, where they landed, was a sea of mud. The snow had been trampled, melted, rutted, and she was careful when she stepped down. The last of the CSR people helped her through the mud. April Higuera idled the engine.

Then the helicopter lifted off again, its shadow moving over the muddy diamond and back up the cliff. The noise went away from her like a motorcycle going around a curve.

She had hoped someone from Ed's office would be there —either Ed himself, or Neil—so she could get her car. But no one was there except the children. She recognized Jason among the ones throwing snowballs.

"Jason, where's Christopher?"

Jason paused in his personal war. "He went to his grandmother's."

"Where's your mother? Does she know you're here? Did she take him out there?"

"She's at the sheriff's office. I ran away." He threw a snowball high into the air in her direction and it splattered on the ground. "Don't rat on me, or I'll hate you." He packed another snowball.

"She'll want to know where you are."

"Just tell her to come get me, then," Jason said. "I want a ride home."

Lorraine shouldered her day pack and climbed the path toward the sidewalk. It wasn't far into town, but the sidewalk sloped up the whole way. Just past the Nugget, where the climb leveled out, she ran into Bud Saunders.

He lumbered toward her along the storefronts, a heavy man in a down vest and baggy jeans and a gleaming gold belt buckle. "Hey, Lorraine," he said. "How're you?"

"I'm okay."

"Sheriff needs to see you," he said. "He wants to see everybody all of a sudden."

"I want to see him," Lorraine said. "What's this I hear about Christopher's being out at Pinnacle Ridge?"

"Don't look at me," Bud said. "That's Neil Shanks. The man has got a talent for messing up. I guess he took Chris out there while we were up the mountain. Vicky didn't know any better. Neil just took him."

"Vicky must have said it was all right."

"And after that he got drunk and broke into your place. Me and Ed found him there last night around midnight."

"Broke in for what?"

"You think I'm a mind reader? He's a pervert and a scuzzball, that's for what. He sure as hell knew you weren't there."

"What'd he say, though? What reason did he give?"

"He was drunk. That's his reason. And now I got to find Finn. It's all Neil's fault. This whole thing. Finn was supposed to show up in town, but he hasn't and now Ed says find him. Bring him in, he says. I thought he was the sheriff around here."

"Aurey said Finn went down the trail."

"Well, I ain't seen him or his truck. I was just going to check the Nugget."

Lorraine looked up Main toward the county building. "Is Ed in his office?"

"He was," Bud said. "That don't mean he still is." He scratched his head. "Where would you go if you were Finn?"

"I might go home to sleep."

"Not Finn. I been there already." He looked sideways at Lorraine. "You think Becky left Finn?" he asked. "You Blythes have got a history of that."

Bud smiled, but Lorraine didn't think it was funny. "I don't know what Becky would do, but it isn't any of your business."

"I know that. I'm sorry, Lorraine. Neil isn't much to leave Finn for anyway. I'll say that. He's a scumbag, that's for sure. Comes into town and sets himself up to buy and sell a few businesses. When he sells that store he's going to have a pile of cash. Finds someone's wife to brainwash with those books. That's my idea. You can't trust somebody who reads like that."

Lorraine tried to ring up Pinnacle Ridge from the pay phone at the pharmacy, but there was no answer. She dialed again and let the phone ring and ring.

Then she went up to the sheriff's office.

There were TV cameras around the entrance to the county building—Channels 2 and 9 from Chipeta Springs and Channel 5 from Grand Junction—and reporters from several newspapers. Charlie Fernsten was stationed at the door of the building to keep them outside.

Lorraine had no problem getting through the crowd and past Fernsten.

"Who's that? What'd she get in for? Is she with the search? Who is she?"

"No comment," Fernsten said.

Lorraine went down the stairs to Ed's office. The dispatcher's desk was a cubbyhole whose space was taken up by a bank of telephone and electrical equipment. Sharon was on the line when Lorraine came in, and she waved Lorraine through to the inside.

Ed was at his desk writing something down, and Neil sat in a chair against the wall, reading. "Oh, it's you," Ed said. "Good."

"I saw the reporters," Lorraine said. "What's happened?"

"Zero," Ed said. *"Rien de tout.* It's publicity. I can't even move anymore. I had to send Bud out after Finn, and I know he's going to do something drastic. I know it. Why can't I have Meeker down here now to hog-tie Finn?" He looked at Lorraine. "I guess you heard about Toots."

"Yes."

"Did you see the *Chronicle* too?"

Lorraine nodded.

"Isn't that a sensation right up to the minute? That's why

these other jokers are here. Your mother only talked to Pop this morning."

"Who brought her in?"

"She drove the tractor," Shanks said. "I saw her coming up the canyon with ten or fifteen cars behind her. It never occurred to me she'd go to Pop Krause or to the Mc-Cradys."

"It puts the pressure on me," Ed said. "We're doing what we can, but that headline begs us to find her. I'm writing down something here—a statement to give to the piranhas—" He stopped. "How are you feeling, Lorraine? Have you talked to your parents?"

"Not yet. I called, but no one answered. I want to drive out there."

"Maybe Neil can take you," Ed said. "He has some explaining to do anyway."

She glanced at Neil. "I heard from Bud."

Ed coughed and cleared his throat. "You can press charges if you like. It sounded innocent enough to me at the time. He says he was drunk and afraid to drive. I can vouch for the drunk part. So will your father. They were together out at Pinnacle Ridge. But it's still a crime to break and enter. I thought maybe you'd like to hear his side."

"I would," Lorraine said. "But first I want to know whether Christopher is all right."

"He was all right this morning," Ed said. "I talked to Wendell."

"It was my idea to take him out there," Shanks said. "I was trying to dissuade Wendell from coming into town, and Christopher had wanted to go."

"I remember that. And I try to keep him away from there."

Shanks nodded. "Maybe you should let him go out more often."

"You can decide later about the charges," Ed said.

"No charges," Lorraine said. "It's done."

"Good. Now, let's think about these reporters out there. If I make a statement maybe I'll get some room to move. I can't stand this office anymore. If I have to stay in this room another half hour I'll have a heatstroke." He stood up and wiped his forehead with a handkerchief. "All right, listen to this." He looked down at the papers and shuffled them around. "I'll say we're still looking. That much is safe. We're thankful for all the help the people have given. That's good politics. We're grateful for their generous support. We want to express our thanks to the Colorado Search and Rescue, the United States Army, the Rotary Club." He looked up. "But I don't want to answer any questions about Finn."

"Nobody asked anything about Finn," Shanks said.

Ed mopped his brow again and put his hands flat on his desk. He seemed to lift himself out of his chair with just the palms of his hands. "I know what they're thinking," he whispered. "And I can't even *find* Finn. I'm trapped in the steam room. How can I arrest Finn when I'm in here?"

Shanks got up and fetched a glass of water from the bathroom. "Take it easy, Ed," he said. "Drink this. Sit down. I saw man once in Belize who had a heatstroke. It wasn't pretty."

Ed stared blankly and sat down.

"What do they think?" Lorraine asked.

Ed drank the water. "They think Finn killed Becky."

"Who does?"

"Everyone." Ed thumbed his hand toward the reporters. "When I came in here they were all asking whether I'd caught Finn yet. Caught him! I haven't even talked to him yet. They think he's escaped. They want me to set up roadblocks. I haven't got the personnel for roadblocks. I've got Bud, who's a lamebrain, and Neil, here, who's a bookman. This county doesn't have the money for roadblocks. It can't even get its own sheriff out of the basement. Escaped! He can't escape if he's not wanted."

"You don't think . . . ?" Lorraine didn't finish the sentence.

"No, I don't think he did." Ed leaned forward over the corner of his desk. "I'm not saying he isn't capable of some-

thing like that, sometime, in a fit of anger. But I don't think
he would have come down like he did in that snowstorm.
He may be a hothead, but he isn't any actor. He couldn't
pull off what you see on TV, not that meeting in my office."

"Then why didn't he ride down in the chopper with me?"
Lorraine asked. "Why hasn't he come in here?"

"I don't know. He wanted to get his truck at the
trailhead. Maybe that's a reason. I didn't say he would help
us. But I don't think he killed her. Now I'm going out to say
something to these hyenas," he said, "so I can get out in the
air."

9

Shanks and Lorraine went out the back way to the Subaru, and on the way to her place to get her car, Shanks wanted to stop by his room. "You can come in if you want," he said. "I just want to pick up something."

He thought Lorraine would wait in the car. She was tired and sunburned and wanted to get home. But when he turned off the engine, she snapped open her door and got out.

Earlene had gone. The bed had been made and the kitchenette cleaned up and his clothes folded. She had put his suitcase on the bed, with a note attached. *Have a Good Trip.*

"Is that from Earlene?" Lorraine asked.

"Yes."

He made no apologies. There were none to make. Lorraine lifted the hawk on its string, then let it down gently.

"What's that sound?" Lorraine asked.

"Water in the flume."

"Is this the hawk you found that day?" she asked. "The one you didn't want to kill?"

"Yes. That's what I came to get."

She looked around his room at all the books. "It's very neat."

"Earlene cleaned up."

"And you were planning to go somewhere?"

"Michigan," he said. "I'm always planning to go."

"That's home?"

"That's where my family is from."

"And what will you do when you get there?"

"I'm supposed to help in the family lumber business. I should be there now."

"Instead of out here?"

"Yes."

He looked in the kitchen drawer for the scissors to cut down the hawk.

"What are you going to do with the hawk?"

"Take it to Pop Krause." He snipped the fishing line and held the bird with one hand under the breast.

He was ready to go, but Lorraine sat down at the table as if she were suddenly exhausted. She looked out the window toward the alley where the Centennial Restaurant was blowing smoke out into the air.

"Did Becky come here very often?" Lorraine asked.

"Sometimes. Three or four times, maybe."

"Is that all?"

"Yes."

Lorraine got up again and went to the bookshelf as if she'd seen something she wanted. She examined a few titles, then stood by the bed and looked out the side window toward the flume. "Becky used to say you knew things," she said.

"I read books," Shanks said. "That's not the same thing."

"She was impressed by the way you talked."

"I didn't mean to impress her."

"No, I didn't say you did. But she admired you." Lorraine turned around and faced the room. "She'd never encountered anyone else like you. She knew cowboys and hunters and Finn's friends. She knew how to deal with them. But she didn't have confidence in herself. I used to tell her how smart she was and what she could do if she tried, but confidence isn't something you give to someone with words. I think it had to do with the way my parents were, especially after Toby died. Becky could ride horses and rope a calf and hit a softball like a man. And she could hunt and fish. But underneath somewhere she was wanting."

"You make it sound as though she's gone," Shanks said. "She's not gone."

Lorraine smiled, though it was a tired smile. "I know," she said. "I have to go out to Pinnacle Ridge and see Christopher and talk to my parents and tell them she's not gone. Everything will be all right."

"It will be," Shanks said. He cradled the hawk gently so its fragile wings wouldn't break. And when he looked up, Lorraine was right in front of him. He put his arm around her and held her gently. "It will be all right," he said. "Wait and see."

He dropped Lorraine at the A-frame and helped her shovel out her car from under the wet snow. Then he pushed the car out and he waved to her as she drove away. Shanks headed back up the River Road to Pop Krause's. The plow had been through again and had scraped the snow down to the gravel in places, piling it up on both sides of the road in dirty mounds. There was a wall of snow in front of Pop's dilapidated mailbox. Someone had left a sack of aluminum cans hooked onto the mailbox door.

Shanks parked and lifted the hawk from the backseat. On his way in he picked up the cans.

It was colder along the river than it was on the hill in town. The plowed snow was already frozen where it was, and Shanks climbed over the rim of snow and went up Pop's unshoveled walk to the side porch where the door was open and the screen door locked.

He knocked, rattled the cans, and called through the screen.

There was a deer carcass in the kitchen. It had been skinned out, decapitated, bled, and its forelegs sawed off below the knees. A rope secured through the bones of the hind legs ran through a pulley on the ceiling and was tied off to the drainpipe under the sink.

Pop appeared barefooted in the doorway to the living room, holding a shotgun. His wild hair looked like gray sparks flying from his head. "Oh, it's you," he said. "I thought you'd be here."

He put down the shotgun and unlocked the screen.

Shanks came into the kitchen. There was no fire in the woodstove, and the smell was a dull odor of drying game.

"I thought it was elk season," Shanks said.

"The deer don't know," Pop said. "Me and the deer have an agreement to keep each other alive."

"Like this?"

Pop's beard twitched when he smiled. "I don't let hunters go up on my land," he said. "The deer pay me back."

"No hunters but you."

"I take a weak one," Pop said. "One that'd die anyway. I'm a scavenger. That bird you got there is a hunter."

"Red-tail," Shanks said. "I thought it might be something you'd like. I can't take it with me when I go back to Michigan."

Pop came over and circled the bird. "You didn't shoot it?"

"No. I found it alive. Wendell Blythe said its wing wouldn't heal."

"You should have brought it to me," Pop said. He took the bird and held it in the air above his head. "Come in. Come in."

Shanks followed Pop through a blanket covering the doorway into the living room. The other room was warmer. A smooth heat emanated from the potbellied stove in the corner and flowed through the air. It was darker too. Shanks had been there once before—it seemed long ago now, as if it were a room he had not remembered.

"Sit on the sofa," Pop said.

He hung the hawk up on the light fixture in the center of the low ceiling.

Shanks took off his jacket and settled on the soft cushion.

The wall in front of him facing the street was blank, and Pop had stapled plastic to the window frames. Through the plastic the TVs were a blurred mountain, half buried under the snow. The air in the room seemed heavy, like blue-gray dusk.

"I came to ask about ancestors," Shanks said. "Yours and mine."

"You came to ask about Martha's daughter."

Shanks nodded.

"My people are gone," Pop said. "But I will tell you what you want to know." He stood for a moment, gazing at Shanks without speaking. "Wait. If you have come to listen."

Pop laid a stick of wood in the stove and then went out through the blanket.

Shanks had come to listen. He had come to ask what had happened to the Uncompahgres who had gone up over the mesa into Utah. And he wanted to know about Becky. He had believed the photographs of the Indians marching up the hill with their horses laden with their possessions. But the story in the *Chronicle* had not touched him. He supposed he was like many who thought what could not be touched or experienced or deduced logically from external sources could not exist. Yet he believed in the power of dreams. He trusted the senses to give reliable images of smells and colors and textures of air. In dreams he had lived other places, dimensions which could not be the here and now, though they were places without time. He believed in worlds within worlds, inside and out, larger and smaller, worlds shifting constantly, expanding, compounding. Which world was he in? Which did he glimpse at any moment?

Where was Becky, then? Miles away. Nowhere. In one of the worlds he dreamed of.

The blanket lifted from the doorway, and Pop Krause appeared again, dressed in pale deerskin. His shirt was beaded with turquoise and red beads at the forearms and on the breast, the leggings along the outside seams. He wore a headband which kept his gray hair tight around his face.

Dust floated through a strip of errant light, and the room seemed to grow smaller in the heat. Shanks did not move.

Pop crossed the room and drew the curtains over the plastic on the windows. The room faded further into dusk. Pop stood in the center of the room with his back to the hawk.

For minutes he said nothing, as if he were waiting to hear the call of the hawk behind him. His feet were set apart, his knees bent. His gray hair flowed down the back of his pale leather shirt.

The air tightened.

"We begin with light," Pop said finally. "We are the spring of light." He turned around slowly and faced Shanks. He began a low chant, in a voice reminiscent of an animal's soft whine.

The whine rose, lilted into song, the notes gathering their own inertia. Shanks felt drawn into the rhythm, as if into the current of a river.

Then Pop stopped abruptly. His eyes opened, harsh as the hawk's, then eased. He spoke calmly. "There lived one moon a man of light, a man whose skin was like light and whose eyes were like light, and light flowed from him to his people."

He resumed chanting softly, murmuring.

He stopped.

"The man whose eyes were light was the leader of his people, but there were elders among the tribe who understood the nature of the chieftain's great gift. The elders wished to capture the light and keep it forever. Light was the great spirit. The elder spoke with the chieftain, who wished also to give the light to his people. He consented to give the light if there could be found a way."

Pop closed his eyes and made no sound for a long time.

The room seemed to darken further, as if, beyond the curtains, clouds had blocked the sun from the Amphitheater.

"The elders built a tepee of buffalo hide and the leader stayed in it for many suns. The men of the tribe brought him the flesh of rabbit and the heart of a frog and the cheek of a prairie hen and water from the spring. They sat with him and talked of many things.

"Then the elders tried to contain the light, but they could not. It was still in the man."

Pop chanted like a lute, more music than animal sound. He stopped again.

"The elders put the chieftain in the kiva, which was dark and cool in the ground, and the man of light agreed, believing it for the good of his people. The men of the tribe brought him roots and wild berries and the meat of a bear and water from the spring. They spoke to him through the small slits in the adobe and told him of the width of the sky and the level of the river and how they had hunted the bear.

"Then the elders tried to catch the light from the kiva, but they could not, for it was still in the chieftain's skin and eyes, and it flowed from him into the people."

Pop chanted again, and Shanks stared into the darkness of the room as if it were a cave. The only sound was the music of the voice.

"The elders found a great cavern and put the man of light into it. And this, too, the chieftain allowed, believing it for the good of his people. They rolled a boulder in front of the cavern so no light could escape, and this time they did not bring him food or water from the spring. They did not allow the men of the tribe to visit him to speak of the color of the morning or the sound of the night, thinking that the light must flow and be lost on the voices.

"They stayed away from the cave for many suns. When they returned and pushed away the boulder, there was no light. They called into the cavern, but received no answer."

Pop's voice fell away into soft music, and Shanks stared into the darkness. He began to float in the darkness and from far away he heard Pop's voice calling to him, as if the distance between them were years. Yet the sound carried. Even a whisper was clear in the still air.

He wanted to speak, to answer the voice calling him, but he could not reach the words. He could not speak, though he thought of what he wanted to ask, could hear Pop calling.

A smooth clear lake appeared to him. It stretched before his eyes—transparent, deep, endless. He wanted to bathe himself. The air was so hot in the room. He was dizzy with the heat.

Then he was in the water, felt the cool fragrance of wind which stirred over his skin, the wind whose rippling hid the depth of the water. He sank down, and water filled his mouth and lungs and eyes. In the hawk's eye a faint light glimmered, no larger than a mote in the air. It was suspended above him, and he heard another voice—Becky's—call from far away, though he could not hear her words. He could make out only the voice and the light.

10

Shanks drove the River Road from Pop's to the corner of Prosperity Street. He left the car there and climbed the hill past the Panorama Motel. He was extraordinarily happy. The air was crisp and cold, and though the sun was gone from the river and clouds had begun to edge over Whitehouse Peak, he felt exhilarated. He was not concerned about the weather now. He was glad for himself and for Becky in ways different from before, in ways he had never conceived of. He was neither cynical nor naive. He knew his imagination had tricked him into thinking he had heard Becky's voice. At the same time his sensations had been as real as breathing the cold air was now on the slope above the motel. His feet broke through the crusty snow in the shadow. He heard the cries of children on the sled hill blocks away.

When he got into the spruce trees, the snow was powder again. It was deeper there, too, and flew away from his boots with each step. Across the river the cliff walls were red, and white with snow, and dark red where the water from the melt had run down. Already ice was forming into falls, which in the morning would be blue verglas.

Nothing was so certain now, nothing so fixed. That was

what gave him such pleasure. Becky had been right about that. There was no predictable future. It had not come to him in a moment at Pop Krause's, either, but rather in the way all things are realized—by living through the days, by accretion, by trial and error. Little by little, if one paid attention, the world sifted down to the heart.

She had taken the risk to flee. Not from Finn: that would have been too simple. She had left the people who knew her and what they expected of her. She was alive. He was certain of that. No one knew where. That was what she had meant to accomplish: to separate herself from the past.

He paused at the rim of the canyon where the trail broke down to the Xanadu. Through the mist he could hear the rushing river, high now from the day's melt, and downriver through the breaks in the mist, the whitewater swirled through the granite cliffs. Hot water meeting cold air: steam rose from beneath him, floated up the canyon wall, dissipated when it reached the rim into the wider air.

The trail was steep, snow covered, and he climbed down slowly through the mist. Becky, he knew, would have skipped down this path as she had the night in the dark when she had surprised him. But he had been trained to be more careful. He placed each step, dug in, tested his weight. That was how he had been taught, what he had learned. He went at everything cautiously.

He made it down, but even when he was on the smooth rocks at the river, he could barely see the spring. Steam hovered like thick fog across the water. The Xanadu was the same clear pool, green and blue, like a geyser.

The Indians believed in the power of the waters. The hot springs cured not only the wounds of battle and the diseases of the flesh, but also the losses of the spirit. That was what Shanks knew he suffered. Losses: he wanted the waters to heal his fear and sorrow.

He took off his clothes and lay facedown on the warm smooth rock beside the pool. The river roared through the canyon, echoed from the walls above him. He felt the cold spray of the river like cuts of ice on his skin. Becky was there. He could feel her all around him.

He did not know how long he lay on the rock, whether minutes or hours. Clouds had covered the V of the canyon above him with a steel gray. He wondered whether he had slept and dreamed.

He edged to the pool and immersed himself gradually into the hot water. Feet, ankles, knees, thighs. He stood on a rock ledge underwater, lifted his hand high above his head, stepped down. Chest, shoulders, neck. He lowered his arms straight out over the water.

When Shanks arrived back at the sheriff's office, Vicky said Ed was on the roof sending a message to Aurey.

"What happened?" Shanks asked.

"The helicopter just called in a report," Vicky said. "They spotted something."

"What?"

"I don't know what. All I know is the helicopter called in to the airport, and we got the message." She shifted her chewing gum to the other side of her mouth. "Why don't you go up and ask Ed?"

"Did Bud come back?"

"He's in the office."

Shanks didn't want to see Bud, so he climbed the stairs to the roof. Dixie Garcia was in the stairwell.

"He told me to wait here," she said. "He said I should keep people out."

"He means reporters," Shanks said. "Did he say what was going on?"

"No."

"Well, I have a message for him."

Shanks pushed on through the door and out into the fresh air. Now that the clouds had moved in, a pall had settled over the town. A few children were still sledding on the top of Placer Street, but not so many as before, and the euphoria of the morning's sun had given way to the prospect of more snow.

Ed was sitting on the low wall which bordered the flat roof. In one hand he held the sender and in the other a cigarette. His posture was bent, and he was not looking at the view. He was staring at a map he had laid out on the tarpaper roof.

"I'm telling you what Sid Towe down at the Chipeta sheriff's office told me," Ed said. "I know what Finn said. That's the report. That's all I have. It looked like something red buried under the snow."

"Where again?" Aurey's voice came through the static. "Tell me where exactly."

Shanks went over and knelt down by the map. Ed had circled a portion of the quadrant in red, where the isobars were nearly touching one another. There wasn't a speck of green in the area, and the only blue was the thin line of Winchester Creek which had its headwaters below Red Cloud Peak.

"Northeast flank, Red Cloud Peak. Do you read me? Northeast. North thirty-eight degrees, by east one hundred and seven degrees thirty-four minutes. The pilot said there was a rock slide there, and whatever it is, is buried on the north edge of that slide. It's steep terrain or they would have landed. You hear me? Over."

There was a pause in the receiver, a humming noise. Aurey did not come on.

Shanks tried to picture the terrain from the lines on the map. He imagined the sweep of mountain peaks, the sky spreading outward, rimmed with clouds, the gently curving earth over the horizon. The backbone of the Divide. White. All the ravines and gullies and forests were white. In that immense white, one speck of red.

Aurey came on. "I hear you," he said. "That's a boulder field. I know the place. All right, I'm on my way. Over."

"Be careful," Ed said. "Check back in. Over."

Ed hung up the receiver, but he still stared at the map. He took a long pull on his cigarette, held the smoke in, crushed the rest of the cigarette against the wall. Then he snapped the butt out into the air and exhaled. "I don't see

how she could get over there," he said. "Here's the Depot."
He pointed to an X on the map and moved his finger toward
the red circle. "There's no line. And it's a long way. She
could never have made it that far in the snow." He looked
up at Shanks. "And where was she going?"

11

Ed went in the back door of the theater through the alley. Flash kept the door unlocked for his customers, Ed guessed, at least up to the second floor where there was another door and where you needed a signal to get in. Someone was there because Ed could hear music pounding through the floor, reverberating in the metal railing on the stairs.

The stairs were poorly lit, a violation he would have to remind Flash about, since the theater had an emergency exit through the back. He paused on the landing, tried the door into the theater which was locked from this side. He knew he should have kept a tighter rein on Flash, but the commissioners hadn't given him the budget he'd asked for. He'd wanted to hire an undercover person—he could think of several people who would have liked the money—but people in town had the idea that drugs only existed in Miami. So Ed had to be content with a few spot checks at the fastfood window which had finally closed, a few searches that Flash always smelled out well in advance.

Ed had already found Finn's truck in Flash's garage. The broom handle had been snapped off getting it under the low clearance, and the bed was filled with snow, but other than that, the truck looked as it always did. There were three or four beer cans lying on the floor of the cab, tire chains loose behind the seat, a matted *Field and Stream* on the split plastic upholstery. The only thing he'd found out of the ordinary was a woman's watch in the glove compartment.

He knocked at the metal door on the second floor with the butt of his pistol, and the music went off. After a minute Flash came down the stairs from the loft.

"Who is it?"

"Ed Wainwright."

Flash opened the door right away. "Hello, Ed." Flash scratched at his halo of dark curly hair, smiled halfway. "You want to see a movie?"

"I want to see Finn."

"You can come in and look," Flash said. "Him and Hank went over to the Golddigger."

"Hank Tobuk? I thought he went up with Weedy."

Flash turned his hands palms up. "They wanted to play some pool. I got a movie to screen before I show it out front."

"What's Finn's truck doing in your garage?"

Flash shrugged. "A parking place off the street," he said. "Seems every time Finn drives, Pork hands him a ticket."

Flash moved aside and let Ed go on up to the loft. The projection room for the theater was up there, along with a reel room where Flash had a splicing machine and a shelf full of silver movie canisters. Along one wall were two sofas facing a white screen.

Ed lifted the screen like a window shade. "This where you saw Becky from?"

Behind the screen a plate glass window looked out south toward the Panorama Motel and Ptarmigan Pass.

"Am I being interrogated?" Flash asked. "Should I call my lawyer?"

"You can call your mother if you want," Ed said. "I want to know whether this is where you saw Becky go up to the Xanadu."

"Yes."

"And you followed her?"

Flash came over to the window and looked out. The clouds had not yet come down low over Mt. Abrams, which was a pristine white cone to the right of the river gorge.

"Where did you get all this?" Flash asked.

"I got it," Ed said. "Let's leave it at that."

"I followed her," Flash said. "I saw Neil go up there first, and I can add one and one and smell a fuck. I don't like to see friends of mine get foxed over."

"Nothing went on," Ed said.

"Right. And my name is Mother Teresa. I was there, man. I saw them."

Ed turned and stuck his face two inches from Flash's. "It was *dark,*" Ed said. "Pitch dark. Lots of stars."

Flash turned away.

"You didn't see them, did you?"

"Okay, so I didn't see them exactly. But they were up there."

Ed kept looking out the window. "They were up there. Yes. Is that what you told Finn?"

"I wasn't going to tell Finn," Flash said. "I remember once when Weedy said something about Becky. Just an innocent remark, a joke about whether Becky was a good lay. Finn jumped across the table and smacked Weedy so fast, no one could grab him. It took three of us to get him off."

"So you filed the information away?"

Flash smiled. "It's all timing. Anything worth anything is timing. You have to know when to make your move."

"And you waited until you saw Hank."

"That's right. I figured Hank was the kind of man who could make something happen."

"Which he did," Ed said, "by going to the McCradys."

"Something like that."

"Tell me."

"Hank had the idea that if the McCradys published a story that Becky wasn't up in Bear Creek no one would go look for her. He didn't want a body found."

"He thought Finn killed her."

"At first he did. When he heard the news Sunday night and found that note. He put it together like a lot of people."

"But now he doesn't?" Ed said. "Is that what Hank got from Finn?"

"I don't know, man. You'll have to ask him. I'm just a movie freak."

The town filled with dark at the same time the searchers and hunters came down from the mountain. Pockets of light were everywhere—windows lighted in motel rooms, restaurants opened, headlights moving up and down Main Street. Ed had left instructions with Shanks to take down Hugh Menotti's recommendations for the next day. He'd get with Menotti later. Of course it depended on what Aurey found up on Red Cloud Peak.

Ed didn't go into the Golddigger very often. He was not a drinking man, and when he was, he preferred a quieter place like the Little Italy where people didn't bother him. As long as the Golddigger didn't need him in a professional capacity, he didn't need it. Besides, he thought he might develop bad habits if he spent too much time in a barroom that was loud and smoky.

The immense mahogany bar was on his left as he went in. It was a piece of carved wood that had been brought up from the Nugget when Ernesto had taken over the café. It had two separate mirrors in it, each four feet high and ten feet long. A hundred bottles of liquor were reflected in the glass.

It was busy for a Monday. There were a few hunters, but most of the tables were taken by college students helping out on the search or the locals who had come in after work. Ed recognized several reporters, too, who had been out in front of the county building.

"Here comes the villain," someone said, when Ed passed. Ed didn't bother to see who it was. He had his eyes on Finn.

Finn was leaning over the rail of the pool table, his left hand on the green felt and his right sliding the cue through the bridge of his fingers. A rectangular Budweiser lamp

spread an even light across the array of colorful stripes and
solids still on the table.

"It's a scratch," Hank Tobuk said. "It'll never go. No
way, José."

Finn sighted the cue ball, his dirty blond hair falling forward over his cheeks. He splayed his legs out a little farther
on each side.

Then he stroked the white ball hard. It hit the striped
yellow nine ball, which caromed from the cushion and back
out into the middle of the table. The cue ball clacked down
into the corner pocket and rolled underneath the table.

"See?" Hank said.

Finn stood up slowly. "Ed made me miss," he said. He
picked up a long-necked Coors bottle from the table where
Hank sat.

Ed ambled into the light. "How was it up there?" he
asked generally. "You get a workout?" He leaned down and
picked up the cue ball from the return.

"It was real shitty up there," Finn said. "But it would
have been a good day to hunt. A super day, if there hadn't
been all those turkeys all over."

"They're trying to help," Ed said. He looked at Hank.
"You made a quick trip up and down, Hank."

"Well, you know, Sheriff, when Finn came down, I got to
thinking I ought to be cheering him up instead of being up
there with the horde. I was worried about him being lonely
and all."

"We all are," Ed said, looking back at Finn. Finn was
bleary eyed from sun and lack of sleep and beer and whatever it was Flash had given him. He looked as if he had been
tagged with a solid right.

"Goddamn, Ed, we been *looking,*" Finn said.

Ed nodded. "I know. I just have a few more questions.
Just a few."

"Fire away."

Ed tossed the cue ball into the air and caught it again.
"Well, no. There are these reporters all around, and I'd
rather not speak in front of them." He pulled a piece of

paper form his shirt pocket inside his coat. "This is a search warrant for your trailer," he said. "I thought we could take a little drive."

Finn didn't say much on the way out. He slumped in the front seat of the Blazer and closed his eyes. He asked Ed once what he hoped to find, and Ed had answered, "Nothing," and that had been the extent of it. Ed had hoped Finn would just talk.

When they pulled up in front of the trailer, though, Finn suddenly came to life. He jumped out and ran inside, and Ed didn't try to stop him. By the time Ed got out and had taken a look at Bo Jack and climbed the stairs, whatever it was that Finn had in the sugar bowl was long gone.

Finn was sitting down on the sofa unlacing his boots when Ed came in.

"I wasn't after the dope," Ed said.

"What dope?"

"That's what I said." Ed smiled and sat down in the La-Z-Boy, though he didn't lean back.

"What's this search warrant for, then?"

"Scare you," Ed said.

"I ain't scared."

Finn pulled off his boots and socks. His feet were white from the dampness, and his heels were rubbed raw.

"You've been up the mountain a long time," Ed said. "Friday, opening day Saturday, all of Saturday night when it snowed. Then out Sunday morning and back in again. No wonder you're tired."

"I'm not tired."

"You look tired. You want a cigarette?"

Finn nodded, and Ed tucked matches inside the cellophane and tossed the pack across to the sofa.

"Did you hear the helicopter spotted something? This was about an hour ago. Something red they thought was buried in the snow."

"Is that so? Whereabouts?"

"Up on Red Cloud Peak."

"Becky's not up there," Finn said.

"That's what I said."

"Not on Red Cloud Peak, not anywhere. Hank's right about that. She's long gone from up there. I know what she's done. She was never lost. She suckered me. That's what she did."

"You don't think she's on Red Cloud Peak?"

Finn lit a cigarette and threw the pack back to Ed. "No."

Ed stood up. "I did get this warrant for a reason," he said. "I wanted to come down here with you to see whether Becky has been here. I knew I couldn't tell. The only person who could tell that was you. Would you do that for me? Take a look and see whether you think anything Becky might have wanted is missing?"

"Hank was here," Finn said. "I know that from the empty beer cans."

"Just look around," Ed said. "Check Becky's clothes, dresser drawers, that sort of thing."

Finn shrugged and got up and walked barefooted down the hall toward the bedroom. One the way past he flipped the thermostat, and under the trailer there was a soft explosion of propane. A fan came on.

Ed followed him along the carpet and stood in the doorway.

The bedroom was tiny, just large enough for the bed.

"You want me to look in her closets?"

"Anywhere," Ed said.

Finn crawled over the bed and riffled through the closet. "I don't even know what she owns," Finn said. He slipped the hangers along the racks. "It'd be hard to tell what's gone. Maybe Lorraine would know."

"What about money?"

"What money?"

"Could she have taken savings, something like that?"

Finn picked up the stack of bills on the dresser. "We were waiting for the lottery," he said.

He went through a couple of drawers. Papers, socks, underwear. From the bottom drawer he emptied out sweaters.

Then he stopped and held up two books which had been folded into a blue cardigan. "What is this shit?" he asked.

He threw one book on the bed toward Ed and opened the other.

"Neil Shanks, Gold Hill, Colorado," Finn said. "This is Neil's book."

Ed picked up the other, which was *Ceremonies*.

"This other one is stories," Finn said. He flipped through and read a couple of titles. " 'Tell Me a Riddle,' 'I Stand Here Ironing.' Books, man, these explain something. These explain a whole lot."

"Like what?" Ed said.

"Nothing."

Finn crawled back across the bed and found some running shoes, which he carried with him to the living room. On his way past the kitchen he got a beer from the refrigerator.

Ed brought the books.

"So tell me a riddle," Ed said.

Finn sat in the La-Z-Boy and put on his running shoes. Then he stretched back. "Nothing to tell. The goddamn son of a bitch."

"Neil?"

"Fucking A."

"Why don't you start with the note," Ed said. He set the books on the orange-crate table in front of the sofa.

"What note is that?"

"The one you left for Hank Tobuk. Vicky found it when she put up Bo Jack. If I recall, it said something about a sugar bowl, and that Becky was pissed. What was Becky mad about?"

"She was always mad."

"But *this* time?"

"She was mad that Weedy and Hank were coming up to hunt."

"Not about the woman at the Black Canyon Motel?"

Finn drank from his beer and looked away. "That was before," he said. "Flash borrowed my truck."

"So what about this time?"

"I don't know why she was mad this time. She's as nuts as her mother. They're all nuts, all the Blythes. You got another cigarette?"

Ed got out the pack but waited.

"Becky was always on me for things I didn't do."

"Like what?"

"Like one time in Junction I came back from bowling, and she accused me of setting up this dope deal. Shit, all I did was bowl a few frames with Hank and watched a half of *Monday Night Football.*"

Finn looked over. Ed threw him the cigarettes.

"Could you stand that?" Finn asked.

"What happened up at the camp?" Ed asked.

"When?"

"Friday night."

"I told you. We had dinner and went to sleep. We didn't even have a fire."

"You didn't talk?"

"Becky was always talking. She never shut up. Even when there wasn't anything to say, she'd keep on like there was. It drove me crazy. You want to know what she said? I'll tell you. I can't remember exactly. That's the truth. We talked about the bet I made with Weedy—who was going to get the first elk." Finn paused and lit his cigarette, thinking. "So we get into the sleeping bags early, right? I figure it's dark and we'd been arguing a little and maybe she'd come over to me. You know what I mean? But no, she gets into her own bag and zips it up tighter than a nun's cunt. I'm lying there on my cot thinking maybe she's playing hard to get and wants me to make the move. But then she starts whispering about some goddamn book! That's what struck me just now. It was something about ironing or something. She goes on like that, whispering, and I can't tell whether she's talking to me or to herself. It was gibberish."

"What did you say?"

"Finally I had to tell her to shut up. She was going to scare the elk doing like that." Finn drank his beer.

Ed considered that. He went over to the window of the trailer and looked across the valley. The countryside was covered by the dark now, but a few lights of the ranch houses shone out from under. "What was she like the next day?"

"Saturday she was fine. She was real quiet, though. We got up early when it was still dark out, and we had a quick bite to eat and got packed. We were trying to be quiet. And it was cold too. We wanted to get moving up the meadow."

"You didn't notice what she took with her?"

"It was *dark,*" Finn said. "She could have taken a couple of dresses and a wad of twenties and I wouldn't have been able to tell. I was getting my own gear together."

"Then you climbed the meadow?"

"We went over that in your office."

"I know we did, but that was yesterday. She didn't say anything? When you rested, didn't you talk?"

"We didn't talk much," Finn said. "Anyway, Becky stayed a pretty good distance behind most of the time. I can't say whether that was her or me. Usually she keeps up, but maybe I was anxious to see elk more than she was. I wanted to have the first shot."

"What about when you split up?"

Finn drew on his cigarette. "We had kind of an argument then, but it wasn't about Hank and Weedy. We were planning how to get through the trees, like I told you, and we agreed about the Depot as a meeting place. But Becky didn't have her watch, so that pissed me off."

"You gave her yours, as I remember."

Finn drank from his beer and slid the can down beside him in the chair. "She had to have some way to tell the time," Finn said.

"Is this the watch?" Ed took out the watch he'd found in Finn's truck and brought it over.

"Where'd you get it?"

"From the glove compartment of your truck," Ed said. "The warrant covers that."

"That's not what we argued about," Finn said. "The

thing was, Becky wanted to take the ridge, and so did I. That was the better place to see from, and elk usually move uphill. We went around about that. She said I'd been leading the whole way. I said she could have kept up. I offered to flip her for it."

"And?"

"She said she didn't trust me. I told *her* to flip the coin. No, she didn't want to. She wanted the ridge and if I went up there, she'd go too. Can you get that? It wouldn't be any use to pinch the elk in the trees if we both took up top. So finally I let her."

Ed thought for a minute. "What can you see from the ridge?"

"The back of the Amphitheater. Bear Creek. Down into Wounded Knee on the other side."

"Into the trees where you were?"

"She couldn't see much into the trees. It's dark timber. The ridge is a little higher, but the trees work right up near the top."

"She'd be above you, though, is what I mean. She could see you, but you couldn't see her."

Finn didn't understand.

"What I'm getting at is what Becky might have been thinking. You wouldn't say she was real angry when she went up to the ridge?"

"She wasn't angry at all. She got what she wanted. But I see what you mean now. She was planning the whole thing out. She left her watch in the truck because she knew I'd give her mine."

"It's possible," Ed said.

"Up at the Depot, when it was snowing like a bastard, I didn't think of that. I thought she'd gone back to camp. And when I got back to camp I wasn't all that worried either. She was holed up somewhere. But the longer she was gone, the more I started thinking about it. Maybe she fell. Maybe she hurt herself. It got dark and I couldn't get the fire going, and the wind was whipping the snow everywhere. I had this bottle of Yukon Jack, and I started thinking how

12

Aurey climbed steadily up the meadow with his over-
loaded pack on his back. He carried the skis and the
walkie-talkie and his sleeping bag and the one snowshoe he
had carried the night before. As soon as the clouds had
come in, the wet snow on the meadow had started to freeze,
and the glaze made the uphill more slippery than ever. His
boots snapped through the crust, and the soft mud underneath gave way. Dirt caked on the waffle soles.

He worked his way up to the crest of the high meadow
where he gave a last signal to John Meeker down at the
main field headquarters. Meeker waved.

The ground had been tracked all day by searchers, and
with the evidence of so many people, the country did not
seem so wild to him anymore. It seemed more like a well-
traveled country road. He skirted the meadow to the right
and went into the aspens where Finn and Lorraine had
come down. The leaves had fallen now, killed by the cold
night and pushed down by the weight of snow, and they
littered the snow like ocher petals of flowers. A hint of elk
musk, days old, lingered in the air.

The helicopter made a pass over the ridge above him, in
and out of the clouds and the sun, apparently on its way

Becky was probably back in town. She'd left me up there
before the snow ever came in."

"We don't know that," Ed said.

"In the morning I was crazy," Finn said. "I was pretty
mad and I thought of my friends down here laughing at me.
I went up and got Bo Jack because I didn't know if I could
get out alone, and when I saw Toots there, I spanked her
out of the corral too. I'm sorry for that. It wasn't her fault
Becky bolted on me, but I hied her out of there, and she
took off through the trees. I guess she went down the trail.
You know about that."

"Yes."

"Then when I got down, nobody had seen Becky. I figured she *was* lost, so I went back up with everybody else. I
thought I'd read it wrong, though she still could have left
me. I didn't know about Neil until Hank came up this
morning."

Ed shook his head. "There isn't anything to that."

Finn nodded. "Who'd have thought she'd go for Neil?"
he asked. He sat forward and kicked the orange-crate table.
Then he threw Becky's watch against the wall.

down to the field station where Menotti was. Aurey expected to talk to Menotti from the Divide.

The clouds had come up within the past hours, and he could not tell from where he was whether they might bank in or dissipate in the colder air of the evening. For the time being they seemed harmless—mostly stratus scudding high over the Amphitheater.

He had never been on the northeast flank of Red Cloud Peak, though he'd seen it from above. He and Raymond had climbed the wall and the cornice on the east, and from the summit they'd looked out over the slide and Winchester Gulch and Pinnacle Ridge to the northeast. The slide had run eons ago, a massive break from the summit which had left boulders strewn for two square miles below the wall and all the way down to the lip of Winchester Gulch.

Winchester Gulch was rock and scree and clay cliffs dropping off into nothing. It had been badly eroded into a myriad of small gullies and ravines which petered out miles down into Difficulty Creek. If Becky had tracked an elk in that direction, she'd have had to cross the Divide, and he couldn't imagine an elk's heading northeast into the slide when it could just as easily cut to the northwest and into the dark timber in Cutler Creek. On the other hand, an animal was prone to err, too, and a bull could panic.

There wasn't much red that occurred naturally in the high country. Down lower there were pine grosbeaks and purple finches and sometimes in winter a red crossbill. But the birds of the high mountains had no red on them—eagles, hawks, falcons, pipits, ravens. A ptarmigan had a red eyebrow, visible from a few feet. Rosy finches, contrary to their name, were more brown than red. Deer, marmots, picas, elk, coyotes: mammals had no red. There were flowers, but none that bloomed in October in the snow.

There were other possibilities, though. The red could have been litter blown from somewhere, or a bandana lost from the top of the peak. Most likely it was blood. The only natural red was blood, and blood showed up on snow from a great distance. Like Toots. A wounded animal might have left a trail too. That was plausible. An elk shot in Cutler Creek might have come around that side of the mountain. It would run if it were hit, not knowing where the pain was, and when it was weak it would lie down. Then it would move again. He'd seen a deer once in November, well above timberline, that had collapsed in the snow and had got up six times, leaving a patch of blood in each place. It had died at nearly thirteen thousand feet.

The fresh kill of a marmot or a ptarmigan was the other possibility. That would have been visible from the helicopter, too, and there were plenty of coyotes to do the killing.

Aurey climbed more deliberately with the mud on his boots. He rested at the edge of the aspens and picked at a fresh antler mark an elk had left on the fragile bark. He could not see the field headquarters anymore. The volunteers had already started back down, either to the meadow camp at the headquarters or back to town. No sign. That was the last report Aurey had had. She wasn't in Bear Creek. That was Menotti's considered view.

Aurey continued to the next rise, crossed a plateau of crusted snow which held his weight, then headed straight up the ridge where Finn said he'd last seen Becky. He could already feel the nudge of the ebbing light, and he pushed himself faster. Clouds were swirling lower now, over the Amphitheater and into the back of Red Cloud Peak. He could still hear the roar of the helicopter down in the valley.

He'd done everything he could, but what he had given had been too little. Wherever Becky was now, she was dead. They were looking for a body. That was the fact. Raymond had always said to deal with fact, not illusion. You had the weather, and the rock, and the objective dangers. Those were the obstacles on a mountain. There was no sense making something up.

He heard Raymond's soft voice. "Who knows why we do what we do?" he'd said once. "We can't worry about that. There was one time I was hanging on a cliff all night long, and when I woke up I thought I was dead. I was dreaming I wasn't. I saw the blue sky through ice. There was ice all over me, a sheet of it, and when I realized the fact I was alive, I was so overjoyed I felt I could do anything. So instead of retreating, I went up. I was nearly dead, but I kept climbing."

Aurey did not feel that sense now. He wanted to consider Becky's death apart from Lorraine. He didn't know Becky well. He knew her as part of the configuration of people who lived together for a time and who then broke up into other lives. That was what a family did. He had seen Becky a few times at the gate of the school grounds when he and Lorraine left on a hike. Or he'd seen her now and then in Matheson's or at the Nugget. He had barely said hello.

So why did it sadden him to think of her dead?

His eyes ached from the sun glare of the day, and his back had developed, beneath the pack, a small abrasion where the metal pressed against his shoulder blade. But he could not stop. If he didn't encounter difficulty on the way, it would take him till near dark to reach the slide, and he had to get there before dark. A flashlight would be no use in the slide.

Higher up toward the Divide the snow was deeper than he had thought it would be after a day of full sun. It took him forty minutes to scale the long pitch between the Depot and the saddle of the Divide.

He stopped there and tried to reach Ed Wainwright, but he could not make a connection over the Amphitheater, so he called Meeker on the line-of-sight far down in the bottom of Bear Creek. The valley opened up and disappeared intermittently through the clouds.

"Any more word from the helicopter?" he asked.

"They'll try to stay in the air till you get there," Meeker said. "Where are you now?"

"On the Divide. I'm about to drop over onto the other side, so I called now. What's Menotti figuring to do? Over."

The walkie-talkie scrambled for a moment, and then Meeker came back on. ". . . report is more snow. But it's supposed to move through. Menotti's going down, but some of us are staying in camp. Myself and Weedy and Granny. We'll be here when you come in."

"Good. I'm moving before it gets dark."

The clouds lifted suddenly and the helicopter loomed above him, threading its way through the mist. Then it was gone again, fading into the clouds, into its own muffled noise.

The northeast face of Red Cloud Peak looked like a black wall of smoke. It was a jagged edge of rock and snow, and through the clouds Aurey could see the wind lifting powder snow from the cornice. He planned to take the direct route to the coordinates Ed had given him rather than to circle around the easier side to the west.

A gently sloping ridge led off the Divide toward Red Cloud, and Aurey skied the ridge and then broke off to his right. He wanted to stay high to give himself the best view of the slide, but after a few hundred yards the terrain turned much steeper. Beyond a rock outcropping he scared up two bighorn rams, and he followed their tracks lower and around the slope to a couloir.

Tying into the mountain would slow him down, but on the other hand, a slip would send him rolling a good quarter mile to the bottom of the chute. So he compromised: he tied in at one edge. That was the careful option, and one which could save himself time in the long run.

He had often climbed alone. He had teamed with others, too, mostly Raymond and his friends, but he liked climbing by himself. Some people didn't. Raymond, for example. Raymond liked to have other people around to watch him take risks. What to ordinary men seemed like risks were to Raymond ordinary exercises, but they looked impressive to someone who couldn't do them. He could do anything on a mountain in any weather. He had that confidence in himself. Aurey had never seen him lose his nerve in a tight spot.

Maybe that was the audience. The show had to go on. Raymond was the celebrity, the star, the man-who-would-not-die. But he died. That's what the paper said, and the friends who had written Aurey about the death. They had watched him fall.

He had been unclipped from the belay for a few seconds, making a simple traverse over dry rock. Weather perfect. Clear. No wind. Then a chunk of ice had broken away from above him—not that large a piece, really, but it had fallen through the air a long way. He hadn't seen it coming from above, hadn't heard it. It had struck a glancing blow, just hard enough to knock him off balance. He'd tried to keep hold, but he'd leaned backward that half inch, still with his feet on the rock, and for a moment they'd all thought he would lean inward again, grasp the rock and hold on.

But he hadn't. Couldn't. He'd tipped back in agonizing slowness, and at the last instant had grabbed his ice ax and had thrown it at the rock. And then he fell. It was that gesture Aurey had not understood. If you fell, your only chance was to keep hold of the ax. It was the only tool which might keep you from sliding. Raymond threw it.

There was a second couloir after the first, no less dangerous. On a normal day Aurey would have walked it without a rope. He'd have danced across it. But he was tired now. Slower. Beneath him the couloir fell off into the pale blue snowfield of the gulch—not all that far, maybe three hundred feet.

Aurey banged a piton into a rock at one side and played himself out on the rope to the middle. Then he rapped a wedge into another crack and pendulumed himself down and away to a point lower on the other side of the chute.

He had to climb back up the edge to get a vantage point above the slide.

The boulder field was a chaos of huge stones tossed by giants, a natural disorder. At one moment in time certain forces holding the rock together had weakened just enough to give way. Water had frozen and thawed for thousands of winters, expanded, pushed the stone apart. Air had destroyed it. Air: fourteen pounds per square inch, two thousand pounds per square foot, year after year, for eons. The rock had weakened, and the debris had been strewn where it now lay before him.

From where he was he couldn't see across the rubble. The boulders interlocked with one another imprecisely, forming hundreds of caves, wells, holes, shelters. If Becky had found the slide from this side and it was snowing, she'd have taken refuge here. But the pilot had reported the red from the other side: the north edge of the slide.

He climber higher still and scaled a big boulder to look out. He had hoped to see something which might mark the spot—a flock of ravens rising up from behind the boulders. But all there was was the odd configuration of stones piled one on another, snow-covered or rimed with ice.

A brisker wind had risen, and he couldn't hear the helicopter anymore. The wind drove the clouds hard over the cornice above the face, and he could feel the nicks of snow against his face. No doubt the helicopter had turned back, vulnerable to the weather now, the low clouds, wind, poor visibility, night's falling.

He scanned the gray air with binoculars. The boulders coalesced in the flat distance, and it was not only the clouds which obscured his vision, but the snow. He could not tell whether it was drifting over from the cornice or sifting from the skimming clouds, but it made him hurry even more. He had climbed all that way, and now the red might be covered again by new snow.

He labored over the rocks, skirting the large ones, climbing over the smaller ones, jumping from one to another when he found a series of them that were dry enough for good footing. Now and then he paused and measured the slide from a changed perspective. He did not expect to see anything.

He made time as best he could, scrambling over the boulders, slipping down into a crevice, and ducking through the openings between the larger rocks. Halfway across he stopped again and scanned.

It wasn't red that made him steady the glasses. He didn't see any color. What seemed out of place was the black line.

It was a heavy line, barely distinguishable through the light snow and the dusk, a line which could not have been the edge of a rock or the remnant of a tree splintered in the slide.

He scrabbled forward quickly to a higher point where he looked again. He knew what it was: a rifle barrel angled up into the gray mist.

He jumped down again, slipped, caught himself, clattered with his skis over the rocks.

"Becky!" His voice flew into the air.

He skirted another boulder and ducked through a gap among three large stones.

"Becky!"

The light diminished around him, and he scanned again for the rifle. He had veered too low in the slide and had to backtrack. He took out his flashlight from his pack and shone the beam in a line to the rifle, focusing on a dark space among the stones. That was a landmark he headed toward.

He repeated this twice more until he reached the spot.

The rifle was a .30-30 half buried in the ice and snow, and beside it was a red glove frozen into the crust, dusted with new powder. That was all he found. He dug under the snow, searched the nearby caves, circled a broad perimeter with his flashlight. He called her name a dozen times.

But she wasn't there, not close by, neither dead nor alive.

13

He made his camp out of the wind in a niche between two boulders. The snow had not drifted there, and he rolled out his sleeping bag on the rough ground and set the Primus stove in a hollow spot in the lee of the rock. He had one pot and several freeze-dried dinners and the cheese his mother had given him. The sun had melted the snow at the edge of the slide, and he gathered bits of dead grass and some tinder he found under the rocks. He arranged this under the shelf of an overhanging boulder. A stunted spruce had grown up in the crevice among some stones, and he stripped the dead gnarled branches.

But he didn't light the fire. He knew it would not last long, and he wanted to wait. Instead he climbed up a short distance into the slide and sat on the crown of a big rock. The snow had come down quickly with the night. He felt it against his face and it made a small *pock* on the material of his coat. The wind had calmed.

The boulders around him were great unfinished sculptures, monoliths emerging from the earth with incomprehensible slowness. If only the air were not so cold and the hearts of these creatures would quicken and the blood would flow! The jagged owl silhouetted on his left, unfolding its twisted wing, could shake away the thin mist of snow and take flight. Or the armless woman whose shoulder was turned to him could speak. But their hearts did not stir or catch fire, and the snow drove them into the darkness.

But the coyotes were alive. Their high-pitched barks, muted by snow and clouds, rose from the fading ravine and from the caverns of the slide. They circled and called from different places. Their voices were distinctive. The same one which called first from Winchester Gulch cried out again from the edge of the slide. One would call and another would answer, speaking in mocking voices.

Aurey understood them, and once he called back to sound his own presence.

He had expected to find Becky huddled in her parka in one of the crevices. Asleep. That was what she would look like dead. He had thought of her blue-black skin and her eyes frozen closed and her body hard as stone. She would have gone to sleep.

He had combed a radius of a hundred yards around the rifle and the glove. There were snowdrifts on the east flank and expanses of snow which curved in arcs like fields of white grass. There were crevices filled with snow. He had searched as thoroughly as he could in the waning light. He could not explain why there was only one glove. He had uncovered an empty sandwich bag and a half-full box of shells. The rifle had been fired, but he could not know how many times, nor could he guess why.

He had tried to reach Meeker, but Red Cloud Peak and the poor weather made it impossible. And he could not reach Ed. What could anyone do, anyway, so late in the evening?

The snow was a misty powder which came from within the clouds, a cold dust settling from the air. The temperature had dropped and was still dropping. He could feel it minute to minute. The snow covered the boulders and the legs of his trousers and his boots.

This was not a county for those with a faint heart, but he was comfortable there. He was not afraid of the dark or of the snow or of being alone. He loved the country. But something made him uneasy, and he pulled the parka tightly around his neck and tucked his gloved hands between his legs.

He had believed what Raymond had said about the flame. There would be a time one would know, a moment when the gift would become clear, and a man would see his own connection to the world. But it had never happened to him. He had thought it would happen some night he was haunted at the mine, some peace would come to him. But nothing came. The days melted into one another without progress, without particular pain. He worked hard. The seasons changed around him. He noticed imperceptible differences in the weeks, catalogued the movement of birds, the temperature of the air, the amount of rainfall. He was not bored with that life. On the contrary. He loved the life.

And he had been more successful than anyone else knew. He had found gold. He had been for months stockpiling ore outside the cabin where he lived. Not millions, but enough for himself, his parents, for Raymond, who was dead. One day he would find a reason to tell someone.

He climbed down from the boulder in the dark and made his way with his flashlight to his bivouac in the niche in the rocks. But still he did not light the fire. He stoked up the Primus first, put water on to boil. Even out of the open air it was cold, and he pulled his sleeping bag over his legs. He could see nothing from the opening of his niche: no stars or moon, not even the snow falling.

He ate a ration of hot beef stew and macaroni, cupping his bare hands around the metal bowl. Then he peeled the orange his mother had made him bring. It was sweet in his mouth, cold to taste. He ate each section by squeezing it against the roof of his mouth, then chewing the meat. He ate the peel last. Even the peel tasted as sweet as anything he had ever eaten.

He was not in danger. He was not about to die. The nights of sleeplessness and the days of physical exertion had only made him disoriented. A weakness. He was cold and tired. He set the match to the kindling, and a small flame erupted under the rock. He set in the scraps of gnarled spruce, kept the flame hot with his own breath until the spruce caught.

It was good to feel the warmth of the fire. He held his hands over it, moved his face near. The flame curled blue and orange and yellow against the gray rock. Heat spread into his cheek. He felt it in his eyes. He hadn't known until then that his face was so cold.

In the morning he would search for Becky. With the daylight he would be able to make out a track where she had gone, and he'd follow her. Whatever she had with her couldn't be much—not enough to have kept her alive for three nights in the slide or in Winchester Gulch. Not in the snow Saturday night and the cold Sunday night and tonight. She was dead, or she wasn't there.

He checked his watch by the flame: ten minutes after eight. Early still. Hours to get through. He peered from his cave and the fire illuminated a small circle where the snow was falling. It was too cold to snow much, just a gentle drift over the darkness.

Something was watching him from the dark. He felt it beyond the circle of the firelight, a coyote perhaps which had come in close to investigate the smell of the stew.

Aurey crawled to the edge of the shelter. Wisps of snow touched his face. He didn't see anything.

"Hello?"

He ducked outside and stood up.

"Hello!"

There was no echo. No one was there. No one else could have been there except him and the coyotes which still called from below him in the ravine and above him in the slide.

He shone his flashlight out around him in the dark, but it illuminated only the snow falling lazily out of the blackness. A coyote called again, and Aurey answered it, mimicking the yip and howl.

He took a few steps away from his niche and looked back.

How small it seemed against the immense darkness of the mountain. The small flame flickered in the pitch of the spruce bough, ebbed, came alive again.

That warmth and light would have helped Becky, but it did not help him.

He thought of Lorraine then, how she had looked running down the snowy meadow that afternoon. She was gone from him, but he would live through that too.

He called into the dark again. "Hello!" This voice faded. There was a new weariness in the voice, as if the fatigue in his muscles had carried over to the sound he made. It was a dreamlike voice.

Imagine being ice covered and going up! Aurey could not imagine it. He had his fire and his sleeping bag, and the cold was no worse than a hundred other nights he had endured in the high country. But it was not the same.

And he knew he had come to that one moment Raymond had meant, the instant when he understood what the hardest thing was, and it was not what he had thought. Not weariness or weakness or death or being lost. The hardest thing was love. The hardest thing was not feeling love, and he knew he did not have the flame. He was cold and in the darkness on the flank of Red Cloud Peak at twelve thousand feet, and he did not have the flame.

He stood outside his cave until the fire had burned down to the embers and the snow had stopped. Only a dusting had fallen. Over the summit of Red Cloud a few stars began to shake through the clouds. He could see farther around him. No one was there. No one had been watching him.

He climbed back up to his camp and rolled his sleeping bag and packed his cooking gear into his pack. Then he stashed the rifle and the half box of shells and the glove deep in a crevice under one of the boulders in the slide where no one would ever find them.

He would head north around the mountain and drop down over the Bridge to Heaven and into Cutler Creek. He knew the way, and with the clearing sky, he would have no trouble. He could ski the open country along the flank at least as far down as the trees. And if he didn't stop, he could make it all the way back to town by midnight.

14

Hugh Menotti's press conference was in the court-room at the county courthouse. The high windows reflected the artificial floodlights of the TV crews, and the lawyers' table in front of the mahogany bench had plenty of room for microphones. Menotti still had on his green jacket and red pants.

His first announcement was that the Colorado Search and Rescue Team would not continue to allocate resources to the search for Becky Carlsson. "Our people have had several other requests," he said, "and like any organization, we have limited means at our disposal and only so many men. We made our best effort today, and we feel local volunteers can continue tomorrow. We have two hunters trapped on Mt. Yale in the Buena Vista area and a skier missing near Independence Pass. These calls deserve our attention at this time."

"Do you think Becky Carlsson is still alive?" asked the reporter from the Grand Junction *Camera*.

"I wouldn't want to speculate on that," Menotti said. "The terrain in Bear Creek is extremely rugged, and our time today gave us no leads. But there is always a chance. We also still have part of our team in the field on its way toward Lakeland. We expect a report from them within the hour."

"What about the patch of red that was seen from the helicopter?"

"One of the Gold Hill volunteers familiar with the terrain has been dispatched to the area to take a look. There should be some word tonight."

"Was it a body?"

Menotti beamed a smile. "It was a patch of red."

"How many people are staying through tomorrow?"

"I have no way of knowing that. I'm only pulling out those who are connected with the CSR. I'm certain the local authorities are considering their manpower and the options they have open to them."

"Could a person, in your estimation, survive two or three nights in this kind of weather?"

"Oh, yes. With proper equipment and a knowledge of the mountains, a person could survive."

"But without proper equipment?"

"It would be more difficult."

"So you think she isn't alive?"

Menotti shook his head. "Bear Creek is many square miles of territory, and there is a good deal of snow on the ground. My appraisal is that we covered the ground reasonably well. If this woman were up there, we would have found her."

"If she were alive? Is that what you mean?"

"I mean we didn't find her."

Ed watched this news conference on the television at the Little Italy. He had driven the two miles from Finn and Becky's trailer and had a beer. It was past six and dark outside.

The McCradys had also appeared in the news clip. "We report what's news," Jerilyn said, defending her story in the *Chronicle.* "Becky's mother came to us. We didn't invent the details. They were given to us. What you believe is your own business."

Ed had come on briefly, looking red eyed and jowly. He'd been stunned to see himself with the shirt of his uniform untucked and sweat stains under his arms. He spoke as though he were chewing dried apricots. How many people had he thanked? It sounded like a telephone book. "We're doing everything in our power to find this lost woman." God. He winced when he heard that.

He drank his beer quickly. He was angry at Menotti. Not only was he pulling out his men, but he made it sound as though he invented the search effort himself. He didn't even mention Aurey Vallejos by name.

And he was angry at himself too. He had come across like a small-town sheriff making a pitch for reelection. He disgusted himself.

He asked Rico to use the phone, and he called the dispatcher's desk, hoping to get Sharon. But Neil Shanks was there in the office by himself.

"It's pretty quiet right this minute," Shanks said. "I'm reading some books I got from upstairs. Lorraine called from Pinnacle Ridge. The press has taken a break for dinner. It's snowing a little up here."

"Is Bud on the roof?"

"I guess so. The team from Lakeland checked in. They're camped at Lake Fernanda at nine thousand feet and hoping to go in tomorrow to Lakeland. I told them to check in with Brannon."

"Good. What about Aurey?"

"No word yet. There have been a few calls about the plan for tomorrow. I've been telling people to come in. We need whatever help we can get."

"Tomorrow and the next day," Ed said. "However long it takes. It's snowing here too." He looked out at the snow covering the windshield of the Blazer.

"Did you talk to Finn?"

"He thinks Becky left him in the lurch. He's pretty rocky, I'd say, but I think he'll come around. I left him at the trailer to get some sleep. But tomorrow I'd stay clear of him, Neil. God knows what stories Hank and Flash have told him, and he found two of your books in Becky's bureau drawer."

"I'll stay clear," Shanks said. "What's your plan now?"

"I'm heading out to Wendell and Martha's from here. What'd Lorraine tell you?"

"She says they're doing as well as she can hope for. Wendell wasn't drinking any, and she thinks it's good for Martha to have talked to Pop. Christopher's still there. I guess he's been some solace too. He's going to spend another night."

"Where's she now?"

"Out at the A-frame. She's tired. But she said to call her if you need any more help tonight."

"We should be all right," Ed said. "Things will taper off once Menotti's out of town. And the hunters are busy with the snow. I'll be in to relieve you in a little while."

Ed had another beer. He sat at the bar and stared at the sweat on his glass, the piece of polished wood on which the glass sat. He didn't want to go home. That was the last place he wanted to go. Wherever Louise was. He wasn't that bad. He was good and bad like everybody else, not a prima donna like Menotti, not a hothead like Finn, not a wizard like Neil Shanks. He was just a man who made mistakes and they cost him. That was the bottom line.

He'd make more before he was through too. That was the pattern he'd got into. He hadn't meant any harm. Neither had Paula. He hadn't meant to do anything wrong. If it had been against the law to sleep with Paula, he probably wouldn't have done it. Which didn't make it right either. It wasn't something to be proud of. It was a lapse, that was all. Bad judgment. Sad.

He drank his beer and ordered another.

Rico tilted the mug under the tap and let the beer siphon down. "What is it, Sheriff? You look beat."

"I'm beat," Ed said.

Rico wiped the bar and set the beer down. "Must be getting old, Ed. I don't think I've ever seen you like this."

"I'm getting old, Rico. That's the way of it."

"Shit," Rico said. "I'm kidding, Ed. There's nothing wrong with you that twelve hours of sleep wouldn't cure."

"Maybe," Ed said. "Except I don't have twelve hours of sleep coming."

He stared for a minute at the beer glass with a bit of foam sliding down the side.

Patterns were something to consider. Everybody had them, he supposed. You could look at Finn Carlsson, for example, and say there was a man destined for trouble. He drank in bars and took dope and shouted at his friends and enemies both. He was in no-man's-land, eking out a living for the short term, and someday something bad would happen. Or you could take Rico, moving day after day through his television shows to the grave. Or say, Aurey's friend, Raymond Jernigan, the climber. You knew one day you'd pick up the newspaper and see his obituary. That was what his pattern led to.

And that was what worried him about Jerry and Louise. Patterns. How did they get that way? He supposed he was at fault. He let things ride too long. He thought you could smooth over trouble with a smile and a few calm words, like on the job. Wait and see what happened next. That was what he did. That was his pattern. And if you saw your own pattern and didn't like it, you had better do something before it was too late.

He stared at the amber beer, the smooth wet glass. Then he got up, and without a word to Rico, he went out and got into the Blazer.

A feathery snow blew against the windshield, not enough for the wipers, and Ed stared out into the white rain and the darkness. The Blazer gripped the wet road, slithered a little on patches of ice. Not so much snow had fallen this far north in the valley and the roads were sketchy. Flicks of gravel put down by the highway crew scattered up under his car.

From some distance he could see Paula's bungalow. The

arc light marked the yard and the Ford Escort parked in the drive. She wasn't expecting him, but he knew her schedule, and unless she'd been in town, which she wasn't, she'd be getting ready for her shift at ten. They had to talk. That was what he'd realized in the bar.

He pulled into the driveway and left the motor running and the lights on behind the silver bumper of her Ford.

He got out and left the Blazer door open and rang the bell at the back screen.

"Eddie," she said, "what are you doing here?" She had on a robe, and her hair was piled on top of her head. Loose bunches of it fell down her neck and over her ears. "I was just about to get into the shower."

"Don't call me Eddie," he said.

She had no makeup on her face, but she didn't need it. Her skin looked soft and smooth without it.

"All right, Ed." She gave him a slight smile.

"I can't stay."

"I have to go to work," she said. "I was having breakfast. Would you like something to eat?"

"No, thanks."

"You want some tea?"

He stood just inside the back door, as if he were afraid to come too far into the kitchen.

"Did she find out?" Paula asked.

"Who?"

"Sharon."

Ed looked down at the floor. "I don't know. I think Louise has. I didn't say anything."

"And you think she'll tell Sharon?"

"Don't you?"

Paula looked straight at him. "I don't know Louise."

For a while they didn't say anything. Ed stared at a wall calendar pinned up above the toaster. The days were marked off in large green X's, though he didn't know what for, what Paula was counting off or waiting for.

"I can't pretend it hasn't happened," she said. "Is that what you want me to do?"

"No. I don't mean it that way."

"How do you mean it?"

Ed tried to think of how he meant it. He was too old, was what came to mind. He was too old, for sneaking. Lies proliferated, changed from what was not true to something invented, then to something you began to believe yourself.

"I'm going to tell Sharon myself," he said. "I'm not much for confessions, but I think I have to."

Paula nodded and bit the edge of her lip. "You could look at me, Ed."

He looked at her.

"You want to know about this calendar? You see how I'm marking the days? I'm not pregnant. Nothing like that. I been marking them off for no reason. It reminds me that I ought to be waiting for something. I don't know what. Night to fall, maybe. Day to come. Something to look forward to. That's what you've been, Ed. Something to look forward to."

"I wasn't much," he said.

She smiled, but still held her lip in her teeth. "You were all right, Ed. Nothing marvelous, but all right. You were what I had. You got me through the days. Which are long, Ed. The days are long sometimes."

He nodded, but said nothing.

"I have to get ready for work," she said. "Nursing isn't a profession where you can be late." She pushed her hand up into her hair and held a bunch of it in her fist, then let it loose again. "Maybe it's the hours. Maybe it's eating breakfast at nine o'clock at night. It does something to my head."

"It's a pretty head," he said. "A very pretty head."

Then she floated to him across the room and stopped before she reached where he was standing. "You'll come and see me again, won't you?"

"All right."

"We'll talk," she said. "That's all. We'll just talk. You're a sweet man."

"I'm not a sweet man."

"Now you go on," she said.

She put her face next to his, the smooth cheek against his. Her body gave way into his, and he stroked the hair that was loose at her neck. He held her for a long moment, scared, staring at the calendar behind her, at the large green X's.

15

Ed tried to make the situation appear hopeful to Wendell and Martha. Finn didn't seem to be directly involved. He'd just talked to Finn, and Ed was convinced. There were many people who thought, along with Martha, that Becky was alive. They just didn't know where. That was the impression Ed wanted to leave. Menotti and his men may have left town, but that didn't mean they'd stop looking. She might be sheltered in someone's else's hunting camp, injured maybe and unable to travel. Or she could be in the Lanier Fork–Horseshoe Basin watershed, which included a dozen tributaries. It wouldn't have been too difficult to wander out of Bear Creek and across American Flats. There would be another team going up tomorrow.

Then, too, there were people close to Becky who thought she wasn't in the high country at all, that she'd got clear of Finn and went off on her own somewhere for a while. She'd be back when she was ready.

Of course he would let them know right away about any further developments. If there was anything at all to report, he'd call.

After that chore was done, there was nothing to do but go back to the office. He had to wait for Aurey to call in, and then he'd decide how to proceed in the morning. Neil could help. Vicky's children would be in school, so she'd be available, and Bud too. He expected a drop-off in the number of volunteers. Maybe by half. School would be back in session, and people had jobs to go to. Besides that, the urgency was gone. Everyone knew Becky did not need rescuing anymore. She was either alive somewhere else or dead. She needed to be found. That was true, but she didn't need to be saved.

The snow had nearly stopped before he'd cleared the sandstone spires coming up the canyon toward town. He felt only a little better having talked to Paula, a bit more self-satisfied. He still had to face Sharon, but his stock had risen now. He wasn't asking God for forgiveness of sins, though as a general principle, forgiveness was easier to ask for than permission. He didn't understand what made it such a big deal. If he'd gone fishing for a couple of days without telling her, she have forgiven him, no question. If he'd binged over in Pueblo and lost a hundred dollars at the greyhound track, she'd have been mad, but she wouldn't divorce him. Even if he'd got fired from his job, she'd have stuck with him. So why should she get so upset about an affair?

Or would she care? That thought had scared him too. Sharon had never seemed to him the kind of woman interested in eternal devotion. If he'd died, she'd have remarried within a year. And she wasn't jealous. She'd never issued him ultimatums about other women, not like Vicky Saunders did to Bud. Or maybe it was that she had never given him the credit of being the object of any other woman's desire.

As he drove around the swimming pool and into town, the lights of the town flickered wildly in the air. It was hardly late—eight o'clock, a little after—but it seemed late. The town looked closed up, sleepy, a place the dusting of snow had made beautiful again. The softball field was white, the snow piled up at the sides of the roads was white. It was a town, Ed thought, where someone could live well.

* * *

Neil was asleep on the floor of his office, right under the
whirring fan. He was lying on his parka with a chair cushion under his head and a book open on his chest. Ed wished
he could sleep so completely himself that he didn't wake up
when one of his children came in the house late.

He picked up the book Neil had been reading—*A History
of Placer Operations in Gold Hill and Lakeland Counties*—
which looked as if it would put anyone to sleep. It was
opened to a page on the placer mill that had been located on
White Mesa Creek and the Uncompahgre River, and Ed
read a few paragraphs.

The mill operated here between 1882 and 1887, but it was
profitable only in its early years between 1882 and 1884,
when it was sold to the same New York syndicate which
had purchased the Midas Touch placer claim in Cutler
Creek Basin. The price paid for the so-called Relocation
Claim was an exorbitant $150,000. There is evidence to
suggest the syndicate hoped to establish a large smelter
operation for other mines in the area and was seeking to
buy properties in various districts. The railroad, however,
was behind schedule in laying its track, and by the time
the line was completed between Chipeta Springs and
Gold Hill, the syndicate had gone bankrupt.

At any rate, most of the gold had already been extracted from the Relocation Claim by the previous owners, J. T. Wells and Darwin Owens. It was not unusual for
men to establish a valuable property, reap most of the
rewards from it, and then sell it to unsuspecting Eastern-
ers eager to cash in on the gold bonanza. *Caveat emptor*
was a slogan to live by.

The Relocation was the farthest north of the placer
operations in the Uncompahgre Valley, and also the latest
chronologically. It was a particularly rich find, perhaps
because of the way the river had silted up at the conflu-
ence of White Mesa Creek, which was known from early
days to have traces of gold at its headwaters (see Brian, et
al., 1888). It was logical to assume gold had washed out

to the river, but the obstacle to development of the claim was that hostile Indians occupied the territory of White Mesa for over twenty years between 1860 and 1882, when they were resettled in Utah to the west and south of Moab.

Ed closed the book and laid it on his desk. Neil had been reading such books off and on for as long as he'd been in town, as long as Ed had known him. So far as Ed knew, he hadn't found much. He supposed a man could spend his whole life digging up his ancestors if he wanted to, but even if he found them, what good did it do? What would one do with all those bones?

The telephone rang, and that woke Neil. Ed answered. "Hello, Ed Wainwright."

"Hello, Dad, it's me."

"Jerry?" He sounded drunk.

"I been talking to Louise," Jerry said. "I wanted to tell you this. You are one fucking, lousy hypocrite."

Ed held his breath for a moment. "Don't talk like that—"

Jerry hung up. That was all. The line was dead. Ed was still standing by his desk holding the receiver in his hand.

Shanks stirred from the floor, stretched, got to his knees. "Who was that?"

"A crank," Ed said.

"You said Jerry."

Ed nodded. He put the telephone back in its cradle, lifted his shoulder to wipe the sweat from his forehead. "It's hot in here, don't you think?" Ed sat down heavily in his swivel chair and leaned back. The pipes crisscrossed the ceiling, some aluminum, some iron, some wrapped in tape. "Isn't it funny I don't know where these pipes go?" he asked. "I've been staring at them for eighteen years, and they must go somewhere. They make all that racket. . . ."

He felt dizzy. The room was steaming. He couldn't think. That was his own son, or was it? The voice hadn't sounded right. Would he recognize Jerry if he saw him on the street?

Shanks was up and moving around.

"You can't get away from it, that's the problem," Ed said. "Can you?"

"What?"

"I mean, when someone calls you on the phone, never mind that it's your own son, forget that part of it, and labels you what I would call the worst name . . ." Ed's voice trailed away into thought.

Shanks didn't answer.

"I can take being called an SOB because I know I'm a pretty congenial fellow, at least for the most part. And I can live with being a bastard to some people. You can't please all the people all the time. But the other is true." Ed looked at Shanks. "And what can I do about it when he calls and hangs up like that?"

"Maybe he didn't want you to do anything."

"Maybe. You could be right."

"Do you want me to talk to him?" Shanks said. "I'd be glad to help if I can."

Ed shook his head. "I know you would, Neil. But there isn't any help in this case. It's beyond that now. I think you'd better go on. I'd like to stew here for a while. Go on home, why don't you? Get some sleep."

"It helps to talk sometimes," Shanks said. "If you want."

"Talk?" Ed smiled, but the smile vanished as if he had considered something and dismissed it. "No, I don't think so. Not now. Talking is the thing I'm good at with other people. I can shoot the breeze with the best of them, but here, see, when it gets close to home . . . I could tell my life story to you, but I couldn't go home and say three words to Jerry."

"So tell me your life story," Shanks said. "I have one to tell too."

Ed pressed his lips together and smiled. "I just want to hold down the fort," he said. He stared at the pipes on the ceiling again. "I wonder how to find out where the pipes go," he said. "Do you think anyone knows?"

16

Clouds still hung in the night sky when Shanks left the county building, but it had stopped snowing. A glaze covered the sidewalk. The underbelly of the clouds reflected the streetlamps along Placer and Main, and the soft gray gave Shanks the impression of being inside a world of turmoil, a dream. He wasn't tired, and even if he went back to his room, he knew he couldn't sleep. His mind was as ephemeral as the moving clouds, floating, spinning, drifting. Now that he knew the truth, what was he supposed to do with it?

He walked down Placer through the new snow, glanced into the window of the Longbranch at the corner, where rock music was pumping from the jukebox and out the open door. A silver light reverberated around the bar, and a few people were dancing, caught up in the sound, while others milled at the bar, laughed, drank, told tales. He passed on, crossed the street, and walked up several stores to his souvenir shop. He looked in the window at the display of Ed's crystals for a moment, but he did not go in.

The truth was not supposed to be a problem to be solved. When he had left Grayling he had meant to get a clear version of Thomas Shanks. That was all. He had wanted to understand and go forward. That was how he saw it now, in hindsight. He had even been prepared to make compromises with what he learned. He was, after all, not responsible for what someone else had done a century ago. He might be ashamed. He might assuage his own conscience with gifts to charity. He might feel compelled to do community service or lead himself a more moral life.

But he was not so anxious for the truth as he had thought. He had put off knowing for a long time. Becky had shown him that, but he hadn't wanted to see it. If he were so dedicated to finding out about his great-grandfather, why hadn't he moved faster? Evolution, he said. He had to give himself time to adjust gradually to the new details, to assimilate ideas, to consider and reflect.

"Bullshit," Becky had said. "You don't want to know."

And she was right. That was evident now. When he approached the truth, he resisted it the way like poles of a magnet repelled each other. He had not wanted to know, and then all at once he had found out. He had fallen into the air and could not stop himself no matter how he tried.

He turned away from his shop. There was nothing for him there. He backtracked toward Placer, stopped at the window of the bank. In the window was a diorama of chukars and a pheasant set among sparse tufts of desert grass and wood. Wendell Blythe's name appeared in gold letters at the edge of the sand beside an explanatory card:

Ring-necked pheasant and Chukar *(Phasianus colchicus* and *Alectoris chukar)*

Two gallinaceous game birds introduced to the United States from the Old World. The chukar favors the dry terrain of the western third of the country, while the ring-necked pheasant is a dweller of brushy hedgerows and fields to the north. Food is mainly seeds which are ground up by ingested stone in the gizzard.

Shanks studied the display for a moment and then went on. He turned left down Placer toward the river, and made up as he went his own card:

Neil Shanks *(Homo sapiens)*

Introduced from Grayling, Michigan. Favors bars and taverns, serious reading, sleeps alone (mostly). Food comes mainly from the Nugget Café.

He found himself, in several minutes, on the bridge across the river. He stopped there and looked for light, but the clouds still swirled above the town. He could hear the river running beneath him, the round stones rumbling along the bottom.

Yes, he had been prepared to admit Thomas Shanks's misdeeds. Reading the letters, he had imagined the petty offenses Thomas could have committed in order to consolidate his fortune. There might have been, perhaps, an episode or two which reflected badly on the family. But he had found no mention of the family name.

And yes, he had wanted to uncover the true history, unembellished by the myths of the generations since. He had suspected Thomas of inordinate greed. A clever man would have glimpsed opportunities others had not, would have taken advantage of loopholes less intelligent men would not realize were there. Such were the variations on a theme common for as long as man had existed. Shanks had been ready for all that, prepared in his mind to mark down the transgressions and then to dismiss them.

He had wanted the truth to be useful in this way, to free him from doubt and ignorance. But he saw now he had entertained the possibility of only a certain kind of truth, a truth within limits. He could accept Thomas Shanks as slightly tainted, within the parameters of human error and greed, but not as the monster he knew now.

The truth had been more terrible than he had imagined, more profound than he had dreamed. That was his difficulty: he had visited this truth on himself. On the one hand he had imagined a pale version of history, and on the other he had discovered the darkest reality. No wonder he had been afraid. It was right to fear what could harm you.

What he faced now was a truth beyond words, emotions which could never be summarized, questions never to be answered. He could never know the pain that had died with the men and women who had marched into Utah. He could not know the slow litany of their unwritten days. And who could explain the traitor?

Thomas must have known there was gold in the river long before he had become friendly with the Uncompahgres. At the same time he was arguing their cause he was bartering away their claims to the land. That was the only conclusion to draw. Whether he had adopted the name Darwin Owens to protect himself from his own people at the time or to cover up the crime, Shanks could of course never know. It was no wonder he did not want George to come west. And for his treachery he was rewarded with a fortune in gold, which had been handed down in ignorance from generation to generation.

But history could not be changed, could not be renounced or denied. The dead could not be informed. The Uncompahgres could not be resurrected from the wasteland of Utah and returned to their homeland in the mountains.

Headlights came up the River Road out of the dark trees. He had lost track of time. The clouds were blowing free of the sky, and as they moved, the stars came after. The sound of the river had lulled him, absorbed him, left him weary.

He crossed back over the bridge and ducked down on the worn path children had made to the water's edge. He did not want to be seen. He did not want to be known by his own name.

He hid beneath the bridge like an outcast and listened to the car thunder overhead. It shifted gears at the bottom of the hill, and he heard the familiar whine of a Volkswagen engine. He climbed the path again in time to see Lorraine's car stop at the stop sign at Main.

The taillights flashed red, and the yellow car brightened

under the streetlights as it crossed Main. Aurey must have called down, Shanks thought. And he started back up Placer toward town.

To whom could he explain what he knew? Who would listen? None of his family would want to hear such a story. Thomas was a man of their own blood, a hero. For reasons incomprehensible to them, Neil had unraveled a story he himself did not want to know. What would it profit anyone else to hear it?

Yet if he kept quiet, wasn't he the same as Thomas?

The Amphitheater arched above the town bathed in starlight. He climbed the icy sidewalk to Main. A good number of cars were angled against the piled-up snow on the sidewalks, mostly in front of the Outlaw and the Golddigger and the Longbranch, and farther up where the movie was still in progress. One of those a little way down from the Golddigger was Finn's maroon truck with the broom handle gone.

The truth: that was what Finn needed to hear, Shanks thought. And he needed to hear it from him. He would explain the books. That was a start. He and Becky had shared books and they had talked, but there was nothing more than that. He hadn't been privy to the secrets which made her leave. She had reasons of her own. She had to leave was the way Shanks thought of it, and she would come back when she learned what she needed to know. They had been friends. No more than that. No less.

He looked for Finn in the Golddigger. The pool table was taken up by four hunters in blaze-orange vests and cowboy hats. Earlene was busy at the bar, setting up beers from the deep-well cooler. He waved to her and looked over the tables, but Finn wasn't there.

Then he went across the street to the Outlaw. Drinks were more expensive there, and it was fancier than the Golddigger, but if Helen Howell or Dixie Garcia were working and it was crowded, they usually could slip a few free drinks to their friends.

The air was gray, smoky, loud. The teardrops of the

chandeliers, doubled in the mirror behind the bar, made the air glitter. Most of the clientele were hunters who didn't care that the trout was frozen or the crab legs a month out of Alaska. They didn't care that a beer was two dollars instead of a dollar across the street. The walls were red velvet and brocade, reminiscent of the era when money flowed from the mines the way it flowed now from the tourists. Someone at the rear of the room behind a crowd was playing ragtime.

Shanks spotted Helen Howell at the waitress's station, but he couldn't get in to see her. A group in front of him was waiting for a table to open up. Shanks craned over their heads, but the room was crowded. Jamie LaMotte behind the bar was serving up drinks as fast as he could, and Dixie had just emerged from the swinging doors to the kitchen with a trayful of nachos and dinners.

This was not a good place to talk. Shanks realized that right away. It was too noisy and there was no place to sit. The Golddigger would have been all right. Maybe they'd play a game of eight ball. But not here where they'd have to shout over Scott Joplin.

He didn't see Finn, anyway, though he picked out Charlie Fernsten down the bar. The bar was crowded with drinkers on stools and standing between stools.

Then a table opened up in the middle of the room. The six or seven people in front of him pushed forward, and the group at the table scattered through the floor tables toward the coatrack. The ragtime stopped, and the bar lapsed into talk and the dead sound of glasses being shifted.

"Neil!"

Finn was coming toward him along the bar, holding up a Coors bottle. He reeled along the backs of the people seated at the bar, keeping balance against them. When he reached the waitress's station, Helen Howell caught him by the arm.

She said something to him, and Finn nodded. Helen let him go.

The chandelier lights glinted through the smoke. And the piano started again—some tune Shanks didn't know.

Finn stood in front of him beside the rail where people waited to be seated. " 'lo, Neil," he said.

Shanks could not think of anything to say. Finn's slurred grin took away what he had meant to say, what in other circumstances he could have said easily. But Finn's grin was the same as noise.

The Coors bottle dangled from a single finger of Finn's right hand. Shanks noticed that. *There were no words* was the only thought that came to him.

Finn swung with his free hand. The blow glanced from Shanks's cheek just under the right eye, and the second impact was the beer bottle coming roundhouse from the other direction. It skidded across skin and bone just under his ear. He had no time to fend off. All he felt was the force of being snapped backward and being able to do nothing. He heard Finn yell something, though he didn't know what. He hit the floor, and in another second, Finn was on top of him, flailing at him with his fists.

17

Ed had the blue flasher on before he and Lorraine left the front of the county building. Bud called down from the roof, "What happened?" and got from Ed, "Stay there." Ed backed the Blazer out quickly and called on the CB for the ambulance.

It was only a block down to Main, but driving was faster than walking, and Ed wanted the blue light. He did a U-turn past the Golddigger and came around into the right lane in front of the Outlaw, leaving enough room for the ambulance to park in front of him. Then he and Lorraine got out. A crowd was waiting around the door, some looking in through the plate glass window or talking about what had happened. Up Main Street, beyond the bank and the row of shops, the ambulance siren started up.

It was quiet inside. No music. The lights had been turned up, and in the back the kitchen door had been propped open to clear out the smoke. Shanks was lying on the carpet near the coatrack. Someone had put a towel on his forehead, and Helen Howell was sitting on the floor dabbing at the blood on his face. One eye was swollen nearly closed, and his lip was oozing blood.

"He goes in and out," Helen said. "One minute he's all right, and then he passes out."

"Did you see it happen?"

"Finn hit him with a beer bottle. That's all I know."

Ed bent over Shanks and took away the towel. There was a clean cut above his eye. "How do you feel?" Ed asked.

"Good," Shanks said. He started to sit up, but Ed held him.

"You lie back. We have the ambulance coming."

"Did Aurey call?"

"No."

"I saw Lorraine. . . ." Shanks closed his eyes and lay back.

"I saw it coming," Helen said. "I told Finn no trouble, and he promised, and the next thing I saw is Finn hitting him with the bottle. It took three people to get Finn away."

"Where is he now?" Ed said.

"Took off," Dixie Garcia said. "He and Hank."

Ed stood up. "What does Hank drive?"

"A Ford truck," Helen said. "Red and white."

"It happened real fast," Dixie said. "No one knew what to do."

The ambulance siren got close, and then whined down outside the door. A minute later two EMTs came in with their bags.

Shanks tried to sit up again, but this time Lorraine was there. "Let them look at you," she said.

"I only wanted to talk to Finn," Shanks said. "I wanted to explain . . ."

"I know."

One of the EMTs was Father Shonnard. He gave Shanks smelling salts, while Missy Delregado examined the cuts on his face. "I've seen worse," Missy said. "We'll clean him up a little and get him down to the clinic. He looks all right, but the doctor will have to stitch the cuts."

"I'll ride with him," Lorraine said.

Ed nodded. "I'll find Finn."

Ed went outside into the cold air and took a breath. The

stars were out now, and though the moon had not risen, the sky was clear. A snowplow was coming down from the pass, the last run of the night, its orange light whirling.

Jerilyn and Homer McCrady turned the corner of Tincup Street and came up Main. They parked behind the Blazer.

"We heard the siren," Homer said. "What happened?"

"Just a bar fight," Ed said. "You get one every hunting season."

Father Shonnard came out and opened the back of the ambulance to get the stretcher. Ed helped him lower it to the ground and roll it down to the edge of the ridge of snow at the sidewalk. They lifted it over the snow and Father Shonnard wheeled it into the Outlaw.

"Who is it, Ed?" Jerilyn asked.

"There are witnesses inside," Ed said. "You can ask them what happened."

He got into the Blazer and turned off the flashing blue light.

Then he radioed the state patrol in Durango and Sid Towe in Chipeta Springs to be on the lookout for either a red and white Ford pickup or a maroon Chevy truck with a jumping-buck decal on the driver's door. "Either one or both," he said.

When he was done, he pulled on up Main. In the rear-view he watched the EMTs bring Shanks out on the stretcher and, with the help of several people, lift the stretcher over the snowbank. Lorraine climbed up front on the passenger side.

That was the pattern for Finn, and for Neil too. He warned Neil to stay out of Finn's way. What good did he think explaining would do? Did he think Finn would believe him?

Finn believed what he wanted to, as most people did. But maybe Ed could convince him that times had changed. He had always tried to do his job fairly, in a way that allowed for people to do the right thing, and he had given Finn that opportunity once too often. This time, Ed decided, he would learn from Meeker. He'd do the job right.

Ed hoped he wouldn't find him. He hoped Finn had taken off and the state patrol would catch him, or Sid Towe down in Chipeta, because after Finn had been caught there was nothing more Ed could do to him. After that it would be up to the lawyers and the courts.

But right now it was up to Ed.

He circled down to the River Road, up Prosperity, and down through the alley behind the theater. The garage was open, but Finn's truck was not there. Ed didn't stop. The truck was not parked on Main either. He drove to the end of the street, turned left before the pass, and climbed to Tin Pan Alley. He turned off his headlights before he got through the first block.

The alley was closed in by fences, woodpiles, the backs of stores. Streetlights illuminated only the major cross streets, so the middle of each block was dark. Going down the alleys at night was like threading a shadowy tunnel.

Finn's truck was two blocks down, pulled off to the edge of the alley. Ed couldn't tell the exact distance, but it looked to be where Neil's apartment was. Ed coasted forward.

Should he flash the lights and make Finn run? Or should he wait? If he waited he might be able to get Finn in the open, at the trailer maybe, instead of in the truck.

Finn crossed the alley and got into the truck and pulled ahead. He had his headlights off too.

Ed came on. He stopped beside Neil's Subaru and got out to check the apartment. Finn had been there, but nothing was disturbed. He had left the two books that Becky had hidden torn up and scattered across the table.

By the time Ed got back to the Blazer, Finn had cleared the alley. He turned down Placer to Main, made a right past the Golddigger just to make certain Finn hadn't gone there, and then headed north toward the swimming pool. Finn's truck was just turning the bend beyond the pool and heading into the straightaway before the canyon.

He let Finn go. All he wanted was for Finn to keep going north, feel the pressure behind him, go slowly. He called the dispatcher's office and got Sharon.

"You're there," he said.

"Someone has to be," she said. "Bud called me. Where are you?"

"On Main heading north. I've got Finn ahead of me, and I'd like to keep it like that. Can you call Sid Towe and have him set up a roadblock down at the county line? He knows the place we've worked before."

"Past the Little Italy?"

"Right. I'm going to slowpoke it down the canyon. If Finn doesn't see me and turns into the trailer, that's fine too. I'll connect with Sid when I get out of the sandstone."

"Why don't you just pick him up?"

"I can't," Ed said. "And will you check on Neil?"

Finn had turned on his headlights in the straightaway and accelerated up to the speed limit. Ed kept a respectable distance, still with his lights off. Forty, fifty, fifty-five. Ed eased off and let Finn go out a half mile ahead.

The road was level for the first several hundred yards, a silken line of packed snow. Ed tested the brakes, slid a little, coasted into the slide, and brought the wheels back. It was slippery, but visibility was excellent. Stars and snow gave off light.

Sharon's voice snapped into the dark interior of the Blazer. "Ed? Come in."

"Here."

"Sid is starting from Chipeta Springs. You should be able to get him in about ten minutes. He knows the place."

"All right. How's Neil?"

"He's awake. I talked to Lorraine. Courtney is sewing him up now, and she thinks they'll keep him overnight."

"Good."

"You still have Finn?"

"I can see his taillights every once in a while when he hits the brakes on the curves. I'm probably a half mile behind. I have him, and there's no place he can go."

"Is there anything else?"

The moon edged out from an angle over the lower wall of the canyon and spread out against the sandstone cliffs on the other side of the road. He drove in shadow, but it was still easy to see.

"I want you to stay on the CB," he said.

Sharon was silent for a moment. "Stay on?"

"You have to make me talk," Ed said. "We have to talk."

He let the Blazer coast through the turns. He could still see Finn down below him, rounding the distant bends, or, when he couldn't see the truck, the headlights reflecting from the sandstone and into the air. The road looked so smooth, descending and curving into the windblown asphalt and patches of snow.

He felt the heat of the tight space, the friction of the car moving through the air. But he did not talk. He sat in the driver's seat and watched the road curve away.

Finn had slowed a little, and Ed had closed the distance. But in the dark Finn still had the illusion no one was following.

"I'm listening," Sharon said.

"Stay with me. Stay on." He tried to think. "Do you know this is the way we always talk to each other? Over the CB. I hear your voice over the radio, scratched and echoed, but I don't see you."

Sharon was silent again. The radio hummed a single tone. Finally she said, "Jerry told me, Ed. Louise and Jerry both."

He could not see her. He was glad he could not see her at that moment. "Well," he said. "Oh, shit."

"They didn't know what else to do. Louise said one of her friends saw the Blazer at some nurse's house, but there wasn't any call in the log."

"There was a disturbance," Ed said. "Out White Mesa Road."

"Don't, Ed. I've known for a long time."

He steered the Blazer into an icy turn. How could she have known? Lies. He was telling lies again. He felt the Blazer slide, and the road seemed to disappear in front of him. For an instant he was driving through air. Then his tire caught the gravel he couldn't see at the edge of the road, and instinctively he pulled on his headlights.

The road burst in front of him into the white light, and he pulled at the wheel, caught the dry edge, and held the curve.

Up ahead Finn hesitated for a split second, like the deer Ed had caught in the headlights a few nights before. Then he spooked. He took the next curve full bore.

"Ed?"

"Finn's making a run for it," Ed said.

Ed pressed the accelerator. The Blazer jumped into the curve, and he turned on the blue flasher overhead, spinning the color out against the walls of the canyon and over the icy road.

The Blazer strained and he tightened his grip on the wheel. It was too late now to ease off. The truck couldn't outrun the Blazer, especially in the canyon. For a minute, maybe two, he closed the gap.

"Talk to me," Sharon said.

He couldn't talk now. The Blazer was pulling up, and Finn was about to clear the last sandstone spires and head down into the flatter ranchland. Ed measured fifty-two through the curves and more on the downhill. But Finn kept the truck on the road.

"Ed, let him go."

Sharon's voice was soft, strained. But he didn't answer.

"You said to make you talk."

He lifted his foot from the accelerator and the gears slowed him. He felt the Blazer drift.

Finn speeded up across the flat land ahead.

Ed slowed still further. The road ran through the dry juniper and pinyon hills. Finn wouldn't stop at the trailer now. But there was no need to chase. Finn knew he was there, still coming on.

Ed turned off the blue flashing lights.

"Are you there, Ed? Come in."

He thought of Becky then, for no reason he knew.

The Blazer coasted. The lights at the Little Italy came into view up ahead of him, needle sharp in the clear air.

Finn was still racing on across the white fields. Now that the moon had risen, Ed could see the billowing cottonwoods along the river and the low hills of the moraine in the distance. He wished he knew whether Becky was alive.

"I'm here," Ed said.

"You worried me," Sharon said.

"I was thinking of Becky," he said. "How long have you known?"

"Years, I think."

"It hasn't been years."

Sharon's voice lapsed into static and resumed. ". . . what I mean. All we have to do is look at Jerry and Louise. Something has been wrong for a long time."

"I kept thinking—" But he stopped. He passed the Texaco station, which had a purplish clock in the window, and then the Little Italy with a few cars and four-wheel-drives parked out front. Then he was back out into the dark country again with the monotonous moan of the engine for company.

"Don't expect me to be glad you told me," Sharon said. "All this time, Ed. Really. How could you do this?" She paused, and then came on again. "I have calls now," she said. "The switchboard is lighting up."

Then she was gone.

He rounded another bend and the long dusty white bend of the mesa cut across the stars. To the right in the far distance he could see the red and blue flashing light of Sid Towe's cruiser stopped at the side of the road.

He tried to raise Towe on the radio, but no one was at the car. Towe wouldn't have set up a roadblock visible from such a distance. He'd have set up flares on the side of the highway first, and kept the car hidden.

Ed accelerated again, and when he got nearer he saw the flares. They were set up as they should have been, about a hundred feet apart. The sheriff's cruiser was pulled off at an angle to the side of the road.

Finn's truck was in the ditch on the left, its headlights angling up through the yucca and sage into the pinyon trees higher up. Steam was pouring from under the crumpled hood.

Ed pulled in behind the cruiser and set his own flasher.

Towe came over from the other side of the road, and Ed got out.

"He wouldn't stop," Towe said. "I had the car parked in the road, and he started to veer around it. So I shot a tire. He wasn't going all that fast when he went off. I was right next to him. He lost control. He's still in there. He looks to have a broken arm is all, and a bump on his head."

"You call the ambulance?"

Towe nodded in the whirl of colored lights. "It's only been a few minutes. I went through the cab for a weapon, but I didn't find one. I thought maybe you'd want to read him his rights."

Ed leaned over and got a flashlight out of the glove compartment. "I'll be glad to do that," he said. "I'm glad it was you that caught him."

18

The North Buttress of Red Cloud Peak was a gently sloping plain above timberline, but Aurey could not see it under the blowing snow. He could see the stars and the moon and the cornice of the peak, but the ground under him was windblown snow. It moved beneath him as he thought the sea might move, in a rhythm of waves. In the storm of Saturday the wind had driven the snow into drifts, and when the drifts melted and compacted and froze, they were hills, covered now by the blowing powder. He skied the waves blindly, letting his legs absorb the rise and fall.

He knew the terrain. He knew there were no boulders here, no sudden drops, no trees. He had been in worse weather on many mountains, higher up than he was now, and colder. But he had never felt such misgivings. It was like a fear of falling, though where he was there was nowhere to fall. Or perhaps, he thought, it was the anticipation of what might happen, though he couldn't say what that might be. He couldn't fall into a hidden snow-cave or suffocate under the snow. He wasn't going to freeze to death.

He hurried, trusting his instincts. His legs absorbed the undulating land. His breathing became rhythmic. He chose his way by line of sight. He poled hard on the downhill, and when the friction of the skis began to slow him, he pushed off sideways like a skater gaining momentum on ice. When he glided, he tucked his body to cut the resistance of the wind.

It felt to him as though he repeated these motions forever —skiing, skating, gliding, tucking down. He had no choice but to endure them. He went on and on until he could not go farther, and then he skied on.

He could see below him the dark trees, and the mountain gave way to a steeper pitch. He traversed the long pitch across the Bridge to Heaven and then he was suddenly out of the wind and down into the trees.

There was no trail, and he abandoned his skis at the edge of the timber. Carrying them would slow him down through the brush. He bushwhacked through deep snow and brush and over fallen logs, down into the creek bottom where he intersected the trail near the Four Quarters Mine. A cabin still stood at the spot, partially roofless and raked over by tourists. But the bunkbeds were still intact. Four men had lived there for six years, until one night one of them killed another in a knife fight over a piece of pork rind. That was the story the other two men told the marshal. It wasn't murder, it was self-defense.

Aurey was tempted to stay the night there. He had made it down off the timberline and through a good mile of dark spruce, and he needed some time to gain back his strength. He should have at least had something hot to drink. But he could feel the cold settling into the trees. He had to keep moving while he still had the impulse.

The trail was a snowy rut carved by the Alpha search team which had come down earlier in the afternoon. Their tracks had frozen in the snow, and the thin powder made it difficult for Aurey to tell where to put his own feet. He tried at first to keep on the edge of the trail where the snow was crusted and frozen, but he kept slipping into holes. After a few minutes he stopped and strapped on the one snowshoe he'd carried for a litter, and after that he limped along like an old man dragging one foot.

After a time—he did not know how long—flashes of pain began to shoot up into his leg. He changed the snowshoe to the other foot. It was a slow process, each step made deliberately in order to keep the pain from leaping to mind. It was not farther than three miles from the mine to the end of Cutler Creek Road, where the trail began. From there it would be a short walk down the road to a house.

He could see houses already through the trees far down below. He took off the snowshoe and began running.

His father picked him up at a chalet in Whispering Pines subdivision.

"What fool thing now?" Ernesto said, when Aurey snapped open the back door of the car to put his pack in. "What is this thing you've done now? Did you find her?"

"No."

Aurey slammed the door and opened the passenger door and got in. His thin frame filled the seat from ceiling to floor.

"I thought you'd find her," Ernesto said. "Everyone did. We all thought you'd find her."

"So did I."

Ernesto reached across the seat and put his arms around Aurey. It was an awkward gesture in the small space. "We prayed for you," he said. "We did everything we could to get you back." Ernesto leaned back into his seat.

"I'm back," Aurey said. "I'm very tired."

"You look tired," Ernesto said. "Are you hungry?"

"Yes, but I have to see Ed."

"We can stop by the Nugget," Ernesto said. "I can make you something."

"I can eat later," Aurey said. "Let's go see Ed first. Sooner is better than later."

There were lights on at the county building, and a dozen cars were parked out front. The sheriff's Blazer was there,

along with what Aurey assumed were press cars. The Mc-
Cradys' green Chevrolet was parked at the foot of the steps.
Lorraine's VW was pulled up in the alley by the window to
Ed's office.

Aurey got out and waited on the steps while Ernesto
parked down by the firehouse. They went in together.

The lights were blazing in the all-purpose room at the end
of the hall, and Aurey and Ernesto stood outside the door
and looked in. The reporters were quizzing Ed about Finn,
and Ed was shifting the chaw of tobacco from one cheek to
the other.

"I don't care what you think," Ed said. "I'm not going to
answer any questions about motive. You can ask Finn."

"Is it true Neil Shanks was seeing Finn's wife?"

"Everybody saw Finn's wife," Ed said. "She was in town
almost every day."

"What's Neil's condition?"

"The last report I had was that he's being held for obser-
vation overnight. He's suffered lacerations and a possible
concussion, but his condition is good."

"Are you going to let Finn go free?"

"I'm not going to let him go free. He'll be arraigned as
soon as tomorrow and no later than Wednesday."

Ernesto held Aurey's arm and pulled him away from the
door. "You want me to get Ed out here? You don't have to
talk to the press. I know you're tired."

"I don't care about the press," Aurey said.

He pushed open the door, and when Ed saw him he
stopped in mid-sentence. He waved Aurey back out into the
hall.

Most of the press didn't know who Aurey was, but Jerilyn and Homer did. "Did you find her?" Jerilyn called out.
She got up from her seat and slid along the row. "Did you
find Becky?"

Ed pushed Aurey back out through the door. "What happened?" Ed said. He looked from Ernesto to Aurey. "Did
you come out just now? Did you find anything?"

"I found something, but—"

"Jerilyn's coming," Ed said. "Let's go down to my office."

Ed grabbed Aurey's arm and hurried him along the hallway and down the stairs. Ernesto followed them. They went on through the empty dispatcher's room and into his office.

He sat Aurey down. "Now . . ."

"Where's Lorraine?" Aurey asked. "I want Lorraine to be here."

Footsteps came down the stairs and Jerilyn burst into the office with Homer right after her. "The people want to know," Jerilyn said. "Were you up there, Aurey? Did you find her?"

"I asked her to wait, Ed," Homer said.

"The people have a right to know." Jerilyn said. "They want to know whether he found Becky."

"Hold it!" Ed said. He spat a stream of tobacco juice on the floor in front of Jerilyn's feet. "I want to hear Aurey's story first."

Jerilyn stopped.

Then Lorraine appeared in the doorway, and Aurey stood up. "I didn't find her," he said quietly. "There isn't a story."

"You said you did," Ed said.

"I found the red on the snow," Aurey said. "It was a dead ptarmigan. A coyote kill."

"That was all?" Ed said.

"Yes."

"Are you certain?" Jerilyn asked.

Aurey looked at Jerilyn. "What do you mean am I certain? I was up there at the slide on Red Cloud Peak. Right on the coordinates Ed gave me. You want to know the conditions? It was twelve thousand feet and getting dark and a light snow was falling. And you're asking whether I'm certain?"

"Yes."

"Of course I'm certain."

Ed stepped forward. "Now, go on," he said to Jerilyn.

But his voice was calm. "I'll be back upstairs in a few minutes. Let me talk to Aurey a little and think about tomorrow." He looked at Lorraine. "And I want to call Wendell and Martha with the news."

19

When Ed got home he saw the kitchen lights on. He parked the Blazer out front and went around to the side of the house through the deep snow. Sharon was sitting on the window seat in the bay window, working on a quilt in her lap. She didn't look up. She was sewing on triangles of blue and red and bright yellow, and caught there in the inside light, she looked distant to him, someone he could not touch anymore. She might have lifted her head —certainly she'd heard him drive up—but she concentrated on her sewing. The small panes of glass in the bay window cast pale yellow rectangles onto the snow.

He went around to the back door and spit out his chewing tobacco in the snow. Then he took a deep breath and went inside. The heat of the room rushed at him, and he felt the sweat rise in the palms of his hands. He took off his coat and laid it over the straight-backed kitchen chair by the door, and he slid off his hat and threw it down too.

"Is that the quilt for Louise?" he asked.

"Yes." She still did not look at him. "How did it go?"

"I talked to them," he said. He stepped into the middle of the kitchen. "Aurey came down."

"And?" She looked at him then.

"He didn't find her. He was all the way up on Red Cloud where the helicopter was."

"Did he say what the red was?"

"A dead bird."

Sharon looked back down at the line she was sewing. "You don't sound convinced."

"It was Aurey," he said, as if the name implied something. "He's the one who knows the mountains."

They were silent a moment, and Sharon lifted a blue triangle from the stack of them on the low table in front of the window seat.

"That doesn't mean he couldn't be wrong," Sharon said. "What I don't understand is why he didn't call down. We had Bud freezing his butt on the roof."

"Maybe he couldn't get through."

"A ptarmigan. That's what he said. A dead ptarmigan." He sat down and stared at the whorls in the wooden table. The lines ebbed and flowed in the grain.

"What about Neil?"

"He's all right. I asked Aurey and Lorraine to go by there and tell him what happened tonight up the mountain and with Finn and all."

"That was terrible what Finn did."

Ed nodded. "But you have to feel a little for him too."

"For Finn?"

"I'm not excusing him. We'll bring the charges for assault and reckless driving. But Hank Tobuk and Flash Toomey were part of it. They made up the story to protect him, and he got caught by it."

"What story?" Sharon asked. She looked up again.

"Hank thought Finn killed Becky so he and Flash concocted a reason they thought might give Finn an out. Flash had spotted Neil and Becky once at the Xanadu, and Hank went to the newspaper with the story about how Neil and Becky were going to meet up secretly somewhere."

"The McCradys didn't publish it."

"I talked them out of it, or they decided not to. This morning Hank went up the mountain to find out what Finn had done with the body. Of course there wasn't any body. At least Finn didn't know of one."

"That's when Finn found out about Neil?"

"That part of the story stuck. Finn had already half believed Becky had made a fool out of him. When he first came down, he thought she was at the trailer. I don't think he knew what to believe until this afternoon when he found books down at the trailer. I was with him, but at the time I was more interested in what he had to say about Becky's state of mind than I was in what he might do next. I guess that when I left, he got Flash to come and get him and bring him back to town."

Ed paused. On the counter by the sink were some of the crystals Neil had brought back from his shop—Ed had meant to wash them before he put them back in their glass cases. But that had been days ago now. But he didn't get up. "They went by Neil's apartment, but he was over at the office. There's no telling what might have happened if Neil hadn't gone into the Outlaw."

"At least there were people around," Sharon said.

"The irony is that Neil was looking for Finn. He wanted to tell Finn the truth. He wanted to explain about Becky."

He watched Sharon's unsteady hand maneuvering along the border of the blue triangle, her gaze intent on the fabric, as if she were concentrating on the stitch instead of the unspoken work that lay ahead of them.

"What does Aurey intend to do now?"

"He wants to go back up tomorrow. There are still lots of mines to sort through. And the terrain toward Lakeland hasn't been thoroughly checked over. There are hunting camps all through those creek drainages beyond American Flats. The Beta team is camped in Henson Creek, but there's LaPlata and Lady Luck and Suwanee. He wants to expand the search area."

"Are you going to do that?"

"I'm going to do whatever Aurey says. There's a lot of country up there."

"Do you think she's up there?"

"I think she's missing," Ed said.

Ed got up and turned on the light above the sink and looked at the pale crystals. They shone in the light, sparkled like the sun on water. But he had only collected them.

He turned around toward Sharon, who was holding the quilt. The outlines of the missing triangles were drawn in, and two long strips of yellow were sewn on the border. The background was gray. She had finished about a third of it, but she hadn't worked on it since the spring.

"It will be beautiful," he said. "The arcs and the triangles and the border."

She folded the quilt in half and laid it on the window seat. For a moment he thought she was going to get up, that she wouldn't stay in the kitchen with him. But then she took a yellow patch and laid it carefully alongside the blue one she had just sewn.

"What did you tell the press?" she asked.

"I gave them the essentials. That's what I'm supposed to do. I told them the facts—what happened at the Outlaw, and Finn's running the roadblock, and what Aurey had said when he came down the mountain. The minimum. I didn't tell them about me."

"I hope not."

Ed smiled, but didn't say anything.

"What didn't you tell them about you?" Sharon asked.

"I don't know that I can stay on the job," he said softly. "Not after tonight. I don't know."

"I already know about tonight."

He shook his head. This was the moment when there was nowhere to go, when Jerry and Louise were in bed, and Sharon had all the time in the world to listen. He wanted her to listen, but he didn't know whether he could say the words. He had thought he could explain it, say the right things, smooth out the feelings. But that wasn't true. He was like the alcoholic who couldn't admit his own weakness.

Sharon looked up from her stitch, holding the needle in midair. "You mean there's more?"

What words? he thought. What words did he use to tell her.

He started talking. He knew the sentences would not fit together. "I thought about what I would do when I found Finn," he said. "Right after I went to the Outlaw. I just wanted to push him. Do you understand? I'm not God. Finn had been drinking. When you said that to me over the CB . . . Remember? I didn't know where I was going, and then . . . No one would have blamed me for getting Finn. Like Meeker blowing up the hot springs. It would be forgotten." He paused and stared, then looked at Sharon. "I never lost control, but I turned on the lights. I'd been driving in the dark. And then the flasher too. I could have killed him. I'm the sheriff. . . ."

He sank down onto the floor. It was as if the whole weight of his body had given way. The muscles had collapsed, too frail to hold on to bone. He was on his knees beside the counter, and his head and arms sagged forward onto the floor.

"Ed, get up," Sharon said.

But he didn't get up. He stayed on the floor. He babbled and cried and shouted so that Sharon had to get up from the window seat and come over.

"You'll wake up Louise and Jerry," she said. "They can't see you like this, Ed. Ed, listen to me."

She tried to lift him up, but she couldn't.

He went on talking.

"It will take time," Sharon said. "One day and then another. Ed, listen to me!"

He would not get up. But he grew quieter. Sharon got down on the floor, too, and held his head in her lap. He talked. He talked so fast, the words were mixed up—everything he could think of—as if once the wall had broken there was so much to say he couldn't say it fast enough.

20

The room was dark and smelled of ammonia. Shanks was awake, sweating, uncomfortable in the bed. The novocaine was wearing off from the stitches, and heat swelled in his forehead and in his eyes. He could feel the skin stretched tight across his jaw.

One of his eyes wouldn't open fully, but he could see well enough to make out the window and the moonlit darkness beyond. The river sighed in the distance like someone's breathing, though he knew there wasn't anyone else in the room. He listened for a long time to the flowing water.

He imagined the river rushing through the canyon at the Xanadu, running under the bridge at Placer Street, down along the road past Lorraine's and out into the ranchland filled with snow. This river ran north, joining the Gunnison and the Colorado. The Colorado ran west and south on the other side of the escarpment, winding into Utah, through the canyon lands of the Uncompahgres, then on into a half dozen dams into Arizona. This was not the river of his childhood, not the Muskegon, which emptied into Lake Michigan, or the Au Sable, which flowed east into Huron. The Uncompahgre was his river now, rising from the melt and the springs, collecting from gullies and flumes and side canyons. This was his country now.

He had discovered a land different from the one Thomas had known, though it looked the same. The mountains still rimmed the high country he had never seen, the water still flowed. But it was a place that had aged and changed. Thomas had sought the future, and Neil the past. That was the difference between them. Neil had expected to find in books and documents a continuous line, as pages were numbered or days went by on the calendar. He had lived in a world of predictable order, counting on what had gone before to tell him what was next.

Becky had changed him. She had shown him a person's history could not tell what a man or a woman was capable of or what he or she might do next. The future could be changed, and the present too. He had other choices than those he had made before. He was freer now to go on.

He heard a commotion outside the door. The door opened abruptly and light from the hallway flashed across the bed. For a moment the wild silhouette of Pop Krause filled the light, and Shanks squinted at him and held up his hand to see more clearly. Pop came into the room and closed the door.

"I sneaked past the nurse," Pop said softly. "Don't turn on the light."

Shanks sat up against the pillow.

"I can't be here," Pop said. "But here I am. I was in the neighborhood."

He crossed to the window and looked out, as if to see whether anyone had followed him.

"It's cold out," he said. "Very cold. I knew you were here."

"How?"

"The ambulance brought you. I saw it go past. I was called."

Pop was dressed in jeans and an old jacket with a worn fringe collar, and where he stood at the window, the side of his face and his beard and hair were silvered by the moon.

He gave a low eerie wail, no louder than a whisper, sliding from one note to another. A current ran through the air as palpable as a jolt of electricity. When the sound stopped, the air quieted and the room was so still, even the sound of the river was gone.

Shanks leaned forward in the bed.

"You are the one who sees the spirit," Pop said softly. "Do not forget the ones who do not forget you."

Shanks was not certain whether he was hearing Pop's voice or imagining it. Pop gave another low wail that moved the air.

Then he slipped away from the window and the moonlight toward the door, and a moment later the light came into the room and departed.

Shanks was left by himself again, puzzled by the words. Had Pop meant Becky? He didn't know. No one knew where Becky was and no one would find her. He believed that. He had made her new, from memory and from words, from landscapes he imagined and conversations remembered. What Lorraine had told him and Vicky Saunders and Wendell were illusions Shanks possessed now. He had recreated Becky like a story drawn from pieces of himself.

It was nearly midnight when the nurse came in and turned on the overhead light. "I have to check your life signs," she said. "And you have visitors."

"Now?" He blinked and slitted his eyes to the light.

"The sheriff said it was all right. I can't reach the doctor, but I told Ed I'd see how you felt and use my own judgment. Do you feel up to it?"

"That depends who it is," Shanks said. "I'd rather not see Finn."

The nurse put a thermometer into his mouth and uncoiled the blood-pressure sleeve to wrap around his arm.

"It isn't Finn," the nurse said. She finished taking his blood pressure and pulse and then made notations on his chart. "You're doing well," she said. "Keep the visit short."

She went out, and a minute later Lorraine and Aurey

came in. Lorraine came right to the bed. Aurey hung back at the door. He was still dressed in his climbing gear.

"You didn't find her," Shanks said.

"No," Aurey said.

"He was all the way upon Red Cloud," Lorraine said. "He came down in the dark. It was a ptarmigan the pilot saw."

"She's not there," Shanks said. "I know."

Lorraine touched his arm. "How are you?" she asked.

"Recovering."

"Did you hear about Finn?"

"I don't want to hear about Finn."

"Finn's crazy," Aurey said. "Crazy."

"And I too." He sat up in the bed and looked at Aurey. "Have you ever heard of Darwin Owens?"

"Heard of him? Yes. Why?"

"Do you know what he did?"

Aurey stared at him, and for a while Shanks thought he would not answer.

"Don't you know?" Lorraine asked.

"He had a placer operation farther down the valley. Isn't that right? It was one of the last placer mines started up in the county."

"But do you know anything about the man?"

"I know he found gold. He sold the claim later on, after he was rich."

"Darwin Owens," Shanks said. "Is that all you remember about him?"

"Yes. It's all I remember."

"Who was Darwin Owens?" Lorraine asked.

"He was the man I came to Gold Hill to find. He changed his name from Thomas Shanks to fool people. But Shanks did not go on. He lay back in his bed and closed his eyes.

"Well, you can be glad he took his money out," Aurey said. "That wasn't the usual practice. Most men who found gold wanted more of it and bought more claims and more machinery, and by the time they were done they were broke again."

"What else, Neil?"

Shanks opened his eyes. "It's a story I'll tell another time." He touched his stitches, and then looked back at Aurey. "Are you going up again tomorrow?"

"We're going up," Aurey said. "We're going to check the hunting camps on the other side of American Flats."

"There are mines too," Lorraine said. "And that side goes into dozens of small gullies before it gets to the Lanier Fork. She could be anywhere over there."

"I want to go," Shanks said.

"All right," Aurey said.

"Do you think I can help?" Shanks asked. "That's the question. I don't care what the doctor says. I feel good. But I don't know whether I'd be a help."

"Everyone can help," Lorraine said. "Everyone can do something."

"I'll do whatever you say. I'll stay in camp with the walkie-talkie. I'll climb the meadow. How many people are still up there?"

Aurey shook his head. "There are some left in the meadow by the corral," Aurey said. "Volunteers. And then Meeker and Granny Watson and Weedy are in the camp. I suspect we'll get a few new people from around the county now that the snow has melted off some. There'll be a good group at the trailhead."

The nurse looked around the corner and into the room. "Time to go," she said.

"We were just leaving," Aurey said.

"What time in the morning?" Shanks asked.

"I'm going up at six. But you can come later. I'll have someone in the camp tell you what to do."

"Six," Shanks said. "I'll try to be there."

Aurey paused at the door, waiting for Lorraine, who was still standing by the bed.

"I'm going to stay a minute longer," she said. "If you want, take my car and I can walk to your place to get it. You must be tired, Aurey."

Aurey and Lorraine looked at one another, as if each one

expected the other to say something more. It was a moment they had made for themselves, Shanks thought, a small moment which had come to them unexpectedly, and he turned his gaze away to the window.

"I can walk," Aurey said finally. "I'll see you, then, in the morning."

Aurey went out and closed the door softly.

The room was quiet. Lorraine backed away from the bed and turned off the overhead light at the switch by the door. How different the room seemed then, changed from a bright cubicle with four walls to a liquid silver space without boundaries. Moonlight slipped through the windows across the white sheets of the bed.

Lorraine glided through the gray room and sat down on the far end of the bed at his feet.

"You must be tired too," Shanks said.

"I am," she said. "I won't stay long."

They watched the light from the window, the snow light sheen on the glass. Beyond that shimmering light was the immense country where Becky was, where he might be, too, when he decided what to do.

Lorraine was the one to speak. "I remember a story about Becky," she said. "Can I tell you?"

"Of course."

"It was summer and a full moon so bright, you could almost see colors. I think Becky was fourteen, because it was just a few weeks after she'd run away to Green River. It was before Toby died."

"She never told me she ran away," Shanks said.

"My mother wouldn't let her ride in the rodeo," Lorraine said. "Anyway, this night she came to my room, very late, and she wanted to go out into the fields, so I went with her. A chinook was blowing from the south, and it was the kind of warm night you don't often get in the mountains. We walked along the irrigation ditch until we were a good way from the house.

"Then Becky decided she wanted to go swimming. You've seen that ditch, Neil. There's maybe two feet of water in it. But that didn't matter. Becky stripped down without waiting for me, and when she was naked, she said, 'Aren't you coming?' 'No.' I said. 'I'll watch you.' Then she asked if I was afraid to take off my clothes. I wasn't afraid. There wasn't anyone there except Becky. I made some excuse—I can't remember what—the water was too cold or too shallow. But I remember it was the sky.''

"The sky?"

Lorraine got up from the bed and went to the edge of the window and looked out. "There was too much sky," she said. "Too much moon. Becky didn't mind. She slid down into the ditch and stood for a long time with the water running fast against her knees. You could hear the rippling sound it makes. Becky looked so solid then, and strong, and I remember thinking that when she grew up I hoped she'd be beautiful.''

Lorraine turned from the window and Shanks could see her smile. "Then she told me she hadn't run away because of the argument with my mother. She said that the rodeo was a reason people would believe. She'd run away because she felt like it.''

"And did you believe her?"

"I didn't know what to think. She might have been saying that after the fact, or maybe she didn't know why she'd run away. 'Why did you feel like it?' That's what I asked her. She didn't answer for a while. She got down into the ditch and splashed in the water, ducking her head under and letting the current wash over her. Then she stood up again in the warm breeze. I knew she hadn't forgotten the question. I could see her face in the moonlight. Then she said, 'I don't know. Haven't you ever felt you had to do something? Just *anything*?' "

"Yes," Shanks said. "But not until now."

Lorraine came back over to the bed and sat down, closer to him this time. "Becky stood there in the ditch with the moonlight over her wet body. The water looked cold, frozen almost, you know the way water looks when it's dark and there's a light shining on it. She was shivering and holding her arms crisscrossed across her body. Then the wind dried her, except for her hair, which was streaked with light. She stretched her arms up over her head." Lorraine stretched her arms into the air of the room. "She looked so relaxed and happy then, in a way I knew I'd never be, as if she had everything she could ever want. And I thought no matter what came later, she would always have that one moment for herself."

Lorraine was silent for a long moment.

Then she said, "I keep thinking she'll come back."

For a long time neither of them said anything. Lorraine's face was turned into the shadow, but Shanks was conscious his own was in the light. Lorraine touched his cheek gently and the edge of his swollen eye. "Get some sleep," she said.

"And you."

She took her hand away. "I'll come by for you in the morning."

"Before six," he said. "I want to go up with Aurey."

Lorraine nodded. "It'll be cold."

"I used to live in Michigan,' he said. "My father and I used to go ice fishing, so I can take the cold."

She stood up from the bed and kissed his forehead and went out of the room.

21

Shanks checked himself out of the clinic early and was waiting in the lobby when Lorraine came for him. It was just getting light at that hour, and a faint blue wash hovered above the Amphitheater and swelled to the north down the valley. It was very cold, and clear, too, though already a few wood fires had begun to curl their smoke into the air.

"I've been at your place already," Lorraine said. "I thought if you could go into my house, I could go into yours. I brought over some breakfast and put it in the oven."

"Good. It won't take me too long to pack. What's for breakfast?"

"Cinnamon toast, oatmeal, fruit."

Lorraine steered up Third Street to Tin Pan Alley and turned left down the tunnel. "Did you hear the weather?"

"No."

"It's supposed to be clear, but colder than yesterday. Warming up again tomorrow."

"How is Christopher?"

"Still asleep. My mother was up."

"But he's all right?"

"She says he is. How do you feel this morning?"

"Good." He craned up to the rearview mirror to look at himself. A smudge of blue-black seeped around his eye, and the stitches looked red. The doctor had given him pills if he needed them.

"It looks like you'll have a black eye," Lorraine said.

"But I'll live."

He smiled and settled back into the seat. The VW hummed down the alley toward Placer where the county building loomed up in the blue light. One pale yellow glow shone from a cellar window out into the alley.

"Ed's there," Lorraine said. "We should stop by before we go up the pass. He'll want to know how you are."

They coasted in behind the Subaru and got out quickly. The snow crunched under their feet like paper.

The apartment was warm. The oven had filled the small space with a cinnamon heat, and oatmeal was simmering on the stove. But the space seemed different to him from when he was last there, and for a moment he stood inside the door trying to remember what it was. The table was set with plates and bowls and silverware, but that wasn't it. "The hawk," he said. "I took the hawk to Pop Krause."

Lorraine was stirring the oatmeal. "You never told me what Pop said."

"I haven't told anyone."

"Does that mean you won't?"

"He told me an myth," Shanks said. "Only Pop could tell it."

"Did you talk to Becky?"

Shanks smiled. He could not answer the question, and he wouldn't try. "Do you want coffee?" he asked. "I have some in the cupboard." He went to the cupboard and got out a can of coffee.

"We haven't got time," Lorraine said. "Sit down. Breakfast is ready."

They ate quickly, and when they were finished, Shanks packed his gear. Lorraine had brought over some skis and boots she said Teddy had left when he left for Nevada, and

Shanks packed his sleeping bag and the small bit of food he had, including the coffee.

"I have a lot of food at the camp," Lorraine said. "And a tent and a stove. There's the camp stash too. The main thing is to bring warm clothes, enough socks, a hat that'll cover your ears."

By twenty minutes of six they were ready to go.

Vicky was getting out of the Bronco in front of the county building when Shanks and Lorraine reached the end of Tin Pan Alley. When she saw them she ran out into the street, waving, and Shanks did a wide turn in four-wheel drive and pulled up. She had on her pink parka and white suede boots.

Lorraine rolled down the window on her side.

"You going up the mountain?" Vicky asked.

"Yes. What are you doing?"

"Ed just called me to work the goddamn switchboard for an hour or two. He's waiting for a call from Lakeland, and he had to take Aurey up to Bear Creek because his Jeep is still up there." She squatted down to the window. "I'm glad Aurey didn't find her. I mean, I'm glad he didn't find her there. You know what I mean." She gave Lorraine a hug through the window. "Jesus, Neil," she said, "you look awful."

"Thanks."

"You got whacked good," Vicky said. "But Finn's a creep. Look, it's cold out here. I gotta go." She stood up and backed away from the car. "I hope Becky's in Denver with Willie Nelson," she said. "Or maybe in Salt Lake or Reno. I've always thought Seattle might be a good place."

"I'll be down tomorrow," Lorraine said. "I'll see you then."

"Take care of her, Neil."

Vicky waved, and Shanks let the Subaru edge forward to the stop sign at Main. Then he took a left and gave gas on the icy street toward the pass.

* * *

There were more than a dozen cars parked in the turnout at the Bear Creek Trail. Deep tire tracks melted into the snow from the day before had frozen during the night into ruts, and Shanks bounced the Subaru across the ice. A crowd was already gathered around Ed's Blazer. It was five minutes after six.

"I don't see Aurey," Shanks said.

He parked and they took their skis off the luggage rack and leaned them in the angles of the open doors. They left the packs on the hood, and then crossed the parking lot to where the others were.

Ed had two topo maps laid out on the hood of the car, and Aurey was bent over them, explaining the day's search plan. He nodded at Lorraine and Shanks when they came into the group.

They were going to head east, Aurey was saying. That was the direction Becky must have gone. They'd concentrate on the drainage of Horseshoe Basin and the Lanier Fork, which was an area of ten or twelve square miles on the other side of American Flats. She might even have slid as far to the north as La Plata Creek, where there was a string of silver mines all the way down to Sheep Mountain. All the country was dark timber and hard to cover well.

"Is the helicopter going up?" Lorraine asked.

"I'll work with the Army on that," Ed said. "The CSR commandeered the one we had yesterday, but I'll see what I can do."

They divided into groups according to what each of them thought he or she could do, and Ed gave them patches of different colors so they'd know which group they were with when they got up to the meadow.

"We'll assemble again at the field headquarters," Aurey said. "When we get up there, we'll add to the groups. If you have any questions, we'll answer them up the mountain so everyone will hear."

They broke the knot and got their gear together. Aurey helped Shanks tie on his skis, and when Shanks was ready

Aurey held the pack for him to get his arms through the straps.

"How does the weight feel?" he asked.

"Heavy," Shanks said. "I'll manage."

"We'll go slowly," Lorraine said. "Use the ski poles for balance. And let me know if you start to feel bad."

"I feel okay," Shanks said. "I'll follow you."

There was no track in the snow, but the trail had been well worn the day before and the new snow barely covered the old footprints. The ground was frozen, so the walking was not difficult. It was only the steepness of the pitch that was hard.

Shanks kept pace with Lorraine, though they dropped back from Aurey. Aurey led a short line of five or six people on the pitch through the trees, but he looked back at them often to make certain they were still coming.

They climbed through the spruce fairly quickly to the first clearing, and continued on the zigzag for another half mile. Then Aurey called a rest. He threaded back through the line to where Shanks and Lorraine were stopped.

"How is it?"

Shanks nodded. "All right."

"Any dizziness?"

"No. Is this the shale?"

"This is the shale. It's all under the snow. But you can see the slash up there where it came from."

Shanks looked up at the cliff, which was red and gray. "And we head for that opening in the rocks?"

"Yes. That's where the trail starts along the cliff. If we have bad conditions, we'll rope up."

"Ice?"

"There could be ice."

"I thought you'd never been on the trail," Lorraine said. "That's what you said."

"Becky told me," Shanks said.

After a minute or two Aurey signaled to start again. Shanks followed Aurey's footsteps on a long traverse across the snowy shale. He could feel the pack rub his shoulders, and he lifted it from underneath with his hands and settled it back in a different place. He was sweating, even in the chill, but the cold on his face felt good. His blood throbbed in the stitches and he could feel the crisp air burn his lungs. He could hear Lorraine's steps on the snow behind him.

Visibility was perfect. He could see across the canyon to the red cliffs above the river, and higher up into the dark trees. The sun line had started down against the shadow on the sides of Mt. Abrams and Whitehouse Peak.

Every turn was a new perspective of mountains and cliffs and valleys. To the south, farther than he could see, was Ptarmigan Pass tucked down among the trees. Below him he could hear the river in the gorge.

He was higher than he had ever been before in that country, but he had barely started. Farther up, beyond the cliff trail—he could imagine it already—were the high meadows covered with snow and the aspens and the dark spruce trees and more snow and more mountains. He imagined the hills rising above timberline, one after another, separated by light and shadow. And he saw Becky, too, bathed in the rising sun, in the new sun, like a hawk soaring through the cold silky air, wherever she was, her shadow skimming over them on the ground.